The Forgotten Memories of The Blue Soldiers

Leo P. LePage Jr.

authorHOUSE®

AuthorHouse™ LLC
1663 Liberty Drive
Bloomington, IN 47403
www.authorhouse.com
Phone: 1-800-839-8640

This is a work of fiction. All of the characters, names, incidents, organizations, and dialogue in this novel are either the products of the author's imagination or are used fictitiously.

Published by AuthorHouse   02/05/2014

ISBN: 978-1-4918-6196-7 (sc)
ISBN: 978-1-4918-6197-4 (e)

Library of Congress Control Number: 2014902414

Fictional memoirs of a street cop

Mary Lou

Some time ago, I was sifting through old police memorabilia. I had amassed over my career, while perusing through various articles; I stumbled on an old clipping that had me travel back through the hands of time. The article contained a short story regarding an elderly lady who resided in my sector. Her residence located in a tough area of the city, which exposed the elderly citizens like Mary Lou, to be vulnerable to predators.

This kind old lady was mugged one rainy night. Her arm broken and bruises about her body, she suffered pain an indignity and the scum relieved her of the grand sum of four dollars and thirty three cents. Mary Lou eventually became house bound due to serious disabilities. A grand old woman who suffered the tragic loss of her husband on D Day on the Beaches of Normandy, years later, history repeated itself as life unkindly robbed her of her only child, a son killed in Vietnam in the DMZ. There are many a mothers and wives that can feel the pain and loneliness that she felt having surviving not only her husband, whom she loved dearly, but her only son as well.

I had the honor and pleasure to meet this wonderful soul through one of my officers. As time went on, my squad would check on her, bringing groceries, giving her lifts to doctors, dentists, etc., etc. We became her adopted sons, for she had no one else in this God's world. She had eyes of blue that danced when she smiled. Hair white as snow and a heart of pure gold, we loved that old lady. Her spirit was always high key. She possessed riches of the soul, millionaires never attained. After a visit and when departing her presence, she would hug you hard and whisper, take care my "Blue Soldier" and God bless. After reflecting on that period shared with this old lady, the title "Memories of The Forgotten Blue Soldiers" was born. Rest in peace Mary Lou, we miss you; watch over all your blue soldiers.

Dedicated to my beloved

Wife Lisa

My Second Rose

Start of watch 12-26-13

"A Breath of Life"

Foreword

There are monsters that live in the underbelly of the city. They come in the form of murderers, rapists, pedophiles and all ilks of demons. They prey on the weak and defenseless. Fortunately every day men and women in Blue pick up their shields and like knights of old go forth to battle these monsters and protect our citizenry and maintain the social order. Very often these warriors develop their own demons to live with and are sometimes called upon to make the ultimate sacrifice.

Who better to tell their story than one of those who carried the shield for twenty five years? Leo LePage served as a city police officer during some of the most turbulent times in American history and has the unique perspective of someone who was there!

Bernie Sullivan Chief of Police, Retired, Hartford Ct.

To Society

The Dream

Boyhood dreams of long ago
Saw the color blue, oh a
Policeman's what I saw
And what I'd want to do
And those dreams did lead
Me on dreamlike though they
Seemed.
Now dear friends thank God
With me I became what I dreamed.
Other dreams have I today
Brought in spite of fears
That I'd blight the color blue
And be untrue to you
You thought of me while on
Your knees for I served
You true.
While in that uniform of blue
I gave my all for you.

The Critic

It is not the critic who counts

Not the man who points out how the

Strong man stumbled on where the doer

Of deeds could have done them better.

The credit belongs to the man who is actually

In the arena, whose face is marred by blood?

Dust and sweat, who strives valiantly; who

Errs and comes short again and again, who knows

The great enthusiasms', the great devotions,

And spends himself in a worthy cause, who, at the

Best knows the triumph of high achievement,

And who at the worst, if he fails, at least

Fails while daring greatly, so that his place shall

Never be with those cold and timed souls

Who know neither victory or defeat?

Theodore Roosevelt

A Letter

My Friends,

In my first novel the reader was able to walk along side officer LaPore and witness through his own eyes the demons that men and women in blue deal with on a daily basis. The Badge, The Street, and The Cop was an honest attempt to expose, to you the reader that Satan does lurk in our society. Officers of my era gave their all to safeguard our streets. However, everyday breaking news reveals our attempts were futile. Why human beings butcher each other has always evaded me. Good men made the supreme sacrifice to no avail. I pray their souls lie in peaceful repose.

I have often felt that my past sins would come back to haunt me. In my new novel you will glimpse just how they did. Blue memories will lead you through LaPore's struggle with his demons and how he fared in retirement. It will also once again have you walk the streets with many men and women in blue as they go about their duties. I pray that you enjoy this book and when finished have an understanding what your thin blue line is battling everyday to safeguard our streets for you and your children. I thank all of you in advance and wish all my readers Godspeed. I was proud and privileged to have once served you. Thank you all.

Prologue

The rain fell in a soft mist; his feet left soft imprints on the soil as he walked. LaPore gazed off into the distance where rows of grave stones stood as sentinels honoring those who rested beneath them. He was older now and his gait was slow but he walked erect head held high in pride as he continued through this quite place. His mind brought him back into his distant past, when the color blue was his life. When the wail of a siren made his blood gush through his veins and when the laughter and tears of his comrades mingled with his own. He had spent his youth and his strength combating the demons of the street, had married, raised a family, and had brought life into the world. As well as, dispatched several demons from this world in the line of duty yes I was a cop thought Lapore. It was a calling one that I loved and cherished. Oh, to go back, to be young and strong once more to serve his fellow man and community. His eyes were wet with moisture; was it from the rain or was it tears that left a lined trail on his cheeks. Memories stamped in his heart pushed him forward. He had come here to soldier's field to pay his respects to an old comrade, to a brother cop that years ago had saved him from the jaws of death. The scene took place on a late night domestic only for him to have fallen some weeks later at the hands of a deranged killer. His travels though the field ended as he stood at the grave of Officer Henry Jenkins, killed in the line of duty on May 27th 1964. Reading the etched lettering on the grave stone, LaPore on his knees felt the sting of tears in his eyes. Now aged he had made it through life thanks to this good man who lay motionless beneath this plot of earth. He had lived to see wonderful things, had watched and assisted as his children grew into adulthood and had enjoyed the joy of grandchildren. LaPore had experienced a great marriage to a great lady and had made it to retirement. The world had revolved many times, since the death of Officer Jenkins, but LaPore never forgot the night these brothers in blue had forged a sacred bond. Standing erect now, LaPore whispered a private word of thanks and gratitude to the Memory of Jenkins. Hank LaPore began, I've let you down my brother, I've hit the skids, and alcohol is now my constant companion. I can't face life without it. I've disappointed family, friends and mostly my kids. Hank you and I and many others who were the blue walked Hells byways, I could deal with that, but the loss of my wife Joey was too devastating. I no longer care, life is meaningless, maybe someday I'll find myself, I don't know, maybe somewhere, somehow, someone will give me the will to live again. Maybe you and so many others who have gone before me will nudge me into the road of life. As he prepared to leave his old comrade these words he had once heard somewhere in youth flashed in his mind.

Saluting the grave, they rushed forth,
This great evil, where does it come from?
How'd it steal into this world?
What seed, what root did it grow from?
Who is doing this?
Who's killing us?
Robbing us of Life and Light
Mocking us with the sight of what we might have known.
Does our ruin benefit the earth?
Does it help the grass to grow, the sun to shine.

Turning his heart heavy with grief, he departed from this silent humble grave. Filled with despair, he wondered what future would now befall him. Whispering a silent goodbye, LaPore shuffled away, ashamed and broken; alone he strolled out of soldier's field to face an unknown, unpromising future.

Acknowledgements

In writing this book it was my sole intent to attempt to present to you, the reader, the dedication and sacrifices made daily by the countries interior blue soldiers, the thin blue line. I owe thanks to so many and hope I slighted no one.

To my current wife, Lisa, my second rose, for being there now and rescuing my soul.

To my deceased wife Joey for being there in perilous times rendering love and comfort.

My son, John, who saw a story in accumulated scrap books that were started and preserved through the years

For Chief Bernard Sullivan, H.P.D., who rendered such support in many hours of need and for his wisdom, guidance and patience for everything

To Officer Paul Mangiafico, E.H.P.D., who encouraged me to tell it like it is.

For Betty Torri, who encouraged me long and hard with this project

To Officer Hank Charland, a brother in blue and a devoted, loyal friend who labored long and hard to get the first, "The Badge, The Street and The Cop," and second book "The Memories of The Forgotten Blue Soldiers," off the ground.

To Dave Owens, a Hartford Courant reporter, who encouraged me along the way and served a literary liaison in this whole process

For Wilma McKelvey, who was like an adopted daughter to Joey and myself, who rescued me, in order to allow me to not only have a break, but allow myself time to continue to write the first book with an easy of mind.

To Eric Hitchcock, who encouraged and pushed the book among strangers in order that he may give people a chance to learn about it and that they may share it with others.

To Angela Andreoni, who saw a story in a dusty manuscript and sent it into be published.

But most of all, to all my brothers and sisters in blue who by their support and back ups got me home

To you the public thanks for letting me, a humble son serve, as one of it's finest and to those who serve and go in harms way, I say thank you for keeping the Hun at bay.

To those who gave their all, rest in peace, you the peace makers that share God's embrace.

Chapter 1

The dead lifeless eyes looked right through him. The sweet sickening smell of dry coagulated blood filled his nostrils. The howl full wail of sirens going in harm's way could be heard in the distance. His subconscious mind retained the image of the blue uniform soaked in blood lying on the floor of an old sleazy hotel. He sat upright in his bed and the room he lay in was blanketed in darkness. Outside he could hear the mournful howl of the wind. The rain was beating a tattoo on the window pane. He knew that the demon had come to him again as another nightmare in the night. His body was covered in sweat and his breathing shallow. His hands shaking uncontrollably as he rose from his bed. Stumbling, he made his way to the kitchen and sighed with relief when he saw where he had left off with his whiskey. Reaching for the bottle, he took two swift gulps. The fiery liquid spread through his tortured body and the warmth comforting him. He sat in his recliner, lit up a cigarette and inhaled deeply. It was then the tears came rolling down his cheeks. Dropping to the floor, his hands were shaking uncontrollably. The liquor and lack of sleep taking his nerves. Off in the distance, the wail of a lonely train's whistle sounded in the night. He sat there alone, forlorn, frightened at what he had become, ashamed that alcohol had become his constant companion. Why not he thought? There's no one else. His life was in a shambles. He was lonely, and no longer possessed the confidence that had once graced his being. From which he obtained from wearing the blue uniform that helped him cloak his community in safety. That had propelled him to the top, made him a line sergeant in law enforcement, a leader of men, and a guardian to his community. Once he had stood tall and had had it all. Now he had become a reclusive shell.

One who no longer cared. Life was no longer precious to him. Too many demons and the sudden loss of his wife in his arms had devastated him.

That night his soul mate of forty nine years died, caused a domino effect and in essence his very soul had died with her. Lapore gulped down another whiskey. He had found that if he indulged enough he would find the sweet blissful peace of sleep. Firing up another cancer stick, his mind traveled back in time where so many demons waited to torture his soul, gulping yet another shot, he gazed out his window where the first rays of sunlight pecked over the grey horizon. Ah, another day of shit he thought. How to get though, it was always a challenge, only those trapped in the tentacles of drink would understand. He knew he had reached the depths of despair and was feeling sorry for himself and didn't give a damn. His cigarette had burned down and ashes lined the floor, he chuckled softly to himself, knowing he had reached the low point of his life. He gazed at a portrait of his wife and wondered what the future if any awaited him.

His drinking had accomplished its goal, the shakes had ceased. Sitting there alone in his solitude, LaPore contemplated what he would do to get through the day. Rising from his recliner, he headed into the bathroom where he shaved and showered. He then dressed finding his cleanest dirty shirt, had a humble breakfast of burnt toast and a slice of cheese and made his way out the door.

LaPore hated being alone and had never been alone in his youth for he had shared life with his parents and siblings. In the marines he was always surrounded by comrades. From the military, he married his beloved Joey of forty nine years and had children right away. Now with his wife's passing he found the nights lonely and his days unfulfilled. He jumped in his car and headed to the coffee shop. He hated it. Nothing but gossips from the local buds filled his ears over cups of endless coffee. It wasn't his thing but it was better than nothing. As the morning progressed he would head to Wal-Mart just to be around people. Strangers, though they were, there was a semblance of life around him. LaPore would wonder through the store browsing reminiscing of happier days long gone. After a short while, he would head to his watering hole and pick up his jug of whiskey, two packs of smokes and head home where a long lonely day of drinking would be his only companion. Often he would pay his respects to his wife in the cemetery where he would stand mute and alone with his thoughts, memories and heartbreak.

LaPore also, from time to time, would head to solders field where he would silently pay homage to Officer Jenkins, who years before had saved his butt. He would think to himself, but why and for what reason am I still here? Once home, he would sit in his old beat up recliner, smoking and downing his liquor. He would endeavor to watch an old meaningless movie, which he paid little attention too but then proceeded to blame it on the TV.

Occasionally, the phone would ring and it would be friends calling to check on him. They were sincere in their concerns and they knew he had reached the skids. Even with all of their efforts they were unable to pull him out of his downward spiral. His life was on automatic between the drinking and frozen TV dinners. This had become his way of life, sad as it may have been. It had become a meaningless cycle and he prayed for death. LaPore felt there was nothing left for him to do. His mind drifted back to a time when he served his country, mankind, had been a son, a brother, a husband, a father, and a grandfather. He had done so with love and felt he had been in an honest and honorable man. But what was left? In the last 3 years he had moved three times looking for something or someone who would never be there. Depressed, he would find himself at different points of the day in tears. Attempting to reach out and bring back that which he once cherished.

After a day of drinking LaPore would often find himself in the prone position on the rug in his living room not knowing how or when it had occurred. He would chuckle and roll over and once again pass into a peaceful stupor. But the demons would always return. The twisted body's of murdered children. The carnage of fatal accidents and the lonely eyes of kids, with that of a thousand yard stare, that he could not help. The grotesque bodies of those burned horribly in fires. For those vivid images of dead brothers in blue, who had given their all and to what avail? The sadness of those tortured souls marred in drugs. The shame of young girls, for reasons known but to them became night walkers. The battered rape victim, with their irreversible pain and physical abuse, would face a life of mental anguish and fear. His heart was grieving like so many others who donned the blue in that you couldn't save them all. LaPore had too much time to dwell on societies sins. Like so many cops across this land he had given his very soul to his calling only to realize in his old age that it was futile. Day in and day out, his life was being drained from him. The nights were torturous as he relived walking the streets of hell.

Each day was a challenging adventure he wandered though the days in a mist uninterested in anything around him. The things he loved most like music, reading, sports he had forsaken. He lived each day clinging to old memories reliving his past wishing he could go back through time. He knew in his heart that it could only be the anguish over his loss. He even dared to damn his God; his soul was lost floating in a distant limbo. LaPore had sought help through shrinks, priests, and ministers. All turned out futile. When the nights set in he talked to his dead parents, his wife, and old comrades and waited for answers and help that never came. He was trapped in the pit of hell and could find no comfort from the demons that plagued him. Or how to pull himself out of this state of life that he had allowed his soul and mind to dwindle in to decay. He knew that if help or a loving heart did not reach out to him soon, his soul and mind would, like a cancer eat his life away.

As the days turned into weeks and months, he found himself in a mobile home park where he had purchased a home. Here he hoped and prayed he would find peace and tranquility. Abutting a cemetery, he gazed out over this hallowed ground where the flags of veterans at rest, rippled in the wind. He felt that these deceased sentinels would grant him the peace he sought. It was here in this place that he met his Lisa.

My Lisa

There was a time
when I was down
My life was in the
ground.
I couldn't seem to
turn it around.
But then one day
the sun shone bright.
I finally found the
light.
For there within my
rasp so tight.
As the sun shed its
light.
I found my Lisa bright.

Chapter 2

It was a sunny day in May, and as he went about unpacking small items from his car and hand carrying them into his new mobile home, there was a soft angelic voice to the left of him stating, "Hi, welcome to Red Hill Park, I'm your neighbor across the street. I live at number 33 and my name is Lisa Twohill." LaPore somewhat startled, turned and gazed into the grayish eyes of a slim attractive women with a very pretty girlish face. She had a smile that just lit up her entire being and made the person it was meant for feel an instant comfort and ease. Smiling himself he took her small outstretched hand in his. The handshake seemed somewhat prolonged maybe because he delayed releasing his grip. They exchanged small talk for a few minutes when she turned stating "I have to get dinner for my son, nice to meet your and good luck." LaPore watched as she headed toward her trailer and then continued his labor of unpacking.

From time to time, the two would chat in the street, oh about anything and everything about life in general. In October, Lisa became gravely ill and had the task of taking medication intravenously at home. A major storm had cut her power, but LaPore was fortunate as his power, for reasons unknown, was restored quickly. While sitting in his recliner on that cold day, in October, there was a knock on his door. Setting down his perpetual drink, Lance opened the door. It was Lisa, cold, trembling, her color ashen; she asked if she could come in. Certainly, replied Lance. Opening the door to allow her access with a caring voice, he asked, "How can I help you?" Her lips trembling, Lisa responded, "I need a big favor, can or would you help me." "Fire away with your request," shot Lance. Well Lisa continued, "I have to administer several medications intravenously on myself and the nurse who will instruct me its application will be here shortly." "However, I have no power which means I have no lights or heat, may I use your place to do this?" "No sweat, my humble abode is yours, replied Lance."

After watching the nurse instruct Lisa for four hours, Lance was appalled at what she had to do. Suddenly the nurse stated "well we are finished, you're on your own. Hope you digested and got it down." As Lisa began to gather her equipment and prepared to leave, Lance spoke up. "Where are you going? You can't possibly do that at home without electric lights or heat." "Where can I go responded Lisa?" "You'll stay here in my spare bedroom. It's warm and safe and I won't bother you and you can stay as long as necessary."

And so a journey was begun, by two souls, who each suffered tragedy. Lance with the loss of his wife and Lisa the loss of her husband in a tragic motor vehicle accident. She returned to her home in a week but unknown to each of them at the time, Karma had been set in motion. They continued to meet and chat in the street and it soon it developed into a breakfast date from time to time and then an occasional lunch. Several times, they had dinner at Lisa's home and as the weather got warmer Lisa would come and chat with him on his deck. It was nearly two years that this quiet friendship continued. One day the two embraced and emotions for both were put into play.

The foundation for a romantic interlude for the two was laid one night in LaPore's living room. As he guzzled another rye and water, Lisa gazing at him with sad eyes, and in her soft voice stated, "Lance it's such a shame, you served your country with honor and dignity, you were a hell of a cop and you have written a successful book, any you're going to end it as a fucking drunk." She had finished what she had to say and quickly exited LaPore's home. Lapore sat there stunned, bewildered and confused as to what just happened. He gazed at various mementos on his walls and knew she was right. But now he feared she would never return.

Much to LaPore's surprise, Lisa did return the following night and quickly started. She said "Lance you know I have feelings for you and I think you do for me, but I must tell you that you have an option here. It's either me or the booze, I won't tolerate it," and once again she was out the door. She did not wait for answer and was giving him time to think about what she had suggested for their relationship to continue.

LaPore sat there in the dark and did some soul searching. His emotions were mixed. He knew he had strong feelings for this girl, but there was an age difference and he was confused and afraid. He did not want her to slip through his fingers. He realized that maybe here was a chance to redeem his life. It was a no brainer. The booze was discarded and he and Lisa started a serious relationship. After three and half years of hell, God sent an angel to rescue him. They became engaged, thinking it would be that, and that alone, one night in the privacy of his home, with the stars sparkling in the sky, Lance approached her. He took her hand, and went down on his knees, and he began, "honey, I don't want a boyfriend –girlfriend relationship. I don't want a shack up." Lisa looked at him intently simply asked then "What do you want?" Lance replied, "Honey I've searched my soul and it's simple, I want you as my wife."

So it came to be on a quiet December 26th with several close friends in attendance, the two exchanged vows. They became soul mates. Lance had felt that God had rewarded him for his past sufferings. He had sent him an angel, a chance for happiness in his final years. In exchanging vows these were Lance's tributes to his bride, "Lisa, in the spring the rose grows, it lives through the summer, withers and dies in the fall, but the following year, another rose takes its place. How lucky I am, you are my 2nd rose, and so now we will embrace life together. Our souls ready to face life's challenges, love, happiness, sorrows, success, and failures together. Hand in hand we will walk together, till death do we part."

Cop Talk

Black Sam

Greg Slyth, Dick Jardin, Lou Ray, and LaPore along with Big Hank were once again at the Lucky Leaf Cafe. Doing battle on the topic up to this point when Big Hank bellowed out, "Hey do you assholes remember when Black Sam had his first kid and what was done to him?" "Yeah, pipes up LaPore, the poor bastard is ecstatic all happy and bouncing around like a pig with menstrual pain." "Yeah, that's right," agrees Slyth. "He get's to the hospital, Hartford Hospital and I believe. But some of the asshole cops beat him there. They zone in on pediatrics. Garner, a young nurse and threaten, carouse, plead and beg her to go along with them. That it will be the prank of the year and she will be held in high esteem by H.P.D. Reluctantly she agrees." "So what happened!" shouts Ray getting impatient. "Alright, hang on!" shouts back Big Hank.

"So Black Sam gets to pediatrics, states who he is to the H.P.D. influenced nurse. She smiles and states I'll be right back with your son. Mean while, the culprit cops are hiding in an utility closet observing it all. Stifling laughs, they watch as the nurse returns with a small bundle wrapped in blankets to Black Sam. Well officer meet your son and God bless. She unwraps a portion of the blanket revealing the kids face. Black Sam gazes at the face before him. He starts to quiver and shake. He let's out a piercing howl. He begins to jump up and down and pummels the wall. Spittle drips down his check. His eyes are bulging. The young nurse terrified retreats slowly." "Repeating often that it was only a joke orchestrated by his comrades in Blue." "Well, why the fuck did he go so ape shit?" asks Slyth. "Because you big dummy, the face Black Sam saw was white. Sam starts screaming "sacrilege! sacrilege! I'll kill those bastards with my bare hands!" "All four were laughing now, choking on their beers. "Who was it," asked Ray. "Who were the crazy bastards. Well, pipes up Big Hank, I think one is among us, right LaPore? LaPore smiling sleeplessly, I ain't saying nothing. All I know is three guys took a weeks comp time to escape Sam's wrath. Some orderly was over heard two days later in the cape, saying I never saw four cops running so fast down the stairwell. Must of been some incident somewhere. But nobody knows nothing."

"Man that's just wrong," stated Ray that's fucked up, "What'd Sam do? "Oh he just put it on the back burner and waited to take his revenge."

Chapter 3

Four old men sat at the round table against the wall in the rear of the Lucky Leaf Café. They had come here for years to unwind and swill a couple of cold one's. Kept their backs to the wall in order to see who entered the bar. It was a defensive posture learned from experience and heart ache.

Big Mike, taking a pull on his beer broke the silence. "Well Lance, you old fuck, how's the new bride and how's everything going with you guys?" LaPore looking refreshed and younger smiled with his response "good Mike. I've got a great girl. She has breathed life back into my soul. It wasn't looking good for me for awhile." Art chimed in, "yeah, that's because you'd become a balky you asshole. Scared the shit out of all us, and we all thought you were a goner and it would have been a shame, you're not a bad guy. Just a dip shit, glad you're off the sauce and that girl's got to be something with putting on the right track. Now you can enjoy retirement." Ah well, Piped up Joe Buyak, "she's lucky the old fuck can't go on to much longer so she won't have to put up with his shit to long." All four laughed at the pun. There was mutual respect among the four buddies of blue. Three were retiree's from H.P.D. only Buyak was still active, currently wearing a star as a deputy chief and enjoying not only a great respect from retired officers, but also among those on active service.

The four ordered another round and as usual the conversation drifted back into the world of police work. LaPore opened the door to past exploits and memories. "You guys remember when Baly was shot?" The room grew silent and somber; John Baly was a young aspiring officer, who was killed in the line of duty on Palm Street years ago. Deputy Buyak prodded LaPore on vaguely "Lance, what happened that day? How did it go down?" LaPore gulping his beer gazed at a distant photo of old time cops hanging on a wall behind the bar. He began his story, "well it was about 15:30 hours (3:30) the switchboard in commo, lit up like a Christmas tree. Numerous calls reporting a white male in front of 122 Palm was shooting up a car with a shot gun. The male was pointing the weapon in all directions. The neighborhood was in a panic mode and Officer John Riley was dispatching and thanks God because he was the best. Anyhow John growls over the airways, "Units 17, 16, 15 attention 44(line Sergeant) reports of a deranged man is shooting up a car in front of 122 Palm Street with a shot gun. The suspect in question is threatening residents with the same. Be advised that address is on the hot list and we've responded to that location numerous times on all shifts. Be advised one Bob Honaque resides at said address and is considered 10-44 (mental case). Precede Lion, (light's siren) but use caution, party in question is subject brandishing the 10-83 (weapon). The first units on scene advise of activity. 10-4-17 unit 17, 10-4 unit 16, roger unit 15, 10-4 unit 44 and unit 44 to responding units, do not front park at scene, repeat no front parking. Take positions a half block away. Will form up at 66 Palm Street reconnoiter and setup a perimeter till we know what's going down. 10-4 unit 44 understood forth came the response from units 17, 16 and 15."

With the distant wail of sirens, heading in his direction, Honaque made a quick retreat into his house. He was sweating profusely and breathing hard. His eyes were glassy and red rimmed. He had been drinking shots of whiskey all day. This angry man had been arguing with his wife and slapped her around. Enraged he had grabbed his shot gun from his living room closet, a 20 gauge pump. He had loaded it full and placed a box of rounds in his pants pocket. He then exited the house where he commenced to pepper his wife's vehicle with numerous rounds. After shooting up his wife's vehicle, he returned to his living room all the while keeping low. He peered out of the living room window and observed several police vehicles. Their strobe lights rotating and had positioned themselves a half block from his location.

"Fuck them he thought! Let'em come! Take me!" "Robert put the gun away those cops won't play pleaded his wife. Come on all there is right now is damage to my car. Please end this quick begged his terry eyed wife before it escalates and becomes too late." "Fuck you woman!" screamed Honaque as he slammed her against the wall. "You're lucky I haven't shredded you with my toy. Here, get the fuck outta my way! Get in the bedroom and shut the fuck up!" Making his point he then smashed her in the chest with the gun butt, she screamed in pain, clutched her chest and she fled into the bedroom and locked the door behind her. Honaque roared with laughter as he took a deep pull of whiskey from the bottle he had placed on top of the TV. Creeping back to the window he observed several police advancing towards his home. Standing up-right Honaque swung the window open, leveled his shot-gun through the open window at the advancing cops and roared with laughter. As the men in blue scattered diving for cover, he took another pull on his whiskey bottle and waited. Delighted to see what action the cops would now initiate.

Sergeant Don Drillow, in the prone position behind some shrubs, located approximately three hundred feet from the target's home; spoke quickly but calmly into his portable radio, "unit 44 dispatch." "Dispatch go ahead unit 44." "Dispatch confirming we have a male party at address in question, brandishing a shot gun through an open window on North West side of residence. He appears to be a white male. I am unable to determine if anyone else is in dwelling and request additional back up units and notification to S.W.A.T. I will establish a command post in the rear of 244 Palm Street. Residents in immediate vicinity will need to be evacuated post haste. Acknowledge dispatch." "Dispatch unit 44 messages received and understood, watch commander has been notified and all notifications in the works and unit 44 from watch commander hold your position till he arrives on the scene." "Unit 44 dispatch 10-4, I am to hold our position, Roger that. What about those additional units?" "Dispatch unit 44, units 18, 12, 20, 22 have been advised on landline and enroute to your location. Have unit 44 and all units respond to 122 Palm Street and switch to the F-4 frequency."

Sergeant Drillow now accessed the situation. He had several officers, within range of the target. But his concern was for surrounding residents and also he was aware of vehicular traffic for he knew he had to shut down this roadway. Contemplating his actions his thoughts were interrupted by the voice of Lt. Mulchaey over his portable, "unit 50 to 44, have been monitoring the situation and are having footmen picked up and brought to your command post. I am enroute to your location. Is there anything else you need? 10-4—unit 50 I have Palm Street shut down between 400 Palm and 650 Palm Street with no traffic north or south."

The command post was now in the control of Lt. Mulchaey, who was shortly joined by the watch commander captain Heinwich. Officers were directed to commence evacuating nearby homes and to use extreme caution in doing so, as they were in the line of fire from the targeted Honaque residence. As officers fanned out to initiate the evacuation process, others were directed to surround the Honaque home using whatever cover was available. Once the perimeter was established, Captain Heinwich with the use of a megaphone, and in an authoritative voice directed a command to Honaque, who now in a defensive mode in the interior of his home. "Robert Honaque, the voice resounded throughout the neighborhood, you are completely surrounded. I implore you to come out with your hands raised; no harm will come to you. Do it now and this episode can end peacefully without further incidence." Honaque weighing his options coward behind his fortress, sweating profusely, he swilled another shot and remained silent. Again Captain Heinwich repeated his message and waited, silence was the response. Putting down the megaphone Captain Heinwich spoke into his portable radio, "unit 50—dispatch!! Dispatch come in unit 50, unit 50 has S.W.A.T. been notified?" "Dispatch unit 50 that's a 10-4. They are mobilizing and an E.T.A. of 20 minutes for arrival at the scene is contemplated." "Unit 50, dispatch 10-4 and ascertain if tear gas is available," "Stand by unit 50, checking on that request. Dispatch unit 50 10-4 on item requested, S.W.A.T. responded they have ample supply of gas." "Dispatch, thank you and has unit 300 been notified?" "Dispatch unit 50 roger that unit 300 and 100 are enroute to the scene." "Ah, that's good thought Captain Heinwich. The chief and chief of operations notified the cavalry and their closing fast. Whatever happens next is their decision, thank God. Well, better let them know what's being done prior to their arrival. Unit 50 to units 300 and 100, unit 300 is on. Go unit 50, that's a go for unit 100 and 300—unit 50. 50 to 300 and 100 have command post set up at 220 Palm Street. The target house 122 Palm is surrounded by officers, and neighboring homes have been evacuated. S.W.A.T. is enroute and also fire apparatus is in the vicinity in case gas is necessitated. Two ambulances are also in place some 100 yards in rear of command post out of range of gun fire.

Unit 300 to unit 50, 10-4 how many officers involved in operation? Unit 50 to unit 300, I have 30 officers at my disposal. Evacuations have been completed and targeted residence is completely surrounded. Unit 300 to unit 50, very well hold your positions and take no action until myself and unit 100 arrive and access the situation. Unit 50 to unit 300 10-4 sir, we'll remain in a holding pattern.

Honaque is in a drunken stupor, as he watched the blue uniforms converge on his property and then simply disappeared behind various types of cover. His property was surrounded by trees and thick brush. The denseness of shrubbery made it impossible to track the officer's movements. Cursing he stumbled into an adjoining room, in an attempt to observe more from a different venue. But the denseness of the vegetation again marred his view. In a rage he returned to his original position. Lighting a camel cigarette, decided to play it out and see what the fucking cops had in mind. "Fuck them he thought! Let them come." "We'll see who's still standing when the smoke clears. Honaque was now in a pugilistic mood and he was becoming more aggressive with another snort of whiskey. He had even pissed himself but didn't care. "Life was a hassle. His wife was a bitch, his job sucked and his bills were out of sight. Fuck it all! Fuck the world and most of all fuck everyone, especially the fucken cops!!" Leveling the shot gun, he pulled the trigger. The explosion ripped through the neighborhood. He giggled with glee, like a school girl, that'll scare the shit out of them. Make'em think. The shot resounded in the quiet and the cops surrounding the building tried to dig even deeper.

In whatever cover they possessed not knowing who the son of bitch was shooting at. Revolvers drawn and aimed at the house, they waited for a command that never came. Discipline was the champion of the moment as they held fast. Reciting silent prayers and thinking of loved ones. This was a cop's worst nightmare, a barricaded nutcase with a weapon and a possible hostage. Discipline and precision were the working brothers here. Restraint had to control emotions, fear, and be cast aside. This was what it was all about, the training, the praying, and the donning of the blue.

Here was the great test, the quest to preserve life and property. To serve and protect these men in blue held their defensive posture. Sweating and praying, amongst them with a firm resolve to discipline and waited for orders from those in command.

Captain Heinwich approached his chief, threw a salute and brought the chief up to the standard operation procedure that had been implemented. "Oh, chief S.W.A.T. is now on the scene." "Good" responded the chief. "Have Lt. Horwan report to me like yesterday." "Yes sir, will do." Lt. Horan stood at ease while the chief relayed his orders. He knew Chief Culligan knew his stuff. Lt. Chief Culligan began, "Deploy your men at strategic locations and make sure they have close fields of fire at the suspected target. No one to fire unless I give the order, is that understood?" "Yes sir understood no firing unless ordered by you." "Correct Lieutenant; join your men and good luck.

S.W.A.T. sharpshooters were now in position. Each had chosen a fire zone where field of fire was unimpaired. The targeted home was now under full police siege. Time would unveil what action would occur. There was a sudden commotion on the south side of the targeted house. One of the S.W.A.T snipers reported a woman climbing out of a window. She was disheveled and hysterical. Several officers risking injury rushed to her aid and assisted her to a waiting ambulance. Lt. Horan to command post unit 50 go ahead S.W.A.T one. "Sir, we have the wife in our custody. She states Honaque is alone in the house. But he is very intoxicated and is in possession of a 20 gauge shot-gun with ample ammo. She is uncertain if there are any other weapons in the home, "unit 50, S.W.A.T one 10-4 very good, all officers hold your positions."

Honaque, in his defense perch, continued to observe the scene lay out before him. Cops were everywhere. He knew S.W.A.T. snipers were at this moment zeroing in on him. His mind was in turmoil. He swallowed a stiff shot of whiskey and sat on the floor. He was hoping he was out of the line of fire. Chief Culligan beckoned Captain Heinwich. "Have our officer's close in quietly and cautiously. Let's see if we can't force this asshole's hand. Have Sergeant Drillow's team prepare to lay down tear gas." "Yes, sir, I'm on it."

As the officers fanned out in an attempt to flank the house, officers Baly, Snyder, and Topaz crawled through dense brush. Their revolver at the ready for they were in anticipation of what was to come and with their heart beating rapidly. They came upon the small clearing, and started to sprint for additional cover stumbling on a twig or rock, Officer Baly was propelled towards the ground. Falling hard, he heard a loud retort that resounded through the neighborhood. His weapon had discharged, Baly eying his two comrades asked did I just shoot you? At first he had felt nothing, and then a searing pain exploded within his stomach. Nauseated, turning gazed, he gasped once then laid still. The bullet had entered his body through a small opening in his bullet proof vest. Officers Snyder and Topaz horrified at first were able to gain composure. "Unit 16 to command post, and dispatch we have officer down in rear of target home. Officer shot himself in side, as a result of a horrific fall. Need help and fast. The officer is unconscious."

As Chief Culligan and his staff listened all hell broke loose in the command post. Culligan ordered Sergeant Drillow and his team to lay down a barrage of tear gas into the Honaque home. Whoop, whoop, whoop, the swish of three tear gas projectiles were discharged toward the target. Honaque sitting beneath his window heard the smashing of glass. Peering behind him he saw and felt the stinging heat and odor of the tear gas. As the gas enveloped him, he began to cough and had trouble breathing. He couldn't think straight. He stumbled towards the door. His craving for air propelled him forward. He had to free himself from this agony. Officer Snyder and Topaz continued to render whatever aid to their wounded comrade. They knew he was in tough shape, but medical personal were unable to move to their position until the suspect Honaque was in custody and secure.

Captain Heinwich on the megaphone knowing one of his men was injured, spoke into the megaphone with a tremor in his voice, he repeated his earlier message. "Robert Honaque come out with your hands in the air. Do it now or suffer the consequences of your actions."

Honaque terrified moved to the front door. Grabbing a white towel, he opened the door waving the towel. Hands in the air, hands in the air, screamed numerous cops. Honaque doing as he was told was suddenly tackled by several officers, roughly frisked and rolled on his back and cuffed. Get up you prick cried one of the cops. "You've had your little sortie for a long, long time asshole."

As Honaque was led away in cuffs and the paramedics rushed to aid the fallen officer Baly. As the medical personnel approached officers, Snyder and Topaz, who retreated a few yards to give them ample working room, their faces displayed their deep concern for their critically injured brother. The small group was soon joined by Chief Culligan and Major Dellaher, chief of operations, concern for their wounded officer masked by years of discipline and courage. Officer Baly was rolled or his back and paramedics Tyrone Ellis quickly took his vitals and calling to his partner, Sheila Gritte, his findings. "Blood pressure 85 over 50, pulse low and failing rapidly and he's in rough shape. Let's roll and get him on the stretcher and get him in the wagon. Head for Mt. Sinai Hospital as it's nearby." Lights and sirens blaring the ambulance sped off leaving the officers who remained fearful for their brothers well being.

Chief Culligan addressing Major Dellaher stated, "Have chaplain Cleary picked up and brought to Sinai. This isn't looking good." "Yes sir, "already in the works." replied Dellaher. "Who's picking him up," Frank asked the chief. "Sergeant LaPore, the south boss. He's enroute as we speak." "Very Good, oh and also have Captain Heinwich at command post reach out to his, honor the major. Bring him up to date. Also find out the where about of officer's Baly's wife and send a police escort. She'll need to be brought to the hospital, post haste." "Roger, Chief Heinwich is on top of notifications and who needs to be brought where." "Okay, let's secure this scene and get our people back on the line. Have the dicks and evidentiary services process this scene and Frank, you handle the press. I'm going to the hospital." Okay, chief can do. Hope the kid's going be okay." "Yeah pray, Frank, pray," with that Chief Culligan head bowed, headed towards his unmarked, oblivious to his officers salutes.

Mary Baly was just typing a report nearly completed when she was startled by the sudden appearance of her supervisor, Ann Bell, who touching her, and softly related that two officers were in her office requesting Mary's presence immediately. "Why?" asked Mary. "Don't know, but they said it was imperative to see you." Mary ceased her typing and followed her supervisor into her office. She was startled to see a Sergeant with gold braid on his hat and another officer pacing nervously. Extending her hand to the officers she simply stated "hi, I'm Mary Baly, can I help you?" Sergeant LaPore had been down this road before. His eyes locked with Officer Harland's. No words were exchanged between the officers. It wasn't necessary. They'd experienced too much grief though the years to even have to exchange the actual words.

LaPore, hat in his hand, gazed at Mary, long and hard, found her to be young and attractive. Masking his inner feelings, he addressed this young woman with as much compassion as he could muster, "Hello, Mrs. Baly, my name is LaPore, this is Officer Harland. We've been directed here to inform you that your husband, John, has been injured and you're needed at Mount Sinai Hospital. I'm afraid I don't have all the details, he lied," not wanting to cause her undue duress, especially here at her employment.

Mary Baly felt a tinge of fear in her bowels, her mouth dry, and her breathing now became labored. She was able to stammer, yes sergeant, I'll just get my coat and purse.

In the meantime, the E.R. personnel were working relentlessly on Officer Baly. His vital signs continuing to deteriorate and Dr. Martin Brach, one of the attending physicians, made a quick decision. "Let's get him to surgery we're losing him. Let's move people, let's move."

Chief Culligan along with a large contingent of officers had gathered in the waiting room. Grief, anger and fear displayed on their faces. Several officers were assigned and directed to keep the press at bay.

Sitting in the front passenger seat, Mary Baly was locked in quiet thoughts. She had just found out she was pregnant at 1:00 that afternoon. Their first child, what unknown she was heading for? LaPore heading towards the hospital operated his cruiser at a good speed. But he had made his decision of no lights or sirens, in order not to cause more anxiety to this young woman to his right. Officer Harland, in the head seat remained silent lost in his own thoughts was it happening again, was another blue centurion about to muster out from the thin blue line.

In the O.R. surgeons cut an incision into Officer Baly's stomach. As they entered the cavity, they were appalled at the effect the bullet had caused. Major organs were, devastated; laboring feverishly in a heroic attempt to affect major repairs and stem blood flow. It was futile. Halfway through the surgery, the anesthesiologist bellowed flat-line, flat line, he's flat lined. An attempt was made to message the heart to no avail. Officer Baly aged 28 now belonged to the ages. He expired at 17:10 hours. Doctor's wiping their brows, stared at nothing, saddened and frustrated that their skills could not save this brave officer.

Mary Baly, LaPore, Harland entered the hospital though a gauntlet of officers, who lined the corridor. A respectful silence followed them as their footsteps echoed and announced their arrival. Mary was rushed to the waiting room and was shocked when she was greeted by Chief Culligan and father Cleary, the police chaplain. Each placing a hand on each of her arms and assisting her into a somewhat comfortable chair, Chief Culligan steadied himself and related to Mary in a short summation what had led her husband to this hospital. Trembling, tearful Mary joined the others in the suspenseful fearful wait. Little was said. The tick tock of a wall clock breaking the silence, hands clasped in her lap. Mary prayed and waited, in horror and nausea gripped her. She could only hope. Hope that her man would survive his ordeal.

Conversation was muffled as the waiting room was hushed and subdued as the family and friends of Officer Baly suffered in anguish, solitude. Some were reciting prayers and others chose to stare off at nothing, alone with their thoughts. The honk of a large truck outside their window broke the silence. Suddenly the door to the waiting room burst open and standing there in his green regalia was Dr. Peter Stern, the head surgeon in charge of the operating procedure on Officer Baly. All eyes were tuned in on the doctor. He walked slowly towards Mary, now flanked by Chief Culligan and Father Cleary, taking her hand in his, his eyes locked with those of the chief and father; he then returned his focus to Mary. Speaking softly his voice was just audible, "I'm so, so sorry, we did everything medically and humanly possible, but the damage inflicted by the bullet was to devastating to your husband's major organs. We lost him at 18:25 hours, please accept my sincere condolences, he must have been a brave man."

The room swirled about Mary Baly, letting out a loud gasp, clutching her chest she fell back onto the couch guided gently by the strong hands of Chief Culligan and Father Cleary. "Water, someone get a glass of water." Commanded the chief, and all those not family members clear the room, thanks for the comforting support and company. Mary, her head spinning, heard faint voices calling to her. They sounded so distant. She gradually came around. It was then the shock of Dr. Stern's words sunk in. Letting out an agonizing scream, she began to cry hysterically. Tears cascaded down her cheeks and fell onto the carpeted floor, for her heart was broken. Her life was now shattered. She could only feel the emptiness that engulfed her.

Satisfied there was no more to accomplish here, Chief Culligan and Father Cleary led the young pregnant Mary to an un-marked cruiser. She would now journey to an empty home and her man in blue was gone. Rendering the supreme sacrifice, her mind flooded with fears of the unknown. What was she to do? A new life was stirring in her womb and her husband never knew for she hadn't had the opportunity or time to tell him. "John, I love you," she cried and succumbed to the medication given to her.

Mary Baly stood tall on the church steps gazing into the distance. Her brain numb with pain as the funeral cortege carrying the remains of her husband drew even closer. She snapped a photograph with her mind's eye of the event unfolding before her. Hundreds of police officers marched in step to the rear of the hearses. Their footsteps echoing across the landscape, a sea of blue, 8 a breast, they kept a sharp cadence to the mournful sound of muffled drums. An honor guard of blue stood somber and proud waiting to receive their deceased brother. Thousands of onlookers lined the street, some sad, some indifferent, but all curious to this spectacle of blue paying homage to their brother officer. Off in the distance a bag pipe sounded its mournful wail. A soft rain began to fall as though even the angels were crying.

All this registered in Mary Baly's subconscious as tears streamed down her cheeks. Clutching her stomach she softly whispered, my child you'll never know your father and he will never know you, but you and I will never, never forget him as long as we both shall live. For his memory will live on in our minds and hearts.

As the casket ascended the stairs to the church, the crisp command of attention and present arms resounded over the crowd and officers now at attention. An over flow crowd was in attendance. Mary was forced to listen to the services on loud speakers. The Reverend Father Cleary began his eulogy as the crowd listened attentively. "Cherished family of Officer Baly, loyal friends, and sister and brother officers, we are gathered here to pray for our brother in blue. Why it is that good is often cut down by evil? Why is it that a young man who chose to serve humankind lies here before us in peaceful repose while the person directly responsible live to begin another day? None of us here can answer those questions. None of us understand. Is there a great plan? One only knows. I can only attempt to offer solace and comfort. I can only praise Officer Baly for his courage and sacrifice. I can only thank him and all in law enforcement for their courage, sacrifice and devotion. Officer Baly belongs to the ages now. He sleeps with our maker. He was loyal and devoted to his oath of office, to serve and protect. His was the ultimate sacrifice for his life was lost in ensuring that others were shielded from harm. He along with thousands of officers throughout this great land treads in harm's way to safeguard the comfort and security of citizens. They swore to protect the thin blue line, is one short today, but more than that an unborn child will never know the physical presence of a father. A young mother and wife must now ponder what the highway of life will lead her. Speaking softly, just above a whisper, Father Cleary addressed the bereaved widow, as though the two were alone, isolated from a cruel, harsh, unforgiving world. Mary, difficult as it will be you must be strong and brave. Not only for the honorable memory of your husband, but more so for the unborn child resting in your womb. The hand of God brushed your brow at the moment of conception. This alone seals the bond between you and John and the child to be. Yes, John is gone, but his spirit will always be in our hearts. His history always in our minds, and good men wherever they see a blue and white will take a moment to remember. My friends, this casket before me contains the mortal remains of Officer John Baly, a devoted husband and honest and loyal officer and a child of God. We will grieve. We will miss him, but his soul will live on in our hearts. He rests with the Lord. For Christ himself proclaimed, blessed are the peacemakers for they shall see the kingdom of God. Words are futile I know. All we have left is prayer. Pray, my friends that today, that tomorrow, the world is a little better because of Officer Baly's and others in blue who gave their all. The supreme sacrifice, so others may live."

The assembled crowd was silent except for muffled sobs from Mary. The service had ended, now the difficult and torturous journey lay ahead. The march to lay officer Baly in his final resting place continued at a slow and steady pace. The soft rain had ceased and a gentle breeze now whistled through the grave yard. Those in attendance stood in mute silence, alone with their thoughts. Mary, sitting with her family, head bowed gazed at her husband's casket. Tears lined her face as she whispered her private goodbye and thanked him for the love and time shared and for the child she would soon bear. Father Cleary finished his litany for the dead. The attention was given. Hundreds of blue clad officers snapped to. An explosion of heals clicking together cascading throughout the cemetery. The order present arms rendered. Hundreds of white gloved hands raised in a hard salute. Off in the distance positioned on a knoll. Seven officers raised their riffles and fired their volleys. The echo startled Mary. Officer's tears in their eyes, stared long and hard at the flag draped casket and private whispered farewell. A soft mournful tune flowed across the fresh cut and well groomed landscape. Taps, the final homage to fallen soldiers in blue, filled the air. Few dry eyes could be found.

Chief Culligan folded the flag, with it in hand, knelt before Mary Baly, and spoke to her. "On behalf of the State of Connecticut, The City of Hartford, will you accept this flag as a token of our deep respect and thanks to your brave husband for his sacrifice? His was an honorable act." The service was over. The crowd of mourners, and officers shuffled off and were gone. Mary alone, stood off in the distance. She whispered softly, I love you John, rest in peace. She turned and headed for a waiting vehicle. But the words of the patch of the Hartford police offered comfort.

Post Phoebus Nubila

After the storm-the sun

Cop Talk

Domestic Adventures

Big Hank, LaPore, Art and Deputy Chief Buyak were sitting at their personnel table at The Lucky Leaf Café. Deputy Chief Buyak speaks up, "Hey you guys didn't hear what happened at 17 Liberty the other night?" "No pipes up," Hank. "So spit it out Chief, what the fuck happened?" "Well, the guys are constantly reporting there on domestics seems these two are always at it. The old lady, Marge weighs 650 lbs and her husband Nate, is just a little bit of a guy about 5'2. I don't think he weighs 120 lbs. Well, anyway, the officers respond again last Friday, B squad and found the old lady sitting on top of Nate. His lips were blue and his eyes are bulging out of his head. He shit his pants. He's deader than Hell. Suffocating for he couldn't exhale. At this point it took six cops to pull Margie off of him. When questioned, she states, "She fell on him and couldn't get up." The boss on scene makes a decision and they charged her with manslaughter to cover their asses. What the fuck? You've gotta death here. They go to put her in the paddy wagon and the wagon tilts all the way over to the right. They drive all the way to the P.D. like a crippled elephant leaning to the right. The guys try to be professional but they can't stifle their laughter in the hallway. You know how it is cop humor to keep from going over the edge. "So, what the fuck happened to Margie," asked LaPore. "If it took six cops to lift her off Nate, the prosecuting body believed that she could have fallen and couldn't prove she sat on him like the guys suggested. The judge does tell her, "If you remarry go on a strict diet. Case dismissed next case."

He laughs, Art says, "that's pretty funny, but look at the one we had some years ago on Kent Street, same scenario. The cops are always responding to a domestic to the William's home every Friday night. Well this one Friday they responded and the door's ajar. Nobody answered the cops' knocks or yelling. So they entered the apartment. The kitchen walls are swath in blood. Old man Williams is lying on the kitchen floor on his back up against a kitchen cabinet. A steak knife is buried up to the hilt in his chest. Blood and shit everywhere, the place stinks like a shithouse, garbage everywhere, dead mice, etc, etc. So they enter the living room and find the old lady, I think her name was Ethel, lying on the couch bare ass. She had pissed all over herself and covered with blood and shit holding a pint of Calvert's. One of the cops jabs her with his finger and she grunts. Rises from the couch, she stinks like a pig farm. She wailing, "What the fuck you Gestapo want now?" The cops glance at one another and the one says, "Hey Ethel, you fucked up this time. Your old man's in the kitchen deader than his dick." "What y'all talking about!" she shouts back. "Well seems you buried a steak knife in his chest and he's gone, Ethel, gone, gone, gone. Ethel yells at the cop, spit flying from her mouth. "Mother Fucker gone!" Where the cop fires back, "I don't know maybe to Hell, but this time you stabbed him to death." Ethel stares off in space for a minute, then let's out a loud fart and a half babbling states, "What the fuck you say man, I stabbed him before, he never died." The moral to the story, "don't piss off your old lady."

The four cops burst out laughing, finished their drinks, said their goodbyes, see you later; they all have tears in their eyes from the laughter as they head home to their old ladies for they will take Arts words to heart and not piss off their own.

Chapter 4

"Recruits! Attention!" The command was given by Captain P. Dullivan. It echoed through the academy hall. Sixty recruits sprang to attention, waiting patiently and apprehensively as to what instructions would follow. "At ease and be seated," ordered the academy's commander. Captain Dullivan paced slowly back and forth a trick he had implemented years ago. He did so purposely, let the recruits stew. Let them squirm; this was no high school curriculum. This was about a profession that dealt with life and death on a daily basis. His mood was somber. Determined that these police recruits, those that survived, would be capable police officers prepared to serve and protect the City of Hartford and those who traveled its byways.

Recruit Barbara Horiaty sat erect and silent. She was the lone female in this recruit class. Upon entry she was warned of the hardships to be thrust at her. More so than the male recruits for the reason most police administrators harbored strong opinions that females were meant to deal strictly within the ranks of the juvenile division. But, times were changing, crime was on the incline. Sex crimes had peaked and educated people peered into the future and recognized that female officers would almost certainly be an asset to the police vehicle.

She listened attentively, as Dullivan laid out the curriculum regarding their training. Three months of physical hardship and hours on retaining the rules of law, and strict adherence to discipline. Two hours of intense hand to hand training and followed up with many hours at the firing range. She was a very attractive woman and eyes were always passing over her physical being. She was familiar that there was snickering behind her back and knew that those instructors on the side lines were out to discourage her. But her mental resolve had steeled her. She sat erect and proud and was determined to prove that she could take whatever challenges that were thrown at her. This was her dream and she had always aspired to being a police officer, to don the blue. She had passed the tough entrance exams, which had propelled her into the academy. She would not fail. She would demonstrate to all she came into contact with that she, Barbara Horiaty, would measure up to the vigorous standards that was required to inherit the title of COP.

As days turned into weeks, recruit Horiaty impressed her instructors with the level of her skills that were developing. Barbara had even put a hurt on some of her partners in judo. She fired expert at the range. Not only with the police service revolver, but also, with the shotgun. Through sweat and sometimes private tears, she was prevailing and had earned the respect and admiration not only of her fellow class mates but also from the academy staff. At times, there was solidity to this grueling training. For example, when it was time for her to be the victim pretty, well endowed, who could blame these sweating males for the chance to practice C.P.R. on Barbara and perhaps slipping in the process and who knows where ones hands night land. However, the instructors were quick to recognize this and a dummy figurine drafted to replace the human victim.

Days turned into weeks filled with lectures from states attorneys, doctors, and instructors and from numerous agencies, such as the F.B.I., treasury A.T.F. secret service, lawyers, psychiatrists, D.C.F., state police, forestry, and the list was endless. So much of the law was to be digested and retained along with periodical exams were used to net out along the way several recruits. They were summoned to Captain Dullivan's office thanked release. Through it all Barbara continued to excel and outperforming most of her male counterparts. She found herself standing tall and proud. Her final grades had stamped her #3 in the class. She had accomplished her personal crusade and she would graduate with an exemplary standing in her class. Her dream was about to come true.

"Recruit class 75," bellowed Captain Dullivan. Tension, as all of the recruits sprang to attention, sharp and proud in their pressed uniforms of blue. Their silver shields glistened in the lightening. Their hearts pounding, for they had succeeded the harsh training that police recruits undergo and have to successfully pass. For these recruits will soon be plunged into the byways of hell.

Chief Culligan strode to the podium. His blue eyes gazed out at this sea of young faces in blue soon to join his thin blue line. Memories of his own youth flashed through his mind when he too stood before his chief. Clearing his throat, he addressed his new officers. "Welcome to the ranks of the thin blue line. You will soon join these ranks. Ranks of the Hartford police department. You will be asked to sacrifice yourself on a daily basis, to render your heart and soul to this great calling. It is a profession you have chosen. Do it well and be proud. Protect the good name given you. Do not dishonor. You will deal with many anxious moments in your careers. Life and death will walk by your side. Families will spend holidays alone. You will know temptation and loneliness. You will often be frustrated with society. When these shallow moments occur, remember your oath of office. Let fire in your hearts remind you that your duty is to serve and protect. Bear in mind that your actions will be monitored by the public you serve. You have the power to arrest and if necessary to kill. But remember, respect that power. Guard it with your very soul. For our maker is watching. Good luck and God bless. Oh and remember these words on our uniform patch are etched the words, Post Phoebus Nubila, which stands for, After the Storm, the Sun." Family and friends in attendance rose as one and clapped and cheered. They had smiles on their faces and some had tear rimmed eyes. All knew that this was a dangerous calling and that the blue line was all that kept Satan and his demons, of the street, from devouring the young, the old, the poor, and the impoverished. It was a battle that would continue till time stood still.

Officer Horiaty parked her vehicle in the rear parking lot of the police department located on Jennings Road. Grabbing her gear, she entered the station and headed for the female locker room. A bit nervous, she had been assigned to the grave yard shift. She dressed quickly eying herself in the full length mirror. Correcting what small flaws existed in her appearance. Entering the squad room she was greeted by silence. Cops already seated eyed her with curiosity and with some suspicion. Not one approached her and she was left seated alone in silence. She was startled by the swish of the squad room door opening which allowed a small trickle of air admitted to the stuffy atmosphere. Captain Heinwich entered flanked by his lieutenant and sergeants. The command of "fall in for roll call" was bellowed by Sergeant Honoly as he stood at the podium. He then began to call off the roll, Murphy! "Here," Gonzalez, "here," Primo," aye, here, my Sergeant Joseph, wish I wasn't but here now, sergeant." "Alright, can the shit guys," shouted Captain Heinwich! "Let's have a proper roll setting here. Damn he thought to himself these vet's can be ball busters. The roll continued. Finally, coming to Officer Horiaty, all eyes were trained on her as she responded, "here sir." Captain Heinwich apprised the female officer who stood at stiff attention. His first thought, "What the fuck, they sent us playboy, now I will have to worry about one of my shit heads making an ass of himself. Locking eyes with Officer Horiaty, officer you're assigned to unit 16. Your field training officer is Officer Toone. Pay attention and learn. He's one of the best. Now you begin your real education in police work." Cat calls and lewd remarks were directed toward Officer Toone. Hey Toone, stay on the line, no cruising in the parks. Hope mama's been to you the jabs continued. Officer Horiaty just smiled. She was determined to earn respect. She knew she would have to deliver to deserve it. Finally the hassling ended. "Okay, let's hit the road," Sergeant Honoly, bellowed. "Use caution and keep your backs to the wall, extra attention to the bars, it's Friday night. Try to hover around their locations at closing. Fall out and make sure you check your cruiser equipment." Toone approached Horiaty. "Let's saddle up and hit the streets. Just play on me. The first couple of nights, I'll take the lead on complaints. When you're a little more comfortable with your surroundings, maybe in two or three shifts, I'll let you take the lead. See what you've learned and how you handle situations. You've been well trained and you had to impress a lot of gold braid or you wouldn't be here. Don't let the troops rattle you. They're good guys, but, you understand you will be tested. It's only natural. Don't be afraid to ask questions. No matter how petty. Someday you'll be on your own, so now's the time, okay let's hit it."

Barbara took an instant liking to this Officer Toone. His appearance was sharp. He spoke in a soft menacing voice and eluded an air of confidence which were the results of 15 years in the trenches. Finding unit 16, they checked their equipment. Satisfied all was in order, they fired up the engine and roared into the night. Toone grabbing the mike spoke calmly, "Unit 16 Officers Toone and Horiaty, on the line." Barbara felt a surge of pride and adrenaline as the dispatcher's voice acknowledged, "Unit 16, Officer Toone and Horiaty on the line 00.15."

The two weeks under Toone's tutoring proved to be un-eventful. Several domestics, motor vehicle accidents, loud noise complaints, more or less broom and dust pan complaints which were handled with ease. But the one thing she had observed is that Officer Toone responded to his complaints with compassion. That he always displayed a semblance of respect to individuals he dealt with. He entered a call for service as a lamb, but could change into a lion on a dime if so provoked. As their last shift spent together came to a close, the two shook hands. Toone final advice to her, "trust and believe you'll witness human depravity at its worst. We're here to keep the lid on the garbage can and to assist all in time of need. Good luck kid, be humble and fair, you'll do alright." With that Officer Toone turned and was off. She stood transfixed watching his silhouette swallowed by the night. Officer Horiaty would never forget the lessons and secrets he passed on to her while going in harm's way.

Officer Horiaty was feeling a little more comfortable and was getting the feeling for the streets. She was now assigned to a second field training Officer Hank Harland who at 6'3, 240lbs. was an imposing figure, who commanded respect. Their assignment was the Albany Avenue beat, a hot spot in the city, where several bars were known as trouble spots. Where drugs, and prostitution ran rampant. Shooting's were frequent and decent citizens bunkered down early as the dark and its street demons settled in. It was when the thin blue line was most alert. The men and women in blue knew the drill. This was the hour when predators of fellow man would abound.

Hank was another staunch teacher. Entering the bars and taking control immediately when situation warranted. True to his size, discouraged up start trouble makers, but there were always the fool hardy whose brains were cooked by drugs and booze who thought these officers could be defeated. One night in the red ash, while patrons were dispensing, as the joint was closing, one such jackass pulled a weapon and shot two men standing next to him. Officers Harland and Horiaty had just entered through a rear door, and witnessed the accuse attempting to flee though a side door. Officer Horiaty tackled the man known as Willie Hightower, aka big bear, to the floor, while Officer Harland kicked him in his loins and disarmed him all in one motion. "Down on the floor, fuckhead ordered Harland! Place your hands behind your back! Do it now!" Meanwhile, Officer Horiaty was administering first aid to one of the victims. She knew the first victim, was gone. She had found no pulse, no heartbeat from the victim. Big bear now cuffed and secured was thrown into a booth by Officer Harland, also known as big hank. Several officers had arrived as back-up. The crime scene secured, the dicks notified, an ambulance was enroute. At 12:55 hours, in her third week of patrol, Officer Horiaty was involved in her first homicide. Unfortunately there would be many more. But when their tour ended she felt some elevation. She had assisted in her first murder arrest and had stood tall and reacted to the incident like a coiled tiger. Both she and Officer Harland were commended for their actions, but, Officer Horiaty knew it went further than a medal. She was earning the respect from her comrades in blue.

Barbara was impressed with big Hanks style of approach to various crimes. He never once used his size as intimidating. Rather, he approached people with a certain respect. True his size was intimidating and his strength was readily available, but he practiced patience and restraint. Barbara picked up on these traits and storing them in her subconscious for future references. After one particular shift, enroute home she chuckled to herself, remembering some of big Hanks advice. "Remember kid, most of your career will be spent among gutter sleuths, the depraved, the druggies, the perverts and the witness episodes which the average person would not think possible and would not believe it. We're here to clean up the garbage, to protect the meek and innocent. Never forget that, but remember this, you may be able to save the world, but not everyone in it."

The two weeks with big Hank flew. Having responded to numerous felony calls and assisting to several apprehensions, she was fast digesting the fact that human depravity abounded on the streets. The words, mother-fucker, fuck, cock-sucker, bitch, homo were added to her repertoire by the animals that prowled the streets. She had saved a life, delivered a baby, held a dead child in her hands, fought back tears. She could not falter for she was on her way. She was determined to honor the blue. The time had arrived when she would enter Dante's Inferno alone where life and death decisions would hang in the balance by seconds.

As she went about her duties, days turned into weeks, weeks into months, and with inexhaustible energy, she patrolled her areas with vigor. She paid attention to the poor, the vanquished, the lonely, the aged, youth, always ready and willing to listen to their troubles no matter how small. She went out of her way to ascertain where disabled persons were house bound determined that they would not perish through neglect. She checked on battered women and assisted them with finding the proper help. Often on her own time her reputation with her peers continued to excel. Citizens gazed at her with respect. Criminals knew they were messing with a tigress. She had dropped many a male with knowledge of judo, quickly with the eye, she could spot scumbags in seconds and her felony arrest sheet climbed upward. Comrades marveled at her activities in police work. Officers felt secure knowing she was working an adjoining district. They knew that if she was your back-up some dirt bag was in a world of shit. Yes, she was proving that the female officer was here to stay. That yes they measured up to the high standards of policing and that in some cases, they outshone their male counterparts. Administrators had sat up and taken notice realizing that this officer was a God send.

Plans were being implemented in the heart of headquarters where ranking officers of the intelligence divisions and vice and narcotics had taken a keen interest. They would soon utilize this officer for the good of the department and community. Barbara sat in the semi darkness of her living room reflecting on her life. Her eyes darted about taking in various family photos and memorabilia. They settled on a gold rimmed frame, which already contained two distinguished services medals and two recent awards and several written commendations. Smiling to herself she felt contented. Feeling good about herself and her career as a cop had been a pinnacle of success. She enjoyed the respect and affection of her peers. Five years on the job, she was currently high on the sergeant's list. Barbara felt elated, loved her job and the few rewards it bore her.

The ringing phone startled her, rousing her from her solitude. Reaching to the end table, she retrieved the phone. "Hello," she half whispered. "Hello Barbara, this is Lieutenant Dellaher. Sorry to disturb you, but I need to talk, are you busy?" Barbara sat upright. Her curiosity peaking, Lieutenant Dellaher was the commanding officer of vice and narcotics, "good evening lieutenant," she responded. "No sir I'm not busy. Just sitting here, gearing down. Had a busy tour today, you know what it's like." Dellaher chuckling, "yeah sometimes you get the bear and sometimes the bear gets you. Okay, here's the scoop, can you be in my office tomorrow at 10:00 hours?" Barbara's mind was in overdrive, thinking to herself, "What can this be about? Yes sir, of course 10:00 hours tomorrow can do sir." "Ah, very good then, I'll see you in the a.m. Sleep tight." The phone went dead. Barbara rising from the couch, yawning was excited and curious. Heading for the bathroom, she drew a hot bath. She was in thought mode. "What could the commanding officer of vise and narcotics have in mind?" Oh well she thought, "We'll know soon enough."

At 10:00 a.m. the next morning, Barbara sat across from Lieutenant Dellaher seated behind his desk. Dellaher smiling was impeccable in his appearance, tall and straight. He was always well groomed, sharp and in top physical shape. It was the old marine in him. His office was humble but the walls were aliened with numerous photos from his service days, police career. There were numerous citation and commendations adorned the walls.

Clearing his throat he stared long and hard at Barbara. "Officer Horiaty, he began, I don't have time to fuck around here. So, I'm going to come at you hard and straight. Prostitution in Little Hollywood is on the rise. (Little Hollywood is a mixture of homes located in the Westside of the city) As a result, street crimes have soared, muggings, robberies, burglaries etc., etc., you get the drift. The department is under pressure from civic groups and the arch-diocese to gain control of the situation. The uniform division is too busy to effectively address the issue. So it falls on my unit to implement a plan of action. You're wondering, at this point, why you're here? Okay. Understood here's the skinny and listen hard and long. Digest my request thoroughly and then make your decision.

The bulk of our problem out there comes from suburbanite John's looking for a cheap thrill. They're naive and stupid, but the chaos, their creating is causing havoc to our stats and has inflamed area residents along with the arch-bishop. You're here for this reason and I'll explain. No offense, but you're a very attractive woman. Have proven time and time again, your actions have earned you the respect, not only from the troops but your superiors and public as well. I and the department wish to use these attributes to our advantage. Are you still interested and should I continue?" "Yes sir," replied Barbara in a barely audible whisper. "Okay, coming at you. Here it is. We would like you to go undercover. That is dress very sexy. You'll work the evening shift and be tied to my unit. Your job will be to lure the John's. You'll be wired and unmarked chase units will be close by to snatch violator's. You understand that the John's have to commit in order to effect arrest's. I'm not going to print a pretty picture here. This is dangerous. You will be standing alone and you and I know what lurks out there. I'm not issuing you an order and this is strictly voluntary. The decision rests squarely with you. No offense will be taken if you decline. Do you need time to consider?" Barbara sitting transfixed and attentive, didn't bat an eye, "sir when do I start?"

Dellaher once again stared at her only this time with a slight smile. Her reputation as a street cop had reached to commanders throughout the department. He felt a deep respect for this young woman and a tinge of fear. He knew he was planting her in harm's way. But this was the job and it went with the territory. A plan had been forged now it had to be implemented. "God be with her," he thought.

"Okay, thank you officer. You'll report to Sergeant Howan's team. Evening shift tomorrow and be here early. You'll be briefed and prepped. You then will be wired and all that shit. Also the department will purchase several sets of dress attire that you'll be wearing. Hope you don't take offense because they'll be alluring outfits. I thank you and good luck. I don't have to tell you to be careful. I and the department have full confidence that your actions will prove this operation a success."

Embarking from the lieutenant office Barbara ran smack into the bulk of Sergeant Howan smiling. He simply remarked "Whoa, girl, what's up. You're like a detracted locomotive. You damn well knocked me over." "Sorry Sarge. My mind is wheeling. I just left the boss's office." Howan smiled. Her reference to the boss told him she had accepted the assignment. His heart pounded. He was ecstatic. He had always looked forward to someday working with this girl. She had time and again proven her mettle. Howan felt confident that she would only be an enhancement to his team and the operation that was about to unfold. Chuckling to himself he thought not hard to look at either. "Okay Barb, we will see you tomorrow. We'll kick ass and give 'em hell. Hey, the cavalry is enroute to the Westside. We will give the streets back to the good guys. It won't be easy and it will take time, but hey the Hartford Police Department will prevail. When we do see you tomorrow kid, be prepared and ready."

At 16:20 hours, Barbara was briefed by Sergeant Howan and was given her instructions. She was told to strictly comply with his plan. She was to traverse Farmington Ave. west from Sigourney Street to Forest Street. Then do an about face and retrace her route east to Sigourney Street. Unmarked vice units would be positioned in the rear lot of Saint Joseph's Cathedral and in the parking lot of Hartford High School; their listening devices had been thoroughly checked. Reception was loud and clear.

At 17:10 hours, Officer Horiaty, was dropped at Farmington Ave. and Flower Street. The decoy action was now imitated. Heading west on Farmington Avenue, she was a striking figure attired in revealing shorts and a tight fitting low cut white blouse and red high heels. Sergeant Howan felt that there would be little difficulty in effecting arrests. Howan turned to his partner Detective Schlitz, "well, it's begun, and she's alone out there." Grabbing his mike he whispered, "Alright be on your toes. The goose is loose, pay attention and be alert. Now we apply the heat."

Barbara alone with her thoughts, commenced with her journey into the night. Her emotions two fold, one of excitement and the other a tinge of fear. Predators would be out in force, on Friday night, Johns would be canvassing the avenue seeking thrills and pleasure. She would have to practice restraint, play the role, to perfection. Barbara had to act and sashay in the manner of a street hooker. She checked the hidden device in her low cut bra and was satisfied all was in order. She whispered softly, "Babs to unit 223, how do you read?" Sergeant Howan's voice responded, "Read you loud and clear. Be advised we're in position and on you" She had reached Farmington and Sigourney. It was a warm evening, but a cool breeze caressed the tree's lining Aetna Insurance. With traffic heavy and groups of people congregating in front of businesses, and apartment complexes, all enjoyed the sweet ripple of air through the streets.

Barbara began her trek heading west when suddenly she sensed movement to her left. A black Pontiac had pulled alongside with two white males smiling and leering at her. No doubt she had their interest. "Hey baby, interested in a night of fun asked the passenger. You're a beauty and we could make sounds and music all night, just the two of us." As instructed she continued her march. They had to totally commit to a monetary transaction for sex in order to affect a caller. She gave a sweet smile and responded with "oh yeah honey, what's on your mind? What is the agenda?" The male passenger continued his tirade. "Come on sweetheart. We really can have a good time. We'd take you to paradise, experience ecstasy. Come on girl don't be shy. You're looking to fine. Bet you look awesome in the raw." She chuckled and continued walking with the vehicle cruising slowly alongside. "Okay baby, no more graveling, we'd like to fuck you and suck you for hours. What's it gonna cost? We're go $200 for a piece like you, interested or not?" As the exchanged echoed through the chase cars radio, they revved up their engines on hearing Barbara's response, "See me in the rear of 220 Farmington Ave. It's an out of the way lot. I'll meet you there; have to watch out for the fuzz.

You know us working girls have to be careful." "Hot damn baby we'll be there. My tool's just longing for you."

The Pontiac sped off, turning into a narrow driveway. They roared into a small lot, weeds and garbage covered the small landscape. As they killed the engine and lit up a couple of Marlboros, they were anticipating a night of lust and pleasure. Suddenly two black vehicles barreled into the lot. Their vehicle covered in lights. One vehicle parked to the front and the other in the rear. Both subjects were dumbfounded. Was this a heist was their thoughts, but their thoughts were shattered when an authoritative voice commanded them to exit the vehicle with their hands in the air. The words of the police ringing in their ears and thrown against the vehicle, they were quickly frisked, read their rights and told they were under arrest for soliciting a prostitute. So began the cleansing of the Westside.

The night proved a tremendous success. Twenty-two arrests were affected. The operation continued for three weeks and slowly the word trickled out that the area was a hot spot. That police were clamping down in force. Repeat operations were put in motion in other annexes of the city. Their duration lasting till crime stats declined. Always Barbara Horiaty was place in harm's way as the decoy. As a result of her heroic actions, hundreds of arrests were affected. Her courage and intelligence and spread throughout law enforcement. The brass were elated and pressures on the department subsided. Tributes and accommodations toward Barbara poured in from everywhere. Residents, businesses, police administrations, her colleagues, the arch diocese, once again she had displayed in a humble fashion that her credentials as a cop were impeccable. That indeed she was a deserving and grateful asset to the Hartford Police and law enforcement as a whole. Was this action by police necessary? A simple yes now women, mothers, young girls, wives could once again travel the avenue whether to the store or just exercise without fear of deviates harassing them. Husbands, fathers, could embark to work with less worry, muggings, robberies, and assaults. Burglaries declined considerably. You the reader be the judge.

Chief Culligan entered the conference room. He waved his senior commanders to remain seated and planted himself in a chair at the head of the conference table. He was anxious to begin the weeks briefing, as there was a ton of inter-division intelligence to decipher. His eyes bore into Major Dellaher, "Major why don't you begin the proceedings." "Aye Sir," responded the major, "this past week we had four officers injured in line of duty, two on a domestic on Sigourney Street and one up in the Clay Hill section on an active burglary. As you may know, Officer Bordello was shot and slightly wounded in the South Meadows on a motor vehicle stop. His prognosis is good and he should be discharged from Hartford Hospital within a couple of days."

Culligan interrupted, "the family okay? Do they need anything, Frank?" "No sir, they're in good spirits and I've assigned an officer to assist with their needs." "Okay, Frank, very good, continue on." "Well chief, you know we're short of personnel. Merchants throughout the city are demanding there be added police patrols. We've beefed up the Albany Avenue area, due to several drive byes. But we're robbing from Peter to pay Paul. It's a band aid response but, under the circumstances, the only effective alternative." "Frank, we have a recruit class of 80 starting next week, so suck it up and give it your best. The ranks will swell soon and anything else questioned the chief. One more thing, start hitting the nomads and comancheros, for those gangs are getting feisty again. I don't want a fire ignited here and a repeat of last summer, gang warfare." The chief turned to Major Ahern, commander of the plain clothes units. Major Ahern was antsy. His division was currently dealing with Arabic deviate on the loose throughout the city. "John, the chief directed his attention to him, what's the situation on the funeral home cases. We've had two more in the past month. I know your guys are beating the bushes and wearing out shoe leather. Fill me in; pressure is mounting from everyone who is someone and those who are no one. I've got five enraged and anguished families on my ass. The Mayor is up tight and like the rest of us is pissed off and horrified. We can't allow this to continue having some nut case, who is breaking into funeral homes, and who is having sex with deceased women. Give me something concrete here. I've got a press conference in an hour. What can I give them?"

"Chief we've been rousing all known deviates, and anyone with a past sex history. We've been in contact with area P.D.'s soliciting any information they may have on known sex offenders. We've canvassed the areas where these sick crimes occurred and questioned hundreds of area residents, motorists to date. We've got little or nothing to go on. The perp's mo. is he enters those funeral homes via the burglary route, usually as far as we've been able to determine, in the early morning hours. Suspect has left no clues, no prints, and no semen. He's got to be committing those acts wearing a condom. We've staked out numerous funeral homes to no avail. There's really not a pattern here. He hits sporadically and keeps his appetite under control as he strikes usually every couple of months. We have gone deep on this one chief and we're pressing informants, street walkers, junkies and even cabbies, maybe just maybe we'll light a spark and shed some light on this caper. I can't give you more than that chief. I apologize, but I've got nothing you can give the press.

The room grew quiet, Chief Culligan lit up a camel cigarette and inhaling, he blew blue gray smoke towards the ceiling. Drumming his fingers on the table and his mind in over drive, "this was not good. A sicko was on the loose and the rope had been laid and stretched by the noose was not bound, not yet, not yet." He grunted his displeasure. His eyes roving over his commanders and he barked, "Fuck! Fuck! This prick is making ass-holes out of this department. Here I sit and I am told by my chief of detectives, we've got shit. I've not happy. God damn it! We've got to get control here. I want this son of a bitch before he goes after live bait. You commanders kick ass and get the fire burning in your troops. Your sitting in this room because your suppose to be top cops. I want ideas! No matter how asinine or silly they may appear. One of you Hollywood cops come up with a sound reaction plan and do it like yesterday. We're the god damn cops. This is our city. I cannot and will not tolerate this to continue. Best you all understand where I stand. Get on top of this and I mean quickly." The chief red faced stood abruptly and strolled out the door. He had terminated the staff meeting prematurely. He had to before his anger boiled over for he knew that his temper was being put to the test. He walked briskly into his office, stopping for a brief moment to instruct his secretary to forward his calls. He was not about to take calls in the steamy mood he was in. He wanted time to reflect and prepare for what he anticipated to be a long and arduous press conference. The media were like hyenas circling a prey. They would be on him like flies on shit. The funeral home capers were hot and he sighed, he had no answers.

Chief Bernard Culligan sat in quiet solitude at his desk. He pulled open the middle drawer, extracted a pack of camels and fired it up. The nicotine rush relaxed his nerves and temper. The press conference had been catastrophic. The media had been all over him. He had remained professional but the beating he had taken had frayed his nerves and temper. He was an honorable man and had always thought that honor was a gift a man could give himself. But the frustration he felt was intense. His city was being terrorized by a depraved sick animal. Raping dead women in funeral parlors and creating havoc, chaos in families of those poor souls who were violated, were in the throes of agony, at the most vulnerable time of their lives. While in deep grief, they now suffered this terrible anguish.

Captain Ray Haufman cautiously and quietly had approach the closed door of the marked office of the chief of police. Stealing himself to confront his chief with what he felt was a plan, probably, if opened, the only possible door to apprehend this sick perp. He knocked twice, when a gruff voice bellowed from behind the glass, "enter!"

Haufman entered the spacious office. He approached the chief's desk, saluting his superior and murmuring a soft "good morning chief." The chief eyed him with interest. He liked this captain, respected him for reasons he had appointed him to head the intelligence division. He knew his right flank was secure. That he would always be appraised of activity within his city. "Good morning Ray, have a seat. There's fresh coffee, help yourself, and if you wouldn't mind pour me one too. You know the drill black no sugar." Now face to face, seated across from each other, the smoking lamp lit the chief, stared into the captain's eyes hard and long. "What's up Ray, what have you got? Please throw something good my way. As you know it's been a tough morning. About now, I need an upper. Go ahead shoot and be frank, at this point, I'm all ears." "Saw the press conference chief. Sorry you were raked over the coals. Tough times eh, chief" "Yea, Ray but the city's in panic mode and the medias not helping. Hopefully, we'll catch a break, today, tomorrow, or whatever, but it better be soon or my ass is grass; well Ray, you didn't come here to render sympathy, what's on your mind?"

"Chief, I'd like to run something by you. I've been thinking on this long and hard. I realize this investigation is the bureaus, but I've an idea that could work. Let me run it by you. You ingest what I say, mull it over, just hear me out." "Okay Ray, okay fire away I'm open to any reasoning here."

"Well chief, I think we should plant a decoy, set up a prop, and sort of speak so tempting this shit stain will be unable to resist. I believe we plant a phony obituary in the paper and play it up real zesty. My gut tells me this bird scans the obituaries in order to satisfy his desires. He hits on a deceased female of his interest and strikes. This has to be his method. He goes underground for long periods and then is forced to feed his hunger."

The chief fired up a camel, nodded his approval for the captain to smoke and gazed at a photo of his family. This could be a great ambush, quite possible the method to put this bird in a cage. He remained silent for several minutes pondering the strategy laid before him. The room was quiet only the ticking of a wall clock could be heard. Finally, he rose stepping around his desk. He placed a hand on the captain's shoulder, "sounds like a plan, Ray, but an article in the paper is one thing. Obviously you've thought this through, how would you proceed?" "Well, we contact Farley & Sullivan Funeral Home, we work cohesively with them. We'd have to have a wake. It's got to look real. He'll certainly seek and peek, if he likes the bait, we're set. There's no doubt he'll strike. We'll have to use a live set up, laid out in a casket. The scene will and must appear to be the real thing. It'll be hairy, but with luck we could bring it off." The chief gazed at a decoration on his wall which read, in part, Chief Bernard Culligan, for gallantry and his outstanding ability to lead and initiate quick and difficult decisions. Returning to his seat, he was searching his soul. He knew the captain was right on. He made his decision, "okay Ray, I agree now we need a decoy and we both know who it must be. Don't we." "Yeah chief, it can only be Officer Barbara Horiaty." "Ray sequester her in your office, it has to be voluntary.

I cannot, and will not order anyone to lie in a casket for God knows how long. This is one dangerous game. An assignment like this will take big balls. Let me know her answer. But I caution you, hers and no one else are to be privy to this action. No one! If we initiate an operation only a hand full of trusted and handpicked personnel will share in this operation. Is that understood captain." "Yes sir." "Then fine, you're dismissed and thanks for coming by. This just might work. We've got nothing to lose and no choice but to go ahead. This bastard has got to be nettled and fast."

Barbara stared at the flag standard to the left rear of the captain's desk. She also focused on the Hartford police logo framed on the wall directly behind him. Her love for both had brought her to this moment in her career. Looking at the captain with straight eyes and without hesitation she simply stated, "Yes sir, I'd be honored. I'd love to take this son of a bitch down."

Captain Haufman smiled extended his hand clasping hers in his. "Very good, Officer, hang in for a few, I'll notify the chief." Chief Culligan picked up his phone on the third ring. "Chief, Ray Haufman here, that's a go. Officer Horiaty has accepted the assignment." "Okay Ray, very well, have her here with you in my office tomorrow at 0900 hours. I'll reach out to those personal who will be involved."

Chief Culligan was in a somber mood. Deep in thought seated across from him was Officer Horiaty. Too her right stood Captain Haufman. Both officers had entered the chief's office at 0900 hours, as directed. The chief firing up a camel sat upright in his chair appraising both officers. His gaze was fixed and stern. Stubbing out his smoke, in an engraved H.P.D. ashtray, he broke the silence. "Officer Horiaty, good to see you." As his eyes roved over her, he was impressed; she was impeccable in her blues. Ribbons adorned her chest. She sat ram rod straight. Their eyes locked. "Barbara I'm grateful that you've accepted this assignment, but I caution you this is a dangerous and perilous assignment. You'll be on your own in a dark room. If you have a change of heart no one will ever question your courage." "Chief no sweat I accept the challenge. It's what we're about. Danger is our shadow every day. I'm here sir and I await my orders."

Culligan turned to the captain. "Ray, reach out to Lieutenant Lanzi. Instruct him to pick four sharp and trusted dicks to assist in this operation. He or they are directed to reveal nothing to anyone. I emphasize anyone. The team assigned will meet tonight at 19:30 hours at Vincent's Steak House to formulate and finalize our course of action. I want no leaks, no big mouths, and no heroes. What I do want is collaring this sick asshole. Oh and Ray, a Doctor Mcguirk will be joining us at the diverse meeting you'll both understand fully when we discuss the issue at hand."

Chief Culligan sat at the head of the table. An exquisite dinner had been laid out for the officers seated to his left and right. The chief, through connections with Springfield Massachusetts Police Department, had been able to procure a private room adjoining the main dining area. Here they were out of sight of roving eyes and sharp ears. Culligan began, "we all know the reason we're here. I know you're curious as to why I chose this venue. Simple no one is to know what we're embarking on but this group right here. I caution you all to keep a closed mouth. You are not to discuss what transpires here tonight with anyone. That includes wives, girlfriends, boyfriends, whatever, not even your pets." The chief knew he was a bit tight. He retreated by introducing Doctor Mcguirk to the group. Apologizing for his rudeness, the doctor had arrived shortly after the meal had ended. "Okay, everyone knows one another. We're all bed partners in this episode, so Ray, addressing Captain Haufman, spill out your plan of action. Be a brief as possible and lay it out simple. I want no misunderstanding or confusion. This must and will be a cohesive effort. We all want this sick fucker where he belongs in a dark cage with rattlers as roommates, commence, captain, commence. Oh one more thing, you're all wondering why the doctor is here. That explanation is coming just sit tight. You'll have your answers. You've all been chosen to share in this covert operation because of your spotless records and trustworthiness. Okay, I've blown enough smoke up your asses. Sorry, Ray, Go ahead, and lay it on us."

"Well," chief began Haufman, his eyes roving over the group as he spoke. "We're all aware of this pig's m.o. He strikes early am. Long after the funeral parlors close. My plan is simple. We place a phone ad in the obituary page of the central paper. We play it up big time, photo and all. Barbara will be the bait to lure our boy to us; of course, there'll have to be a wake. We'll need people to attend as mourners. The show has to appear realistic. I believe this shit stain checks out his victim while attending wakes and observing while in line. If he is turned on by what he sees, he reconnoiters the home and seeks accessibility attempting to minimize discovery. I've been in contact with Peter Weinstein, Director of Farley Sullivan; He has been strongly advising to remain mute about our intentions and has demonstrated complete cooperation."

Addressing Officer Horiaty, the captain continued. "You understand Barbara that the risks you'll be undertaking, you'll have to lay in a casket in the dark. If the son of a bitch takes the bait you'll have to practice intense restraint. You can take no action till the puke gropes you and attempts to remove you from the box. He usually strips the body and takes his pleasure on the floor. We'll have an officer positioned in a casket in the adjoining room. As well as, an officer will be in the basement and another in the john and in concealment one will be in prone position. Just to the rear of you camouflaged by flower arrangements. We'll make sure there are plenty, of course, and you'll have your 38 as a bed buddy. No pun intended. Now here's the fun part, Barbara you can't be breathing regularly during the wake, so we contacted Doctor Mcguirk, who is in attendance. The reason we had to know how to control normal breathing at low risk to you. So I give the floor to Dr. Mcguirk."

An imposing figure, Dr. Mcguirk stood 6'2, burly in build and gave off an air of confidence. Looking at Chief Culligan, he simply stated, "propanol it's used in surgery. It places a patient into a deep sleep. Respiratory activity is minimal and there is very little breathing, very minimal. It could work, but remember in surgery oxygen is in full use. You won't be able to conceal such a device with the action you're planning. There is a risk here. Can it work? Yes, very possibly. Can there be a major setback, such as respiratory failure, hell yes! It's never been tired this way. Not as far as I know. That's all I can enlighten you on. I'll be glad to assist in anyway. I'll be there to administer the medication and I am more than willing and able to remain on the premises in hiding should things turn sour. That's it. I can't tell you anymore," looking at Barbara with respect and concern. He stated "good luck officers. I pray your courageous actions are a success."

He awoke early, had spent a sleepless night. His hunger torturing his soul and he needed relief and soon. He stumbled into the kitchen. Beer cans litter the counter and floor. His hairy ape like hands reached for a can sitting lonely on the kitchen table. He gulped it down in one swallow. He fell into an old dilapidated recliner. His mind recycling, his one thought of sex ruled his every thought. He needed the cold flesh of a woman. His depraved desire was what satisfied him. It had been a while since he had sex with a lifeless female. He loved that there was no resistance, no whispers of love, no commitment, no need to feel or care. Just gratification of his needs and be on his way. Women had hurt him throughout his life, scaring him and ridiculing him for his grotesque features. The dead did not laugh or belittle him. He experienced great heights of pleasure fucking them, fondling them; he didn't need warmth or companionship. Just a naked body to, toy with, to enjoy, to experiment, to spend himself and then to be on his way. God he hungered! It's time, my loins are on fire. I need to fuck soon. Put my cock in that cold hairy paradise. Ride that vulnerable body to my heart's content.

Oh, please let there be a beauty in today's obits. Trembling and wobbly, he wondered into the living room, opened the door and retrieved his morning paper. Foam seeped out of his mouth as he opened to the obits. The photo of a deceased beauty exploded from the page. His heart was beating rapidly. He couldn't control his shaking. He perused the script beneath the photo. Barbara Jean Moylan aged 26, passed from this life suddenly on Tuesday, May 10th, scanning quickly through the article; he quickly found what he was looking for. Friends may call at the Farley, Sullivan Funeral Home, 10 Webster Street, Thursday, from 4:00 to 9:00 p.m. A smile creased his tortured face. Staring at the photo of the deceased, he felt a stirring in his loins. An erection quickly ensued. Thank-God, he thought soon my hunger will know satisfaction. He began to masturbate, two days, he thought. He began to chuckle, soon his cock would find refuge between the un-resisting legs of a woman who could not laugh, scorn him or could not ridicule his twisted body. His soul found refuge in the dark. He did not care; pleasure was once again within his grasp. He began to plan his method of entry but would view the body first. He laughed aloud as a grieving mourner. His orgasm was an explosion. He sighed with relief and gulped another beer. His time to strike at womanhood was at hand.

Chief Culligan, Captain Haufman and Lieutenant Lanzi, sat having coffee within the sanctuary of the chief's office discussing the event that was to unfold shortly. It was Thursday and all aspects of the operation were covered. Culligan glanced at the wall clock. It read 15:15 hours. Soon the drama would unfold. Culligan felt some apprehension. His thoughts working on the welfare of Officer Horiaty for he was not keen on her being medicated to induce a deep sleep. No one had knowledge if it had ever been attempted. There was no documentation it would prove effective. His concerns were valid but orders had been issued and the mission set in motion. At 15:50 hours, Barbara looking resplendent in a low cut blue dress entered the casket. Her 38 placed by her right side covered by white silk lace. Her heart was racing. Fear flowed through her being. Her hands trembled over so slightly. She was fully aware of the risks involved here, but her strong resolve and confidence inspired her. Smiling at Lieutenant Lanzi and Dr. Mcguirk, she laid back in the repose position. Dr. Mcguirk had a hypodermic in his hand, smiling, softly whispering "Good luck. I respect your courage." That said he plunged the three inch needle into her right arm. Barbara gasped slightly. Felt a strange sensation. The walls grew distant. She uttered her act of contrition and then blackness.

Lieutenant Lanzi then took his position lying prone to the rear of the flower arrangements. Detective Joe Bastando, laid peaceful in a casket in an adjoining room cloaked in darkness. Detective H. Dullivan positioned himself in a utility closet located nearby. Detective Joe Chatz took his position in the bowels of the building for this assigned location in the basement lead to a stairwell to the viewing parlor where Barbara lay in apparent peaceful repose. Dr. Mcguirk checked her blood pressure. It read low and slow. Her breathing was minimal and as far as he could determine, unnoticeable. He quickly exited the area and hastened to join Detective Chatz in the basement, should medical services be needed. The stage was set all was quiet. Soon the door for mourners would be opened for attending mourners. The officers remained fixed in their positions. Their mouths dry, their pulses beating rapidly, restraint would most assuredly be practiced as to control their adrenaline rush.

Captain Haufman sitting in an unmarked with Chief Culligan suddenly proclaimed, "chief, God damn it, we didn't cover the entire basis. Shit, it's supposed to look authentic, but mourners, we forgot about mourners. The prick we're after will surely observe the lack of grievers, and bolt for sure."

Chief Culligan smiled slightly, "Ray, relax. I'd placed several phone calls today to the commissioner of state police for West Hartford and East Hartford police chiefs. They asked for volunteers and we'll have a pretty good showing. Also Bloomfield P.D. and Windsor have been involved. Sit tight Ray we'll be fine-a-okay. These people who as we speak are gathering in the home's parking lot and have no idea why they're attending but were willing to assist when I explained to their leadership we needed help on a covert case.

The props had been set. Mourners acted their part in fantastic fashion. Filing past the casket, even kneeling to pray and pay respects. Low murmurs echoed through the room. Mourners coming and going as the hands of the clock continued to inch forward. Outside light turned to grey and then suddenly as the sun pecked it's goodnight from the west, darkness.

He had stood in line for 15 minutes. His excitement increasing as he inched forward to view his chosen prey. He was impatient wanting to see the sleeping form that would soon grant him his perverted pleasure. He was annoyed that he would have to restrain his heated desires until later when he would ravish this lovely creature. He approached the casket his eyes devouring his prey. Oh God, he thought she is a beauty. He shuffled forward sweat trickling down his armpits. His cool strained in anticipation to the pleasures he would soon enjoy.

The clock struck 21:00 hours. Visitors had long departed. Weinstein strolled through the home performing security checks of the restrooms and ensuring doors were locked. Satisfied all was in order, he flipped off lights throughout the interior. Officer Barbara Horiaty, now lay there in deep slumber. One small candle burned in silence, its light casting an eerie glow dancing off the walls, and bouncing around the casket and form within. Silence enveloped the funeral home only the soft tick-tock of the even watchful clock cast a soft echo through the darkness. The funeral home lay clocked in darkness only three exit lights burned softly in the night like sentinels. Turning right onto Webster Street, he took note of the empty parking lot. He proceeded south on Webster and parked his dented and rusted Pontiac within a block of the home; traffic was light. A young couple holding hands strolled by s he exited his vehicle. He walked briskly north on Webster Street. Turning into the walk of 12 Webster, heading to the rear yard he halted. His eyes scanned the area for any hidden danger for he was shielded in the shadows. His eyes now accustomed to the dark continued to scope his surroundings. Observing nothing, he climbed the chain link fence, which portioned the residence from the funeral home and parking lot. Scaling the fence he landed hard on the asphalt lot. Righting himself, as he had stumbled upon landing, he continued his trek towards the home for he had reconnoitered the premises earlier. He had gone undetected and discovered a small window located between the garage and main building. He retrieved his gloves from his jacket pocket. A small hammer from his waist-band and a thick cotton cloth from his rear pocket, placing the cloth against the window and began his labor. The blows of the hammer, muffled by the cloth, he chuckled to himself, special forces had trained him well. His mind drifted into his distant past. He was bitter, angry with the world and his government. His body was ugly due to wounds he had suffered in the Nam. Once he had been an imposing figure of a man but now he was hideous and women found him repulsive. Thus, his quest to ravish deceased females, realizing he was in pity mode, he took control, thinking could fuck him up. There was a loud crack as the window shattered falling into the interior of the building. Ah, he sighed with pride, success, I'm in. I'm coming baby. I'm coming. I'll give you one hell of a final send off. Detective Chatz heard the tap tap on the window, glimpsed a silhouette and then the sound of exploding glass. He dove under a desk for concealment and in a defense mode waited.

The animal pushed himself through the now exposed cavity and holding on to a window sill; let himself down ever so slowly. It was about an 8 foot drop. Having reached his maximum decent, he dropped the last three feet to the floor. Again, he waited for his sight to accustom itself to the darkness. He then retrieved a pen light flash light and played it about the darkened room. There was a door to his left and he moved stealthily towards it. Gently pushing it open, ahead of him lay as stairwell leading to the main area and its viewing rooms. Soon he would know joy and multiple organisms.

He inched his way up the stairwell slowly. His senses in fine tune even alert for any peril he had placed himself in. His body language revealed a man stalking someone or something stealthily. Yes, he would soon devour his pray. Reaching the top of the stairs, his breathing labored from his climb, he stood transfixed and scanning the semi darkness intently. Two large rooms loomed beyond him and a small candle flickering and dispatching small sediments of light dancing along the walls and ceiling. He studied the name mounted on a stand to his left negative the name it bore belonged to a male deceased. He then focused his interest on the room to his right. Advancing slowly, his pen light shone on the placard. Ah, he gasped in excitement as the name exploded in his voice.

Barbara Jean Moylan

He stood perfectly still for his eyes adjusting slowly within a minute, his special forces training kicked in. He advanced into the room. His eyes darting left and right, his ears in overdrive straining for the slightest sound satisfied he was alone, he continued his march The casket came into view, within seconds he was alongside. He peered down into the serene face of his victim lying in peaceful repose.

Midnight Barbara began to stir. She experienced weakness and the desire to crawl back into the peaceful abyss of sleep. But the whispering of Lieutenant Lanzi penetrated her semi conscious. He had grown concerned that she had remained in a deep slumber, satisfied she was withdrawn from her stupor he returned to his perch which offered good surveillance. The hour was late and if the demon they hunted were to strike it would be soon. Barbara's mouth was dry, and she felt wetness between her legs and knew she had urinated. Oh well, she thought she thought it couldn't be avoided due to being shelled between the confines in this tight box for eight hours. Apprehensive clutched at her heart. Her brain was sluggish, and screaming to exit this box that held her prisoner. Several times she had attempted to open her eyes but they felt like cement blocks and would not function. Her body felt like it was submersed by heavy weights. What was she doing here? Was this a nightmare? Slowly her eyes began to focus. Darkness engulfed her and the light of a small candle acting as a beacon for her to focus on. The sweet aroma of flowers as she inhaled filled her nostrils. Her arms felt dead and her hands resting on her stomach. Her motor movements were semi-curtailed the result of being confined in the reposed position for such a long duration. She attempted to move her fingers the pain excruciating. Slowly they gave ever so slowly. Her legs were immobile. Terror engulfed her being. She felt trapped and her mind in confusion. Spittle seeped from her mouth flowing down her chin. Oh God, she thought, help me. Tears of fear and frustration flooded her eyes, trickled down her cheeks. Fuck she thought enough of this self wallowing. Reaching deep into her soul she garnished every ounce of resolve and strength she could muster. She had a job to do and do it she would.

Lying there trance like she heard a soft creaking sound to her right. She steeled herself and waited every muscle in her body waiting to uncoil. She felt a presence standing by her self—imposed prison. Heard raspy breathing and a voice whispering, you are a beauty my dear and my loins crave your secret treasures. Before they plant you sweetheart, old Eric here will send you off into eternity with a fucking never experienced in life. His right hand reached to her breasts and began to fondle them and squeeze. Oh, they feel full and round under my grasp he thought, such large and luscious orbs as he licked his lips in anticipation. What a feast. I shall enjoy putting their nipples in my mouth. Chuckling, he reached around her head and began to lift her from the coffin. His guard down, he was stunned when he felt the cold steel piece under his chin. The sound of the metallic click of a hammer cocked resonated in the dark stillness. The voice of his prey penetrated his hearing, "move mother fucker and your dead!" resigned to his fate, he muttered "please full the trigger be merciful free my soul from this body of hell." Officer Horiaty could not believe her ears but she held her composure and continued to hold the revolver to his chin.

Lieutenant Lanzi sprang from his concealment. A coiled rattler in action, his flight propelled him forward. Air bourn his body weight drove the suspect to the floor. Detective Dullivan burst from the utility closet. Detective Bastando exploded from his casket. He flew into scary darkness rendering assistance to Lanzi. Dullivan also joined in the Frey. Detective Chatz sprinting up the stairwell two steps at a time halted in his tracks as he determined that Lanzi and Dullivan had secured the suspect now on his belly in the prone position. His hands cuffed behind him. The two plain clothes officers were in the process of frisking him. Satisfied he was clean they read him his rights.

Captain Haufman seated at his desk in the intelligence division, was edgy, glancing at his watch. He was startled to see it was 0255 a.m. The silence of his phone concerned him. He would rather have been a participant at the scene, waiting wasn't his fort. He jumped as the ringing phone disturbed him from his deep thought process. Grabbing the receivers, he bellowed, "Intelligence Captain Hoffman," Lieutenant Lanzi's cold voice on the land line, put his nerves to ease. His heart rate slowed to normalcy when the words echoed in his ear. "Captain, subject is in custody and all is well in cop land."

Haufman quickly reached out to Chief Culligan, unknown to the captain, the chief was in his unmarked parked in the vicinity of the funeral home. The voice of the dispatcher blasted from the car radio, "Unit 300 come in, unit 300 dispatch!" "300 here, sir from unit 250 (Captain Haufman), the animal has been trapped and in custody." "Unit 300 to dispatch —thank you and dispatch, dispatch two blue and whites to the Farley Sullivan Funeral Home. They are to assist our personnel at the scene. Have the south boss also respond further. Have the detective division assign personnel to that location immediately." "Dispatch unit 300 10-4"

Farley Funeral Home was now a beehive of activity. Crime scene tape had been placed at the scene. A uniform officer guarded the entrance to the viewing parlor. Technicians were busy matching the suspect's finger prints to those on the casket. Yes this crime was treated as a homicide due to the heinous of past assaults. The chief expected an airtight case and his demands would be honored an obeyed. Officer Horiaty was taken to Hartford Hospital. She was treated for dehydration. Her blood pressure brought under control and two days later she was discharged and would receive the Distinguished Service Medal for her extreme bravery.

Chief Culligan seated at his desk, perused his press release, he chuckled at the use of Captain's Haufman's two dollars words. Satisfied at its completeness, the chief rose from his chair, exited his office and with a hearty smile on his face, greeted the press, "well boys here it is and commenced to enlighten the media of a police action well-done."

Eric Alden a highly decorated Special Forces vet had been apprehended by outstanding police work. He was brought to justice and was sentenced to life without parole to a mental institute.

Tribute to Barbara

Barbara was an excellent cop, excelling in a dangerous and forgetful society. Serving with distinction, courage and a firm resolve to protect and serve. She earned the respect of superiors, clergyman, citizens, politicians, but treasured the respect received from peers, and grunt cops. On numerous occasions she risked serious injury even death. Take for example, on a blistering, hot summer day, she responded to a violent active domestic. Arriving at the scene, she walked into a volatile situation. A burly male who had stabbed his wife while the children watched was wielding a large knife. Two other officers were laden as the victim and her children had sought refuge in their rooms. Barbara noted the two cops were in an awkward position and unable to halt this threat to themselves or the victims. They had no line of fire. Barbara sprang into action, she placed herself in a defensive mode and shielding the group, she exposed herself to imminent danger. The suspect when confronted screamed and charged Barbara, but she never wavered. She ordered the subject to freeze, weapon at the ready and in extreme danger, Barbara fired. The bullet hit the bull's eye and the subject collapsed to the floor shot between the eyes. Her courage and fortitude preserved the welfare of the victims and the brother officers who had been rendered immobile at a critical moment.

This writer was both honored and privileged to wear the same uniform. You knew your back was secure. She was one hell of a back up. Sadly fate was unkind to this blue warrior she passed at the age of 42. Illness putting her down where evil could not. We her brothers and sisters officers will never forget her. Barbara's courage and devotion was an inspiration to all.

I pray that female officers of this day emulate her perseverance and loyalty to the cop's code, to serve and protect. For she paved the way, proved that females are capable and a valued asset to law enforcement. March on my sister's in blue, march on. We, who preceded you, respect you and thank you for going in harm's way and keeping the Hun at bay.

Cop Talk

Afternoon Fun With The Troops

Harper, guzzling a beer, "Look what Harland and Joey C did to Hotchkiss." "What?" asked Striker "Seems Lee was walking beat 13, Union Place, ate in some shit hole and started experiencing abdominal pains. He tried to ignore them but it became too much even for that Big Bastard. He has the district car run him up to St. Francis Hospital ER. The asshole thinks he's got food poisoning." "Yeah so what happened," pipes in Gomez. "Let me finish, shit for brains. Anyway, he's examined and admitted. The fuck is so big and strong he didn't realize it was appendicitis. The doctor operated early the next morning. Now it gets good. He's in his room that afternoon sleeping, when in walked Harland and the mini lama, Joey C, ever the asshole kicks Hotchkiss rack. He opens his eyes, thinks he died because two ugly assholes are at the foot of his bed. "Hi guys, what's up?" Joey C threw a pornographic book at him, sued a gutter slut. Hotchkiss is all tubes and needles. "I don't think he wants to look at naked broads." Well in walks a nurse to give Lee a shot for pain. She pulls back the sheets and Lee lies there exposed for just a moment. It's all Joey C needs. He roars out, "Hank did you see that? That guy is built like a tank, but his dick looks like a prune. My God, How do you fuck with that? It's just enough to piss with." The nurse is holding her stomach for she's crying from laughing. Hotchkiss turns beat red. You little wimp! I'll get out of this bed and throw you out the window! I'll kill you, you little fuck!" Joey C fired back, "you big fuck, you can't do shit. You look like a machine with all that shit in you." "Joey, when I get out of here, roars Hotchkiss, you better take a leave of absence. I'm gonna get you." "Yeah, promises, promises." Lee is so angry his heart monitor goes sky high. Finally the nurse tells those two screw holes they better leave.

Harper laughing say, "Joey C is in deep, deep shit. "Yeah, but Hotchkiss don't run so good," states Striker. "Yeah and Joey C isn't wrapped to tight either and he carries a 44 on him all the time." "Good thing, says

Harper. That's the only caliber I think might penetrate Lee." Laughing and some of the days issues forgotten, they finished their beers and each fired three rounds into the barrel. Well, see you tonight guys, "yeah, right on, tonight!"

Chapter 5

Captain Haufman, seated at his desk was busy reviewing intelligence reports, choosing only the serious cases. For the moment, his incoming reports spilled over from the file. Incidents and infraction from officers, citizens, and in formants created a back log of intense review. His brain was in overdrive. He had been spending late hours and his soul-mate at home was becoming disgruntled, perusing the reports was alarming. Six shootings in the past week alone, three occurring in the south end of the city and three in the north end, were all drive byes. The detective divisions work load was enormous and all plain clothes units had been directed to assist and assign personal from their units to shore up the bureau. Haufman was dismayed. Three of the victims were D.O.A. and three critically wounded. Sipping his coffee, his thought process in high gear, he concluded that the street gangs, notably the savage nomads and comancheros, had terminated their alleged truce and street warfare had exploded. Rubbing red rimmed eyes, he felt edgy, tired, frustrated, all their patrols and covert operations to kick a lid on the situation were proving futile. He sensed danger to the city and its inhabitants. He dreaded the upcoming chief's meeting. Past experiences in this nature, enraged Chief Culligan. He knew the shit was about to hit the fan. "What the fuck chuck?" he muttered to himself. The man needs to know already does, I'm sure. Glancing at the clock, it was time at 08:58. He exited his office steering himself to the office of the boss. Other division commanders were assembled in the chief's outer office. All were somber. Fatigue lined their faces. Fifteen shootings in the past month sat heavy on their shoulders.

The door to the conference room flew open. Assistant Chief Joe Lawler, with a solemn expression on his face, beckoned them to enter. Haufman whispering to Captain Weinstein, Head of the Detective Division, "fuck a duck, the old man's gonna be pissed" Haufman took his seat at his usual place. He took note of the hushed whispers of other commanders. He noticed that they too were bleary eyed. They suffered as well from the same pressure as him. The self imposed berating, shared the chief's angry venting. Haufman, placing his briefcase on the table, he removed stacks of reports, filtered to his division by line officers, detectives, plainclothes men, informants, citizens, he carefully laid them on the table. One report captured his attention:

To: Captain Haufman, Intelligence Division

From: Sergeant Huxley, unit 43, Patrol Division

Subject: Street activity.

Re: Nomads – Comancheros

Sergeant Dan Huxley cruised west on Park Street. His mind occupied with thoughts of the recent shootings. He was alert and tense. He felt a sense of foreboding. Aware that a volatile situation was unfolding and that Hartford Police Department would be hard pressed. It was certain that a warlike atmosphere had woven itself on the city's streets. Like a cloud of vaporous gas it was devouring youthful males on a weekly basis. A murderous rampage that had citizens cowering in their home from the fear that was all too real to them. Lighting a Marlboro, he took note of the streets activity. Congregating on street corners, battling the heat, their homes like furnaces due to the oppressive heat wave, street walkers glanced his way, some smiling, while others were raising their middle finger. He laughed; fuck them he thought, losers, and no soul. Look at their eyes, thousand yard stares. They know they have no future. Poor bastards, life and their diseased surroundings led them here. He passed the El-Dorado Café, loud music blasting from the interior, two derelicts staggered into an adjacent door. A homeless disheveled old man, pushing a shopping cart full of bottles, turning right on Broad Street, soon was swallowed by the night. Traffic was moderate and radio traffic from dispatch was at a minimal. His sector units responding to all familiar noise complaints, domestics and some minor assaults, barking dogs, must be the heat he thought. Humming to himself he hooked a sharp left onto Pope Park Highway. With his heart pounding, his brain on high alert began his tour. He had received a call from his five star informants and had arranged to meet behind the now defunct Hart Manufacturing Company. His squeal had been excited. His squeaky voice on the landline decimals higher in volume than usual, hinting that he had explosive info for him. Something big man, something big, the words echoed in his mind. The rodent had never played him dirty. Past info had always proven fruitful. Some actually very rewarding, two murders, three robberies, a rape solved due to the rodent's contacts and sharp eyes and ears, his underground sub squads farmed out like tentacles within the city's womb.

Chuckling, Huxley thought, rodent, the name suits him. He slithers around in the night, his ears are fine tuned and he smells trouble like a rat smells food. Turing into the North West corner of the parking lot, he observed the rodents red Honda. It blinked its light twice revving up the engine Huxley was soon parked alongside a breeze puffed between the two vehicles. The rodent, his eyes glistened red like in the dark, smiling, "good to see you man. I got good shit, for big time shit, best you cops get going, quick. Bad happenings coming, gonna make them recent street shootings. Look like Pluto and Goofy had a ruckus. Now I be in a hurry, my man, you listen. I'll talk, then baby I'm gone outta here. Heading Deep South can't be around, some ones gunning for the rodent." "Okay listen up", the rodent began, stars glistened above the soft gentle sign of the nights slumbering wind embraced his cheek. The rodent never ceased rambling on and on. The info that spilled from his lips, shocking, and frightening, Huxley appalled listened attentively. Jotting down registration numbers and alias of suspects, suddenly, the rodent finished his narration simply stating, "you got it man, now I'm outta here." Gunning his engine, he roared into the night. His rear lights blinking little red beacons. The Honda disappeared swallowed in the dark. Huxley sat transfixed. He lit up another Marlboro and exclaimed "Jesus, Mary and Joseph and the pour fucking donkey." He uttered aloud, "This is hot" grabbing his mike. He whispered hoarsely, "unit 43 enroute to 10-2.

Have the watch commander contact unit 250 at his home. I mean like yesterday." The dispatcher's bored voice, acknowledge, 10-4, 43, copy you, your off on a 105D, HQ.

Captain Haufman, unit 250, entered the watch commander's office. The wall clock read 0400. Bleary eyed, he took note of Sergeant Huxley. Banging away on a type writer, oblivious to his surrounding, the furies pounding of the keys expelling words like a machine gun expelling rounds. Haufman was on edge, tired; his uneasy sleep broken by Captain Heinrich's land line. The previous week had been a living Hell. He was near exhaustion and his unit and the entire department under siege by gang activity. His ulcer burned like Hell, two much coffee and lucky strikes no doubt the villain. He greeted Heinwich with a nod and a "what's up." Heinwich sipping a stale coffee, "Hell's fire is about to unleash sir." Huxley's detailing a very volatile report for your eyes only. Aw-fuck, thought Haufman. The fire in his stomach burning, "fuck a duck, I'm tired, pissed off, hungry and horny, it stinks in here, I've a meeting at 0900 with the boss in the morning, shit talk about the bear getting you. The old man's livid, that conference is gonna be a cluster fuck. He'll be on us like flies on shit. Well, like I always say "What the fuck chuck. Let's see what the Serge's planting on the door step."

Chief Culligan entered the conference room. His mood sour and his face haggard and flushed for he was in no mood this day for whinny excuses. He would not accept finger pointing or back stabbing for the most part he had a competent staff. But a couple was bandbox commanders who he would dispatch soon. His first call of this tour came from the mayor, "another shooting last night chief. What the fuck is going on here? Have your cops lost it? Should we run up the white flag? Maybe surrender or negotiate away the city? Come on, Bernie Where's your troops? Are they asleep or retreating? Please tell me I'm wrong. Okay, chief forget what I've said. I'm just frustrated same as you. You know you have my confidence but get control though, and quickly. You can't believe the pressures and calls I'm getting." "Yeah, good morning to you and to your demons, no sweat I'm about to break heads in fifteen minutes. We'll get on top of this." "Okay, chief, I believe you." The mayor hung up the phone abruptly.

The door to the conference room burst open. Chief Culligan flanked by assistant chief Lawler, strolled briskly into the room. The chief appeared reserved and strode directly to his seat at the head of the table. Planting himself into the chair, he scanned the room noting that his contingents of commanders were all present. Addressing his echelon the chief spoke so gently resisting the urge to explode and release the anger and frustration festering within.

"Gentlemen, the city is under siege. We are supposed to be its guardians, the cavalry, and the watch dog, whatever. However in the eyes of the media and lets emphasize, our citizens, we are performing beneath the boy scouts. Breaking news everyday is embarrassing. Society is questioning our abilities and confidence in this department and we are at ground zero. Now, listen up, and listen good, my ass is sitting in the chair, thus I and I alone am in the hot seat and rightly so. As I wear the stars and I'm sitting here staring at your faces. I recognize indecision and fear in your eyes. I will not tolerate, ineptness, not now, not with a mounting crisis confronting us. You are supposed to be the top cops of this department instead I'm thinking I'm surrounded by a palace guard. Those punks on the streets are an embarrassment to this department. Those streets are supposed to be ours. What the fuck is occurring here? Is this a repeat of Custer's last stand? Or maybe we'll just in a full scale retreat, for Christ sakes, fifteen shootings in the past week, no collars. The streets are running red. Where the fuck are the bluecoats? I've been out and about the streets at various hours, you gentlemen know that. The bureau, itell, vice and narcotics, those divisions' offices should be bulging with witnesses to say the least. Yet, when I stroll through those units at 0700 in the am, I see a couple of dicks pecking away on their fucked up typewriters. The chief red faced, rose from his seat, slammed his right hand on the desk, I'm warning you gentlemen, if you can't get a grip and get control out there, I'll draft street supervisors and replace you fat cats. You earn inflated pay checks, while the city is experiencing open warfare. You pretenders with gold braid are home, fucking your wives or girl friends or for all I know spineless little boys." "Aw, come on chief," piped up Deputy chief Harlan, "that's just wrong, that isn't right." "Fuck it isn't!" Culligan roared. "I've been out there cruising every night. I haven't seen one of you bureaucrats out in the trenches. I'm beginning to put faith in the song that perhaps we should send in the clowns. You! Gentlemen know me; know where I'm coming from. I'm pissed, degusted and fast losing confidence in my command structure! Like Custer's chief scout was quoted, "What the fuck, look at all them Indians." "Well, get this, and digest, ingest, whatever the fuck the Indians are in the fort and you my darlings had better formulate plans post haste! I want those scumbags evicted and quickly! I want my blue coats storming their lairs. I tell you now certain politicians and citizen groups are clamoring to transfer this cluster fuck that exists in the city to the jurisdiction of the state police. This I remind you that it has never occurred in the history of this department. You bet your wives asses and your own it won't happen on my watch. The vacation for you hotshots is over. The days of peering in a full length mirror, from lurking about and ego's soaring, because you look oh so sweet, in all that gold are here are now curtailed. Your bimbo's are gonna get off your asses, roll up your sleeves and get fucking dirty alongside those poor bastard grunts out in the field, with all the ordinance, pulsating through this city. It's a question of time before some poor cop gets his ass in a sling."

Captain Rowan seated at the far end of the table, timidly raised his hand. Quickly dropped same and lowered his eyes when the chief staring long and hard waved him off. "I've no time for whining or excuses. You people get this issue turned around. I want suggestions and I want a successful conclusion to this. Get me a plan of action. No more dicking around. Your wives and mistresses or however you pleasure yourselves, have been put on hold, as of this moment. I've sat here berating you top hats for the past ten minutes and I'm concerned. I'm worrying when God handed out brains you received trains instead. I'm sick of the Chinese fire drill we've invented on the streets. Fuck! Fuck! Put whatever limited thinking process you possess. I want those streets back in our possession, we're better than those squirrelly shit stains. We better be or we'll all be cleaning shit houses soon. Okay, you know how I stand! Beware, I meant what I've said! Quote me if you dare. If you're insensitive to my outburst, hand in your resignations; otherwise, stand tall present me with a bonfide plan within twelve hours. Your top cops play the role even if for a spell your actors. Get it done gentlemen! Like shit paper my patience is worn thin!"

The chief stormed from the room. Silence enveloped the top command of Hartford Police Department who sat stunned, angry; with the tongue lashing they received by their chief. The quiet was broken only by the audible sighs of several and the shuffling of paper. Briefcases were snapped and quietly several commanders shuffled from the room to smoke, piss and grab a coffee, relieved to escape further wrath from their chief. Assistant Chief Lawler, they've been granted a fifteen minute break, to the brains of the department. A short respite from bulging pressure, in 15 minutes they would gather in the conference room, review, preview, exchange intelligence reports from the field. From citizens, informants, street honkers were high on the list. Men were known to spill their souls when frolicking in a comfortable bed with a woman. They would dissect all information hoping that piece by piece all would come together like a giant puzzle. Now they would earn their inflated salaries thought Captain Reynolds. A smirk on his face, for within the confines of his briefcase, sat volatile information, perhaps the ammunition for a loaded hand was the answer to their mode of attack.

The brass of H.P.D. filed slowly into the conference room. Lost in thought, Chief Lawler was already seated at the head of the table. Once seated, the assistant chief scanned the room and took note of the crest fallen faces of the department's top echelon. The chief had ruffled their feathers. Now it was up to him to light a warm fire. Cohesiveness was the recipe to terminate this cancer plaguing the city.

Gentlemen, he began, we've been enlightened as to how the old man feels. The heat is on and the pressure cooker is about to explode. You and I are expected to execute, to oversee our troops bring down the Hun. Together we have no alternative, but to initiate a police response that is within the scope of the law, and to serve and protect the citizens of Hartford. We've suffered wounds. We've bled now the wounds were scabbed and the clock is ticking. We've got to muster our resolve and take back the city. Those grunts in blue are looking for leadership, that's us, so we must roll up our sleeves and before this night is over we'll implement a plan. We'll begin by flipping through all Intel reports, concentrate on the nomads and comancheros leadership. We know who they are. We just have to pin point their safe houses, so gentlemen, let's get it done. Good citizens are bunking down in their residents and lives are at stake and our guys are certainly in harm's way out there. It falls on us to destroy these vermin. I've lectured long enough; the floor is open to suggestions and ideas.

Outside the sun was beginning to peek behind the horizon. Dark shadows inched their way onward cloaking light of day. Night fall was descending the city braced itself for another night of terror.

The room was quiet an occasional cough slicing through the silence. Papers were being shuffled audible whispers between commanders echoed in the room. The solitude was shattered by the voice of the Intel, Commander, Captain Reynolds. Addressing the assistant, he spoke calmly, but confidently, "sir, I believe I have the information here before me that will break those scumbag's backs." He had opened his briefcase and laid out before him were a stack of reports relating to the shootings in question, photo's, spent shells, the caliber of weapons and various evidence collected at the scenes, as well as, IDs of victims and suspects questioned, detained, then released for lack of proof. Standing, he held a loft one particular report, "Sir, this is a new report that was submitted to me at 0500 hours this a.m. by Sergeant Huxley, unit 43. It contains information of a highly volatile, in turn; it is frightening in its content. However, I believe it's the piece of the puzzle that completes the big picture. Huxley's informant is reliable and his info in the past has led to outstanding results in cleaning heavy case loads. This is the break we've been waiting for. I believe we've got these scumbags by the balls. Now we apply the squeeze." Lawler listened attentively; all eyes and ears were on Reynolds as he settled back in his chair. The assistant remained quiet for a time. He gazed out the window into the night, whispering a silent prayer that Sergeant Huxley had struck pay dirt.

The assistant gazed long and hard at Reynolds. They had worn the blue for years and had once been partners in the field. They shared a deep affection and respect for each other. "Okay Ray," he whispered, "lay it on us, be concise, gentlemen no interruptions please, until the captain completes his presentation. Then we'll sum it up and react and pro-act, accordingly."

Reynolds rose from his seat. His 6'1" frame expelling an aura of confidence. He strolled briskly to a large wall map of the city, studying it for a short moment, turning he faced his fellow white shirts. "Gentlemen, the information stored in the packet placed before us is the fire which will cleanse this city of the plague that has established a foothold. It is imperative that you know that as head of itell, I took the liberty to contact the State Police, New Haven Police and N.Y. P.D. as the information given Sergeant Huxley, involves their departments. You will notice on the map two red circles are located at 36 Lawrence Street and the other at 43 Belden Street. Now the information you will receive here today is I must emphasize highly confidential, it must not and cannot leave this room. Hand picked men of this department and the state police are already being briefed. The chief early this a.m. contacted the state police requesting manpower assistance. A mode of attack was submitted to the boss and received his approval. This operation will demand a large influx of personnel, thus the request to the state police. Now the State Police will be at our side in force. We will be the one in charge of the operation. This arrangement was agreed to by both the chief and the commissioner of the state police. So as to eliminate the confused looks on your faces, allow me to dictate a summation of what is transpiring here."

"Apparently the nomads receive ample supplies of drugs and ordinance on Thursday nights between the hours of 19:00 and 2100. Delivery is usually affected under the cloak of darkness. A purple van with yellow stripes bearing New York tags is the carry all. The bastards always have a blue Honda with four Hispanic occupants ride shot gun to the rear of the van, said vehicle also bares New York tags. Note gentlemen, these scumbags are far from stupid. According to the informant, they have a radar system in effect at all times. Lookouts saturate the area via roof tops, porches, windows or just plain walkers. They also place females with baby carriages strolling back and forth. Looks pretty innocent but that street is a camouflaged haven for their purposes. Okay, you'll have an idea of their MO. I need not tell you the area is highly surveillance on both 36 Lawrence Street and 43 Belden Street."

"Before you ask, let me emphasize that the MO for 43 Belden is basically the same. Only their source of supply is out of Springfield and yes Springfield Mass. PD has been notified and fully involved. Several of their drug units have been assigned to assist us as they have access to numerous photos and IDs of members most likely involved. The Comancheros have established a credible fortress of their own on Belden Street. Their garbage is delivered in a phony ice cream truck. Also enjoys a shot gun escort a red Toyota bearing MA plates. The occupants of all vehicles mentioned are well armed and must be considered extremely dangerous as are the occupants at both locations."

"For your ears only, Lieutenant Lanzi will be field commander. For the raid at 36 Lawrence Street, Lieutenant Mulchaey will head the charge at 43 Belden. Both forces will be under the direct command of Major Dellaher. I can tell you this; a plan has been formulated and will be initiated quickly. We are attempting to gather sufficient information to obtain search warrants. If there is time, however, if proven necessary in order to protect life, we'll act on speed. I am not at liberty to reveal how our surveillances of these locations have been supplemented, only that they are in effect as we speak and will continue around the clock till we feel there's enough juice to strike."

"The chief, Major Dellaher, Captain Weinstein and yours truly, held a cloak and dagger meeting at 0600 hours this morning. We all feel that due to Sergeant Huxley's report, which tied the knot that convinced us we've pinpointed the Nomads and Comancheros strong holds. Reports from line officers, detectives, itell investigators, citizens, parallel one another, so we have concluded that a strike is imminent. The state's attorney has been advised and has been brought up to date. Hourly reports from surveillance teams are filtering into itell and I will say the results are proving that we are on target. Please accept my apologies, it was not meant to keep several of you in the dark; however, the sensitivity of this operation had to be addressed. Gentlemen a word to the wise, what has transpired here in this room is meant for your ears only! I cannot elaborate any further. I will tell you this we will be hitting them hard and strong. Both striking forces will muster a minimum of 25 personnel, consisting of our people, state police and F.B.I. also members of the DAs investigative unit. For the moment I've no more info to render, any questions?"

Would blue blood soil the streets? Would innocents be injured with these thoughts clouding their thinking? All came to the same conclusion. No choice. The street toughs were out of control. Cops going in harm's way could and would take back the streets returning them to decent citizens. His summation complete, Reynolds with a nod, walked briskly across the room. Closing the door softly he headed toward the chiefs office. The brass of the department sat in stony silence exchanging anxious glances. Tension filled them like a fog enveloping the shore line. Disappointed and angry their minds in overdrive, wondering why they had been kept in the dark, and passed by, by their boss, low murmurs echoed in the room. Whispers of men with frayed nerves had they lost the chief's confidence? Were some destined for unwanted transfers? Their brains clouded by negative vibes. Many questions, so little answers, as their adrenaline slowed, most realized the significance of secrecy. Blue blood could flow in the streets, a survival occurrence. Two major operations to be launched simultaneously, would it succeed and at what cost, eventually Captain Lawson broke the quiet solitude. Well guys, time to pick up our big boy panties and move on. The old man's right. Limit the opportunity for a leak. Our boys are heading in harms way. We've got to be cognisant and support the boss and our soldiers in blue. Let's saddle up and prepare to plug what gaps could occur. May God smile on this department today? Slowly filing from the room, the commanders headed to their various commands, harboring a sense of apprehension.

Two CL&P trucks parked at each end of Lawrence Street. Their workers assigned to the job at hand. One remained on the ground and his two co-workers ascended to the top of the pole and began their labors occasionally scanning the area for any signs of activity. As they continued to work and the time approached mid morning, they spotted several nova sedans that had pulled in front of 45 Lawrence Streets. Two pretty nurses carrying medical bags in hand entered and once in the hallway they knocked twice on apt.1a and the door opened immediately. They were ushered inside they began to setup various equipment. A gas company truck began drilling in the street in front of 43 Lawrence Street. A jack hammers resonating throughout the neighborhood. Four laborers wipe their brow and continued their labors. Two clergymen in a black ford pulled to a stop in front of 34, quickly entered the building. Their hands laden with assorted religious articles.

Raoul Sanchez, on a perch located on the roof of 36 Lawrence observed the activity below him. Dragging on a Marlboro, thought all's okay. There is nothing out of place here. I do not hear, nor do I smell pigs in the area.

Engine Company parked directly across from 43 Belden Street. Fire fighters like exhausted bee's were clamoring in an about the building checking for carbon dioxide leaks. Two SNET repair trucks pulled too a stop in front of 49 Belden. Four workers exited unraveling coils of wire and were placing traffic cones to the rear and alongside their vehicles. Angel Sanchez observed the activity from his perch in the cellar of 43. Satisfied all was quiet, he stepped from the box supporting him. Smiling, he thought shit ain't anything happening. It's warm and cozy down here. All our babies in the corner resting peacefully for their work ahead think I'll catch some z's for 5. Fuck, up all night with nose fueling. I'm beat man and there's nobody here but us. The rest of them mother's upstairs getting high, getting some pussy, fuck them, they worry's for nothing.

In the apartment of 45 Lawrence Street, Officer Rita Blancette H.P.D. and Trooper Joan Teal activated their long range night scopes. Darkness descending quickly had forced them to act with haste. L&P workers continued their labors as did the gas crew in the street. Two men in clergy attire sat in observation mode peering through a rear window which presented them with a view of the rear of 36 Lawrence. Except for the reverberating sound of the jack hammer and an occasional car horn sounding, the street was quiet. As an occasional lonely pedestrian strolled the street. An old disabled woman turned into 36 Lawrence Street heading to the rear of the apartment. Her cane cascading along the walkway and Raoul Sanchez studied her and thought God she's one ugly bitch while firing up another Marlboro and returned to observing the street and having lost interest, in the old lady and brushing her off as harmless.

At 43 Belden Street, Angel Sanchez nodded off to sleep. Dreaming of his island and safety where he received his share of bounty. Upstairs his street tough comrades frolicked and made merry, secure in the knowledge they were untouchable. In the bowels of the Hartford Police Department sixty men and women of various law enforcement agencies, stood at rest. They listened attentively to Major Dellaher as he drew a final dress rehearsal of the impending operation. Flanking him on either side were Lieutenant Mulchaey H.P.D. and Lieutenant Martin S/P. For the later three supervisors, who would lead the actual attack, on the Nomad's and Commancheros lair? An occasional cough broke the monotone of Dellaher's address. He continued his dialogue in a baritone voice. The words, caution, safety, and common sense noted in his remarks several times and the large map behind the chiefs desk, contained etchings of how, when, and where officers would attack. Dellaher paused for a moment. The only good news at the moment is we have secured warrants for both addresses, with that in mind; I will not belabor this briefing. You're all professionals. You've been trained, briefed, and your going in well armed. I'm proud of you all and personally gratified that so many law enforcement agencies function as a cohesive unit. Good luck and God be with you and be safe out there.

Major Dellaher strode from the podium. In 22 years in law enforcement, he couldn't remember an operation of this magnitude. The young faces who had gazed at him so attentively played in his heart. As a silent prayer, thank God for such devoted men and women who live their lives in harms way.

Night was descending on the city laying its tarpaulin of darkness. Night birds began their peaceful chattering. Stars twinkled in the twilight.

Here and there pedestrians scurried to their homes seeking refuge from the demons that ruled the night. Vehicular traffic was moderate and motorists crawling slowly through city streets enroute to destinations known but to them. The sentry perched on the roof of 36 Lawrence kept a strict watch, noting that the gas company was now laboring under the glare of night lights. He kept the street under strict surveillance noting that CL&P was now hoisting heavy cables at their assigned work stations located at both ends of the street. Nothing appeared suspicious. Soon the delivery would be arriving. Then plans formulated late information in the wee hours of the morning. Hear-say an attack within Comanchero's territory was in the making. He was tired, lit up a smoke and sat with his back resting against a small brick wall. He was unaware that unseen eyes were locked on his every move.

Lieutenant Lanzi had briefed his men a final time. Thirty strong they huddled in a blue & white school bus with large blue lettering identifying itself as H.P.H.S. Athletics somber and edgy they caressed their weapons anticipating the command-blue birds are a go. They waited in silence, each with there own thoughts. This one of a wife and kids and that one with a sweetheart and another worried for a sick parent on it went. All hopeful they will once again see the sun. These were the men and women in blue. Their hearts pounding and mouths dry, they had talked the talk when sworn to protect and serve. Now they would walk the walk. The bus idled in the Aetna parking lot, hidden from prying eyes, as dark wrapped them in its peaceful tarp. They prayed and waited. At exactly the same hour Lieutenant Mulchaey marched his men into a green and white bus with the markings Weaver High Athletics, parked in the lot of the Holiday Inn. They appeared to passer byes as revelers celebrating a victory. Like their brothers and sisters south of them, their hearts raced with anticipation. Their thoughts of loved ones, while some prayed and some showed false bravado with jokes. All perspired profusely and soon they would confront armed subjects. They were trained and heavily armed. The unknown lay before them, these soldiers in blue waited with a disciplined quiet. Lieutenant Lanzi glanced at his watch. It read 20:10 hours. All was quiet for there was nothing from the surveillance teams. Lieutenant Mulchaey sighed; the night marched on in quiet solitude. All this planning and logistics would it be for naught. Lanzi's and Mulchaey's portable radio's squelching broke the silence. Men and women in blue instantly alert in the confines of their bus. Reports from the surveillance teams advised that pedestrian traffic to both 36 Lawrence Street and 43 Belden Street had increased dramatically. The signal street rats in their nests, in force, be advised, both streets extra quiet. Appears something about to go down wait for me to advise, the radios fell quiet.

A full moon cast its eerie glow basking the city streets in dim light. The wind rustled softly and one could feel its hot breath. An old lady with the assistance of a walker hobbled on the gravel walkway alongside 43 Belden Street. She passed unmolested as Angel had slumbered off at his post. The purple van exited I-91 North banking a right at the Airport Road exit. It continued north on Airport Road accelerating as the operator and occupants were anxious to reach their destination and discharge baggage. They were uneasy due to the freight piled around them was volatile. Juan the driver, eased off on the pedal when his side kick, Annocio, "barked slow down, fuck lips! What you want? Fucking cop on our ass! God damn fuck! Learn, baby, learn or the man, Phillipe, off your ass!" On their ass was a Honda, cool thought Jesus. Cool, we okay. Gonna be there soon, dump the shit get some brews and pussy.

Heading south on I-91, the red van entered the city. Proper Spanish music resounded softly through the interior. Operating the vehicle was John Victor. His demented grin displayed gaped broken teeth. He feasted on the adrenaline rush. Devoured the risks involved and lived for the excited high of danger. John took pride in that he was on Springfield's P.D. wanted list for homicide. Laughed aloud startling his counterparts, he'd kill again, which gave him a feeling of power the Beretta in his waste band an equalizer to any man.

The red van slowly pulled to a halt in front of 36 Lawrence. Blowing its horn twice, The Honda close behind both pulled into the driveway and parked in front of a broken down garage. Killing their lights, they exited from their vehicles, stood quietly waiting for assistance. Raoul had neglected his post. He had left to check out the old woman with the cane, as she had ventured toward the cellar. He felt secure approaching the old lady as she descended down the stairwell. "Hey you old bitch, where the fuck you think your going?" There was no response as a large hand grabbed him by the throat. A large fist cracked into his jaw and he was thrown bodily down the stairs where he lay prone in an unconscious state. Officer Lee Hotchkiss leaped to the bottom of the stairway, relieving his victim of his weapon. Rolling him over, he cuffed and gagged him. Grabbing his portable he whispered calmly the lookout is secured. 'All units go, go, go." The surveillance teams from CL&P and the gas company exploded into action. Weapons drawn they advanced on the double. Quickly surrounding 36 Lawrence Street for the Nomads waiting in the rear were quickly over powered and whisked away by rough hands. Lieutenant Lanzi barked to his driver, "Let's roll on the double!" Within minutes the blue and white H.P.H.S. bus rounded to a stop at 36 Lawrence Street. Thirty law enforcement personnel swarmed the building, half ascending the front stairs and the other half the rear. Screaming police, smashing doors, occupants thrown against walls, frisked and cuffed. Resistance was minimal and the Nomads had been caught flat footed. Faced by an army of blue and heavy ordinance, they meekly surrendered. The event took place with the smoothness and quickness that the H.P.D. was known for. Many lives would be spared this day, thanks to our blue soldiers.

At precisely the same moment a blue van traversed itself west on Belden Street, followed closely by the red Honda. Both made a hard right into the driveway of 43. Three horn blasts signaling their arrival. Cutting their engines, the occupants chain smoking and edgy, sat in a moody silence. Soon their comrades would exit the building and relieve them of this hazardous cargo.

The old lady with the walker had continued her trek. Reaching the rear porch, she found the cellar door unlatched and began descending slowly, moaning in pain. Raoul heard the clack, clock of the walker. Striking the cellar stairs, springing from his slumber, he arrived at the bottom of the stairs. He was amused at confronting this old disabled ugly broad. "Hey mama what the fuck you want? No place to be old woman." The old lady grunted her apologies muttering she was old and lost. "Well, mama, turn around and get the fuck out." No other words emitted, as a crashing blow struck him in the face. As he staggered back against the wall as a foot exploded into his balls. He vomited lunch and nausea gripped his stomach and pain clouded his thinking. Then smashing blow to the head. Mercifully to be relieved of his pain, for blackness enveloped him. Officer Fred Dewis stepped over the prone body. Reached down and retrieved a 45 caliber from his waist band. He then commenced to latch the cellar door. Reaching to his right leg, he retrieved a sawed off shotgun. Taking position at the bottom of the stairs, he sighted on the entrance. Raoul had been secured to a ceiling beam in a standing position and gagged.

As the van and Toyota sat motionless, five firemen sprang into action. Quickly grabbing shot guns and automatic weapons from the idling fire engine, they quickly surrounded both vehicles. S.N.E.T. workers also imploded on the area blockading the front entrance and rear entrances. It was at this point, Sergeant LaPore rasped into his portable, "unit 265, to field command, and eagles nest, all is a go, go, go!"

The green and white weaver bus roused into life spilling from the Holiday Inn parking lot. Its acceleration engine startled arriving guests. Rolling into the night, it screeched to a sudden stop in front of 43 Belden Street. Discharging its cargo of men in blue, who quickly broke into two groups, one crashed through the front door knocking over occupants and obstacles for the word police resonating through out the darkened interior. The other cascading through the rear entryway and thus enveloping the occupants in a text book pincher movement. The sea of blue and its arsenal of weapons were deployed so rapidly they rendered the Comancheros immobile blinded by the police high powered lightening. They were helpless.

Officer Fred Dewis had successfully killed power to the strong hold. Lieutenant Mulchaey was ecstatic. No shot's fired and the premises fully secured in15 minutes. Now a methodical search could be lunched. The scenario repeated itself at 36 Lawrence. The Nomad fortress rendered immobile in minutes. A search of the premises was already in progress.

Major Dellaher inspected both locations satisfied that searches were conducted thoroughly and professionally. Concluding his tour at the sites, he had land lined the chief, who was ecstatic. He reached out to the mayor, and indoctrinating him on the nights events and success. Disconnecting with the mayor, he had summoned Captain Reynolds, itell commander, instructing him to handle the forth coming press release. Finishing his instructions, he had driven to the sites. He was proud of his men and was overwhelmed with gratitude that the raids proved successful, a textbook operation. Much work lay before him. Outside agencies had to be thanked and not to be short changed. The utility companies would receive his personnel thanks for the use of their trucks and equipment. Sergeant Huxley would be highly commended as well as several other officers. The police brotherhood had marched shoulder to shoulder and decimated two powerful street gangs in a single sweep. Reports of large catches of weapons, drugs, and money filtered in. Not to mention evidence collected linking the gangs to numerous crimes, burglaries, robberies, and muggings solved as a result. Cases would be cleared and filed away.

The long arm of the law had prevailed and many lives preserved. The media was in a frenzy to siphon info for their headlines. Chief Culligan, alone in the solitude of his cruiser, monitored transmissions which crackled through the airways. He was relieved that officers were not injured. The lightening speed of the operation was a complete success. Chief Bernie Culligan felt haggard and tired. He departed to headquarters sure all was well. Heading north on I-91 homeward bound, he sensed the presence of comrades long gone whispering in his ear, duty, honor, integrity, accountability, responsibility. He lofted a crisp salute to the heavens. Yes, my brothers, those words were honored and carried out by your brothers and sisters in blue with conviction this very night.

The foray into 36 Lawrence Street and 43 Belden Street disabled the savage Nomads and Comancheros so critical to bring the streets back to the innocents. They would cease to function again as a terror to the streets. The damage inflicted by law enforcement was a death knoll drive byes would cease. Once again decent citizens could walk and enjoy their streets. For how long who knew? New demons surface, but the thin blue line would stand their watch.

Both raids resulted in the confiscation of 92 hand guns, 33 riffles, 10 sawed off shot guns, 22 shotguns, thousands of rounds of ammo, 33 machetes, 98 hunting knifes, thousands of dollars in stolen goods, large quantities of drugs, $150,000 in cash and the arrest and conviction and incarceration of 36 gang members. During the aftermath and as a new dawn peeked over the horizon, a young officer was over heard exclaiming these words, post phobias nublia "after the storm, the sun."

Cop Talk

Bellevue Square

The juke box was softly filling the bar with an old country melody. It was raining drops beating a soft tattoo on the window, next to five old timers. They sat reminiscing about days and incidents long gone. "Hey," Jardin croaks out as he belches his last swig of beer, "you guys remember the Grotte incident at Bellevue Square.?" "Hell yeah, the others yelled out." "That was fucking funny." "Hey LaPore," you were the boss that investigated that incident, right?" "Yeah right," groans LaPore. "Well Old Sarge!" shouted Big Hank, "Tell us about it. Spit it out and leave nothing to our imagination."

"Okay," begins LaPore. "I was the northeast sergeant that day, unit 42. I think I was in grade only two weeks, when the dispatcher bellows over the air, "unit 18—16 attention unit 42 assist the officer, 13-B Bellevue Square." "He never called a 10-0 (officer in trouble). Anyways, we all acknowledged the job and head pell mell to the Square. 18 was the first on the scene. Unit 16 and I roared up within 5 minutes. What's the first thing I see but 18, Officer Halloway, standing on the stairwell holding his stomach. At first, I thought he was hurt, but on closer scrutiny, he's laughing his ass off. I'm thinking to myself, what the fuck chuck? What the Hell's going on here? I approach Halloway, John, what's going down? But he can't talk. He's laughing so hard. He just points upwards on the stairwell. So, John Howan, who's in 16, and I ascend the stairs. Well you guys all know Gerome, you know Gerome Whitehead the neighborhood drunk." "Yeah," the gang answers. "So continue Lance," pipes up Big Hank.

"Well, Officer Grotte responding to an intox party in hallway urinating confronts Gerome. Now we all know Gerome is harmless, what he weighs all of 96 lbs. Grotte goes 6"2 230. He commands Gerome to flatten against the wall. You know all that sop shit. Gerome tells him to go fuck himself and pushes Grotte aside to make his exit. Grotte goes ape shit and throws Gerome against the wall. Gerome starts to snarl and spit and tells Grotte to piss off or he'll kill him. So what's Grotte do, he pulls his revolver orders Gerome to the deck. Gerome starts screaming, "He's trying to kill me! The cop's gonna murder me!" Doors fly open all through the building. Gerome leaps at Grotte, Grotte backing away, stumbles, his weapon discharges. The round ricochets off of all four walls and strikes Grotte right in the ass. Grotte is lying there in pain. Gerome is hollowing incoherently. The residents are up in arms. What the fuck do I do? I call for an ambulance, quickly dispatched Grotte to St. Francis Hospital. We got Gerome out of the building and charge him with intox. What the fuck? I had no choice. I've got a wounded officer, who shot himself in the ass. Now we're all laughing hysterically. The neighbors think we're all nuts." "So how the fuck did you submit your report Lance?" asked Big Mike "God Damn, it was a bitch, typing it up I couldn't stop laughing. Captain Heinwich, the skipper, thought I was demented until he read the report." "Wow, he goes hysterical with laughter. The whole department finally got wind of it. Laughter echoed through the building."

"So what happened to Grotte?" asked Lou. "You guys wouldn't believe it. The guys pitch in and sent him one of those rubber donuts, you know, the kind that you shit with. They also sent him a rubber gun, a real bullet and a pint of Gerome's whiskey and a card signed by Gerome, stating hope you shit for a week. Anyway, Grotte recovered and shortly after resigned. He had no choice for whenever he went to his locker; there was a picture of Gerome and a photo of the department medal of valor."

Laughing hysterically, all five comrades stood. That's a beauty LaPore. You must have had the report of the week. "Yeah," retorted LaPore. "Later guys I'm outta here." All got up and headed homeward bound.

Chapter 6

0830 hours Officer Lynette Dolsen had just completed school traffic. The blue goose dropped her at Trumbull and Pearl Streets upon completing her assignment. She began her patrol and was assigned to a foot beat in the heart of downtown Hartford. Traffic was heavy at this hour and the streets crowded with pedestrians. Coming to Dunkin Donuts, she entered, and stood her turn as the line snaked long through the ship. The java business was brisk and chaotic at this hour of the day. Officer Dolsen was concentrating on a young couple making merry in a booth. Startled when a voice asked, "Can I help you" Smiling at the clerk, she ordered a black with one sugar. Found an empty seat facing the street and she took a seat. Ah . . . hot, she thought, but good. Coffee jumped started her metabolism. She needed it bad this morning. She'd been up late the night before studying at the community college, majoring in political science. Customers came and went for some acknowledging her with a nod and a smile while others ignoring her presence.

The portable radio on her gun belt spit out transmissions steadily and the dispatcher's soft melodious voice directing units for a multitude of calls. She had studied the crime bulletin attentively and knew crime was on the incline in the downtown district with numerous snatches, muggings, snatches and grabs at various businesses. Her beat was right in the heart of this mounting crime wave. Lynette was given instructions, at roll call from her sergeant, to contact business owners. Be visible to them, perform P.R. Public relations is a tool that police were working diligently to upscale. Finishing her coffee she exited on to State Street crossing west on Main, she began her area of patrol. She headed west on Asylum Street checking the south side and moving several vehicles doubled parked. While discharging passengers, she noted that the majority of businesses had ye to pen. Most began their work day at 0900 hours. However, she scanned the street attentively concentrating on the crowd of pedestrians heading to work stations at the Travelers, Phoenix Building, The Hartford, etc., etc. Thousand of souls flitted about. Many obviously to prying eyes of predators looking for fresh game for she stood in the foyer of Savitt's jewelers, ever alert and transfixed she received immobile semi-camouflaged from the street. She watched as Joe the weasel scampered along darting between pedestrians. The weasel was known to cops as an ace pick rocket and purse snatcher. He would stalk his prey and strike in a flash. His was a lightening stroke. Strike and he was gone. Disappearing into the throngs of citizens, her strict observance paid dividends. The weasel struck like a cobra and slamming a middle age woman into an alley by the five and dime, in a heartbeat, he had her purse. Her cries were muffled by the enclosed alley walls and the roaring noise of vehicular traffic. Dolsen sprang from her observation post and a college sprinter, she ran like an elk. The weasel walking quickly so as to avoid notice and detection was surprised as he was suddenly was grabbed from behind and slammed to the pavement. Blood seeped from a head wound sustained when he struck the pavement. Rolling over he moaned in frustration. He was staring into the barrel of a police 38 special. Broadsided by Officer Dolsen smiling, Dolsen ordered him back on his stomach. "Okay, shit bird," she rasped, "hands behind your back, Give me any shit and I'll step on your nuts, understand!" "Yeah, oh yeah officer'" whined the weasel. Cuffed and secured, Dolsen spoke into her shoulder mike, "beat 12, dispatch" "dispatch come in beat 12." "Beat 12, dispatch, I have Joe the weasel in custody, Asylum and Trumbull. Ding dong mugged a female and she's approaching me now. Send me the wagon; I'll advise if a 10-10 is needed for the victim." "Dispatch beat 12 that's a big 10-4. The skipper will enjoy his mornings brew, Good job! Are you okay?" "Beat 12, dispatch 10-4. But the wagon boys may have to swing weasel. From here to Hartford Hospital, seems he sustained a head laceration." "Dispatch, beat 12, 10-4 we'll advise unit 68, they've just saddle up and enroute to your location."

Joe the weasel, aka Joseph Boumto, a white male, DOB 7-15-37, was charged with assault and larceny. He'd finally been netted and would spend a lengthy spell at the Somers hotel.

Lieutenant Mulchaey swung into the service road which paralleled the Connecticut River, in possession of two coffees. He reached for the radio mike and compressing the transmit button reached out for unit 43. "Unit 50 to unit 43." "Unit 43 go, unit 50." "Unit 43, meet me at the fox's lair." "Unit 43 10-4 unit 50" The fox lair was code between the lieutenant and his sergeants. A prearranged meeting place out of the eyes of the public and his blue and whites. Five minutes later, unit 43, Sergeant Huxley, pulled along side of unit 50. Returning courtesy salutes, Mulchaey handed his Sergeant a coffee light and parked in a manner as to be face to face with the two line officers conversed about the various issues. Gossip was occasionally enjoyed for everyone thrives on gossip. Who's fucking who, who divorced, who were the good cops and who the deadbeats were, etc. The conversation lapsed into an arrest which had been front page news. "Some dickhead in the suburbs had been raping a seven year old girl, initiated when she was one and had been ongoing for seven years. A real piece of shit, a scumbag prick, should be shot, related Huxley." "Naw, I got a better solution for the maggot," shot back Mulchaey. "What Lou?" "Well Sarge, I say take the prick, put him in an outhouse, staple his dick to the toilet seat. Set the fuckers shit house on fire and then hand the goat's turd a rusty saw. Huxley laughed. "Hey that's a thumbs up Lou. The prick would really be in a hot pickle." "Fuck him," rasped Mulchaey. "Too many shit birds like him out there, you know my sergeant, you take a rabid animal, there's no trial, no bleeding heart liberals pleading for mercy. The animal is simply destroyed. What the fuck is the cock sucker? Jesus, when are we going to learn and wake up anyway? "Don, nice job by Dolsen this morning, did you slide by?" "Yea, Lou. She's okay. Good cop sense. For we got the weasel and the dicks figure he's good for a hundred snatches downtown in the last four months." "You gonna commend her?" "10-4, Lou. I'm putting her in for a merit award." "Good show Sarge. I'll notarize it. She deserves it." "Them jack offs in the anticrime unit couldn't collar him, shit; the only thing they've caught far as I know is a cold. Okay, Sarge stay alert and keep me appraised of happenings, say hello to the bride." Touching his cap Mulchaey sped off. Hurley followed the blue and white as it departed the area in a plume of dust. Smiling, Huxley murmured to himself, "what a boss, the best God damn Lou, in the department.

Robert Grillo exited the bus in front of the old state house at 09:55 hours. Debarking with a modest amount of passengers, he headed directly to a deli where he ordered an egg sandwich and washed it down with a medium ice tea. Grillo's eyes surveyed the area of Hartford's downtown bristling with assorted business outlets. He was thrilled with his observation. Pedestrians and vehicular traffic was congested. He liked that because it insured his plan would be successful. A young woman in sexy attire passed by brandishing a huge smile and her white teeth glistened in the florescent lighting. "Fuck her he thought, just another slut conniving to fuck me or some other poor slob. Bitches they're all alike got no time for their bullshit." Grillo was a tormented man. Hated the world and despised his fellow man. Pitied himself, his marriage had recently terminated. He inhaled deeply while anger steered his emotions. His life in shambles and he'd lost all his worldly possessions. Worse he'd cloaked his very soul in a dark abyss, faulting the world for his misfortunes. He felt the bulge in his waist band. "Ah, he thought there's the power. There's the equalizer and the key to my future." Again feeling the bulge, he whispered, "patient my old friend soon we will strike and you will soon display yourself and together we will once again climb the ladder of success." He giggled with excitement happy his blue wind breaker offered refuge to his trusted friend.

Completing his meal, he rose from the small table and stepped into the sunlight. He mixed with the crowds thinking "this must be what it's like to be a worker ant." Crossing Main Street, he headed north. He paced himself slowly. Grillo could not let adrenaline cloud his thought process. He had planned this mission for months and had reconnoitered the area. His target loomed large in his mind and grew closer as he approached Pratt Street. His concentration was momentarily shattered by the jostling of a passerby who unwittingly bumped into him. Pushing the elderly man, he cursed, "you old fuck, and watch where your going, get the fuck away from me!" The old man mumbled an apology and scampered away ingested by the crowds of passerby's heading for various destinations. Several people had halted abruptly and stared perplexed by his sudden out burst. But his twisted lips scowling at them set them scurrying away. Approaching Pratt Street, he halted and leaned against the building. Lighting a cigarette, he checked his watch. 11:00 am. Beautiful he thought right on schedule. He walked to the corner peered west on Pratt Street. His heart racing, he grinned broadly. Ah-ha, there it is. An armored truck stood immobile by the sidewalk. It was parked in front of 66 Pratt Street. He scanned north, south and east and west. He felt exhalation, no cops in sight. His months of surveillance was about to pay dividends. Patience he thought discipline yourself. Fingering the bulge under his jacket, Grillo spoke softly in audibly, "almost time my friend". In 15 minute your power will nudge me upward and return me toward the good life.

Officer Lynette Dolson had entered the Adam's Furriers, chatting with Ben Ardren, the manager, implementing public relations as instructed at the morning roll. They were exploiting the merits of real fur versus synthetic, while engaged in this conversation the door flew open. Two customers chatting wordy entered. As she turned to face the intruders she caught a glimpse of Grillo standing in front of the United Bank. Back against the wall his head swiveled side to side scanning the street. His motor actions disturbed her. He appeared as a hunter engrossed with movement in the street.

The armored car had expelled its contents and slowly pulled away from the curb. Dolson watched as Grillo once more checked the area. Noting his right hand disappeared under his wind breaker with a final glance backwards, Grillo entered the bank. He studied the interior. Four tellers lined the counter, and no guards in sight and two customers were engaged in business activity. He strode to the last teller to the left. Smiling cheerfully the teller welcomed him with "may I help you sir."

Grillo placed his left hand on the counter and his puerperal vision showing the customers leaving the bank. "Ah good" he thought, "do it now." Gawking at the young teller's face, he whipped the 45 caliber from his waist band, swinging his right arm in an upper ark, it pointed at the teller's face. "Yeah bitch lips, give me it all, tell your friends act nice and no one gets hurt, Fuck up and your all dead. I don't fuck around," pointing at the teller, Mary Whiscomb, an attractive brunette, he barked, "go lock the door, do it now bitch quickly, don't fuck up, whore and don't piss me off!"

Mary quickly moved to the front door locking the mechanism in one swift motion. A potential customer startled, halted in his tracks. Pale faced and nervous, Mary advised the customer, "the bank would reopen momentarily and that their alarm was malfunctioning." Just give us a few minutes. Bill Hallisey stood facing the door, "okay missy, just hurry or I'll be late for work." In the meantime, Grillo had the victim teller placing several bundles of green backs into a large shopping bag. His eyes locked on the third teller. "Get on it slut! Get those stacks of green ready I'll be through with this fucking whore in a minute!" Bank manager, Bruce Holcomb, strode from his rear office, confused at the eerie quiet, customers were usually lined up. Only one patron stood at the end of the counter. He moved in that direction, froze when he saw teller Doris Risto stuffing stack of money into a brown shopping bag. Alarmed he addressed her directly, "Hey, Doris what gives? What's going on?" His pulse raced when the male at the counter raised a hand gun above the counter. "Shut the fuck up! Faggot! What are you an asshole? This is a hold up! Get you fat ass on the deck and stay there! Move and I'll blow your balls off!" Holcomb collapsed to the floor, sweat forming on his face. "Damn'" he thought, "This is real!" He felt wetness run down his legs. "Shit, I pissed myself. Oh God, let us live!"

Grillo continued his travels along the counter stopping only long enough for the tellers to drop the green booty in his bag and the 45 swiveling back and forth threatening the terrified employees. He approached the last teller watched with amusement as the teary eyes terrified girl nervously placed seven stacks of money topping of his booty bag. Hey cunt, you're real pretty. Get your ass over to this side of the counter. Come stand by me and be quick. I've no time to fuck around. The horrified teller Mary Epstein evacuated her assigned station. Quickly walked around the counter and had stood by Grillo's side. His eyes ogled her lustfully. "You know baby, I've been without poo-tang to long. You're coming with me. Remember, waving his 45 in the air, my big brother here. You'll walk by my side like we're a couple. Fuck up and your dead. I've nothing to lose. The rest of you assholes stand fast. Any sudden movement or if I even think you are, your dead, understood? Dead! Alright, down on the floor. Hug it hard like your gonna fuck it! He laughed at his remark. Goodbye and thank you. Have a nice day, fuckheads." With Epstein in tow, he backed slowly to the door. He felt elated, "Yeah, I've done it" he thought. Reaching the entrance way. He turned dragging the terrified Epstein along.

Dolson hidden behind a large fur coat had a clean visual of what was going down. She grabbed her portable. "Beat 12 to dispatch. Send me back up I've a 10-87 in progress at 66 Pratt Street. The United Bank suspect is a white male. Approximately 6", heavy set, with a blue wind breaker, blue pants, brown hair and has a hand gun in his possession. He is backing towards the Pratt Street exit door and appears to be towing a female hostage with him. Have responding units shut down and secure Main and Pratt and Trumbull. I've the culprit in my sights."

John Riley listened attentively. An experienced dispatcher, he immediately went over the airways. "Units 12, 14, 10, attention 43, 10-87 in progress, at 66 Pratt Street, the United Bank, and Suspect armed. Officer on scene, observing." "10-4 unit 10," "roger unit 12," "10-4 unit 14," "10-4 unit 43", came the response, "unit 43 to responding units, take defensive positions. Unit 10-shut down Main and Pratt, 14, you secure Trumbull and Pratt. Dispatch, roll me two more units." "10-4, unit 43, Units 16 and 18, head over to the Pratt Street area. 10-87 in progress," "10-4 unit 16," "10-4 unit 18, we've copied on the way." "Unit 43 to units 14, 16, 18 close up on me in front of the civic center. We're going it on foot. Do not use sirens and no front parking. Be aware of citizens. The area is a beehive of pedestrians. 10-4, unit 43" "All units acknowledge, units responding." "All copy Sarge, civic center, on Trumbull, that's an affirmative."

Grillo reached for the door pushing hard as he was now in a hurry and bent on a successful exodus from the area. Holding Epstein by her left arm, they stepped out onto the sidewalk. Looking left and right, he snarled to Epstein. "Move it bitch I'm in a hurry." He turned right to head east on Pratt, and froze when he spotted a blue and white screech to a halt at Main and Pratt. Making an about faced, he was planning on now heading west towards Trumbull and cursed when a second blue and white roared to a stop at Trumbull and Pratt. Realizing both ends of the street were now manned by cops, he had no other option but to seek escape through the rear of an unsuspecting business. Glancing about he was shocked to see an officer approaching from the opposite side of the street. Weapon drawn, the officer ordered him to freeze and discard his weapon. He yanked Epstein back into the bank. Holding her close he needed time to think. The situation had turned sour. He knew the cops were on to him and closing in fast. How he didn't know. It didn't mean a fuck. Escape was his only thought. Fuck'em! He had his hostage. Use her as a shield and tie the cop's hands. "Yeah, you mother-fuckers, I'll force you to back off. The girl is my refuge. Yeah I'll abscond with this bread and orchestra a successful escape"

Dolsen scampered to cover behind a parked pickup. She had a perfect angle on the entranceway. Pedestrians observing her 38 pointed at the bank's door, retreated quickly like a herd of cattle. They stampeded towards both ends of Pratt Street seeking safety. Women screaming and men running in a panic was in motion. Escape was their only thought. Holcomb had crawled along the floor. Reaching the rear door, he reached up and unlocked it. He didn't know why, for he just did it. He then returned to his position quickening his pace when he heard Grillo returning his loud cursing warning Holcomb to remain in the prone on the floor.

Lieutenant Mulchaey screeched to a halt in front of the civic center. Units 14, 16, 18, were already there. Unit 43 was in deep conversation with his officers planning what action they would initiate. Mulchaey shouting "Sergeant Huxley, take two men and move cautiously towards the Bank! Stay on the south side and use the buildings to conceal your movements! Try to get right by the bank's entrance! Do not enter and await my orders!

Unit 18 is coming with me! Stay in touch by radio. Okay move! Let's go earn our pay."

Officers Liscomb, Kahill, and Johnson advanced cautiously east on Pratt Street. Hugging the walls, unable to have visual, they strained their hearing. Keeping Officer Dolson in sight, the street had emptied of civilians and both ends of Pratt Street having been shut down by police. The early morning mist had evaporated. The suns rays warming the city and foot by foot the three officers wormed their way to the bank's entrance. Weapons at the ready and beads of sweat dripped from their faces. Sweat strains appeared under armpits and adrenaline rush incarcerated their heart beats. Fear and excitement dictated their emotions. All three inhaled deep breaths and then they were there!

Mulchaey and Officer Lindstrom lined strong had negotiated their trek towards the bank through alleyways and over fire escapes. Leap frogging from roof top to roof top. Clamoring down a side fire escape of a record business, they arrived at the rear of the bank. The beige colored door appeared forlorn and debris strewn about the small lot. Vagrants empty bottles stood like sentries against the wall. Mulchaey whispered to Lindstrom, "Let's go, stay alert, be ready, the bastard could fly out the door any second. If he's armed, Fuck'em! We take no chances. We'll send'em to hell!" "Hey Lou, wonder where's he's from?" piped in Linstrom. "Who the fuck cares", fired back Mulchaey, east bum fuck, who gives a fuck, and it's where he might be going that counts! He fucks around and he gets a nice cot at the coroner's office in a body bag!"

Grillo felt trapped in a fish tank. The only ace he held was Epstein. He pulled her close, shielding himself from the bead Dolson had on him. Glancing around he noted the employees remained in the prone position on the floor. His brain was a whirlwind and perhaps a retreat through the rear door. Naw, changing his mind, the pukes will have that covered. The gun to Epstein's head, he stalled, for he needed time to gather his thoughts.

Mulchaey and his partner pried the door open slowly needing to practice discipline and caution. Innocent lives were in peril. Mulchaey made his decision. Entering the bank on his belly, he advanced at a crawl, Officer Lindstrom close behind him. Inch by inch, they advanced, confronting Holcomb on the floor. Mulchaey whispered "be quiet and stay where you are. We are at the ready. Both officers reached the end of the counter. Mulchaey inched himself to the corner. Peering around, summing the scene, displayed employee's lying on the floor in several locations. His muscles grew taught inhaling slowly. He was confronted by the suspect's back. The pistol pointed at a young female's head and was held firmly in a bearlike embrace. "Fuck," he thought, "what to do?" Lying still he made an instant decision, rising from the floor, he charged Grillo. Grillo intense on the front door was startled by the sound of pounding feet to his rear. "Aw, fuck one of them tellers is taking flight!" He rotated both he and his hostage, disturbed by the activity behind him. He and the hostage were propelled backward and crumbled to the floor. Struck by a large apparition in blue, legs and arms swinging threw and fro. Mulchaey grabbed for Grillo's gun hand. Both were punching each other. Fists connected with flesh and bone. Mulchaey screaming, "Drop the fucking gun, asshole! You're fucked for there is nowhere to go!" "Grillo fired back, "Fuck you! Take it if you can! Try mother-fucker!" Mulchaey was soon joined by Lindstrom entering the Frey, like a lion in heat. He pounced on Grillo, landing several blows to his face. Blood spewed into the air covering all four combatants. as Epstein was clearing and kicking at Grillo, the bank employees screaming in terror, had taken refuge behind the counter. As the battle ensued, the four cops stationed in front of the bank charged through the door. As the struggle escalated a loud retort echoed during the mêlée, Epstein yelped in pain. Grillo's weapon had discharged striking her in the right thigh. Screaming, "I've been shot!" Tears cascading down her cheeks, she was rolled from harm's way by Officer Kahill. The officers swarmed over Grillo. Lindstrom wrestled with Grillo at the bottom of the combatants, relieving him of his weapon, bleeding profusely from lacerations inflicted in the battle, Grillo was rolled onto his belly, arms roughly pulled behind him and cuffed. Officer Dolson and Kahill administered first aid to Epstein who had blood spewing from a gun shot wound. Using compressions and soothing words, the officers were able to stem blood flow. A tourniquet was applied and her legs placed in an upright position. Grillo was moaning and had shit his pants. He began whimpering then bust into a fuselage of tears. He'd fucked up now there would be hell to pay.

Officer Dolson, manning her portable hissed into the mike, "Beat 12 to dispatch," "Dispatch come in beat 12." "Dispatch slow any other units down, suspect in custody. Request two 10-10s to the scene. Female hostage suffered gun shot wound to right thigh. Suspect will require medical attention for facial and bodily lacerations. No other injuries and scene is secure." "Dispatch beat 12 10-4. Notifications of the proper authorities have been initiate, as we speak. Inform our officers, job well done. As well as the Detective division and Feds are enroute to your location." "Any unit needing dispatch, come in." There was no response. The voice of John Riley resonated throughout the airways. "Attention all units the 10-87 at 66 Pratt Street, United Bank, has been secured. Suspect in custody. All units not needed clear the area. KCA330 the Hartford Police at 12:45."

Robert Grillo, age 37, DOB 2-16-1940, received medical attention requiring several stitches. He was facing a long haul in the federal hotel. Miss Epstein recovered from her wound after a lengthy rehabilitation. The officers involved were commended and were awarded the distinguished service ribbons. For Officer Dolson, her performance on that sunny day was the essence of police work and received two awards. United Bank employees suffered mental trauma, but returned to their jobs and no doubt tense whenever a customer strolled through the door.

Police patrols continued in the business district resulting in further arrests. Their presence discouraged the vermin and predators and expelling them from the area. Crime dwindled and merchants and citizens going about their business once again felt free and safe to return to the streets to window shop. Stroll hand and hand or have enjoyable meals at the 4 and 5 star restaurants. The thin blue line of soldiers of the interior, always in harm's way, for their motto is to protect and serve. Thank God for the blue. Yes, they would always be there for you and I and for our kids. Taking for granted, they deal with and rid the streets of demons and predators everyday. This was such a day for the men and women of H.P.D., "The Thin Blue Lines."

Cop Talk

The Out of the Way Jail

The four old vets sat at their favorite table located in the rear of The Lucky Leaf Cafe. Reflecting on days long gone. Jardin somewhat sober for the hour bangs the table. "Listen up you dinosaurs. Hear what Langavon pulled." "Nah," barks Harland. "What'd the crazy bastard do now?" "Well the scuttlebutt has it he was assigned to the Blue Hills beat. Walks into toe the barbers. Glances around observing several patrons in waiting. Joe asks, "Yes, officer can I help you?" "Yeah, responded Langavon, "How many ahead of me?" "Five," retorts Joe. Langavon grunts and walks out. He returns the next day with an instant replay. "Hey Joe, How many?" Joe not looking back replies, "five." So dickhead Langavon makes a quick exit. The next day same scenario. Langavon strolls through the door. "Joe, How many today?" Joe annoyed retorts, "Don't you count six?" "Fuck so Langavon departs the premises. Joe the barber beckons Willie Slim, a street person who takes refuge from the elements in the shop. Joe says, "Slim follow that cop I can't figure what the hell his problem is?" Slim happy for the diversion, skips out the door. Returning a half hour later, Joe asks, "Where'd he go?" Slim smirking simply replies, "your house."

All four laughed heartily. "Shit had to hit the fan," chuckles Jardin. "Nah," replied Harland. "Joe was happy for him and his old lady were on the fritz. He just walked away. Langavon got away clean again. That guy lives, breaths, eats, sleeps with his dick in his hand. Someday an enraged husband will deliver the "coup de grace" with a silver bullet." "Yeah, someday someone's gonna put the squeeze to his pecker in a vice." Harland pushes out of his chain heads for the pisser. Returning "Hey, you refobates, How about Hotchkiss?" "What about the Big Bear," pipes up Gutsomovich. "Unfucking believable," puts in LaPore. Lieutenant Mulchahy, cruising down Allen Street spots Joe the Balls Gucci cuffed to the chair link fence across from the Mercedes Dealership. He grinds to a stop at the curb and walks over to Gucci. "Hey, what the fuck is this? Who the fuck put you here?" Gucci smiles sheepishly, "Mister Hotchkiss." "What the fuck for?" Growled Mulchahy. "Shit, I pissed him off. Fuck up in the Connecticut Lunch." "Jesus H Christ," mutters Mulchahy. He jumps into his cruiser grabs the mike, "unit 50 to beat 13." "Beat 13 come ahead unit 50." "What's your location?" Orders Mulchahy. Unit 50 I'm standing tall and proud in front of the eatery." "10-4 stand by be there in a cow's fart," replies Mulchahy. "He roars up to Hotchkiss and they exchange salutes. Mulchahy grimed faced barks, "What the fucking Christ are you thinking of? Did you shit your brains this morning?" "What?" Lou asks Hotchkiss all innocent. "Fuck you and yours! What? retorts the Lieutenant. You got balls! Gucci is cuffed to a fence. It's high noon. Have you gone south on me? For Christ sakes Lee. The Civil Liberties Union would have a field day. The liberals would experience organisms. You must be mad or you haven't got laid. Jesus Lee, is this your own precinct here. "Aw Lou, you didn't release him did you?" Now Lee is getting hyper. He hates being hounded by bosses, as we all know. "God Damn it Lee! I don't give a rat's ass how you run your beat! But keep it clean, but your exposing not only yourself but the department to ridicule and criticism as well as a possible civil suit! Now get your ass up there and release that little prick!"

Lee throws the Lieutenant a sloppy salute and walks off muttering, "Fucking scumbags get all the breaks." He uncuffs Gucci, drags him to 15 Allen Street where he's tight with the maintenance supervisor. He's already negotiated with the super, aka Papa Al, for a small space in the bowels of the basement. It's one of those commercial building, you know the ones that line Allen Street. So no one but Papa Al travels there. Well, anyway, located in the cellar are 3 large bins. Meshed in iron screening each contains a hard wooden chair and three buckets. A couple of rolls of ship paper. Lee's thought of everything all three have connecting water hoses. He drags Balls Gucci and tosses him in the center cage bellowing, "you know the drill you little prick!" I'll release you in two hours." "He had his own private jail," exclaims Jardin. "Yeah, shit for brains. The bears had that location up and running for two years. What the big fuck does, if someone pissed him off on the beat, he incarcerates them by the hour. Depending what they did." "Give it to Lee,!" yells LaPore. "He hates paper work, so he solved the problem, of course felons arrests go to H.Q. He only fucks with the drunks and derelicts." "yeah," echo's Harland but he fucked up one night. He got caught up in a shooting and forgot all about Lenny the Fish Murphy. Woke up at 4:00 am and flew out of the house put the pedal to the medal, like a big ass gazelle thundered done the stairs only to find the Fish sound asleep. Like an innocent puppy. Only Lee could pull a stunt like this those street people feared him and knew he'd kick their ass. If they whined or complained." "You know, stated LaPore when I was the line boss I often wondered where all those vagrants were, when Lee was on. Union Place was always clean and neat. Gotta give it to the old bear, his was a tight ship. He always had my respect. No question. He was the strongest toughest cop to don the H.P.D. blue. Hope he's faring well. Yeah Jardin remember when he stuck your ass in your locker?" "Yeah," replied Jardin, but he never did it again." "How come?" asked Harland. "The Big Fuck was afraid of me, pulled my revolver told him I'm gonna blow his cock off. He'd never fuck with me again." "You know Lee if he thought you were 10-44 he gave you a wide berth." "Yeah ups LaPore, you had to have fun for it took the edge off. We all fucked with the bear. He knew and loved us and the affection returned to him ten fold from his great brothers and sisters." The clock struck 12:00 midnight "Aw shit," whispered Jardin, "we're all in a world of shit. Let's take a 105D and head home." The table sat bare, slowly the interior lights dimmed and died out. Left behind to the hands of time were a thousand memories shared by old warriors. The stories would fade but the souls of these old comrades would roll free and clean as they shuffled to the final roll call.

Chapter 7

Captain Reynolds itell commander whistled sharply than took a deep breath. Exhaling slowly as he perused the field itell report. His secretary had just handed him. On his desk sat the morning paper. He glanced at the headline embossed in large black type. Vietnam protest planned for this weekend. Vietnam vets against the war, was the main theme. They wanted to make a statement that the government would stand up and take notice for the injustice that the vets have been experiencing.

Reynolds was perplexed, word via intelligence reports hinted that as many as 35,000 protesters would be in attendance. Firing up a Marlboro, he reclined in his seat, closing his eyes attempting to rest his brain. As commander of itell, pressure was experienced on a regular basis. His job and that of his command, was to keep abreast of activity within the city, together with dissecting, analyzing and directing the flow of information regarding crime and its associates to police commanders within the department. He needed to maintain a respectful re-pore with law enforcement agencies, be they locals, state, or federal, earning their trust and retaining it was a daily exercise. He could ill afford to make mistakes. Rubbing his temples, he inhaled deeply, expelling blue smoke towards the ceiling. "Fuck" he thought, "another crisis. It fucking never ends." Late nights would be the regimen and meetings with agencies directly involved with policing and maintaining peace and security of this event.

The potential for violence is a strong possibility. It was wide spread throughout the nation. "Shit! Shit! Fuck a duck!" Grabbing his sheath of reports, he rose from his seat, strolled out the door, walking briskly to the end of the corridor. Entering a large complex, the sound of type writers and ringing phones dulled his senses. Surveying this beehive of activity, he halted abruptly and then knocked sharply on the door, marked Chief of Police. "Come!" was the immediate response given. Opening the door quickly he entered the inner sanctuary of his boss. "Good morning, chief." "Good morning, Ray. Take a load off, have a seat," requested Chief Culligan. Smiling broadly, "what's up Ray?" Reynolds dropped into a chair facing his boss. Placing his papers on the edge of the desk, "Chief, have you seen this mornings headlines?" "No, Ray, I've been going over the unusual, but your here so it must be a 10 on the Richter scale." "Right on chief seems that antiwar protests have caught up to us." Captain Reynolds reached for the chiefs paper, swirled it towards him. There it is chief, Maalox tonic time again. The chief glanced at the headline perused the article. Slamming the paper on his desk, he swiveled around facing out his window deep in thought he uttered fuck. We'll be up to our asses in whale shit. Son of a bitch, there's no reprieve in sight. He swiveled back facing Reynolds, "okay, well captain you know the drill. Contact all of our commanders. You know your lot here. Lot's of notifications with surrounding towns and state. And Ray step softly on this. We're going to need all the help we can get. Christ, Bushnell Park. Talk about a geographical nightmare. According to your itell, and the media, 35,000 assholes will be frolicking in the heart of the city. Shit to fuck, we've got to protect the business district. Alright, fuck it get on it like yesterday Ray. We've no time to lose. Yell, scream, cry, plead, and beg, I don't give a shit. But set up a conference for tomorrow at 0900 hours with all the agencies this cluster fuck will demand. Get together with Major Dellaher and Captain Weinstein. Today let's tighten our end. Hells bells, your dismissed Ray and keep me informed."

"Yes sir," Reynolds was on his feet and walked briskly out of the office. His somber mood mirrored the chiefs. Concern and worry would top the law enforcement menu for the reminder of the week. Returning to his office with a glance at his desk calendar told him it was Monday, May 23rd. Rubbing his eyes, he felt nauseous. He keeps saying to himself, "four days, only four days to prepare." He experienced feelings of doubt and foreboding. Pressing the intercom, he instructed his secretary to reach out to Major Dellaher and Captain Weinstein, requesting they report to his office forthwith.

Major Dellaher, flanked by Captain Weinstein sat facing Captain Reynolds. The tick-tock of the wall clock grating their nerves and all three knew too well they would be confronting massive crowds and that it would be hostile and unruly. It fell on them to create an operational plan that would offer the city and its inhabitants secure and safe.

Reynolds spoke shattering the silent gloom that permeated the office. "Major, captain, thank you for your expeditious arrival and I know you're familiar with what's going down. I've met with the boss and he directed us to formulate and initiate an operational plan that will ensure a successful conclusion. The department will be direly strained, as you know. Manpower is a major concern, as well as, logistics, equipment and ordinances, also topping the list, major we'll have to siphon most of patrols personnel. Captain Weinstein your division will also be cannibalized. Detectives will be in uniform and swell the ranks of the field services bureau.

"Now I've compiled a list of sister agencies and commercial business who can assist us. Feel free to interrupt if I've left any thing uncovered. Here are the facts gentlemen:

1) State police, five surrounding P.D.'s West Hartford and East Hartford, Wethersfield, Bloomfield and Windsor.
2) The fire department, a request for six pumpers, should the need for pressure water hoses be necessitated.
3) Connecticut transit authority, for use of eight buses placed a strategic locations, there use to book and transport detainees arrested.
4) At least a dozen ambulances, we'll endeavor to get more if possible. But the minimum is a dozen.
5) We'll utilize our motor cycles in partnership with state police motorcycles. This should ensure that we'll show a force of at least 50 strong should we be forced to confront and dispense unruly crowds.
6) Again, we'll assign our mounted horse cops with that of the state police and surrounding towns that loan their horse cops to us. I

figure a total of twenty five will be deployed and again to disperse unruly crowds.

7) Gas and CL&P should be on sight

8) Portable toilets placed at strategic locations throughout park. Hell I don't have a clue how many. We'll have to guess and with hope we'll guess right for 35,000 souls we'll need several hundred. Where we get them is up to city yard. They're been informed and have personal scouring. Surrounding towns and scavenging from the parks and various construction sights. The yard will place as many as they can beg, borrow and steal in the park this Friday afternoon.

It is imperative that strong barricades ring the downtown business district. No spill over's into downtown can be tolerated. Already the merchants are in a furor, clamoring for protection. Commo's phones have been off the wall since these mornings' headlines. Also gentlemen the state police and the National Guard will render air surveillance. This is good from above they'll have a broad spectrum of streaming crowds. Be advised my personnel are engaged in contacting the agencies I've previously mentioned. The chief has called for a 0900 hour strategic meeting with representatives of those agencies in the conference room, tomorrow. Well gentlemen, that's my table spread for the day. We roll our sleeves up and we get the job done. We've been in this game for years. We know what confronts us and we've been there before. In effect we will be fielding a blue salad. A cohesive effort by law enforcement of all levels, with God's help. When the plume of dust settles, the sunset will settle over a peaceful and successful conclusion. Oh, one more thing, feds will be circulating throughout the crowds getting Intel and advising when and where weapons may suffice. Thank you major, thank you captain, until tomorrow then, keep the faith."

The conference room door flew open. Through the door strode Chief Culligan and Colonial Russ Stought, Connecticut State Police and Colonial Paul Reyes, Connecticut National Guard, walking tall and proud. They took seats at the head of the conference table Chief Culligan at its head flanked on either side sat Stought and Reyes. The room was crowded with and impressive cast of ranking officers and from surrounding towns and various laws enforcement agencies. There to gather, collect, disseminate, add or delete intelligence that could inflate or deflate what course of action should be implemented. Brass sparkled in the dense room. A collection of brains and brawn and united in a brotherhood to endorse a plan that would unfurl and set into motion this day. Chief Culligan opened the meeting addressing the group. He welcomed them and expressed gratitude for their attendance and assistance. He sat erect as he made eye contact with all present, advising them that the governor had ordered the National Guard to mobilize and prepare to assist law enforcement. One thousand guardsmen were to be in ready alert status in stand by mode concealed within the confines of the state armory. The guard had supplied police with ample supply of tear gas. Military grade a stronger version then that of civilian texture. Also ATF was now involved and would also plant undercover agents with the crowd of protestors.

Advice and opinions circulated throughout the room. It's interior ranked of stale smoke and each member volunteered a course of action. Deliberating amongst themselves, most were thrown out. They were deliberate and disciplined in their discussion. All knew when they entered this chamber they would not emerge ill a solid operational plan had been instituted. At 1200 hours a lunch break was enjoyed in the small cafe two floors below. The conference room over lunch, the brains and commanders of the operation tossed options back and forth. Nerves frayed, tempers sometimes flared common sense prevailed and calm was the forte. At 1500 hours, the meeting adjourned. The representatives of various agencies returned to their respective commands. Intel reports in their possession. A plan of operation had received the stamp of approval and would be put into action. The consensus was a defensive mode should be the course of action with emphasize to safe guard the business district with whatever force was necessary as dictated by crowd activity.

Chief Culligan sat staring out his window. He'd put his stamp of approval on an operation to combat a critical threat to his city. A stand up guy, he alone would suffer untold ridicule and agony if things went amiss. If successful the cohesive command would share in the accolades. "Ah," he thought "Fuck it, the riots, the sexual revolution, now this, this department and my troops have had no respite." On a positive note, however is they're experienced as hells fire, tangling with unruly crowds is nothing new. My guys could write the manual on crowd control. Five years of riots have created a steeled legion of veterans." "Yeah", he whispered signed softly, "we're doing well."

Saturday, August 28th, dawned quietly, the sun peeking over the horizon cast a fiery glow on the rippled waters of the Connecticut River. Life stained in the bowels of the city. Vehicular traffic crawled through the city streets. A slight breeze caressed the trees. Chief Culligan reconnoitering the city proper for the city was alert and tense, and the feeling of the calm before the storm was present. He sighed, his mind in overdrive. He felt nervous. Lots of worries in his heart fear for his men. Agonizing if the protestors could be contained and controlled or would they burst, like flood waters and roaming into the heart of the city. The image of chaos and irreparable damage danced before his eyes. Plans for a well laid operation had been formulated, but what if things went awry. "Fuck," he thought. "Get a grip; I command a determined and professional department and their experience in situations of this magnitude second to none."

Traveling south on Main Street, he noted groups headed toward Bushnell Park. Several handling placards denouncing the war, as he neared Pearl Street, he observed a steady stream of protestors marching west on Pearl. The majority turned south to Haynes Street an access roadway leading directly into the park. Reports from field intelligence filtrating through the airways painted a bleak picture. The park was quickly filling with large crowds continued to flow through city streets. Traffic was backing up congestion of main arteries causing concerns for the flow of emergency vehicles. The die had been cast, Bernie Culligan, Chief of Police, his unmarked idling, sat in stony silence, observing the large multitudes. "So it begins, God be with us." Slowly, he accelerated towards advantage point enroute to field command.

Roy St. Pierre, lay on his couch, sipping an energy beverage fueling his torn body in hopes of surviving another day. He had drifted off, day dreaming which had turned back the clock, taking him back to another time, another place. The ringing phone startled him. Shaking cobwebs to clear his mind, he answered on the third ring. "Hello." "Hey Roy, Peter Burke here, did you see this morning's news edition?" "You mean the anti-war protest?" Roy asked. "Yeah gonna be quite a spectacle of goof balls from up and down the east coast swarming the city, should be a whopper." Roy remained silent after a lengthy pause, Burke barked, "Roy you still there!" "Yes Peter, give me a moment, I'm thinking." Roy back on the line spoke rapidly and excitably, "Listen Peter, activate our notification system. Let's get our boys involved. This is a golden opportunity to make a statement. Get on it right away. Okay Peter. Make sure the word gets passed down the line. We're assembling at 0900 hours Saturday morning at the H.P.H.S. parking lot." "Hey, good show Roy!" "Yeah, we'll make a good show. Fuck we've been talking the talk and now its time to walk the walk. One more thing, Peter, instruct everyone to wear what military gear they possess and to display their decorations and ribbons." "Roger that Roy. Can do I'm on it, over and out. "

Roy reclined back on the couch. He unleashed the Vietnam Veterans against the war. These vets had been outspoken for months preaching the futility of a war. Their government had not committed to win. Now these veterans who had been there, done that, would en-mass echo statements made by "Vietnam Veterans against the War" across America's landscape.

Roy had just finished an evening meal of tomato soup and a ham sandwich. He reached for the phone on its first ring. The voice of an excited Paul Burke reaped through the land line. "Roy it's on unfucking believable! Fifteen hundred guys from throughout the state have pledged to show. We'll stand tall Roy, Trust and Believe!" "Okay Paul, everyone's has been told to assemble at Hartford High, right?" "Roger that Roy, and to don in military apparel and ribbons and you were emphatic on the time. Roger Roy, everyone's got the word 0900 hours formation, we're good to go." "Okay Paul, Good job. See you Saturday. Keep your balls tight we're kicking those yellow politicians' hemorrhoids up their asses." He disconnected.

St. Pierre lay back on the couch closing his eyes. He let his mind drift off. As top honcho of the "Vietnam Veterans against the War," he directed thousands of state veterans who had witnessed first hand a futile scourged war. Tears welled in his eyes as he reflected on so many comrades who gave their all and for what? His top man, Paul Burke traveled life with one arm lost in a cause going no where. He deluded deep into his soul seeking questions that would never be answered. Sitting up he spoke to the four walls. "Yes we'll make our statement. We'll display pride and discipline. We will refrain from violence, unless we are goaded." He signed nothing wrong with the country, just the leadership. He lay back with a heavy heart full of bitterness, hate, betrayal, drifting off to sleep. His first thoughts were for a peaceful solution. Bring the troops home. Enough waste of young lives. Two many forests and alleyways were home to vets. All who gave some and sadly some gave all.

Bushnell Park was near over flow. Crowds continued flowing into the city. They debarked from buses, trains, and private vehicles. As the park filled, chants of:

Stop the war!
Stop the fucking war!
Baby killers!
Baby killers!
All!
Hey! Hey you fucking say!
Stop fucking Johnson's war!

Chants echoed throughout the area. Like a bottle full of steam reaching the breaking point. The crowd grew silent. One could hear the soft whistle of wind caress the trees. All eyes glued to the knoll by the state capital. A sea of blue had suddenly appeared a thousand strong. They stood on a line and their shields glistening in the sun. Night sticks at port arms; they displayed an aura of discipline and determination. Soldiers in blue, they stood shoulder to shoulder. Commands from ranking officers, clear and authoritative, resonating throughout the park. They stood tall and proud and would stand their ground. Well armed police manned barricades at strategic intersections. Their job to prevent unruly protestors infiltrating to the business district this show of force discouraged those souls who have contemplated such fool hardiness.

Major Frank Dellaher stood at the head of his troops. Flanked on either side by the state police, field commander, and commanders from other departments, and agencies and no action would commence unless ordered by field command, which housed Chief Culligan, the commissioner of the state police, and the brigadier who commanded the sequestered National Guard troops. On the left flank of the massed blue line, their engines silent stood 50 motorcycles manned by Hartford Police Department and Connecticut State Police. The right flank in tight formation was the horse cops, 25 strong. The unit consisted of H.P.D. and C.S.P. mounted officers. The naying and snorting of the horses drifting over the heads of the protestors, some hundred yards away and to the rear of the blue ranks, set in a line, were a dozen fire pumpers. Their powerful water hoses were uncoiled and set for immediate action. Above this impressive display of force, the wop, wop, wop, of police helicopters could be heard crescendo, monitoring the swelling crowds. At field command radio traffic was intense. Transmissions of rock and bottle throwing squawked through the airways. The brass listened attentively. Their eyes intense from their vantage point on the knoll. They surveyed the huge crowd. They dissected reports filtering through the airways of disturbances occurring in an around the park. Conversation was limited and there was no time for talk now. The die was cast. The end of this day would reveal a peaceful solution or a catastrophic event.

Chief Culligan studied the operational map to his front were the massed assembly of blue. His cavalry, chuckling to himself, hope the fuck this day is better then Custer's. He noted that Connecticut company buses were manned at six concealed locations and meant to detain parties arrested. Searching further he noted that a dozen ambulances also were assigned to strategic points concealed from the public. "Well," he thought "we've implemented all we could muster viewing this crowd and its magnitude, I wonder."

Roving units assigned to roam the business district reported groups of trouble makers detained and arrested within the forbidden zone. He was startled as the protestor's having observed his force began jeering at the sentries in blue. It escalated into a thunderous roar. The crowd now in an ugly mood, pushed forward foot by foot. They advanced on the silent blue wall undaunted by the advancing mob hurling projectiles. The police stood fast and the crowd was 100 yards away, continued its advance. Police commanders paced back and forth to the front of their silent ranks. Fingers tightened on nightsticks. Beads of sweat trickled down faces from beneath riot helmets heated by the sun. Major Dellaher wet his lips as the mob moved ever closer. He cocked his head to the side. "Detail tension!" he bellowed the thunderous roar of a thousand pair of boot heals crashing together resounded over the park. The sudden display of riot shields slowed the advance of the crowd. They halted in their tracks. The police had switched from defensive mode to attack alert. The crowd now leery began a slow withdrawal and continued to heave projectiles which bounced off blue riot shields. The knoll had become a hive of activity. Motorcycles revved up their bikes as one. The roar was deafening. At a command they shifted into a v formation. The horse cops guided their horses into a line prepared to disperse those who dared an attempt to bridge the police line. Culligan thought "events are moving quickly. A clash is imminent." Dellaher anxiously waited, silence! No order had spewed from command. "What the fuck chuck?" He thought. "I could spit on the assholes if they charge first their momentum and weight in numbers will sweep through us, Jesus, chief give the order to advance on line."

As tension mounted between police and their adversaries, a hushed silence descended within the park. All eyes turned toward the Rochambeau Arch, for there snaking its way through the twin arches marched a sea of green clad figures. Military cadence echoed loud and clear, "hup, two three, four hup, two, three, and four." The rythmatic thunder of fifteen hundred combat boots cascaded through the park. The green rank marched forward proud and disciplined. Heads held high, as they neared the potential combatants. Observers noted the gleam of be medaled chests. They gasped in admiration as disabled veterans hobbled along on crutches, wheel chairs. Many sporting white canes assisted by comrades, missing arms, and legs. These tortured souls would not be denied their right to march with upright brothers. Roy St. Pierre led the contingent. Flags flanked him. The stars and stripes resplendent in the morning sun led the way. The red white and blue rippled in the wind. The colors enhanced by the sun's rays. A large banner declared to the world, Vietnam Vets against the war. These once wholesome, healthy men, had once stood tall and had lived the dream, now with shattered dreams and broken hearts, they marched on. Soon they formed a curtain which acted as a shield. Police and protestors now separated by green, stood transfixed in silent tribute to men of broken dreams. The vets led by St. Pierre, continued their march. The command, "Detail halt!" bellowed loud and clear, and the sea of green halted as one. Roy St. Pierre, bellowed "Detail Right Face!" A thunderous explosion of boots coming together echoed as the order was obeyed. St. Pierre was eye ball to eye ball with Major Dellaher. His eyes roved over the lead officers noting their ribbons earned in Korea and what this demonstration was about. Vietnam!!! Many a young boys dreams litter the fields of that hell hole.

Officers had been instructed to don military ribbons, for this event. St. Pierre snapped to attention. Raising his right hand, he fired off a quick salute to Major Dellaher. "Good morning sir. Sergeant Roy St. Pierre, 27th calvary reporting. This detail of veterans means no harm and no threat. We have arrived on scene and hoped to signal a statement of negativity to a futile and unjust war. We've come to place our stamp of disapproval, nothing more."

Major Dellaher snapped to attention returning St. Pierre's salute. He noticed his gleaming medals which hung in dignity across his left breast. He spoke softly, as his eyes locked on an empty left sleeve which fluttered in the wind. "Welcome Sergeant, we are here to preserve peace nothing more. It is our profound hope that this day be remembered as a day of atonement and not of entombment. These officers, to my rear shall remain tight in ranks unless pressed into aggression. We both know the drill. Your cooperation and example here today sergeant could save the day." Roy St. Pierre, smiling, whispered softly "major sir, may I address the crowd?" Dellaher surprised, simply stated, "Yes go ahead, as long as its not defamatory." Dellaher took St. Pierre by his good arm and led him to an outdoor speaker close to the command post. "There you go soldier. Leaning close he whispered to St. Pierre, "Tell it like it is. Let the world know. Give em hell." St. Pierre stepped to the microphone noting the four large amplifiers positioned facing the crowd. Clearing his throat he gripped the mike with his right arm. The crowd grew silent out of curiosity. They leaned into a soft breeze. Their interest buoyed by the apparition of masses of men in blue and green facing them.

As St. Pierre spoke, his voice thundering was carried by the caress of soft wind drifting over the sobered crowd. "People I, we, he pointed at his contingent of green clad brothers, are here to embrace you. For hand in hand we hope to produce an emotional stamp of disapproval on continuing an immoral and unjust war. We have returned to our native soil, bitter, disheartened, frustrated, and disappointed. You are not isolated in feeling betrayed by our government. Think, for a moment. Reflect hard and long. Let your hearts and souls be the judge. Look at these men standing to my left. These down trodden soldiers gave their all. You see before you the remnants of once were highly trained and disciplined troops. They proudly followed the flag. They trusted our leadership and witnessed horrors you cannot imagine for both to us and the innocent souls of Vietnam. We are not here to cause blood shed or to inflict damage. We have experienced personally the horror of in corrigible decisions. The media refers to you as a mob and I say the true mob exists in Washington. Buffoons, who hide behind impressive titles, and live the high life, while sending youth through the gates of hell. Tears flowed down his checks. Everyday somewhere across this land the echo of rifles fill the air and the sad notes of taps embrace the hearts of loved ones. The final farewell, the final salute, to a boy turned soldier, who never had the chance to live, many who never experienced the love or sweet embrace of a woman. Military hospitals and the V.A. Hospitals are over flowing with wounded and disabled Americans which are your fathers, brothers, husbands, and your sons. Here facing you stands a small contingent of those who once served in good faith. Many as you see made this track in a wheel chair, with crutches, canes, unseeing. They bear these wounds, having served their flag. I ask you, what sin did they commit by serving their country? You see the physical wounds they bear, but your eyes can not reach into their tortured hearts and souls. Images of horror stamped on their souls, till the peace repose of death releases them from their torment. You have heard of the carnage inflicted on that country we have lived it. We do not ask for approval or forgiveness. We acted in good faith, but the countries leadership is weak and hypocritical. That is why I stand here before you this day. I implore you to continue the pressure. But in a peaceful manner, yes bring the troops home. End the war! But let us not shed each others blood. Here on our hollowed soil. Facing the men in blue, he continued, these good men confronting you bear no malice. They, like us, are following orders and are honoring their oath of office. Many suffered the agonies of Vietnam, but they remain silent, neutral, and experience their own demons. Yet, they stand tall, proud and disciplined. They are prepared to receive the brunt of your hatred for an unpopular and unwinnable war.

Why? Americans throughout this great land today, stand divided. We are blind, deaf and dumb. Can we not unite and spare future young men from such catastrophe? Those who have served know full well that the people of Vietnam also stand divided over our presences. So where does that leave our soldiers division at home and in the land he has shed his blood, his tears? This soldier has felt the pain of broken dreams, the ache of a broken heart, and not one who has tread that soil returns unscathed, for their minds and souls are tattooed with scars that cannot be addressed or healed. Like a wound, it will bleed, and then scab and the scar will remain. You've done your country a favor and you have come here at your own personnel sacrifice. Some traveled many miles. I now implore you as your brother to disassemble. You can leave with pride and distinction so long as your departure is clean and without malice." Casting a salute to the crowd, he bellowed "Thank you! Thank you, for attending! One day the voices of America's youth will be heard and good men of honor will return to their homes. Thank you!"

He strolled from the microphone. Tears rolling down his face uncontrollably, from the memories of dead comrades who walked along side of him, while he exited the podium. He exited with pride and head held high, so the crowd could witness his strength and honor. He knew his soul would have restless nights. At least he had served with courage and honor, and like all would pay a lonely price.

The crowd stood silent. Tears lined many faces. The tired soldier had hit home. A crescendo of cheers off in the distance began. Soon it exploded into thunderous applause, which continued several minutes. The cheering carried by the wind found refuge in every soul that had shared that day. Protestors began exiting the park in peaceful droves, within the hour the park lay bare in quiet solitude. Only the wind whistled through the trees, scattering debris left behind.

The command post was quiet and the commanders lost in thought, because the disabled soldier had touched their hearts, no doubt. Chief Culligan gazed out at the empty park, thankful. His respect for the Vietnam Veterans, whether for or against the war, had risen numerous decimals. Walking briskly to his communication operator, he waited in patient silence for the field reports to filter in. The radio crackled. The city was quiet and small groups lolling about seeking eateries and beverage. His department had affected 85 arrests for minor charges and no injuries were reported and there was only minor damage in isolated areas.

The blue line stood fast at parade rest in disciplined silence for two hours ensuring the crowd had surely dispersed. The city was secure and they watched in reverence as the contingent of Vietnam Vets against the war came to attention. Their ranks full of pride and their banners held high. They heard the brisk military command of forward march and watched with solemn pride and gratitude as these old wounded soldiers march in peace one last time. Slowly they passed through the Rochambeau Arch. Only the thump, thump of their boots striking pavement echoed through the park. The torch of a stationary figure of a soldier etched in the concrete lighting their way in grateful silence. Chief Dellaher stood tall and quiet in front of the ranks. He hoisted a crisp salute to St. Pierre who crisply returned the courtesy. "Good bye old soldiers" whispered Dellaher, "farewell." His heart was heavy, for he knew that most would not make it.

The order received from field command was given to the major. Facing the blue ranks, he quietly addressed them his voice choking with emotion, for he simply said "thank you, dismissed." The ranks broke. Each going home spared the carnage of a potential confrontation. Each stamping the memory of this day in their hearts for they knew that old soldiers had had their victory and had maintained peace to Americans and their law enforcement bothers. High flapping majestically in the wind, the stars and stripes had shown bright, as if smiling and blessing that many would remember what occurred. Here all the days of their lives.

"Post Phoebus Nubila"
"After the storm, the sun"

Cop Talk

The Voice in the Wall

Jack Striker, Bob Harper, Will Gomez and Tom Reynolds, had just completed the grave yard shift. Twelve midnight till eight in the morning sitting around a small fire at the round table, a little ride away off Windsor Street, safe from prying eyes of the public. A case of Budweiser was to be their breakfast. Striker sounds off, "you guy's hear about Harland?" They all piped in, "No what did he do now?" "Seems he and Gutsomovich are working booking. It's a hot Friday night on B squad and they've got a full house of guests in the cell block. Well, anyway this one dude, we'll call him fucknuts is giving them a rough time. They threw him in a cell of H block and leave. Fucknuts is hollering and carrying on annoying the other guests in the detention hotel. So Big Hank directs Officer Dochaud, who had taken to eating in the little service alley that runs behind H block, now Blair does so. It's a confined space as you know meant to service plumbing to the cells.

Dochaud works his way to the rear of fucknuts cell. He starts tapping on the wall. Fucknuts ceases his hollering. He's looking all around wondering where the tapping is coming from. Suddenly he hears a whinny voice from behind the wall asking "is anyone there? Please help me." Fucknuts approaches the wall and states, "who the fuck is that? What are you doing in there?" The voice sounding tired replies, "is that big cop around?" Fucknuts answers saying, "How the fuck do I know. He must be. I'm in jail here you asshole." "Please, respond the voice. Don't be cruel;" I've been here for 15 years," Fucknuts obviously had taken a back, state "What?! Get the fuck out of here! Who put you there?" "That big cop, that's who, because I gave him some shit." "They can't do that!" "Shouts Fucknuts, this is America; look friend fires back the voice. This is Hartford and these cops are nuts, especially that big guy." Fucknuts says to the voice, "How do you eat or go to the bathroom?" "Oh, they have a little space and they slide some kind of shit beans through it and I shit and piss in a bucket. I haven't bathed in 15 years." The voice now sobbing,

Fucknuts enraged states, "when I get out of here, I'll notify the media, and they'll set you free!" "Oh thank you! Thank you! Shouts back the voice. "I am dying for a hot dog." "A hot dog? You've been in there all that time and all you can think of is a hot dog? What the fuck is wrong with you?" "I love hots, friend. Please get me out of here."

At that moment Big Hank on his rounds stops at Fucknuts cell. "Who the fuck are you talking to asshole? Are you a nutcase?" Now Fucknuts has gone timid, this is the cop the voice is talking about, and he is weary. "Officer, I was just singing." No way is he going to tell this big cop about the voice in the wall. Big Hank stares him down, "You were talking, and I don't like nutcases. I don't want anymore shit, you understand?" "Yes, officer, I do, I do." Hank walks away now. The voice begins again. "Who were you just talking to?" "That big fucking cop and he really thinks I'm crazy." "Oh, don't let him think like that. That's why I'm in here. He thought I was nuts, because I told him when I was in my cell, someone was in the wall." "God Damn! shouts Fucknuts. Then stop talking to me!" At that instant Big Hank reappears with Gutsomovich. He's holding a large syringe in his hand, containing a white substance. "What was in it?" asks Harper. "How the fuck do I know, pigeon piss, for all I know. You know those two guys are screwballs. Anyway, Hank tells Fucknuts, "You were talking again. See this syringe?" "Yes officer, replies a now full terrified Fucknuts. "Well I'm going to stick this up your ass. It contains a sedative that will control that fucked up mind of yours." "No, No, officer, please I'll be quiet." "Last chance asshole, last chance," with that the two assholes leave. Now the voice comes, "What did he say?" "Look you fuckhead! Shouted Fucknuts, he's got a syringe loaded with some white shit says if I'm not quiet he's going to shoot it up my ass." The voice says, "No, no, don't piss him off; you'll be out for a month." "What, they can't do that! Where am I in Russia, here?" "Be careful, says the voice. "Look man! Get the fuck away from me. You're the one pissing off that big guy. Leave me alone! I'm not talking no more. He hears the voice who is not exiting the service space saying, "Good luck. Hope you're not put in the wall."

Fucknuts goes bonkers. He goes completely ape shit. Four cops have to restrain him in his cell and an ambulance is called. He's taken to McCook Hospital, placed in restraints and all the while screaming about the voice in the wall. No one listens. He's given a shot which knocks him out. He spends two weeks in the hospital telling everyone about the voice. Last I heard he was receiving psycho therapy. All four laughed, the moral being, don't fuck with Big Hank.

Chapter 8

Spring was in the air. Tuesday, April 24, had dawned crisp and clean. A slight breeze caressed the trees throughout the town. Main Street hosting numerous pedestrians' shoppers as it housed diversified businesses for their browsing and shopping needs. Lieutenant John Stowe, watch commander, seated at his desk perusing reports handled in the last 24 hours. Radio traffic crackling over the airways was light. The day watch had gone smooth and quiet. Glancing at his watch he chuckled 15 minutes to go and this tour was over.

Out on the street patrol units leap frog through town streets some parked in strategic locations wrapping up final reports. Another day going in harms way near completion. Officer Frank Mallozi was gossiping with a locale merchant assuring him that extra patrols were in effect as his business had experienced a rash of swap and grab larcenies. Officer Frank was a good street cop. Always gave the little guy attention. He played by the rules but always kept circumstances fair for that little guy. Well Frank, see you later. Ending the conversation with the merchant, he headed to his cruiser, looking forward to a pleasant pasta dinner.

Communications had been quiet most of the day. Several larcenies, motor vehicle accidents, late reported assaults, some burglaries and one or two domestics, thrown into the mix, soar 2nd shift would begin filtering in. Dispatcher Art Winkler had just lit up a camel. Clock watching, anxious for his relief, he was excited and nervous. He had a date with a cute chick and he had recently met and worn down for this dinner engagement. Day dreaming he reached for the buzzing telephone. Glancing at the wall clock, it read 3:15. East Hartford police, "dispatcher Winkler may I help you."

Late in the tour he was tired and bored. He came to immediate alert. The voice on the land line speaking calm and cool. "Yeah, you can I'm going to kill my wife and son." "Hey, pal hold on now, where are you calling from?" The male caller sighed. "23 Comstock Place, Apt. 2B, and I'm not fucking around, mean what I say. The world sucks, maybe I'll hurt more assholes too. Well, I've told you shithead. Do what you got to do." Winkler stamping a complaint card, yelled up to the command module, "Sergeant Fred Jepson! Hey Sarge, better roll units to 23 Comstock, Apt 2B. Male caller, states he's going to kill his wife and son, sounded serious, not excitable, spoke calm and slow."

Jepson turned to his dispatcher. "Get a name? Did he mention a weapon?" "No name. Just stated what I told you. Unknown if weapon involved. He hung up too soon." "Shit to fuck, you got a call back number?" "No but, I'm on the phone with S.N.E.T. They're putting an emergency status. I should have something real quick." "God damn it Winkler! You'd better! I've told you before, get names, weapons. You're giving me shit here! The fucking troops out there need to know. Jesus they're the one's going into the lions den."

Compressing the mike, Jepson barked into the airways, "unit 24, 25, 23, attention unit 40, 23 Comstock, Apt 2B, Male caller states he is about to kill his wife and kid. I've nothing further at this time. Added info forth-coming, all units respond" "unit 23 roger" "unit 24, 10-4" "unit 25, affirmative" "25 Comstock Place, unit 40 on the way." Jepson bellowed in response, "10-4 all units responding, 23 Comstock, use caution! Do not front park, use caution! You're off 15:20." Lieutenant Stone eves dropping on the broadcast on his radio, sprinted into communications. Sergeant Jepson, "be advised on of our former guys resides in that building. I don't know which apartment, but he did suffer from certain issues." Looking at Winkler, "anything more you can add?" "I'm on the landline with S.N.E.T. now Lieutenant. They're checking their data. I should have something real quick." "Yeah, well Winkler, should have had it yesterday. Set a fire under their asses. We need to know right now. If it's who I think it is, his place is crawling with weapons. Advise when you know. Sergeant Jepson, be advised I'm headed over there. Have Mallozi in 24 pick me up.

Tell him I'll be at the end of the parking lot on School Street waiting."
He turned and galloped from the room.

Officer Mallozi acknowledged the call. "Fuck!" he said aloud. "It's par
for the course. Fucking shit always hits the fan every time. There goes my
pasta dinner. Hope the fuck this doesn't turn into a Chinese fire drill.
Again his call sign, dispatch I'm on, go ahead!" bellowed Mallozi. "24
be advised pick up the watch commander on School Street, at end of the
lot." "10-4 unit 24, eta 30 seconds" "hope he can run, aw good show,"
thought Mallozi. Stone's a good boss. He's got brains and common sense
and balls we should be fine."

Frank Fecarla hung up the phone. Sweat dripped form his forehead.
His hands shook uncontrollably. He suffered bouts of sporadic tremors
usually when nervous. He grabbed the riffle which lay against the wall
beside him. An M1 Garand, a powerful military weapon. It expended a
30 cal round. On the table, by the phone, a half dozen boxes containing
100 rounds of shells. Each lay opened ready for use. Frank could hear his
wife sobbing and his son crying. He had locked them in the bedroom.
Spittle formed at the ends of his mouth. He felt dizzy, agitated and he
was disgusted with life. Disenchanted with his wife and believed his son
did not belong in this world. He injected an eight round magazine into
the weapon, slid back the bolt. The metallic click assuring him that a
round was chambered. He positioned himself behind a curtain, now he
could observe the street with the gun barrel. Frank shattered the glass
window and now he giggled, "I have easy access and a clear field of fire.
Fuck's got rid of me and now I'll show them all what a real cop can do."
Frank crouched behind the window with the riffle at the ready. "Where
the fuck, are they? Where are those fucking protector cops?" He would
not have long to wait.

Winkler jotted down the information. The S.N.E.T. operator had given
him. He disconnected. "Sarge!" he yelled, "Got the info. Dude's name is
Frank Fecarla at apartment 2B; phone 860-527-6312." "Okay Winkler,
good boy, next time get that information first. Now notify the Detective
Division and get the commander on the horn. I think this is the real
deal. Advise what's going down. I'll notify the chief. Lockhard! He yelled.

Lockhard, an old dispatcher, discarding his paper, get up here and relieve me, I've got to inform the boss."

"What the fuck Sarge? The shit probably gonna hit the fucking fan and you want me in the hot seat." "Just get you ass up here, fuck lips. I've no time for tears. Pull up your big boy panties and sit your ass in this chair and stay alert, you fuck. Don't go south on me! I'll be back in a flash. Besides here comes Sergeant Labbe, my relief so go back and sit on your brains."

Winkler dialed extension 404. The voice on the line answered, "Detective division, Commander Thorns." "Commander, this is dispatcher Winkler at communications. I've been instructed to inform you that we have a possible hostage situation brewing at 23 Comstock Place, Apt. 2b. A trace on the phone number was initiated by S.N.E.T. Id's that residence as a rental to one Frank Fecarla. I took the initial call and he related he was going to kill his wife and son. Hey kid, slow it down, rasped Thorne. "Did he say why? Did he hint as to a weapon? How did he sound?" "No sir, he didn't elaborate as to why. He didn't reveal if he possessed a weapon and he was calm on the line." "What time did the call come in?" "Sir, at 15:15 hours" Thorne glanced at the clock it read, 15:45 hours. "What's the phone number at the apartment?" "Sir, its 860-527-6712" "Okay, thanks, advise if anything further from the responding units". "No sir, they've just now were given arrivals." "Thanks," Thorne disconnected. He then retrieved the phone and dialed ext. 500. Within three rings, the voice of the boss picked up. Chief Drum, "fire away." "This is Thorne. We've got a budding situation in the works." "Yeah, Dan, Sergeant Jepson is here filling me in. Better get Hurley in right away as our negotiator. I'm betting we're going to need him. It's Fecarla's place and he's a special person, as we all know. Oh, and keep your boys on the clock. No one checks out unless I give the word, understood?" "Right chief, I'll contact Detective Hurley right away." "Fine Dan," the line went dead.

Officer Mallozi, along with Lieutenant Stone in unit 24, arrived at Comstock, electing to park three houses down from number 23. As they exited the vehicle, the resounding sound of a gun shot rang. The windshield of unit 24 disappeared in a spray of shattered glass. Both officers leaped a four feet wall facing in the direction of 23 Comstock and took cover in the prone position. Two more successive shots echoed through the neighborhood. Both striking unit 24, both officers drew their weapons. Locking eyes, both knew their 38's were futile and no match for what they were confronted with. "Jesus Frank!" exclaimed Stone, "What the fuck chuck? He's really gone ape shit, really gone south this time. We're going to need help on this one. These toys we're holding, we might as well stick'em up our ass. We need some big ordinance here and fast. Fuck the other units are arriving on scene. Jesus Christ," Stone leaped to his feet. Whistling loud and hard, he signaled to pull over and halt where they were. Another shot rang out hitting the pavement to his right. He crawled back behind the rock wall. Breathing hard, he turned to Mallozi, "Fuck a duck; we're in a tight fix here. Listen you stay here and I'll crawl to the end of the wall. I'm out of his vision down there. I've got to take charge and get things rolling and use one of the units radio to notify those people peering out of their homes. We've got to evacuate the area and shut this street down." "Okay Frank, you stay safe." Stone crawled as fast as he could. Reaching a safe escape route, he scurried to unit 23, parked out of site of the sniper. "Dick, hand me your mike!" "Yes sir, responded Office James Sepetro. "Unit 23, Lieutenant Stone to dispatch!" "Dispatch, come in, unit 23. "Listen and get it right sarge! We're taking fire here on Comstock! Unit 24 is Swiss cheese! My units here are under cover! I don't dare move them! Have additional units close Comstock! No traffic is allowed either vehicular or pedestrian! Notify command staff; inform them we'll need support here! We need heavy ordinance, tear gas and also have an ambulance, and fire apparatus stand by in area! I've got my guys here taking up positions as close to the target as possible, unit 23, out!" "Dispatch to unit 23," Lieutenant your unit designation will now be unit 50, and unit 50 roger on your requests. Hold tight we'll be sending the calvary post haste."

Within the confines of the East Hartford Police, the quiet had escalated into a bee hive of activity. Detectives were donning bullet prove vests. Patrol officers of the 2nd shift were being briefed and soon would be in battle regalia enroute to Comstock Place. Cruisers of the day squad not assigned to Comstock would remain on duty and handle calls throughout town until relieved. Communication was in emergency mode. Day dispatchers would remain on station assisting the evening watch. Phones were ringing off the hook with concerned residents from Comstock and nearby streets calling in fear. The phone lines clogged. Shot's could be heard and the explosive discharge of the weapon piercing the quiet of the neighborhood rang out. Residents barricaded themselves in their homes. Their shades were drawn for fear was in high gear and area was under siege. It would seem like an eternity till its conclusion. Chief Drum and Commander Thorne sped to the scene. Drum moaned aloud, "son of a bitch! The media is already here! God damn, Dan, have some of your guy's shoo'em back. The crazy bastards, they'll get their asses shot off! Shit to fuck this place looks like a circus."

The scene was surreal. News vans pockmarked the landscape. Reporters frolicking in the open battling for a front row seat. Spectators with their numbers swelling by the minute, Drum barked into his radio, "unit 100 to unit 41!" "Unit 41 on, chief go ahead." "Sergeant, have your units clean up this cluster fuck at Comstock! Move these people back before someone gets their heads blown off! Do it quick! We need operating room here! As it stands we have little room to maneuver." "Unit 41, 10-4, 100, can do."

Drum was livid. He had officers in awkward positions within sight of a deranged gun man. "100 to unit 40 set up a perimeter at the end of Comstock. Position your men in defensive positions. Get that building surrounded. Have officers gain access through the rear door. It offers some protection from our asshole friend up there. Inform them to evacuate tenants from above and below targeted apartment. All officers other then those evacuating the interior are to hold there positions until I order otherwise. No one is to return fire unless confronted with the threat of bodily harm or death. We've hostages in there. Use extreme caution." Two more shots rang out! "Fucking asshole!" exclaimed Drum. "Unit 100 to dispatch" "dispatch, come in 100." "Dispatch, have one of your complaint writers reach out to Hartford P.D. Request immediate assistance, advise them we need their S.W.A.T. team and I mean quick. Suspect is held up and has fired rounds intermittingly. Further advise them I've established a command post at no 124 Comstock, out of sight of shooter. Will brief and advise them here." "Dispatch 10-4, 100 in process of contacting H.P.D., Time is 16:15 hours." "10-4 dispatch, advice when contact is made and their E.T.A." Sergeant Labbe turned facing dispatcher Bickford. "You copy Bickford." "10-4 sarge, I'm on the horn with H.P.D. as we speak."

Lieutenant John Slowacki, Commander of Hartford P.D. S.W.A.T was busy inspecting equipment. The shrill of his ringing phone startled him. Grabbing the black receiver, he answered crisply, "emergency tactical services, Lieutenant Slowacki." John, the voice of his Commander Major Dellaher "what's up?" "Not much, major, what's you got?" "You know sir, you don't call unless there's some shit to clean up." "Right John, get your gang saddled up. East Hartford Police has a serious problem and their requesting our assistance. One of their units is standing by at Governor Street and Prospect. He will lead you in. Good luck John. Don't forget to file an unusual report. Be safe!" Click the Major had hung up.

Lieutenant Slowacki a veteran of 15 years sat quietly in the semi darkness of his office. He treasured these private moments of solitude. He was like a prize fighter experiencing an adrenaline rush of someone preparing for battle. Rising, he strode briskly into the gym where several of his men were conducting an intense workout. Strolling to the center of the room, he emitted a sharp whistle. The men immediately ceased their labors and came running to his location assembled to his front, in a relaxed but attentive parade rest. "Alright guys, listen up," began Slowacki. "Get saddled up. East Hartford's in a fight and our expertise is required fast. The situation's is this. There is a dude held up in an apartment, armed with hostages. He has fired on police officers and the fuck is formerly one of their own, who apparently has gone south. You know the drill. We function under their command. We strike only under their orders. Okay, get moving the van departs in 5 minutes. Yeah, Jones you've got a question?" "Yes Sir Lou, any officers been hit?" "No, not as of yet, but suspects in possession of a high powered rifle and has been producing intermittent fires. Oh, and cautions is the word of the day, as always we're under the gun. But this is what we're all about and trained to do. See you in the van. Oh, one more thing get those vests on and double check your weapons."

The blue and white van with emergency tactical services painted on its sides, sped over the Buckley Bridge. The strobe lights flashing and siren whining as a high pitched wail for time was crucial. Not a moment wasted. Lives were in jeopardy. The Hartford Police S.W.A.T. team was about to participate in another high priority situation. Theirs was always a dangerous mission. A close encounters of the third kind. One never knew how the script would unfold. A scoped sniper rifles were fine tuned and oiled this intimidating compliment of men were expert shots that were trained to kill when the order shoot was executed.

Cruising along in the darkness of the van, seven men sat in stony silence each with his own thoughts and prayers. Fecarla crouched low by the window and kept a sharp eye on movement below him. Observing cops taking defensive positions and surrounding the apartment building. His experience as a former police officer warning him that time for him would eventually cease. His mood shifted from anger to deep depression. He was shaking with agitation for he knew he was in the soup and his bitchy wife and kid rattled his nerves with their pleas and crying. "Fuck it all!" he screamed as he fired another round into the empty vulnerable unit 24. Sitting empty and forlorn, three houses down from his sniper's perch. Scanning the area movement to his right caught his attention. Reaching for his binoculars, he studied the landscape. "Ah ha," he cried. "They've a S.W.A.T. Team on scene. I wondered how long, mother fuckers, come get me you Nazi pigs! Let's play cops and robbers! He, he, he," he laughed. "You and my fucking neighbors ain't laughing at old Frank anymore! Got your backs to the wall! And he squeezed off another round at a distant figure. "Look at the fuck! Eating dirt! I'll give these fucking green horns a day to remember."

Lieutenant Slowacki strolled directly to the temporary command post. Approaching Chief Drum, he rasped "sir, Lieutenant Slowacki, H.P.D. commander S.W.A.T. I'm reporting. What are your orders?" Chief Drum smoking nervously studied the Lieutenant standing respectfully for his directions. "Lieutenant, how long have you commanded your unit?" "Sir, three years as of tomorrow is the time period of my command. In that time I've been involved in 21 hostage situations and barricaded persons." Slowacki knew the chief was measuring his experience and leadership abilities. He'd been this route before. "Okay, lieutenant, you've been briefed on the situation pointing at 23 Comstock. He growled that son of a bitch is one of our former cops. He's an asshole with a capital a. You know your job. Direct your men according to S.W.A.T. procedures. I'm aware you positioned yourselves at locations that offer clear view of fire. Do it! But, remember Lou, no firing unless I give the word. Understood! Yes sir. I read you loud and clear. Repeating, no firing unless so ordered by you and only you." Firing off a crisp salute, he about faced marched directly to his men. "Okay girls, let's get it done. In teams of two fan out and seek your vantage points. You know the drill. No shooting unless ordered by East Hartford's Chief. Lets move and for Christ's sake and that of the donkey be careful."

Crowds of gawker's watched as the S.W.A.T. team fanned out on both sides of the street. Leap frogging in military fashion, house to house suddenly they disappeared. Each team had chosen a location in position in order to take the suspect down. An eerie quiet permeated the neighborhood. Rounds were chambered into scoped rifles. 23 Comstock Place zeroed in by expert and well trained shooters. All that remained was a shoot order if the opportunity arose and a clear shot was available. They lay silent in their positions. Discipline would be their forte. The clock continued to revolve. Fecarla jumped at the ringing phone. His nerves were frayed. He waited in contempt knew who it had to be. Picking up the received he rasped into the phone, "Frank what are you doing, come on man you have the town all fucked up. Jesus, Frank your surrounded, there's more firepower trained on your apartment then at Anzio. Come on Frank. Give it up. We'll help you. Think of your wife and son. Get' em out of there. Shit man, you don't want them experiencing what eventually will play out. Frank it can't be all that bad. Come out with them. I promise you'll get proper help. Frank, you were a hell of a man once. Draw on that past on your honor and fortitude. Don't do this Frank. It can only have a tragic finish." Fecarla chuckled, "who the fuck is this Bill Graham? Don't plead with me little dough boy. You want me to come out. Well, play with my balls. Tell the faggot mayor I want a million dollars and I'll terminate the game." He laughed hysterically, you idiot who the fuck are you?" "Frank, it's Dan Hurley, you remember. I broke in on your old squad." "Oh yeah, the nerdy little guy who use to wear girly perfume," didn't you? "What the fucking title you carrying?" I'm a detective, Frank. But listen I just want to . . . ." Fecarla roared into the phone, "You little prick. You made dick. Jesus fucking Christ, no wonder, why the streets are fucked up! You couldn't investigate an asshole with the shits. Now you listen, Dick Tracy, this world sucks. My wife's a bitch, sucked me dry of my worldly treasures. Fucks like a sick duck. My kid's either gonna grow up to be a fag or a junkie. What the fuck chance has he got, anyway? Go fuck yourself lizard face. Don't call back. Aw, fuck it; I'll see that you don't." Fecarla shaking with rage yanking hard on the phone pulled the receiver which exploded from the wall in a shower of wood paneling and wall board. Flushed with anger, he screamed, "there mother fuckers, you've spoken your last to old Frank!" Dan Hurley sighed with frustration. Gazing at his handset as the phone went dead, he turned to Chief Drum. "Sir, the phone went dead and I think he tore it form the wall."

The chief sat stoned faced. Deep in thought, the clock was ticking. The nutcase Fecarla obviously could or would not contain himself much longer. Witnesses had confirmed the wife and son were indeed held prisoner in the apartment. He had the power of the law and many trained officers on the scene. Skilled marksmen who could terminate the suspect at any given moment, yet he had a moral and professional obligation to do everything possible for the safety of the hostages.

Engrossed in thought, Drum was startled by the voice of his aid, Lieutenant Mayors. "Sir, we've a report from the field. Two officers, Mallozi and Sepetro, have gained access to the apartment building and are positioned on the rear stairwell. They have a visual on the rear door to apartment 2b." "No! No! No! Screamed the chief, jumping to his feet, order those officers to retreat and get the hell out of there! What the fuck are they going to do, huh? Knock on the fucking door! Get them the hell out of there! Emphasize, those are my orders! Advise when they're out!"

Mallozi turned to Sepetro, "Jesus Jimmy, what the fuck? What's the boss thinking of? We're here and we could have caused a diversion. Guys could have stormed through the front door." "Hey, Fran, dun no. We're just grunts. Better move, if he spots or hears us in there, all hell could break loose." "Yeah, okay Jim, but I think it sucks," muttering strong disappointment to each other. The two officers exited the building, taking cover behind a full and smelly dumpster.

Lieutenant Stone grabbed the megaphone, "Frank Fecarla, this is the police. You are completely surrounded. Sharpshooters are positioned above, below and beyond your location. Please for the sake of innocent people, end this travesty and come out with your hands held high. You will be accorded respect and receive whatever medical treatment required." The message resonated throughout the neighborhood and was repeated every 15 minutes. Waiting patiently for the response but there was nothing but silence. Major returned approached his chief, "Sir Officers Mallozi and Sepetro have exited the premises." "Okay Major. Good, that's good, don't feel like looking into the eyes of a police window, any response from Fecarla?" "No sir nothing as of yet, he's been quiet as a grave." "Yeah, becoming crunch time and soon very soon, I'll have to earn my pay."

Fecarla was in quite a frenzy, sweating profusely, he gulped down three shots of whiskey in succession. Peering out the window, he fired three quick shots aimed where he thought that annoying loud plea had originated. He was frustrated, losing control and his wife and son continued to badger him and begged for their lives and freedom. "You fucks!" he uttered. He advanced toward the bedroom door, inserting a fresh eight round magazine into his weapon. Now at the door, he slammed into the structure with his full body weight. A big man, there was no resistance and it gave way on the first blow. As the door flew open, his eyes locked on his wife and son huddled on the bed. You could feel the terror that was emanating from their eyes. His wife was still pleading with him to not kill them. But Fecarla, angry, frustrated, heart broken, and deranged, Fecarla raised his weapon, sliding back the bolt. He squeezed off eight rounds into the withering bodies of his wife and son. As the explosions died off and cordite smoke drifted off the barrel of the rifle, Fecarla stood a moment transfixed staring at the bloody and torn bodies of his wife and son. Tears exploded down his cheeks. Desperate for release from a world he could no longer travel, he inserted a round into his rife and slid back the bolt, placed the barrel in his mouth. He whispered I'm sorry and pulled the trigger. Fecarla was killed instantly; he had just had enough of this world that showed no mercy.

"Unit 50 to unit 100, we're hearing heavy fire from inside the apartment, counted eight shots, then a pause and one more single shot. What are your orders? What is your pleasure, sir? Drum knew the time had come to stand tall. This siege had been played out. For sixteen hours, the last report stamped a fueling of foreboding. It was time to take the offense. With trembling hand, he compressed he radio mike that he carried in his hand. "Unit 100 to unit 50" "50 is on go 100." "Unit 50 commenced firing teargas into the apartment. Fire four rounds and wait 5 minutes and storm the apartment from both entranceways. God be with us." "Unit 50 to unit 100 messages received, launching now."

Whomp, whomp, whomp, whomp, and four tear gas projectiles whistled their way towards apartment 2B. They crawled through windows targeted several locations of apartment within in moments thick white smoke mushroomed from the interior of the apartment. The strong sickening odor of tear gas hung in the air. Stinging the eyes of officers nearby and also creating burn like sensations to faces and hands, six officers stormed up the front stairs. Six more took the rear. In unison both doors were smashed with rams that crumpled doors at their feet. The officers swarmed into the apartment weapons at the ready. Coughing with tears lined faces. The officers cautiously searched the interior bed room. Fecarla lay dead in a pool of blood and brain matter on the floor. On the bed, wrapped in each other's arms, bodies contorted in a grotesque position, lay the wife and son. They're lifeless eyes seeing nothing and their mouths silenced in a final scream. Confirmed dead, the officers retreated from the scene trying not to disturb what was now a murder suicide crime scene.

Lieutenant Stone, Frank Mallozi and James Sepetro stood by unit 24. They'd counted 23 bullet holes. They stood silent and their minds trying to cope with the carnage and horror just seen. "Why?" asked Stone to on one. "Why do human beings souls sink to such blackness? How do you slaughter your wife and kid? Yet somewhere in this country it occurs. What a fucking tragedy! Why can't we see? Why can't we stop it? Why doesn't it end? Are we that tormented? So lost or have we lost God? You know guys tonight I'm going to hug my wife and kids. I guess it takes something like this to appreciate life and what we have. I served with Fecarla for a time on B squad. He wasn't a bad dude. What made him so mad?" "Aw Lou. He was an asshole piped, Mallozi." "Yeah Frank, at the end, your right, but what caused him to become that way? He once stood tall and had it all. I just don't know where the rewards of this job will even come from. Go home guys. Have some beers. Snuggle with the wife and hug the kids. Tomorrow is another day. Control your psyches for sure before you retire you'll see more of the same. The streets are a zoo and we are its keepers.

News reports the next day showed head lines of the horrific slaughter. The reports referred to the sixteen hour siege and how officers performed as a professional cohesive unit. What they failed to report was the heavily burdened hearts that the officers would share forever. As well as the broken hearts and shattered dreams of the victims.

Cop Talk

Hospital Escapades For LaPore

Jardin, Gutsomovich, Harland and LaPore back at the Lucky Leaf and swilling beers were having a good old time swapping stories from the deep past. Harland gulping on down, belches and blows a loud fart. LaPore, "remember when you got fucked up on Magnolia Street and spent two weeks in St Francis Hospital." "Yeah Hank, can't forget that what a circus. I got no rest." Harland stifling a laugh, "Yeah, you and that big fat ass nurse, Millie, wouldn't allow beer in the room, pissed us off that one. "Yeah, but she suffered the consequences," chimes in Gutsomovich. LaPore feigning anger, so you sick pricks were involved. "Nah," states Harland, "but we heard through the grapevine." "What went down?" Jardin bleary eyed and unshaven. Lifts his head from the table like he'd been meditating. What went down he slums?" "Ha, Ha, Ha," laughs Gutsomovich. "The bitch was working the grave yard shift."

"The first night, she enters LaPore's room to dispense meds. Turns on the light and jumps out of her skin shrieking. The floor is littered with frogs. She scampers out like a pig in heat. Her mates spend an hour calming her. Anyway the second night she performs a rerun enters dickhead's room and has a piss attack. Three chickens are there, beaks secured are parading around the room again she flies out of there like a raped ape. Same scenario comrades aid in calming her. Okay on the third night she's a bit more cautions. She makes her entry very cautiously activates the light, nothing, she relaxes and breathes easier. Dispenses LaPore his drugs and opens the bathroom door and three ducks ambush her. She screams and literally shits her pants. She runs like hell to the nurses station. Shit running down her legs begs off from work sick and heads on home. The night supervisor is all pissed off. Questions LaPore extensively, right Lance?" "Yeah, you sick puke." "Anyway LaPore is all innocent and is claiming he had pain killer injections and was out like a burnt light bulb. The supervisor accepts his story and departs. Fat ass Millie returns for the fourth night and insist on an escort to LaPore's room. Her requests are honored and the two angels of mercy enter LaPore's room. Like they were on the point, all appears quiet. They administered a pain shot to asshole here, and turn to leave, when they hear a weird sound from under the bed. Both bend to see, and literally go bonkers. A brown and yellow snake slithers between them. Dropping the med tray they flee in unison through the door high tailing it to the nurse's station. Now the head nurse is really enraged. Places a call to the watch commander and commences to berate the P.D. as a haven for nut cases and screwballs. The boss, Captain Heinwich contains his laughter. Defending his department by merely saying," "You don't know its cops." "Who the fuck else would be fucked up enough to perform these acts?" She fires back and disconnects. Anyway, to make a long story short. Fat Millie takes a vacation time refusing to return till LaPore's discharged.

All four laughing hysterically down their beers and head for the door. LaPore stopping for a moment. "Yeah, thought those orderlies looked familiar was to fucked up to be sure. All I know is my room was tabled hostile and only male nurses were assigned till I was discharged. Oh well, fuck a duck. They even assigned security as a watch dog. Prick sat in a chair in the corridor and hassled my visitor's."

Harland, his arm over LaPore's shoulder, chuckling softly, "you know Lance my dad once said, you only take this route once. There are no reruns. Enjoy yourself but don't hurt any one. All four exited the door homeward bound.

Chapter 9

Mary Brocallo completing her bath entered her bedroom. Tired after a hectic day at the office, she'd returned home full of anticipation. For a quiet romantic evening with her husband Frank. She had prepared a lush meal of steak, rice and salad. Now fresh from her bath she donned sexy lingerie. Mary had high expectations of a sexual interlude with Frank. She had been planning the evening in her mind throughout the day. Worried that boredom had crept into their marriage. Frank had been reclusive lately. Maintaining a respectful distance from her, overnight had erected a barrier between them. Confused she couldn't understand why. He'd been coming home at late hours withdrawn and uncommunicative. She'd tried every trick in the book to gain his attention, to no avail. Propped on the couch she'd experienced a sense of foreboding. Was there someone else? Frank had once been so tender towards her. He had placed her on a pedestal. Now she tended mostly for herself. The clock struck 9:00 p.m. Frank was a no show. Her labors spent preparing his favorite meal proved fruitless. His rudeness and inconsideration elevated her emotions from warmth to a pent up fury. She was all imposing women. Men found her an attractive beauty gazing into the full length mirror. A lonely woman gaped back at her jet black hair, blue eyes that seemed to sparkle and a full feminine figure. She'd been faithful to Frank. Respecting her vows married these past six years. She wondered had he grown bored, unsatisfied. She was frustrated. She had never repulsed him, never refused his desires. "Fuck!" she exclaimed aloud. "Fuck him!" I sit here night after nigh like a frustrated nun. Lighting a parliament cigarette she inhaled deeply. Mary exhaled bluish smoke towards the ceiling. Rising from the couch, she strolled to the liquor cabinet, choosing cool bourbon, poured herself two finger of whiskey and downed it. "Down the hatch quickly", she repeated this scenario three times. Now feeling no pain she retired to her bed.

The clock struck 0100 hours. Tears in her eyes, she rolled on her left side, tossing and turning she fell into a fitful sleep. She awoke with a start as she heard the click of the front door latch. Wrapping herself in a pink bathroom, she strolled into the living room. Stifled a soft scream her husband lay prone on the couch, passed out. Her eyes scanned the room. The clock read 03:30. Anger welled within her, but she controlled her desire to confront the son of a bitch. It would be fruitless. He was too intoxicated. An argument could wait till morning. Advancing toward him to kill the lights, she was propelled two steps back by the powerful aroma of perfume that radiated from his person. Enraged, she switched off the lights and fled from the livingroom feeling bewildered and betrayed. The lipstick smear on his collar was further evidence of his unfaithfulness. She crawled under the blankets and a flood of tears gushed down her checks. Mary felt nauseous, light headed and fearful. She experienced a depth of despair that only a rejected soul could suffer. Her worst fears had surfaced. The prick was a cheater and a player of other woman. What the fuck had gone wrong? Closing her eyes, she spent a restless night. Her spirit tormented by hurt, anger, disbelief, guilt, shame, and finally depression.

Sunlight engulfed her room. A soft breeze from an opened window caressed her cheek. She rose from slumber and seated on the edge of the bed experienced dry heaves and the pit of her stomach on fire. Her brain clouded by pulsating pain. Gazing in a hand held mirror, red rimmed eyes covered in dark shadows, peered back at her. In desperation she ran to the bathroom. Mercifully empting the contents of her stomach into the Lysol bleached toilet. Dabbing cool water on her cheeks, she slipped into her bathrobe. Apprehension topped off her thinking. She marched to the living room door determined to confront her Judas husband. She strolled past the prostrate form on the couch, instead detouring into the kitchen where she prepared a pot of coffee stalling the ensuing argument. Experiencing slight tremors, she was successful in pouring a fresh cup of coffee, preferably light and sweet. Seated at the kitchen table, she sipped greedily from the steaming cup, a cigarette dangling from her mouth she contemplated how to confront Frank, he was a slime ball, should she attack from his flanks or effect a frontal assault. "Yeah!" she shouted, "Go after the prick hard ball! No soft shoe antics! Look at him in the eyes and kick him in the balls! God Damn it, he's hurt me!"

Stifling tears, she entered the living room. She stood in the entrance and the sight of her husband seated on the edge of the couch holding his head in his hands infuriated her. "Well, shit for brains! How's you two heads this morning?" "What? What? He responded, what are you talking about? What two heads?" "Well smuck, for one, that cantaloupe you're holding in your hands and the one you play with frequently." "Aw, for Christ sake Mary back off. I've a monster headache!" "Again which one, maybe the bitch you fucked last night got the clap! You rotten son of a bitch! Maybe it'll shrivel up and turn black and rot! Or maybe I'm gonna chop it off!" She was screaming hysterically now. Venom poured from her soul. Poisoned words spewed at him driven from a broken heart and a souls shattered dreams. He recoiled from the onslaught and was ill prepared for this drama. His nostrils flared with anger. Spittle oozed down his checks, his hangover torturing his body. He swayed back and forth on the couch and tried to stand up but was too wobbly. He proceeded to fall back on the couch. She hissed at him, "you stink like a French whore! Okay, you like the ladies, go fuck the sluts! I've had it Frank! Look close at what you're giving up! Get the fuck out, today! Go home to momma!"

"Mary, wait a minute! Look I'm sorry. I never meant to hurt you . . . I . . . I . . . don't know what to say." "Nothing to say Frank, you're a cheater and a bastard! Go! Go! Go! She stormed from the room, half raw into the bedroom. Slammed the door and latching it behind her and threw her body onto the bed where tumult of tears engulfed her. Moments later she thought she heard the apartment door open and close. She crept softly from the bed peering into the living room. Her soul went empty. Frank was gone.

All weekend she felt weak, sick, shook with anger and fear. She felt hatred, then remorse. No appetite she refused to eat, existing on coffee and cigarettes. Rain pelting her window, as she lay on the bed staring at nothing for she had slipped from despair to a deep depression. Rejection and betrayal from the one person she had loved and trusted had pierced her being. This among other feeling had branded her soul with a feeling of hopelessness. No tears were left. She felt that life was frugal and not worth living.

Sunday her spirits ebbed ever lower. The rain kept a steady drum beat on her window. She languished in her bed to wobbly to stand for lack of nourishment. Mary embraced its comfort and feeling of security. She had hoped Frank would at least phone. But the receiver remain ever silent in its cradle. Slowly light of day dipped its curtain of darkness. She shuddered for the fear of the unknown had wrapped its tentacles about her. Mary's mind was a whirlwind of thought. She had tired to hold on to the thought as Frank being her one chance of salvation too what had been a once marred and tarnished life. Her childhood and teen age years, pockmarked with a drunken father who simply opened the door one day, never to return. Then the steady stream of numerous uncles some intimately groping, and ogling her as she blossomed into womanhood. Frank had been her knight in shining armor showering her with a tender love and deep affection. He swept her off her feet for she'd embraced him here was the dream. A chance at happiness and a decent life only her world had detonated. He'd teased her with the promise of happiness and love. He had been unfaithful and continuously lied to his advantage. Her world had imploded and now her soul was dead.

Monday morning she awoke early, groped her way to the bathroom. Once there she drew a hot bath embellishing it with scented beads of bubble bath. She lay back in the comforting water luxuriating in its soothing warmth. Soaping her body slow and methodical with an herbal soap, rinsed and stepped from her cleansing into a thick fluffy towel. Drying herself completely, she glanced around and was satisfied with the fixtures and appliances within the room were secure. Chuckling to herself, she headed to the bedroom closet. Deep into recesses of the closet she retrieved Frank's proudest possession. The 30 odd six loomed large in her petite hands. But she'd handled it many times. Feeling around the floor, her fingers brushed the box of cartridges. Sliding back the cover, she extracted one round. It was all she would need. Siding back the bolt and she chambered the lonely round. Without dressing she retraced her steps to the large bed. Rifle in hand, Mary reached for the phone. Humming an old childhood nursery song, she dialed 527-6300. Her wait was short for a bored female voice answering, "Hartford Police, may I help you." "Yes ma'am, my name if Mary Brocallo and I reside at 79 Evergreen Ave., Apartment 4-H. I'm happy to say I'm going to exit this shitty world. I'm simply going to kill myself. Oh and my front door is unlocked. Your guys in blue can easily enter. They have my permission to enter my home. Thank you and have a nice life."

Mary Brocallo hung up. Lying down on the bed, she placed the rifle on her stomach. Placing the barrel under her chin, she then inserted the big toe of her right foot in the trigger housing and relaxed and waited. Police operator, Anna Halsey, quickly relayed the message to complaint writer John Braxton, who immediately stamped a call for service card and personally handed same to dispatcher, Jo-Ann Rawlins, perusing the call for service card. She compressed her foot pedal. "Unit 11 and 12, 79 Evergreen Ave., apartment 4-H, female caller states, she's is going to commit a 104F. Name is Brocallo. Be advised caller stated front door is unlocked. Use caution. Caller did not elaborate how or why or if any weapons. Units off at 09:10" "10-4 unit 11." "10-4 unit 12" units 11 and 12 Strobe lights flashing zig zagged their way through city traffic. Within 5 minutes they marked their arrival at 79 Evergreen. Exchanging nods and glances the two officers entered the foyer and began their assent up the stairwell to apartment 4-H. Several curious neighbors poked their heads out concerned but committed to minding their own business. The two officers, Larry Burns and John Horvath, ascended to the top of the landing. Turned right down a dimly lit hallway and following its lead came to a stop at the apartment door marked 4-H. Knocking they received no response. Burns muttering "we'll she said she left the door unlocked. Let's find out." A gentle turn of the knob and the door flew open. Both officers with weapons drawn, entered the apartment, once inside, presented with a neat, comfortable looking apartment. The residence was eerily quiet. Only the sound of a ticking clock broke the silence. Cautiously the officers combed their way through the apartment. The atmosphere was surreal and there was no sign of life or sound. Horvath glanced at Burns, "this fucking sucks! What the fuck chuck? Hey, are you here?" He yelled. No answer. Again, "is anyone in here?" Again, no response, suddenly a soft female voice startled the officers. Gaining immediate attention, "Yeah boys, I'm in here in the bedroom. Come to the door but don't dare come in. I kid you not. You'll see why in a second." The officers stepped to the door and peering in they stood in amazement. There on the bed stark naked lay Mary Brocallo. The 30 add six barrel resting under her chin. Her right toe ready to compress the trigger. Burns looked at Horvath. "What the fuck? She's beautiful." "Yeah, I know." "What the bee Jesus do we do?" Both stood agape. Cemented where they stood, the text books didn't cover this. Mary, smiling at the cops with her ample breasts rising with each breath, "now don't come any closer!" If you do I'll press the trigger." "Alright, miss, alright," spoke Horvath. "But why and for what could be the reason? What's the game here?" "No game, officer, no game. I don't like games. My whole life has been a game. An act that's gone sour and I've found that's it's a right handed world and I'm a southpaw. Ha, ha, ha," she laughed. "But miss, spoke out Burns, your not really going to do something foolish here. Come on, nothing can be that critical, can it?" Laughing Brocallo sighed, "Look do I look like I give a shit? Nothings critical anymore, the future no longer looks bleak to me. So stow the feign concern." "Look miss, how can we help? Asked Horvath chuckling." "Get my husband here!" That's how." "Will that stop you?" "Maybe, maybe not, we'll play hide and go seek and see, okay?"

Horvath turned to Burns, "Get unit 43 up here. We're in the stew and I don't want to stir the pot." "Okay John, I'll call downstairs." "Right don't be long. Wait, never mind. Use that phone over there I don't want to be left alone with a naked female space cadet. Although she is a lovely," "Okay, I'll have dispatch reach out for LaPore." "Right, let's get the sarge. Maybe, he has an inkling of what to do." LaPore cruising north on Prospect Ave., was gazing at the park, when his call sign shattered his day dreaming. "Unit 43, 43 come in." "Unit 43 on go ahead dispatch," "Unit 43, head on over to 79 Evergreen, apartment 4-H. Officers on scene,

Potential 104F in progress. They're requesting a boss at that location. Unit 43 dispatches 10-4." "79 Evergreen Ave., apartment 4-H, eta 3 minutes, unit 43, marks my arrival" "10-4 unit 43 arrival 11:00 a.m."

LaPore entered apartment 4-H, greeted by both officers, he received a quick briefing of what was unfolding within this home. Listening attentively, LaPore rubbing his chin nodded at different intervals. Satisfied with the information presented, he stepped to the bedroom door. The scene repeated itself. Brocallo lay still clutching the weapon. Chuckling she stated, "Oh gold braid, makes no never mind. That's as close as you get. I'll say it again I want my husband here and quick."

LaPore turned to Burns, "use the land line and have dispatch reach out to Father Cleary. I want the Chaplin here. Maybe we can save this girl." "Okay sarge, I'm on it." "Yeah, and Larry speak softly. I don't want her eves dropping." Lapore returned to the bedroom door. "Ma'am what's your name? Help me out here." Brocallo chuckled ma'am, my ass. I'm younger then you. But if its worth mud in the hut. I'm Mary, Mary Brocallo, okay? I'm 23, 36-29-36, need more?" LaPore smiled and felt uncomfortable. This girl was naked and beautiful. He had to be objective here and retain a clear mind. Hell could explode at any moment. "Mary, what's the problem why are you contemplating harming yourself?" Laughing hysterically, she responded, "Because my husband is like all you pricks. If you didn't have zippers maybe you'd keep your dicks in your pants." "You think he's cheating?" "My, my, a smart cop. No he's celebret! Don't be naive sergeant. He's a no good fuck. Hell yeah! He's planting his pickle in the garden. "Okay, where is he? We'll bring him here if it will change your mind." "Hartford Screw, he works at Hartford Screw." "Thank you Mary and we'll take care of that. We'll expedite the process and get him here." "Thank you sergeant, I'm tired would like to be left alone for a while."

LaPore stepping forward, halted in his tracks. When she shrilled, "stay back I'll do it now!" "Okay, okay" LaPore with raised hands retreated from the doorway. LaPore stood by Burn's side. "Sarge, why would the asshole cheat on a cutie like that?" "Well, Burns there's an old saying, we were young and dumb and full of cum, maybe he's in that category. They always say that happiness to a man's heart is with a full stomach and an empty cock. Is Cleary on the way?" "Yeah, he gave an eta of 10 minutes. Okay, get back on the landline and have commo dispatch a unit to the Hartford Screw Company on Windsor Street. Advise to pick up one Frank Brocallo and escort him here. Have a 10-10 locate in the area. Also have the watch commander reach out to detective Peters, our negotiator, we need his ass here not passing out lollipops at some preschool folly. "Okay Sarge, anything else?" "Yeah, bring the watch commander up to date. Don't tell him she's naked. He'll be here quicker than you can fart." "Okay, chuckled Burns, you got it." "Stay cool guys, but be cognoscente of that weapon."

The blue and white deposited Frank Brocallo just as Father Cleary exited his unmarked Chaplin's vehicle. Together they scaled the stairwell two steps, Brocallo breathing hard, broke the silence. "Father, do you know what's going on? What's happened to my wife?" "I don't know son. We're both about to find out." Brocallo was anxious; he had noted the three blue and whites parked as sentinels in front of his apartment building. He experienced dryness and sweat formed in his armpits. Heart racing, he and Father Cleary entered the apartment. The three officers had stationed themselves several feet from the bedroom door. They had retreated because Mary had become more and more agitated. Repeatedly, demanding her husband's presences. Brocallo headed directly to LaPore and Father Cleary at his side. "Sergeant, what's going on? What's wrong? Is my wife okay? Why the fuck are you guys here? LaPore locking eyes with Cleary stated "we have a situation here. We're attempting to handle this low key and need you to do the same. You've got to be cool and collective. Show reason and compassion. Frank, I'm going to ask you, no I'm insisting you wait here a spell. I'd like Father Cleary here to try talking to her. Your catholic, am I right?" "Yes, we are," he replied sheepishly and some what embarrassed, but we're not that involved." Father Cleary smiling, "that's alright son. Let's see what I can do. Maybe the collar will offer some comfort." "Yeah, okay, Father, but please I want to see my wife." "No sweat, give me a few." Cleary stepped to the door. Shocked and appalled at the scene. He took two deep breaths. Control here was imperative. "Hi, Mary, I'm father Cleary." "So! What the fuck does that mean? You're going to save my soul. Hear my confession. She laughed, you guys, be real this isn't bible class. The myths you preach its all bullshit. Now go get lost and you're too late! Go away and I mean like now!" Tears welled in her eyes.

Cleary realized her motional level was at the extreme. As he stepped away, she screamed, "Send that asshole fuck of a husband here! I know he's out there. I heard his voice!" As he retreated further, Cleary raised his right arm and in blessing beyond her scope of vision. Father Cleary approached the hushed group tapping Frank on the shoulder. He whispered, "she wants to see you, be strong my son. It's not a pretty picture in there. Act composed and show understanding. She's quite agitated, so you'll have to reach way back for strength. Okay, God bless and I'll pray for the best."

LaPore and the rest watched as Frank stepped to the door. Lapore was annoyed. "He'd heard nothing from the negotiator. Where the fuck is he?" He'd land lined communications was informed they'd been unable to reach him. Shit thought LaPore. This could go either way. That kid in there is volatile. She'd snapped. Damn what a cluster fuck.

Frank stepped nervously to the door. He was shocked at what lay before his eyes. He stood transfixed unable to cope or speak. He stared at his wife of whom he deep down loved, for she made him realize just how much. Mary Brocallo smiled seductively. "Well stud look at what you had and lost. Lost forever, we could have been happy. So long Judas." With that said, the explosion thundered through the apartment. There was blood and brains that had sinew flayed through the air congealing on the ceiling and walls. Frank Brocallo screamed in anguish, his howl resonating throughout the building. She had compressed the trigger. Her tormentor, Brocallo, emptied his bowls and his bladder expelled yellow hot liquid onto the floor. His stomach exploded its contents onto the walls. His eyes bulged and his brain numbed by the photo it registered. Spittle ran down his checks. He pounded the wall with his fist. He was grabbed and pulled away by the cops. Babbling incoherently, Frank Brocallo's mind had imploded. His arms flailing he was wrestled to the floor. The ambulance attendants summoned immediately restrained him with leather straps, given an injection to calm him and whisked away lights and sirens activated to St. Francis Hospital.

LaPore ordered his men to set up a crime scene and called for the dicks. Mary Brocallo was once a handsome woman, vibrant, intelligent and carefree, now lay like a rag doll and her face an empty crater. Lapore and his men stood devastated. Once again, a nightmare had unleashed itself before their eyes. They had vomited breakfast. They would abandon the scene to plain clothes detectives. All of the men in blue, felt like failures. A budding rose had withered and died so hideously. LaPore walking slowly to his blue and white and thought aloud, "why, why he screamed, do we continue to inflict such pain, torment, grief, and anger? Why do we torment each others souls?" Reaching his cruiser he remained and still there were no answers.

Cop Talk

Plants for a Fellow Blue Soldier

Once again the old Vets were seated at the reserved table at the Lucky Leaf Cafe. Squabbling over current events, the political world was in a shambles. The country's leaders were laughable. Unfortunately good honest Americans were suffering because of their ineptness. Jardin swilling a beer as usual barked out "wonder, how the old oak tree is faring?" "Who the fuck knows piped up, Harland. We're all too old and fucked up to negotiate the knoll." "Yeah, whispered LaPore, But I miss it. The oak was a silent friend. Lotta memories sit at its base." "Yeah," slurred Big Mike, he'd had a few and was a little tipsy. He sat up suddenly like he'd been bee stung. "Hey, did you asshole's hear what that hemorrhoid Lancaster pulled." Tell all, tell all," stated Art.

"Well, you all know he fancies the broads, so he meets this cut chick. I'd say a month ago, he wears her down and finally gets a date with her. Anyway the cheap bastard's on duty last Friday, the dates been set for that evening. He's mulling over in that pea mind of his whether or not to bring flowers. He's parked at Maple and Barker, when he spots a funeral procession heading south on Maple, headed to Cedar Hill Cemetery. Ever the thinker, the bastard activates his strobes placing his blue and white at the head of the procession. He provides an escort to the cemetery. People are waving their thanks he acknowledges with a nod and rears off. He then pulls his cruiser into a small knoll surrounded by trees and observes the on going burial service. He fire's up a Marlboro and prays he doesn't get a dispatch. The shyster is continuing his sick mire in over drive.

Finally, the service ends and the group of mourners disperse and on entering their vehicles, departed. Now Lancaster guns his blue and white. He comes roaring out of the tree line and like a rapid elephant, speeds off to the grave site. Leaving his cruiser on idle, he runs over to where the casket site. Alone and forlorn, surrounded by numerous flower arrangements, he spots two beautiful rose arrangements, grabs them both and runs like hell back to the cruiser. That son of a bitch brought those flowers to his date, unfucking believable." "Aw, what the fuck?" pipes up Jardin, Now bleary eyes, more money for happy juice." "Why the fuck not. They only get thrown away." "Aw, fuck you," yells Big Mike. He's a cheap asshole, that's just wrong man. That's fucked up."

Now LaPore spoke up, "Hey, what about the Dullivan thing?" "What, what's that all about?" Babbles Harland as he lets out a horrendous belch and fart at the same time. "Shit!" snarls Big Mike. "You shit your pants, you half a brain fuck. It stinks lie an outhouse in here. Go wipe your big ass! Jesus your disgusting! For Christ sake, half the bar emptied out, God why do I associate with you animals." "Aw, go play with yourself Mike, you got the habit, go in the john and get relief your getting sour." Anyway Harland gawks at LaPore. "Finish your story, ignore this big ignorant masturbator."

LaPore chuckling begins again. "Well, Dullivan's recovering at St. Francis Hospital, after getting shot. Anyways, every time one of the guys comes to see him, they bring him some kind of a plant. Within a few days his room's like a florist shop and smells like Elizabeth Park, when the roses are in bloom. His wife is impressed and grateful. This goes on for a time until the room is over flowing. The plants are now outside his door. Entry is almost impossible to his room. Well, anyway, he's got a room full of visitor's and his bride is sitting by the bed holding his hand. When in strolls the head nun, she stifles a scream, holds her hand to her mouth." "My God, so this is were all the plants have gone." "The crazy bastard cops on coming to the hospital were taken the plants from all the religious figurines and bring them to Ray as gifts." All the vet's roared with laughter. "What'd the nun do?" piped Harland. "She ran from the room and came back with 4 orderlies to retrieve the plants. It took them four hours to complete the task. Dullivan's wife was livid. As Ray state later, "she's never been able to comprehended cop's warped sense of humor." "Hey," piped up Bouchard, "let's send'em a plant." "No!" yelled LaPore. "It'll push his old lady over the edge, yelled Jardin. Hey, I'm outta here." "Yeah," they all chimed in, "outta here, stay healthy!" They all shouted "or see you in the box!" chuckling. All four headed for the door, heading to home with their own thoughts.

Chapter 10

Night had fallen. He lay still in his bed staring out the window. He could observe the stars twinkling above. He grunted as he set up stretching his taught muscles. He'd had a good workout at the gym that afternoon returned home an experienced a dreamless sleep. He walked to the bathroom relieved himself and he'd debated on showering or running a bath. He decided on a hot exhilarating bath would relax him. Settling his thought process the warm water soothed his tense body. He lay back and his mind focusing on his bold plan. Yes, oh yes. Tonight he would initiate his campaign. He would rid the streets and society of the vermin that resided in alleys and under the bridges and along the river banks. Some dastardly scum had the audacity to take refuge in city parks. This could not be tolerated. They were like fleas contaminating whatever they came into contract with. It was his calling to eradicate this blight. The voices as he slept whispering messages. Instructions simple, destroy this cancer, OBEY!!! You've been commanded do not fail.

He rose from the tub toweled himself and returning to his bedroom, he donned black clothing to match the night. He then retrieved a 12 inch hunting knife from his night stand setting same securely in a sheath camouflaged by the long black wind breaker chosen for this night's activity.

The clock showed 9:15 p.m., to early to strike. Rather he sat in his favorite recliner. Leaning back comfortably, he closed his eyes. The visions returned and he was back in time in another era. He was with his grandfather high in the mountains of West Virginia. There he had learned trades most youth never experienced for he mastered how to hunt with the knife, the bow and a rifle and how to skin his kill and to track man or game and he learned to listen to nature and to read and understand its whispered messages. This man of nature, listened to the wind sighed and if he concentrated could pick up the scent of man or beast. For him and his teacher, the sudden quiet of the birds served as warning, you weren't alone. The hunted would give signs of snapped twigs or trampled grass that could point you in the right direction of their location. He had learned how to traverse the stars and how they paved the way for his travels. He conversed with the fox and wolf aspiring to learn their secret ways of the forest. With practice, he learned to mimic cries of birds and to feed off the forest with the delicacies it could offer to preserve ones life.

His grandfather, with much wisdom, taught him to train his body vigorously so as to create a single fatal weapon. He showed him how to prepare his hands, arms, legs and feet; even fingers could be programmed to kill. This strong man ran endlessly until his lungs and heart equaled that of a mountain lion. Once he had taken refuge with, studied its ways, ran with him, hunted ate, slept with until he was his equal in internal skills. His grandfather had taught him the ways of the knife. The art of the silent kill, and the whistle of the arrow, that would eliminate an adversary in a hushed whisper for he had mastered the art of the rifle, and could kill easily from 600 yards. Always and without fail locating his shot in the kill zone for he could survive without food or sleep for days on end. His body was a steeled mechanism. This man had no fear and he prayed to the Great Spirit. He had passed all tests' grandfather and nature threw at him. He was ready, and now it was time to practice his skills. Night called this was his hour. Rising quickly from the chair, clicked off the lights to his apartment, he walked out into the night. He descended the stairs like a cat, unheard by neighbors. Once in the street, the man of nature inhaled the cool fragrant air deeply. Gazing at the stars, marked their location, for he was tense, excited, for this is what he had trained and sacrificed for. He was ecstatic in that he knew his venture would cause havoc, fear and chaos to the city's residents. The fools would not understand nor appreciate. He was embarking on a deadly crusade against lost souls, garbage, germs. He and he alone would be the great extinguisher and destroying the lice that infested the streets.

Heading north on Main Street beginning the hunt and terror, continuing his jaunt on Main, he passed groups of people congregating in front of bars. With couples enjoying a cool breeze strolling hand and hand, this man who had mission, noticed traffic was heavy then realized if was Friday night. Young people alive and merry, happy the weekend was here. He gazed at the full moon its pull leading him on like a magnet that triggered and motivated and captivated him. It was in this time frame he would operate, when the moon was high in the night sky. He halted, leaning against a building, he watched as a ragged disheveled man pushing a shopping cart passed by. He smelled sour the offensive odor of urine emitting from his person. He continued studying the wretched creature as he disappeared into an alley. Still he remained stationary for 10 minutes, then stepped off in the direction of his prey had gone. Reaching the alley, like a skilled lion, entered into the darkness. His breathing slow and deliberate while his sense of smell had already detected the prey for moving stealthy, the hunter approached the old man sitting with his back to the hunter for he was unaware of his presences. Like his friend the lion, he pounced, grabbing his prey around the neck with his left hand. The right was swift and true as he plunged the blade into the right kidney cutting deep on an upper angle and twisting the blade to and from as it bit deeply. The prey moaned softly and slumped to the ground for his life stolen from him in a heartbeat. The hunter had stared at the body, rubbed his blade clean with an old rag. His keen hearing and scent like radar told him he was alone. Turning abruptly, he strolled from the alley. Scanning the area, his vision revealing no one was about. This hunt was a success for it made it possible to mask his feeling of joy. From feverish training, he had controlled his body so his adrenaline rush was a minimal.

He headed south on Main Street, retracing his route home. The voices would later congratulate him. He felt contentment for he knew that he pleased his grandfather. He could rest and plan for the next full moon nestled high in the sky. Completing his first assignment, he felt hunger and stopped at the metro pole restaurant. Scuttle butt had enlightened him to the quality hot dogs served at this eatery. He ordered a coke and three dogs. He sat alone in a booth located in the rear, enabling him to observe the door easily. He drummed his fingers softly on the table top after placing his order. This highly skilled man sat back and felt exhilaration at his first kill, for he hadn't taking life since the Nam. Ah, how he had loved it there. It had filled his hunger and lust for the hunt and the swift kill. In Nam, volunteering to act alone and often scrabbled into the bush at night using the skill he had mastered from brother snake, slithering along the ground, using rock and foliage as concealment, this scent would guide him to the figure of an NVA. Once having them in his site would strike like the cobra, departing quietly and swiftly. The now bloating fly engrossed body of a dead enemy prone in the dirt. Time and time again, he explored the jungle causing fear and terror to the enemy. His exploits earning high accommodations from his superiors and felt satisfaction that his fellow grunts fritted away from him. They were uncomfortable in his presence and thought he'd had gone south. His fellow comrades could not accept that he lavished the kill. At times he was frustrated that he was unable to flush out an enemy soldier. He was undaunted when this rarity occurred for him simply and stealthy stalked into a village and easily dispatched an unsuspecting villager to the happy hunting ground.

A cute waitress delivered his meal. Locking eyes she smiled. "Hi, my name's Jean, What's yours? I've never seen you here before." Shy with women, he returned the smile. "Evening my name, is it important?" "Why no sir, just being friendly is all." "Oh, I am sorry. The name is Jacob Broken Rose." "Come on your putting me on." "No, no, that's my name." "It's quite interesting and quite different. How'd that come about?" "Well, my mother died giving me life, so my father named me Broken Rose. I'm half Indian from my dad and my mother was white." "Oh, I see, sorry about your mom." "It's okay that was a long time ago." "Well enjoy the dogs, see you later." "Yeah sure have a good night." Broken Rose savored his dogs. Sitting quietly and alone with his thoughts gulping the remnants of his coke, he rose from the table and walked into the night.

Broken Rose reached his apartment building preparing to use the rear stairway to his loft apartment. All was quiet and he ascended soundlessly and took every precaution not to be seen nor heard for this was his forte to live life quietly and stealthy. He was cognoscente of his surroundings and constantly on his guard and taking every precaution to flow motionless and invisible. He neither socialized nor chatted with neighbors. Broken Rose remained non existent.

Two days he never left his residence. He retrieved his daily paper and perused the news section and found the article that interested him;

> Homeless man found murdered.
> Police today responded to
> An alleyway at 753 Main Street
> After receiving an anonymous
> Call of a dead body
> Investigators report that
> A middle age, homeless
> Person was apparently
> Stabbed to death
> Victim was described
> Only as an unidentifiable
> White male, no motive
> Or evidence has been
> Linked to this crime
> Police are asking anyone having information
> Contact Detective Reggie Violet at
> 523-6300 ext 214.

He smiled inwardly, "fools there is no evidence. I'm not stupid; well the lawmen will certainly be challenged. I've only just begun." Completing a modest breakfast of one egg, toast and coffee, he studied a wall map of the city he'd obtained at city hall for 75 cents. His finger traced an imaginary line from his residence to the Connecticut River. His recon of that waterway had revealed several homeless people had set up residence in a small tent city near the south meadows. Access would be simple with minimum chance of detection. "Yes," he chortled this would be the objective of his next strike. The voices had instructed him to launch only at full moon. Broken Rose's patience would be tried but he would obey. He would take leisurely walks through the city proper memorizing land marks and available escape routes and potential targets. He would control emotions through discipline and intense workouts at the gym.

He reclined on the sofa. His mind again drifted to another time and place. The spirit of his grandfather embraced him and he heard a whispered voice, like a sigh in the wind warning of caution and self denial. Soft words advising to be lonely like the wolf and smart like the fox. Swift as the tiger and stealthy like the snake. Trust no one only your skills. As the misty image faded, these final words hissed from the vapor form.

> When I was one and twenty,
> I heard a wise man say,
> "Give diamonds, gold, and rubies
> But not your heart away"
> Now I am two and twenty
> And oh tis true, tis true.

Words of wisdom meant as a warning to remain aloof, cold, and cunning, recluse. This structured defense, so as not to grow weak, soft, forgetful, and careless. To refrain from love which softens the heart and short circuited the brain. "Yes, grandfather, you need not worry. Yours were words of a wise man, your thoughts the thoughts of a strong man, and your actions that of a warrior. I will not fail you or the voices that guide me. I will be honorable and obedient to the end. No one shall touch my heart or caress my soul. I only embrace the light of the Great Spirit and exalt life and death."

Broken Rose spent his days at the gym, toning his muscles to be firm and tight. He worked on sharpening his senses and in the nights he patrolled the streets planning his reconnaissance in the early evening when streets were congested with parades of pedestrians. Thus enhancing his chances of remaining undetected, just another stroller, a face unrecognized. He stood in doorways observing the night life, noting when and where cops enjoyed their meals. He knew the hours officers changed shifts and casually held conversations with several. He displayed his good ole boy mannerisms masking his true identity. Broken Rose acted friendly and helpful but never lingered at a location for long. "Hello, how do you do?" was the extent of the conversation and then he would saunter off swallowed in the night.

Returning home early he would call to the voices. Intent on pleasing them, he felt proud and comfortable in that he alone had been chosen for this cleansing mission. That he would act as the lone disinfectant ridding the streets of losers and human parasites. Bedding down early the dreams would return. Their visits a constant reminder of his objective and at times, his grandfather spoke to him in a hushed guttural voice. Refrain from tobacco it encumbers your senses, Ignore spirits it numbs your brain. You are a warrior and born of woman to be nothing else. Practice restraint. Disregard the pleasures of life. Stay focused on your calling. I am ever with you and watchful.

Days turned into weeks and soon the third quarter moon acted as a beacon that Broken Rose should prepare for the kill. Avenge man's plight and destroy the human blood suckers who drained society of valuable resources. He would fall into fitful sleep and the voices fading into the night.

At last the moment to strike arrived. The moon full and bright was his buoy to act. Broken Rose fumbled in the dark choosing dark clothing to camouflage his movements. He descended the rear stairs. Walked briskly to the street and turned right on Main Street. Continuing to Wethersfield Ave. where he continued south to Hyshope Avenue. Crossing to the east side, continued his march east, his walk paralleling Colts Park. Broken Rose paced himself, hugging what vegetation was available. He prowled in darkness, avoiding street lights when possible. He was alert to vehicle headlights plunging into shrubs, careful not to be seen. Sweat crowned his forehead and his mouth dry; he experienced a wave of adrenaline. The excitement fueling his advance and soon, very soon, he would savor the smell of blood. Broken Rose standing still on the bank of the Connecticut River, allowed his senses to guide him. "Ah, the smell of wood smoking and its aroma acting as a beacon pointing the way to his prey." "Brother snake", he whispered, "Guide me as I slither through this foliage." He crawled inch by inch, hugging the river bank. Moon rays shimmered on the water and his keen hearing honed on two voices and their muted voices riding the wind reaching his senses. Ever slowly, inch by inch, he advanced toward their refuge.

Broken brushed aside several shrubs and there, three feet away, sat his prey. A small camp fire exposing a cooking pot and both were smoking unmindful of his presence. He lay motionless, demanding his body to be patient. There was no hurry, for he studied his surroundings allowing scent and hearing to ferry his attack. Remaining immobile, he was instantly alerted, as one of the men stood. "Hey, Pete I'm going to take a piss could and probably will piss a quart." "Yeah, okay, Ed go ahead, I'll stir the stew should be ready in a sec."

Ed moved towards Broken Rose, entering the shrubs to his rear, unzipped his fly and he felt contented, relaxed in relieving himself, oblivious to the coiled assailant inches from him. He sprang quickly and quietly emulating his friend the lion. His right hand crashing a powerful blow to his victim's neck crumpling, Ed was held tightly and placed gently on the ground. The voices screaming in his ear, "Quiet! Quiet!" His victim lying face down all the while he practiced his trade. Lifting his head, he delivered, the coup de grace. Running his trusted blade across his throat, a simple stroke severing the prey's jugular ear to ear blood gushed as a fountain. Not a sound was emitted. He turned from his victim in a crouched position. He moved swiftly to his second victim. Hearing a rustling behind him, his prey turned and felt intense pain in his left eye. His screams muffled by a powerful hand slammed over his mouth. His second victim fell backwards in a curtain of blackness and then stillness, impaled by the hunter's faithful blade which exited the rear of his skull. "Ah, another mission completed." Broken Rose wiped his blade clean on his trusted rag. He strode quickly and quietly disappearing into the foliage. Cloaking his escape in darkness, he fell into a modest jog. Arriving at his residence quickly, again he gained entry successfully, unseen and unheard. The voices would celebrate and come to him in his sleep. They would pour accolades. The warrior in him was disregarding his horrific rampage of death. He was fulfilling and applying his trade to kill.

"Hartford Police Dispatcher, Evans, and May I help you? An excited voice, "Yes sir, my name is John Barrone and my friend and I were out fishing on the river, close to the west bank! Anyway, there are two bodies that appear dead to me! Better get someone down here! There's blood everywhere!" "Okay, sir. Just where are you?" "Oh, just north of the service road and by the Buckley Bridge. We're standing by and we will act as a beacon for your unit, okay?" thank you. But try not to disturb the area. There could be important evidence." "Oh yes sir. We haven't touched anything. Don't want to. Looks like a massacre." "Okay John, thank you. A unit will be there quick as a Bic."

"Dispatch unit 10." "Unit 10 go ahead." "Dispatch unit 10 covering for unit 8, take a possible 10-89 our side of the river and just north of the Buckley Bridge service road. Fishermen boat standing by and the Detective Division is notified. They will meet you there. Secure the scene 10-4 unit 10, on the way."

Crime scene tape fluttered in the wind. Blue and whites parked haphazardly on the service road and unmarked detective vehicles immobile. The officer had to gain access by foot. Detectives Violet and Langin stood off to the side in quiet conversation. As evidence technicians processed the scene. Violet spoke in his soft voice, "Jesus, Bob, There's some butcher out there. Who the Christ would do this, and for what reason? Two homeless lonely souls trying to survive the best they could. It's depraved and some sick fuck is on the prowl out there. Makes no sense these guys had nothing and look at the catch, there cans of Dinty Moore Stew and a package of hot dogs. God damn, this sure wasn't a robbery." Langin in deep thought blurted out, "yeah you're right on Reg, Makes you wonder had that alleyway murder last month. Think they're connected?" "Shit Bob, who's to know, but it's a thought. But for now let's keep it on file. Fuck an ugly duck; we don't need panic on the streets. What throws me, is the mo isn't the same other than victims are homeless. It's going to take shoe leather and beating the bushes on this one." "Yeah, okay Reg, evidentiary is through and the meat wagon is here. Are we through here, you think?" "Yeah, let's head to the barn, send out a type see if any similar crimes have occurred. We'll check with Mass., N.Y., and R.I authority's for now."

The next day's daily news simply reported, two homeless white males found dead by river's edge. A full flown article and not yet anticipated. The calm before the storm settled on the city. But word had leaked through the homeless underground. Wretched souls began an attempt at defense. Showing up their pitiful box refuges as best they could incorporate the buddy system. Pairs gathering together in hopes that in groups it would dispel and discourage whatever predators were on the prowl.

Once into the apartment, he headed straight to the bath snapping on the light. Broken Rose was appalled at his appearance. Covered in blood his euphoria turned to disgust and realizing that a passerby could have seen him or worse detained by a cop. "Idiot," he muttered at his reflection in the mirror. You violated the most basic recon training. He'd fucked up and had disgust for himself. He'd been stupid and had participated in a sloppy kill. He could ill afford a mistake of this magnitude. The voices would be angry and would admonish him in his dreams. His grandfather would shame him with degrading epitaphs. He tore off his cloths drew a hot shower and scrubbing himself raw. Broken Rose vowed there would be no repeat. He would dispose of the clothes tomorrow and bury them far from human eyes. A wave of weariness suddenly came over him for he felt exhausted. He secured his doors and ensuring his lair was safe, he threw himself onto his bed and fell into an immediate restless sleep.

Detective Violet was burning the night oils and had elected to stay at his desk long after his tour had ended. He was poring over the reports of the homicides of three street people. He concentrated first on the incident on Main Street. Digesting what scant information was available; evidence was non existent, no witnesses, no prints and only the blood of the victim. Detective Violet sat back rubbing his eyes, for years as a homicide investigator filled him with forebode. He felt something amiss and that there was a depraved soul on the loose, trying to dislodge his hunch, he was unsuccessful. The thought of a serial killer haunted him. He felt fear, not for himself, but for innocent folks who had fallen on difficult times. He knew they were defenseless and vulnerable. He flipped through the thick report concerning the Connecticut River murders. It was a repetitious. Again no evidence, no witnesses, not even a footprint and the bastard had torn the scene apart ensuring no tell tales signs were left behind. But the past hours were not totally futile; he knew in his heart that the killer would strike only at night and that his targets were people of the night. Retrieving a calendar from his desk he made notations as to date and times. Something unseen was escaping his detection. His mind in overdrive, he inserted the reports in their case files, snapped off his desk light and with a weary mind he rose from his desk. He strolled quickly from the bureau. He was dog tired and tomorrow was another day. A relentless investigator, he would read and reread every detail of these open cases.

Broken Rose had slept fitfully and his hunger for the kill insatiable. How he hated the restraints the voices and his grandfather handcuffed him with constantly warning his strikes could only occur on the full moon. He continued to study the environment surrounding him, memorizing habits of cops, business owners, and employees. He shunned everyone for he would not draw anyone into a relationship. Broken Rose avoided neighbor's content to remain reclusive, his financial status no worry. Grandfather had left him a very modest trust fund and the only record of his existence hidden away in the files of the Marine Corps. This thought kept his brain razor sharp. He must always practice his art professionally. He wore gloves, changed footwear on every strike, should he foolishly leave behind a footprint. He was grateful to his government for having spent thousands of his training. Yes, they had given birth to a natural killer. The Marine Corps had elevated him to Force Recon, where intense training taught him how to apply his trade. Ha ha, he laughed, you taught me well.

Slowly the days slipped by. His appetite grew strong for he suffered tremors from his excitement of the kill. Soon Broken Rose would feast again and he had studied his neat target well, and would strike early just after dark when his victim would commence a habitual exercise. While his excitement barely containable, his next strike would defiantly toss an obstacle into whatever police investigators were looking at. He was exalted with the moon which shone bright and clear through his window.

A sheen of sweat clung to his forehead. He reached into his toy box and pulled out a three foot piano wire. Coiling it, he inserted same into his right front pocket. Flipping the lights off, he exited through the rear door and stepped into the night. He strolled from his residence, heading south on Maple Avenue, repeating his regime in of hugging the buildings and thus limiting street light visibility which would mark his movements. He walked slowly, deliberately so to limit attention. He crossed South Street entering Goodwin Park byway of a foot trail. Reaching the first paved roadway that traversed the park, he lay down among shrubs for he knew he'd have to be quick, to near the main byway of Maple Avenue, he thought. "Ah," but this attack would be launched quickly. He lay confident waiting with deliberate patience. He scanned the park and his immediate vicinity for his prey. "Ah", excellent he murmured. Empty of prying eyes he could only hear shrills of the night birds and croaking frogs that marred the tranquil silence. He grew tense, muscles rippling, his senses alerted into action. He sensed the slight change in the curtain of darkness. The silhouette of movement fanning the cloak of blackness, "Ah, yes there she is." The figure of a female jogger loomed into view. "Fool," he thought here in the park alone. He reached into his side pocket retrieving the wire. Uncoiling it, he wrapped the ends around each hand. His prey was soon abreast and then slightly past him. He sprung like a tiger, clutching her ponytail; he yanked her back harshly, wrapping the wire around her neck. There was not time for a scream, for Broken Rose was swift and accurate. He pulled tightly, his adrenaline fueled by strength twisting and yanking backwards. The lethal wire honed through flesh and sinew, severing cords and arteries. Gurgling once, twice, his victim fell slack. Her head flew from the body with her mouth agape in a stifled scream. Blood like a geyser spraying the trees and shrubbery coating grass a grotesque red carpet. Decapitated the head, it loped about rolling and bouncing finally came to rest at the base of a pine tree. Unseeing eyes frozen in a look of eternal horror, feet away the body lay quivering in death throes. Hands clasped as if in prayer ignored by a monster's hunger.

He stood transfixed admiring his handiwork. Then abruptly he disappeared into surrounding shrubby, the tarp of darkness masking his retreat. Once under cover, he removed the blue jump suit. He'd donned awaiting his prey. Wrapping same in a food bag, he casually joined a group of revelers departing a fast food restaurant. Hugging the security and semi darkness of buildings and avoiding the glow of street lights, he retraced his initial route returning to his lair. Detective Violet stood quietly by the draped body of Pamela Hart. He'd arrived on scene approximately 40 minutes after the ghastly discovery by an elderly area resident walking his dog, whom stumbled onto the grizzly scene. The scene was so horrifying they had to take the elderly resident to the local E.R. for metal trauma. Violet saw with unseeing eyes evidentiary technicians examine the scene with fine tooth comb. His mind was elsewhere, deep in thought for his brain struggling with this latest homicide, the fourth heinous killing within the past three months. But this slaying differed; this was a young vibrant female and the teen aged daughter of an affluent doctor. A star athlete at Buckley High School could be wrong, his investigative talents had led him to focus on a serial killer, but this didn't mesh. This was not a street person. Yet, he shuddered, yet he suspected this brutal assault was enacted by the same assailant. He scanned the crime scene. The gory remains of victim painted a picture of a deranged psychopath. He was convinced by the brutality of the attack that the same hand had lashed out and robbed this young girl of life's dreams and shattered the lives of her family.

His revere was interrupted by the voice of his partner, Detective Langin, "Reg, the techs are finished here. The M.E. I. secured a while ago and the Coroner's wagon is loading the victim and heading out. We've wrapped up the crime scene. What's your play, Reg? Where do we start? Where do we go from here?" "Yeah, Bob, anything jump out at the techs? Anything, Christ! I'll settle for a small amount of bullshit right now. This one's gonna hit the fan, trust and believe the pressure gage will soar on this one." "Yeah your right," both dicks perused the scene one last time, turned and reluctantly departed. Their hearts heavy, both resolved this fiend would be netted and caged. A rabid animal was loose. The city would certainly fall into panic mode. Enroute to headquarters both experienced detectives tingled with fear. Experience pointed to a deranged exterminator running amok.

The brutal killing warranted front page news with a photo of the victim. The face of a pretty girl smiled and crept into the hearts of a frightened public. The mayor's office was deluged with phone calls. Irate citizens concerned for families, demanding that police step up. Earn their pay. Where was the protection? For an entire day the mayor parried calls endlessly. Harried he played dominoes and queried his police chief, demanding a quick resolution as usual when serious crime surfaces. Police, became the scapegoats and the public either ignorant or indifferent to the obstacles and pit falls that malice police investigations techniques. How the law and courts tap dance and coddle the criminal element. How the rights of lawbreakers are protected religiously while those of the victim either placed on the back burner, ignored, or just forgotten. Victims are placating daily across this land. If one were to look long and hard, they'd discover the scales of justice blind folded. There's a bona fide reason for this. She's disgusted? Chief Culligan again was in the hot seat. He ordered his secretary to reach out to his Intelligence Commander, Detective Division Commander and the Field Services Commander, instructing them to report to his office forthwith.

Major Dellaher, Captain Reynolds and Captain Mayer, sat facing Chief Culligan. Their mood was somber for they knew damn well why they'd been summoned. The chief remained silent, and then upon rising from his chair, he addressed his top commander's. "Well gentlemen, I'm thinking you know why your here. The water in the kettle has boiled over and pressure from city hall relentless. The media is getting their rocks off. Well, fuck them. What if anything, do we have in the frying pan, Captained Mayer?" "Sir at this time, I'm absolutely nothing to lay on you. No witnesses, no clues. This bird is a fathom killer. He strikes then is gone disappears into thin air." Culligan grunted stared hard at Captain Reynolds. "Sir we've feelers throughout the city. We've rousted every known nut case. Badgeard Street walkers, junkies, snatch and grab artists, pimps, cabbies, homey's, even homeless squatters. Nothing, zero, zilch, the night has eyes, but lately a blindfolds in place. No one, not even our trusted informants has seen or heard anything." Culligan emitted a deep sigh and turning to Major Dellaher, Frank, Chief my troops in the field are beating the bushes and inquiring as to recent moveins, footmen and sector cars. Familiar with their areas, questioning landlords, area residents as to new faces in town, at least 75 suspicious vehicles have been chased down and registered owners cleared. We're checking and detaining all transits but so far chief, we've struck nothing but bumps in the road. Culligan walked around his desk dropped sluggishly into his chair, addressing Reynolds, he asked, Dan, who's the lead investigator?" "Sir Detectives Violet and Detective Langin" "Hump," grunted the chief. Pressing the intercom, his secretary responded immediately. "Pearl, reach out, A.S.A.P., to detective's Violet and Langin and inform them to report to my office forthwith."

He'd slept fitfully. The voices and that of his grandfather kept coming in the night admonishing him. The voices in peaked up fury berated him for straying from his sole objective. A vaporous image of grandfather with eyes like burning coal, chastising him, "you fool, now authorities will funnel more resources. They'll jumps start a massive manhunt. Fool, now your caution will need to intensify. You've showed me, you disobeyed, you must focus only on freeloaders, and no one cares about them. Now hypercritical politicians will raise hue and cry. Do not detour from the plan and stay the course. We will be watching, always watching."

His secretary knocked and peered into the room "chief! Detectives Violet and Langin are here." "Okay, Ann, tell them to stand easy. Okay, Gentlemen," he dismissed his top brass with a wave of his hand. As one, all three stood and sauntered from the office. "Ann, send them in." "Okay chief right away." Both detectives flipped a quick wave as they passed into the inner office marked chief of police. The chief waved them down into comfortable chairs. "Okay guys, I can't fuck around here. You guys are dinosaurs. Second to none and I'm aware evidence is null. What's your gut feeling?" Violet locked eyes with his chief, "Sir, we believe there's a serial killer on a rampage." Culligan stared long and hard at his detectives. "Reg, what basis do you have for this thinking?" "Look chief, its the violent killings. The prick is sharp for evidence nonexistent. Not a hair, not a print, not even shoe prints. Further more, this monster strikes only when there's a full moon. I made this connection or a hunch. This female kid was butchered under a full moon. I back tracked the other killings and checked with a friend at the weather bureau and he confirmed the three killings were committed under a full moon." "So your thinking we're dealing with a zodiac killer?" "No sir, I do not. I do know we're dealing with one trained ruthless killer and believe he's going to strike again."

The chief shifted in his chair. Swiveling around, he gazed out his window. He respected this team and their experience, well known in the profession and revered. "Fuck if they're right on, we're in the shitter with no ass wipe. Jesus, what defense can we throw out there?" He's got an 18 square mile playpen and a quarter million souls to feast on. God in heaven does a duck suck! He turned back to his lead investigators. How about surrounding towns, sister states? Are there any similar cases?" "No sir and we've queried P.D.'s on the eastern seaboard via NCIC, again negative." Culligan suddenly felt fatigue. Experiencing a nagging headache, he needed to think. He sat in the chair and the life's blood of Hartford's citizens slipping through his fingers. He was determined to insert every available resource to stem the flow. "Reg, Bob, what do you need? We're run with your theory." "Chief, as it stands we need a miracle, a break, pray he fucks up makes a mistake. Chief, this son of a bitch is good, ruthless, cunning and deceptive and knows no fear or mercy. He is well trained and disciplined. He's got Satan on his side. We sure as hell need God on ours." "Alert memos were dispatched to all commands and officers in the department. Aggressive patrols were upgraded and additional patrol cars added to the fleet. Plain clothes units would parallel blue and whites. Delving deep into alley ways, parks and the river bank, surrounding P.D.'s were informed. Police were springing a noose with hopes of tightening the knot.

The patter, patter on his window roused him from a restful sleep. Sitting up he gazed out his window. Rain was falling. Its moisture kissing the street and all it caressed. He liked the rain and loved the fresh smell floating in the air. Rain purified, cleansing the world. In Nam, it had been a faithful ally. He had satisfied his lust to kill on many wet days. Prey left themselves vulnerable. He laughed aloud, it was slaughter. He remembered the look of surprise when he, like brother wolf, leaped from the foliage slashing their throats. Then he would amble away like sister snake slithering quickly back into the forest.

He showered, enjoying the warm tingling sensation that hot water brought to life. Cleaning the fog from his brain and his eyes made of the synthetic cobwebs. Whistling merrily, he exited the bath and dressed quickly. Tight green sweater and body formed jeans; for this clothing were his faithful comrades and black combat boots put the final touch on the natural dress. He sat on the couch, listening to rain drops pelting his roof. Like music lulling him to relax. Smiling inwardly, he rose grabbed his black wind breaker and glancing around opened his apartment door. Stepping into a slight breezy rain, Broken Rose hadn't left his quarters in days serving a self imposed confinement. Punishing himself for betraying the voices and for infuriating grandfather. Daily he begged for forgiveness and sought understanding. Finally in a dream, the voices spoke in hushed whispers. They bestowed their blessings. Grandfather's image a vapory mist appeared smiling, he nodded his approval. In a raspy voice, he hissed, you are young and thus carefree and sometimes foolish. Learn from error. Anger has vacated my spirit. Go, continue your misson. I am always with you.

Heading north on Congress Street, he continued across Main. Lonely, he reached the Metropole Restaurant. His heart skipped a beat, there staring out the plate glass window, stood Jean. In bound, he entered the restaurant. She indicated her service area with her index finger by pointing to an isolated booth to the rear of the restaurant. Knew he liked privacy and to be in position to observe the eatery entrance. She stood by his table and upon her face was a radiant smile displaying her perfect white teeth. Pencil and order book in hand, she locked on his. "Hi again where have you been for I haven't seen you awhile." He sat erect and controlled his emotions. Smiling back he said, "Oh around and I been busy. I'm here on business for my company and I have quite an itinerary planned. Have to follow the schedule." With an awkward moment of silence, "he finally ordered oatmeal, orange juice and black coffee along with one wheat toast." With a cheerful, "You've got it," she scampered off. Broken Rose scanned the interior, noting business was slow. With a glance at his watch showed why. It was already 10:00 am in the morning. The breakfast rush had long gone.

She returned with his order and rushed off to another customer. He studied her ample breasts and her rounded full ass. "Nice legs," he thought. He'd inhaled her scent, fresh and clean like the falling rain. He felt stirring in his loins and had not known a woman for what seemed like an eternity. The voices had commanded he be celebrant. Anger welled inside of him. "Fuck them," he thought, loneliness and a sexual hunger planting the seed of rebellion. He sat picking at his meal for he was in no hurry to leave. He hungered to converse with Jean. For he suffered with mixed emotions and knew he should not share in a relationship. The voices had advised against human weakness, but he was sick of the solitary life chosen for him. He had not chosen this for himself, and resented it at times such as these for he was tired of his inner struggle to embrace life.

Jean returned with his check, smiling as she placed the bill on the table. He felt satisfaction, noting no ring adorn on her finger. As she turned to leave, he gently touched her left hand. "Jean, can you stay one minute. Giggling she stopped short. "Sure for Mr. Broken Rose." "Jean you know I'm alone in this town and I have no friends, nor contracts. You're the only soul I've really spoken to, except for business associates. Please, I've no intent to be to forward, but I was hoping . . . perhaps . . . I could take you to dinner. Maybe a movie or even dancing or whatever you prefer?" She stood quietly absorbing his words. Finally her face displayed a wide smile. "That would be nice "when?" "How about say this Friday? Are you free?" Scribbling her address and phone number on a blank form, she placed it in his outstretched hand. I am off at six. Pick me up at that address around eight. Call if you have to cancel. Thank you. She half skipped and headed to a crowded table. He dropped a generous tip on the table and paid at the register. He left quickly and felt contented. He scanned the streets and turned south on Main Street and headed home. Broken Rose, pleased he had something to look forward too.

Dinner was of the finest and every thing was to perfection, for the five star restaurants was a desirable way to start a perfect evening. They'd enjoyed several cocktails and several hours of dancing. Melting into each others arms with the way thy glided across the dance floor as one. Conversation was mixed and laughter thrown in as a comma between discussing serious business and each other's lives. The hour was late and they shared one last drink and headed to her home, a modest apartment on Retreat Avenue. The night was clear with a soft breeze caressing them as they strolled hand in hand to her residence. Too quickly, they stood in front of 126 Retreat Ave. Broken Rose and Jean stood shyly looking at each other lost in thought and pent up desires. "John, my apartment is on the third floor. Care to come up for a night cap?" "Why, thank you, yes."

Placing his arm around her waist they negotiated their way to apartment 3A. His loins were on fire and he needed physical release. He needed and wanted the serenity of souls embracing in the night. As they reached the top of the landing, he pulled her close with his muscular arms and she came quietly. Raising his hands to her face, he pulled her head slowly closer to him with such passion, warmth and desire until their lips met. Tongues entwining and searching for desire raging through both of them. Broken Rose slid his hands down her back caressing and kneading her full buttocks. She groaned from the shear pleasure of the strength in his hands touching her with desire. She could feel his manhood become harder as he pressed his lower abdomen against hers. Breathing in quick short gasps, inserting her key the door swung open. He continued to explore her body and his body like a poker on fire. Hand in Hand, she led him to the bedroom.

Lust exploded into a frenzy of groping hands and tongues. There was fire between the two lovers hardly containing themselves. It was like they could not get enough of each others body and soul. Naked, they frolicked on her full size bed. He marveled at her ample breast with nipples extended his tongue continued to tease them. The crevice between her thighs, wet with desire, calling for his fingers to probe and go deeper into her womanhood. She moaned with pleasure. Her body rolling side to side, as his tongue slid down to her breast. He lopped his mouth on a sweet nipple sucking greedily, and all the while murmuring words of lust and endearments. His tongue continued on it journey at her firm stomach. Finally finding her lush womanhood he inserted his tongue into her pussy and sucking hungrily on her juices. Jean, raising her hips, for her body quivered in spasms, squeals of delight emitting in the semi darkness. Her hands caressed his back and shoulders. She marveled at the taught muscles that rippled his body. Their souls in a rapture stupor for they came together. He inserted his manhood deep into her treasured delight. Pumping in a lust filled rhythm, he exploded. Bright light flashed as his seed emptied into her secret place. She screamed in relief as an orgasm took over her entire body. The impact was so strong, that it engulfed her whole body for she had experienced total release.

Pleasured in her fulfillment, exhausted they collapsed and fell into a contented sleep. He lay quietly, his head on her chest. He could feel her heart beating. He felt the rhythm of her chest rise and fall with each breath. He inhaled her scent for he loved the musky smell that lingered from their love making. The hour was late. He knew the hour was near that he must depart and leave quickly. The voices would come. He dressed in his cloths that he had removed in haste prior to their love making. Broken Rose had adorned him in the dark and stole a last glance at the naked, Jean. Her body had that glow look with a sheen of sweat covered her body and of total contentment on her face. Reluctantly, he slipped from the room, knowing that he could never return, for the voices would restrict him and admonish him for his weakness of the flesh. Quietly, with a heavy heart, he walked into the night. He would not be back.

The detective division stood quiet. Phone calls were trickling in at minimal intervals. Several major crimes during the night had come to the attention of the CO. A stabbing at 82 Braber St., a minor gunshot wound on Russ Street and a questionable gang rape in Pope Park. Detectives were busy perusing reports, mostly from field officers. Captain Mayer bellowed Violet into his office. "Anything new on the moon murders, Reg?" Violet had stifling a yawn, "no sir, nothing, not even a crumb's scent." We're combing the streets rousting everyone and anyone to no avail." "Okay Reg, stay on it. Keep me informed. Oh, by the way, I reached deep into NCIC and looks like a hot Harpers Ferry W.V. reports similar incidents approximately five years ago. Unfortunately they came up empty. Had three violent murders, same M.O. no evidence could be found. Incidents ceased abruptly." "Right skipper," he strolled from the office.

The dreams disturbed his sleep. The voices came like a wind in the night. His tortured soul reeled from the terrible onslaught. Grandfather's image rose from the dark. His voice was guttural and angry. "You have committed sacrilege! You have defiled your oath! Your weak spirit succumbing to the pleasures of the flesh! You jeopardized the sacred script laid out for you! You shame me! Are you not of my flesh? Does not the blood of our ancestors flow through your veins? You are deplorable! A weak spineless soul! The spirits will shun you! Have you grown disenchanted? Confidence no longer drives your heart! You may well be purged! A place no longer exists for you in the land of spirits. Shame! Shame! Your selfish desires have defiled your honor! My honor! What defense can you offer? No excuse merits forgiveness for such a thoughtless betrayal! Your soul will be exorcized from our ancestor's lodge! I weep for you for you will now wander in limbo and you have lost to our sacred ways!"

Awaking with fury in his veins, he flew out of his bed and shaking a heavy fist at the vapor like image. "Be gone demon, leave my soul; you have spoken your last to me! No longer will I be a slave to you or your satanic friends! I can and will act alone! The sacred misson will be revered by me and carried out! I will succeed, for I will fall back on my own strength and knowledge! I will strike when it pleasures me, not you!" He spit at the image which he now knew revolted him and he no longer had respect for.

A loud hiss resounded through the darkened bedroom. A cloud of mist enveloped him and a low guttural growl passed through him. Then silence. He stood in the dark starring at nothing. He felt relief and he had cleansed himself of the depraved entities. Now he was free to act. Broken Rose would continue to satisfy his blood lust when he wanted to and not when the spirits told him so. Laughing aloud, he would act alone as he had in the Nam.

Dawn peeked its golden head over the horizon. He'd showered, gulped down a coffee and felt fidgety, nervous. Energy propelled him through and from within his sanctuary. "Shit" he yelled. "I need a fix." He went to the toy box studied the implements within. Trembling with excitement, he caressed his bow and arrow. Legend had it that it once served a fierce warrior. He placed the box and quiver of arrows into a large flower container. He'd planned ahead. He could traverse the streets appearing to bring flowers to his lady. Broken Rose exited his apartment. Blinking at the bright sunlight, his eyes were not accustomed to the sunlight. Once again he found himself on Hyshope Ave. He walked briskly, his depraved hunger pushing him relentlessly. Arriving at the river's edge, he chose a thicket of small trees camouflaging him in the thin foliage. Squatting he waited. Missions n the Nam had taught himself discipline. Remaining still and quiet, he was waiting for his query. His patience proved fruitful. Soon a small boat occupied by three fisherman cruised slowly by. Fishing rods were deployed and wheeled out the boats engine was killed and bobbled in the tranquil waters. He smiled they were oblivious to him anchored and no more than 100 yards from his perch.

John Broken Rose retrieved his box and inserted a deadly steel topped arrow. Scanning the area, he sighted on his prey. "Twang", the released arrow flew true biting the wind. Its target to defend less unknowing middle aged father of three, Standing upright the arrow struck him in the in the forehead. The force impaling him with the tip protruding from the back of the head and he moaned in pain, reached to his head. Toppling backwards into the water, a dark red stain marked the area. His two comrades froze in horror. "What the fuck, Tom! Did you see that!" "Yeah! Dave, Jesus, Bill! Bill!" he called, as the body bobbed in the water.

Chuckling John inserted a second arrow. "This was too easy, no challenge like the Nam." But what the fuck it wet his appetite. He released the deadly projectile. It quivered through the wind quickly. The silent weapon impaled the second victim through the neck. The impact ejecting its target slightly airborne and the body hit the water with a geyser like splash. Blood spewing red from a mortal neck wound. Gurgling one, twice, the body went ridged with the arms outstretched in the unsympathetic waters. "Tom! Tom!" Bob was terrified. His two friends impaled! This was no accident; he stared at a small clump of trees resting on a slight knoll and saw movement. His gaze sighting the figure of a man positioned on one knee. He was busy loading another feathered arrow into the bow. Plunging into the frigid river, the last sound he heard was the whispered hiss biting into the wind, missing him by inches.

He stole from his perch. Anger overwhelmed him for he fucked up by blowing his third shot. John knew the intended victim had gotten a glimpse at him. He walked briskly west on Hyshope Ave. cringing for the cries of his missed target echoed across the park. He watched as groups of park goers ceased their activities. Staring off in the direction of the river, several ran towards the cries of the last victim beckoning them forward. He hastened his pace and slipped out of the park with his pulse racing with his heart pounding. He'd committed the cardinal sin for being seen by the victim and worst of all by scores of people. Reaching his apartment, he flopped into his recliner. Disgust and fear added to his anxiety. Yes, police would now possess a description. He couldn't be identified, this he knew. But it was little comfort. John Broken Rose left the door ajar and with arms flailing in revulsion. He worried police would kick it open.

Detective Violet and Langin studied the knoll. They'd found little to go on and a solitary imprint of packed dirt their only evidence. Tom Hallisey and William Downs had been brought to the morgue fished from the river by scuba divers. Dave Henry was too traumatic to question. Evidence technicians swarmed over the area to no avail. Evidence was nil. "Jesus fucking Christ, whispered Langin. We're dealing with a phantom who the fuck is he and why this killing spree."

Although physical evidence was lacking this time witnesses had come forth. At least six people recounting seeing a white male approximately 5'10, walking briskly away from the area carrying a large flowerbox. Two remembered seeing him leave the park and turn right on Wethersfield Ave. Witnesses were in unison describing the male as draped in black clothing. Good physical appearance. Violet had jotted down names and addresses and phone numbers of these potential witnesses. He walked over to Langin. "Well it's not a hell of allot, but it's a beginning to the end. The fox is back in his lair by now, but we know the lair is nearby. Bob, I can smell this fuck, he's not far. He's fucked up for the first time. He'll do it again." "But Reg, we don't know it's the same guy." "Sure we do. He's a hunter, only his game is man. Come on let's hit the hospital, talk to the lone survivor."

The questioning of David Moore was short lived. He fell in and out of consciousness and having been sedated to ease his severe mental trauma. However, he'd confirmed the party he glimpsed was dressed in black. So the witnesses had without their knowledge seen the killer. An A.P.B. was broadcast for a white male, dresses in black, carrying a flower box to all units and surrounding towns. Violet and Langin returned to headquarters. Typing reports on the incident, the ringing phone on Violet's desk creating a short distraction. Violet picked up on the third ring, "Detective Division," Violet speaking. "Hey Reg, this is Officer Don Benoit." "Hey Ron what's going down." "Listen Reg, I don't know if it means anything, but that A.P.B. comro, that just gave out" "Yeah Ron what about it?" "Well, I had a motor vehicle accident, fender bender, really at Main, and a retreat. Listening to that broadcast, something clicked I saw a dude dressed in black, coming from Wethersfield Ave., turn left into Congress Street, He had a long white box. Hell, I paid no attention, why would I?" "Good boy, Ron, no you wouldn't. Listen write that up on a 5 by 8. Get it into me A.S.A.P." "Okay, Reg, I'll drop it off quick like. Have to come to H.Q. on a follow up." "Ron thanks, you may just have given us the key that unlocks the door to this nightmare.

The puzzle was almost complete. Violet informed his skipper of Officer's Benoit's info. Placing the suspect somewhere on Congress Street, a hasty meeting was assembled in the conference room. Chaired by Major Dellaher, strategies were put into effect. Plain Clothes officers in terms of two would comb the Congress Street area. Canvassing door to door, uniformed officers would be assigned to strategic points on the outer perimeter. Prepared to act on a given notice S.W.A.T. was assembled and assigned to position themselves on roof tops and with the use of stealth, the command of choice.

The operation was imitated within the hour. Detectives posing as electric light workers, gas company employees, construction crews, fanned out traversing Congress Street. A dangerous assignment, there was no way of determining what residence lurked. Violet and Langin had canvassed several residents, with negative results. Sporting C.L. &P. hard hats, they stumbled on a teenage boy. Busy painting a foundation, Langin walked over to the youth. "Hey kid, you didn't happen to see a white dude, dressed in black, carrying a white floral box, by any chance." "I did, yeah. He went up the rear stairs to that apartment building." Langin heart skipped a beat. "Is that right? Kid, how long ago?" "Oh I've been here since 8:00." He laughed, drawing an hourly wage, "I'll say about three hours ago, but I didn't see him leave. Oh, yeah, sir," Langin departing, turned back, "Yeah kid," "He went into the top apartment. They're loft like up there. Hey, what's up? He got light problems?" "Yeah kid, he's got electrical problems."

Langin filled Violet with the information. Both retreated to the end of Congress Street and silent signals summoning other teams to their location. One team of detectives, Poiner and Daley were dispatched to obtain a search warrant for Apartment 5A, located at 28 Congress Street. Also for any storage leased to the named tenant, John Broken Rose. 28 Congress was sealed air tight. S.W.A.T. team officers with heavy ordinance had the loft apartment scoped. Patrol officers ringed the area. Pedestrians and vehicular traffic to Congress Street suspended. Residents in the danger zone evacuated. A surreal quiet settled in. Only sporadic coughing and low murmurs of men in harms way broke the stillness. Within the hour, the search warrant was applied for and signed, sealed and delivered. The interviewing Judge Kathy McNamara had dispatched the officers, "with a go get the son of a bitch."

The stage was set, detectives Violet, Langin, Sergeant Knowles, and three of his S.W.A.T. team members ascended the stairwell. Slowly one at a time, there was no talking, not even a whisper, for each man was highly trained. They knew their lot. They stood at the door. Violet standing to one side whispered, "Police." Officer Jim Bownia stuck quickly, crushing the door with a large sledge hammer. Wood and screws splintered in all directions. The door was propelled inward, weapons drawn, the officers swarmed into the interior.

"What the fuck was that!" Broken Rose sprang from his bed with a 45 caliber grasped in his right hand. He moved to the door, gasped in surprise. Officers crouched advancing on him. He raised his automatic. Five officers dripped to one knee. Their order of drop the weapon ignored. They opened fire. Flame and smoke enveloped the apartment and the tart smell cordite filled the bedroom. Collapsing on his back, blood spewed from several chest wounds and oozed from his mouth and nostrils. He felt no pain just a rigid numbness. He tried to sit up there was not strength or mobility. John Broken Rose lay still as the light faded visions of old friends flashed before him. Brother Fox, Friend wolf, sister snake, mentor lion. To late he realized, he'd forgotten and ignored the wisdom of the wise old owl.

The apparition of grandfather vaporized before him in a cold mist. Flanked by the evil spirits, eyes a fire, he pointed a burning finger, hissing the words. "Now you have paid your dues for the loss of my cherished daughter. Your name dishonored forever. As the tarp of darkness enveloped him, his eyes fluttered, and then silently closed forever. His final image brought eternity of the fires of hell.

John Broken Rose served in Vietnam with a marine recon unit. He gave his all and a piece of his soul. He returned home to an indifferent government and thankless society. He is a reflection of many Vets' that could not cope in the world after partaking in a political and immoral war. He was highly decorated. Six innocent lives rest in the womb of their God, while John Broken Rose's tortured soul lies forgotten.

In dishonor, we cannot condone his horrific actions. We may never forgive, however it is not for us to judge his tormented soul, but that of a merciful God. The politicians of that era dispatched our young men to a conflict never meant to be won. Where are they now? How is it that our political leaders can press buttons that cost 58,000 American lives and crippled thousands of others. Not to mention the untold casualties inflicted on innocent Vietnamese victims. Why is it that these depraved armchair generals not held accountable. They fade into the sunset enjoying the good life. Ah, but one day they will be held responsible, For God is forever watching.

Headlines informed the public of the apprehension of Broken Rose resulting in his death; of course they included his service as a U.S. Marine. No where did it mention his broken dreams and shattered soul. A city and its inhabitants can now rest easy, but as with our vets, ingratitude to those in blue marches on. Good men going in harms way, rid society of a rabid psychopath. The cause, you be the judge.

Postscript

John Broken Rose died a twisted tormented soul driven by the psychotic images of his grandfather and spirits. In the end his grandfather enacted his revenge, named Broken Rose as vengeance for his mother's death in child birth, beloved daughter of his tormenter. He was psychologically driven to his tragic dishonorable death.

Chapter 11

Officer Douglas Twohill had just signed on the line. Today he was assigned to unit 14 and his district encompassed the central area of the city, which housed several projects, numerous bars and drug outlets. The area was considered a hot spot as crime ran rampant and one had to be alert at all times. Grabbing a coffee on the run, Twohill had already been deluged with calls. At 9:30 am, he'd handled two late reported burglaries, a domestic and a simple assault. He headed towards Windsor Street where past experience led him to a secluded hide away where he could concentrate on writing his reports out of sight of the paying public. He chuckled as he observed traffic on both I-91 and I-84 reduced to a crawl. "Fuck that! he thought. What a herd, wouldn't want to be part of that confused mob everyday." He pulled into his secret refuge and noticing radio traffic picking up. "Assholes, gonna be a busy tour. Oh well it beats boredom that's for sure."

Joe Murcer had worked for the railroad these pass 15 years. He was a cheerful sort and married with three young children. His attitude lured fellow employees to him like a magnet. His smile and easy temper put people at ease. Humming to himself, he felt contentment and thankful for his good fortune in life, good job, wonderful wife and three healthy beautiful children. He took home the bacon every Thursday. The bills were paid and his mortgage on his modest ranch house up to date. He had a four year old Chevy, which he names clunker and a week's vacation was two days away. As he marched down the line of freight cars, he was attentive to their condition. Doors secured, wheels clear of rust, coupling hoses in place, so far all was in good order. He glanced behind him as he heard the powerful locomotive chugging rearward in order to hitch up to the lead freight car. It's powerful engine to haul the endless line of iron wagons to their various and distant destinations. As he neared the center of the line, he noticed a coupling hose flaying about. He thought it might be a problem but should be easy to correct. Douglas stepped between the two freight cars grabbed the offending hose and attempted to direct same into its coupling housing. Suddenly there was a tremendous shudder. He screamed in horrific pain. The engine, some cars ahead, had connected with the lead car and the force of the vibration, creating a ripple effect, forcing the rearward cars to engage and couple. Murcer was pinned, trapped and clutched by two iron monsters. He was entangled from the waist down. Crushed by tons of metal, his screams for help echoed throughout the Windsor Street freight years. Fellow workers Fellow workers, their skin prickling, sped to his location. Several signaled the engineer to engage to an idle and kill the powerful locomotives engine. Murcer felt little pain. The body's defense mechanism propelled him into shock. Conscious he listened as fellow employees arrived shouting encouragement and offering comfort. His fellow employees were appalled at the scene laid out before them. Their mate was in big trouble. Glancing at each other, they struggled to cope. They had no ideas o n equipment with which to assist and free their comrade. John Barnes, line Forman, assessing the situation pointed at Eugene Drurey, "quick get to a phone and dial the police. Tell them we've a trapped man, pinned between rail cars." Panting with horrid fear, he rasped, "Telling them to send everything and anything, God, oh God, help us."

"Unit 14 and 16 attention 42, on a 104C industrial accident Windsor freight yards. Fire department is also notified, respond code lion. Ambulance is also enroute." "Twohill grabbed his mike "10-4 unit 14. What location in the yard?" "Dispatch unit 14, they're located in the south west section. Look for a piggyback engine. Employees will guide your way to scene. Be advised you're off at 10:21 hours." Twohill activate his light and siren and put the pedal to the medal. He blew north on Windsor Street and his brain in over drive. He negotiated a hard right into the freight yards. His cruiser lurching and bouncing over tracks and debris and he was able to spot off in the distance a long line of freight cars. Muled by two powerful engines, his vision like radar honed in on several workers waving halfway down the line of cars. Within seconds he screeched to a stop. Dust and debris leaving a vapor like trail to his rear. Dust settled on the group an area of panic confronting Twohill. Gesturing and screaming Twohill was propelled between two iron monsters. He gasped as the sight of a human being crushed by metal pincers, gazing at him with a look of dismay and helplessness. Tears streamed down his blackened face, and his breathing short and labored and his eyes reaching in supplication towards him. It was an apparition from hell. A shallow voice said "please sir, please help me, or kill me, please." Twohill moisture forming in his eyes, felt his heart flutter. Nausea in his gut, he'd seen similar injuries in the Nam and knew this was a talking dead man. He needed to vomit but reaped in every ounce of discipline he could muster so as not to. Officer Twohill had to keep his mind from being clouded with grief and sympathy for this forsaken victim. He was startled by the touch of Officer Kahill who joined him in this confined cubicle of hell.

"Jesus," whispered Kahill, "What the fuck? How the fuck, do we help this poor bastard?" Twohill ignoring the question sprinted to his cruiser. "Unit 14, dispatch" "Come in unit 14." "Unit 14, reach out to Hughes brothers and have them get one of those giant wreckers with all the fancy gibberish here A.S.A.P. We've got a man pinned by coupling devices. He's crushed from the waist down and get'em here quick." "Dispatch, unit 14, 10-4 is fire on the scene?" "Just pulling up, dispatch, mark ambulance arrival 10-4 unit14, ambulance arrival 10:33."

Fire Lieutenant Josh Auburn studied the situation quickly analyzing that the victim could not be freed and survive. Yes they uncouple the cars, but once initiated his innards would plummet to the ground and killing him instantaneously. For now he could survive and the powerful grip of the couplings had sealed him tight as a car of tuna fish. Medics ran IV's into his arms and oxygen was administered. Soothing words of encouragement whispered in his ear. Murcer, a Nam Veteran, holding Twohill's hand, "Officer, I'm a goner, we both know that. Please get me a priest and I beg, tell my wife I loved her with my life." "You got it bro," whispered Twohill. "Hang in there," tears streaming down his face, he unashamedly pushed his way through the mingling crowd to his cruiser.

Father Cleary has been out cruising in his unmarked Plymouth fury. He'd been monitoring radio traffic. Police Chaplin he'd planned on hearing officers confessions and just shooting the breeze. He loved the men and women in blue and received ten fold in return received respect and admirations. He jumped when he heard his call sign screech through the airways. "109A, 109A come in." "109A is on, go ahead dispatch." 109A precede lion to the Windsor Street Freight Yards. Units on standby, and they will advise at scene. Your presence is requested by injured party." "10-4 dispatch 109A enroute my eta 5 minutes."

The scene was surreal. Brass from both fire and police had arrived in exaggerated numbers and this adding to the confusion and congestion at scene. Twohill turning to Kahill and in a rasped voice said, "Welcome to the circus where is the monkey running the show." "Yeah, replied Kahill, land of the misfit toys." Twohill slammed his between white shirts and took his chosen place by the victim. "Joe," he said softly "a priest is on the way. Look pal," as their eyes locked, "you want us to fetch your wife?" Murcer, sobbing softly, smiled weakly, "thanks Doug, but no way, I don't want her mind photographing this scene. Please get me the priest. Let us do our thing. Then do what you have to do." Fighting sobs Twohill, held his hand. His grip firm, "Joe trust and believe. From time to time I'll look in on your wife and kids, If you give your blessing." Murcer gasped in pain, inhaling deeply, the rush of air permitting life to sustain a while longer. "Thanks Doug, she's a great girl. If you can make sure my kids steer the right road, one vet to another. Twohill head bowed, "You have my word. I'm so sorry Joe, so sorry." "Yeah, well, like the old adage, sometimes you get the bear, sometimes the bear gets you. I'm fucked Doug, but I had a great run, no complaints; Just sorry I won't share in so many things. You know graduations, holidays, birthdays, marriages, grandchildren." "But you know Ill have box seats." "Yeah, Doug, you will."

Voices rose to a crescendo as Father Cleary arrived. Wrapping his purple stole around his neck, he entered the hellish scene. Those assisting the victim moved away in respectful silence. With the comforting and power Latin words, Father Cleary administered the sacred sacrament of the confessional. "Bless me father for I have sinned. The soft words carried by the wind, fell out of earshot. Of those in attendance, Father Cleary remained with the victim for twenty minutes, exiting in silence tears trickling down his face. He took a position to the rear of the fire fighters who entered hell and their job to disengage the couplings. The decision has been reached. The pain was now excruciating to Joe Murcer. He'd made peace with his maker. Left words of love and endearment in the hands of a blue angel to carry to his wife and children. Firefighters, Bill Henry and Don Wilson embraced Murcer keeping his attention. Wilson had already told firefighter James Boden; when I look at you, release the couplings. "Joe your a brave man. I'll never forget you." As he spoke holding Murcer's head in his arms, Wilson starred hard at Boden. Reaching up he pulled on a line and the coupling released. Murcer emitted a loud groan and exhaled a long breath slumping into Wilson's arms. The bottom portion of his body fell to earth and his spirit leaving his body and returning to the Father, where he will be at peace for an eternity.

Father Cleary administered the last rites and the body placed in a hearse and driven to a place to be cleansed. Joe Murcer would be laid to rest, but Twohill and many others would harbor this nightmare in there souls forever.

Chapter 12

The communications unit was quiet. Too quiet for a Saturday morning, thought dispatcher Peter Cashman. Lighting a Marlboro, he studied his computer, noting that three minor calls for service doted the screen. Inhaling deeply, he was startled by the ringing phone. Grabbing the receiver, he answered softly, Hartford Police, Dispatcher Cashman, may I help you?" The female voice on the landline sounded angry and frustrated, "Yeah God Damn it, that woman Gail Little, in apartment 3B acting crazy again. Her baby been crying hysterically and I hear banging and thumping. You boys better come quickly. Help that little tyke. She gonna hurt him!"

"Whoa, Whoa," Cashman spoke calmly, "Where are you calling from? What's the address?" "Oh, Oh, repeated the caller, it's 42 Liberty Street, 3rd floor, Apartment 3B. But don't involve me, I got's to live here. You know and I be the only black woman in this building." "Okay ma'am we're on the way. Can you tell me anything more?" "Hell's bells man! I just be telling you, she hurting that baby! Best you hurry, she crazy! She be drinking al night! She's a fool and has all kinds of men's there. Drinking and cursing. I swear she the devil!" The line went dead. The caller had disconnected. Cashman stamping a card inserted same into the conveyer marked dispatcher south. "Hey sarge, he shouted, Roll a unit to 42 Liberty, apartment 3B. The Little residence, she's at it again. Caller states loud noises and baby crying. Maybe you should send a back up. Last time one responded she gave the officer Lintell a hard time." Sergeant Vean Trelett retrieved the CFS card and read the remarks. Compressing his foot pedal, his voice traversed the airways. "Unit 6, come-in" "Unit 6 on, dispatch" "Unit 6 take 107D, 42 Liberty Street, Apt. 3B, be advised that's the Little's residence. Be advised unknown complaint but refused

to give a name. Unit 7, swing over and cover unit 6, clear, if not needed."
"Unit six, dispatch units six and seven you're off 09:12.

Unit 6 had just acquired a cup of java from Dunkin Donuts. Revving his engine, he thought "shit that fucking bitch at it again. God damn, DCF, where's their brains, placing that kid back in that satanic environment." His thoughts interrupted by the voice of his backup on the airway. "Unit 7 to unit 6, sir, I am enroute to your location. Meet in front. We'll enter together. Eta 3 minutes, grabbing his mike Lintel responded, "10-4 unit 7, standing by for your arrival." Lintell heading down Liberty Street thought highly of Officer Fred Horhardt, his backup. "Damn good cop, a stand up guy, stays cool and calm. Hell of a mentor for us rookies."

Apartment 3B was a scene from hell. Garbage, bean cans and bottles of booze littered the interior, cigarette butts and burns marks covered the floors. The furniture was torn and wreaked of filth. Gail Little, after a night of drinking and frolicking with several men, stormed through the apartment in an enraged stupor. "Fuck! Fuck! She screamed. My life is hell! Sucks! Fuck it all! She turned into baby Norman's room. Screaming, "Shut up you little fuck! Shut the fuck up! Kicking the soiled crib, baby Norman was propelled air bourn. He slammed into the wall, which enraged the deranged woman to a higher decimal. Grabbing the infant she twirled him around her head and slamming him into the wall several times. Blood gushed from the infants head and torso. All the while the demons in Gail Little's soul continued to taut her. A scene from Dante's Inferno unfolding in that cramped filthy apartment. A loud shriek emitted from the depths of her tortured dead soul. Grabbing the child she flew into the kitchen. Her mind destroyed by her cancerous temper. Carrying the infant she ran to a chard filthy microwave. Laughing hysterically she placed the helpless soul into its bowels. Slamming the door activated the setting at 5 minutes. "Fuck you! Fuck you! She screamed over and over again. Her voice resounding throughout the building for it was the voice of Satin. This mother had finally came to her breaking point. Her mind had snapped for she could not longer take this life that was dealt to her. She then fled out the rear door fleeing into the morning for her destination Al's Cafe. She knew she would find refuge and attention from male patrons at this favorite place, a place to drink and unwind. In the mean time the baby was cooking helplessly in a microwave in the apartment from hell.

Units 6 and 7 arrived simultaneously. Exiting their cruisers, they nodded a greeting. Officer Horhardt spoke softly, "well kid let's get it done, God only knows what she's done this time," fired back Lintell. "We'll know soon enough, "answered Horhardt. Both officers entered the building. Climbing the stairs at a brisk grit, they arrived at apartment 3B. A sweet sickening smell of well cooked meat filled their nostrils. Finding the door ajar, they knocked several times with the announcement police. We've received a complaint, come to the door!

Receiving no response, the two officers entered. Their nostrils flared. They were greeted by the sweet sour stench of cooked meat and filth. The strong odor of urine lingered in the air. Feces abounded throughout the living room they had now entered. They continued repeating and calling out. An eerie quiet descended on them. Continuing their deployment throughout the interior, they entered the kitchen and were driven back by a stench from hell. Both officers forced to cover their nose and mouth to continue their advance into this hellish interior. Both officers eyed the stove thinking that there was meat left cooking but to no avail. Lintell turned to Horhardt, "where the fuck is that odor coming from. There's nothing on or in the stove." Lintell grew silent when he realized his bother in blue had halted dead in his tracks. White faced, he stood frozen his gaze locked on the microwave. His eyes displayed a horror that only men in combat or cops witnessing a horrific crime would understand. Horhardt advance to the microwave, peering through the small window, he groaned in despair. Fell to his knees, whispering "Oh my God, NO! NO! NO! Officer Lintell came and stood by his side and his brain photographing an image from hell, as he grasped his stomach, which had formed a knot, nausea flooding his being. He gasped and fell to the floor on all fours and commenced to vomit. It spewed forth covering the filthy floor. Both officers pulled themselves to their feet. Eyes full of tears. They were face to face with a nightmare. There in the confines of the microwave were the smoldering remains of baby Norman. The small body had exploded within the interior. Viscera lined the walls and window outlets. Blood and body parts congealed on the walls. Both Horhardt and Lintell could not believe what they were observing through the small window of the microwave. Lost in time, the officers remained silent. No training in the world could have prepared one for this. Their brains took a defensive mode attempting to minimize the shock.

Unable to control his sobs Officer Horhardt in an almost inaudible whisper "Unit 7 to dispatch." "Dispatch go ahead unit 7." "Unit 7, roll the dicks. Roll the M.E., roll the ambulance, and roll a priest." His soul wrought with emotion, he continued, "Roll everything." He threw air discipline to the wind. "Inform them all prepare their souls for hell! Unit 6 and I are staring into the face of Satan! Where the hell is God?" Sergeant Tackett listened quietly, disturbed by the tremors in Officer Horhardt's voice. He knew him well. They'd served together for 18 years. "What the hell had they walked into? Uh, Uh, 10-4 unit 7 signed Tackett. Will advise you and roll those units your way."

Sergeant LaPore in unit 43 was the line field supervisor on this watch. Sickness and a shortage of personnel sometimes created this glitch. Scanning the streets head swiveling side to side, he was jolted by the dispatch's voice, "Unit 43, 43 come in unit 43 come in." "Dispatch, unit 43" "start heading to 42 Liberty Street. Unit 7 has requested. The D.D., M.E., an ambulance and a priest, get over there right away. Those officers could not or would not transmit any further." "10-4 unit 43 and unit 43 are they okay?" "Unit 43, physically that's affirmative. Just get on over there. From that location the watch command wants you to land line him." "Units 43 acknowledge enroute to 42 Liberty Street. Dispatch unit 43, 10-4." "You're off the line 10:00 hours."

Captain Heinwich had been listening to the radio transmissions from the field. Dialing ext. 115, Sergeant Tackett picked up on the 2nd ring. "Dispatch, Sergeant Tackett, "Jesus Christ!" shouted Heinwich, "What the fuck have units 6 and 7 got going?" "Capt., I don't really know'" replied Tackett. "All I could tell was those officers seemed frazzled, full of emotion. I've got unit 43 on the way. The dicks have been notified. There was quite an inquisition. I just told them to hustle their asses over there."

"Okay Vern!" snapped Heinwich. "I'm heading over there myself." "Right Capt, if I draw some info out of them, I'll be sure as hell to filter it down to you." "No need Vern, My E.T.A. to that location is 5 minutes. Put me on the line." "Aye Capt. your on in unit 50, 10:10 a.m."

LaPore enroute to Liberty Street Strobes flashing spotted his comrade Dirtbag Trevost patrolling his foot beat, spotting the flashing cruiser lights, the officer stepped into the street. LaPore came to a screeching halt beckoned to Trevost who jumped into his passenger seat. Lapore then geared his cruiser, lurching into moderate traffic. Pedal to the metal he sped towards Liberty Street. "Unit 43, mark my arrival," LaPore barked into the mike. "Dispatch units 43 arrival 10:28 am."

Lapore and Trevost traversed the stairs two at a time. They burst into Apartment 3B via the open front door. Witnessing the carnage viewed minutes before by officers Lintell and Horhardt. Hearing the muted voices of the two officers already at the scene, LaPore and Trevost quickly entered the kitchen area. There to be confronted by their comrades. LaPore noted the tear streamed checks and the horrific look on their faces. Horhardt pointed at the microwave. Both LaPore and Trevost groaned aloud. Curse's emitted from their lips. They turned the wall and emptied their stomach contents. Four highly trained police officers embraced in an attempt for comfort and strength. LaPore reaching for all resolve, ordered Lintell to canvass the apartment. Directly below question its occupants. He instructed Horhardt to secure the rear door and Trevost to station himself at the front entryway awaiting the arrival of the detective division. LaPore had ascertained that nothing had been disturbed by his initial responders, that evidence of the scene was secure. Horhardt, the experienced vet he was, had already laid yellow crime scene tape form the infant victim's bedroom to the microwave. The chime of a clock momentarily clouded his thoughts. Checking his watch, the time read 10:40. He could hear the beats of his heart. He knows he would have to control grief stricken officers, maintain discipline. This scene from hell could ignite an anguish that could explode. They had to maintain their thought process for they had to be cops first, men and fathers second. Wiping his eyes, a picture of his wife and children flashed in his subconscious. The moment seemed anchored in time. He stared at the microwave and felt tears again well in his eyes. He whispered a silent prayer for the helpless destroyed child. He continued to stand there transfixed in the center of the kitchen and impatiently waited the arrival of veteran investigators.

Captain Heinwich shot up the stairs two at a time. He acknowledged Horhardt crisp salute with a nod and a haphazard return. Dashing into the apartment, he was appalled with conditions that felt like he was in the city dump. Met by LaPore they exchanged salutes. The sergeant brought his captain up to snuff and that a Gail Little resided here with the baby. The prime suspect, she had abandoned the premises. He had called in an APB with dispatch, which was just now blaring over the airwaves. "Wanted by the Hartford Police for questioning, in an infantile homicide, one Gail, Caucasian, W/F approximately 5'6, age 29, 135 lbs., LSW black slacks, blue low cut blouse. She is known to frequent area bars and nothing on file with DMV. If found detain and notify detective division. Unit, if party is armed; party has a history of mental disorders. KCA 330 the Hartford Police, at 11:22."

Heinwich observed the anguished faces of his men. Made a mental note to have the Chaplin counsel them and he himself had been horrified by the scene. But as CO, he could not, would not, allow pity me to cloud his decision making. The room grew crowded as members of the detective division and evidentiary services arrived on scene. Photographs were taken of the apartment in depth. The microwave with its hellish contents was dusted, printed and numerous photos are snapped at different angles. The charred remains were left untouched. The officer's investigation however, experienced emotions that the general public would never experience. Rage hatred, grief, helplessness, yet performs their duty. They must, the floor soaked in their tears. What could comfort their hearts? Heinwich, beckoned for LaPore. "You and Trevost hit the road. Cruise the area for this bitch. Pick up beat 19, hosely and scour the area bars. The piece of shit can't be far. Get this demon from hell and do it quick. Throw the book out if you have to, but try to be neat and clean. Okay, saddle up, get your ass out there sarge. Put a lid on your emotions and that of your troops. We're cops this is what we get the big bucks for. This is what we're about. There is no time for emotion that comes later. Go, get the hell out of here and snare that satanic whore." Heinwich eyes moistened and watched as LaPore and Trevost departed the scene. He knew he'd been hard ass and had to be. He had to maintain control whatever the cost. He sighed as unit 43 sped from the scene. The hunt for a demonic soul had begun.

Gail Little staggering from booze, pushed open the door to Al's Bar. An attractive woman, male eyes drank in her swaying form and several shouting lewd remarks. She steered herself to the rear booth where three male acquaintances sat chatting softly and swilling beers. As she approached, Mel Hartren stood, smiling as he spoke softly, "slide in here Gail so nice to see you." The three men exchanged knowing glances. Excitement coursing through their veins, they knew fun and games were in the making for this bitch was hot and easy. A couple of drinks and they'd ball her all night for a cheap piece of ass. Mel snapping his fingers yelled, "Hey Al, Bring the little lady a draft and a double shot of rye. Glancing at Gail, "right that's what you like?" "Yeah, Mel honey, you're right on." Gail needs friends and comfort today, "trust and believe she does." His hand on her thigh, Mel chuckled, "not to worry honey. You've friends and all the comfort you need, right here."

Blue and whites swarmed throughout the city searching for a female animal. The word filtered out. The men in blue were father's, husbands, sons, daughters. A crime of this magnitude tore their hearts, anyone's heart. Bars were high on the list. Cab Companies and their drivers questioned regarding female pickups in the vicinity of Liberty Street. The responses were negative. Buses were pulled over and officers entered scanning passengers. The Dragnet stretched further out and the knot was pulling tight. Plain clothes officers were also canvassing neighbors and what few friends and relatives lived in the area. At 12:15, unit 43 pulled up in front of Al's Bar. LaPore flanked by Trevost and Hosely exited their blue and white. Hosely sprinting to cover the rear door and satisfied the bar was covered, LaPore and Trevost flung open the door. The interior was semi dark. Only two dimmed lights burned at each end of the bar.

The officers stood transfixed. Allowing vision to accustom itself to semi darkness, LaPore spotted Al behind the bar. Their eyes locked. Cops were never welcomed here. Al tolerated them. He'd had no choice. The man had the stacked hand, he was the law.

Hosely burst through the rear door. Entering the interior, quickly observed two doors confronting him. Above in neon lightening was the word restrooms. One marked men's and the other lady's. He made a sharp right towards the bar room. He had entered quietly unseen and unheard. Pacing himself slowly, he halted in his tracks. Cloaked in darkness, he observed a w/f sitting with three males drinking and make merry. "You fuck," he whispered, "we've got you."

He was looking at the face of Gail Little. Taking three paces to his rear, a tarpaulin of black concealed him. Grabbing his portable, he whispered into his mike, "Beat 19 to unit 43." The transmission exploded from LaPore's portable. It resounded throughout the eerie quiet of the bar. LaPore spoke into his mouthpiece. "Unit 43 to beat 19, go ahead." "Sarge, we've got her and she's in a booth here in the rear of the bar by the north wall having a gay old time with three assholes. Ah, wait a sec. She's stirring, for she heard your radio. I've got her covered from where I stand. Come on down quick. She's got no avenue to escape. Now the bitch will answer. Be quick sarge. She's headed my way with her goon bodyguards."

At 43 Liberty, the medical examiner on arrival was horrified and dismayed at what confronted him. Signaling the lead investigator, Detective Ben Langin, he stated hoarsely, "What the fuck! There's little to exam with a toe here and a finger there. This is unfucking unbelievable!" "Yeah, whatever's in there is dead, dead, dead. I've made my pronouncement. Sorry to be tense, this sucks, I'm outta here. Oh, dismiss the ambulance and have the coroner's office send their wagon. Bring the remains to that officer." The task of removing the remains fell to the investigating officer's. A dreaded task as the viscera had to be scrapped from the walls. Photo's taken at each interval. Vomiting, the officers went about their morbid task, for they could not believe their eyes, nor did they desire to, placing sediment and body fluids into a clean plastic bag. All burst into uncontrolled tears when the task was completed. For there etched on the evidentiary containers, in block lettering the words remains of Norman Little, age 6 months, w/m, leaped at them. It was an image photographed by their brains one that would torment their souls for the rest of their lives.

The containers were placed in the coroner's wagon. Those personnel at the scene stood in mournful silence each with their own prayers and thoughts. Veterans of combat hung their heads and their mighty voices screaming to the heavens. Why? Why? Does man commit such savage butchery? They'd thought they'd seen it all. Frustration engulfed their hearts. One cop was heard whispering, "Is God asleep? It never ends."

Gail Little and her male cohorts, on hearing the police transmission, leaped from their booth. Where upon were heading to the rear door. Only three steps taken and they were confronted and detained by the hulking frame of officer Hosely. Whoa, whoa, people stand fast. Ain't no where to go. Mel Hartren glancing at Hosely, "hey man, what's the problem, we ain't done nothing". Not yet anyway, he leered. Me and my pals gonna taking this girl outta here, gonna party at a nice joint. So let us by. You got no reason to detain us. Hosely smiled, his white teeth glowing in the darkness. Your right shit head, you and your two fag buddies can go but she stays. She belongs to the law now. So move, so you don't get your ass in a sling.

Hartren and his two chums, John Willow and Ron Fenton, hated cop's, had yellow sheets from various crimes. Pushing Gail behind them, they growled in unison. Get the fuck out of our way or we'll run over you; suddenly two more cops were at the side of Trevost and Hosely. LaPore addressed them. "Do what the officer says, do it now?" Hartren swung his arm up to sucker punch LaPore. Hartren felt a terrible pain as strong hands held his arm like a vice. He was jerked up suddenly. The bear like hands of Officer Trevost, wrapped tightly around his torso. He was suddenly airborne for he was propelled like a javelin across the room by Officer Trevost. Bouncing off the wall he lay still. Air had expelled from his lungs he was to dazed to move. He remained prone on the floor. Fenton charged at LaPore, but was dropped quickly by three downward claps to his nose. Yelping in pain, his nose broken, blood spewed out onto the floor. John Willow pulling a knife had a go at Trevost. But Hosely's huge hand wrapped around his neck and was driven head first into the wall. A wall frame falling struck him in the face. He felt sudden pain and then blackness. The battle over in 30 seconds and LaPore called for the paddy wagon. Trevost read Little her rights, cuffed her and marched her through the door where upon he placed her in the rear of LaPore's cruiser.

The Hartford PD was cancelled suspect was apprehended. Life in the city would go on. Families would laugh and sing. Lovers would embrace sharing tender moments. The sun would rise and set. Birds would chirp the tender song. The media would print the story of a horrific murder, but time marches on and society forgets. For Little Norman, one cop rasped, "So quickly done, why was he begun?" The case was closed. Gail Little was incarcerated to a mental facility for life. As for the cops, they would go on to battle more demons, see the faces of Satan. They would hug their wives and kids. Their souls would never expel the demons. There's would be a life of torment.

At roll call the next day, Captain Heinwich stood at the podium. He expressed pride and encouragement to his squad. Thanking them for their professionalism and warning, do your jobs but stay detached. Its the only way guys otherwise you'll end up on the skids.

Sergeant LaPore reading the list of overnight crime terminated the roll with these words.

> My brothers and sisters in blue, members of
> the thin blue line. I can only offer these words
> of consolation to you.
> Years ago when I was in the Marines, I befriended
> a Buddhist monk. We called him teacher.
> The last visit I had the honor to share with him
> He offered these words of wisdom from
> The tree of life
> Remember my son.
> The leaves of the tree die, but the tree lives on.
> I simply asked, explain to me teacher.

The leaves signify the experiences
of life.
Life, Love, Hate, Laughter, Tears, Sickness,
Success, Failure, Death
Emotions that guide our path
Storms and tranquility cloak
our existence.
Through it all the tree stands tall.

Cop Talk

Mans Best Friend

Harland, Jardin, Ray and Lapore sat quietly in their faithful watering hole, The Lucky Leaf Cafe. Fresh brews were placed before them. The bar was quiet almost surreal. Conversation had been minimal. Each of them was retired H.P.D. veterans. They sat in the booth reflecting on day's gone bye. Finally Ray spoke up. "Guys, do you realize the shit we stumbled on over the years. It was a walk through Hell. Don't you think?" As he spoke, a sweet melody exploded from the bar's juke box. LaPore, studying the police regalia that adorned the walls, responded to Ray's question. "Yeah, Lou it was a walk through Hell but we'd all do it again, trust and believe. As you all know though there were some incidences we experienced which will follow us to the grave.

One in particular I have to share with my beer buds. "Back in "69", I was working the day tour, in unit six. I'd just revved up the cruiser when dispatch bellows "unit six take a motor vehicle accident car UV D0G Park and Hudson. You're off 0820." "10-4 dispatch on the way. I'll make the story short. I pulled up in front of 4 Hudson Street and bingo there's a car stationary in the intersection of Park and Hudson. I curb the cruiser and head to the scene. Bigger than shit a dead dog, nice golden retriever lay sprawled in the road. A modest crowd had gathered and in the yard is a dump truck. As I grew closer to the incident, this little boy is standing there crying his eyes out. It's his dog and that kid is devastated. My heart fell to my crotch, cause the little guy grabs my arm and with tear filled eyes looks up at me and says," "please officer help my dog." "Holding back my own tears, I glimpsed at one of the yard workers heading to the dead dog carrying a coal shovel. I look at the kid, son wait here I'll be right back. I ran up to the yard worker and man I'm now pissed. Hey, you asshole what do you think your going to do here! He's a smart ass." "Hey pal," he says to me. "The dog's dead! We'll throw the carcass in the truck bed and dump it in the landfill." "Okay, you know we're supposed to be professional at all times, not this moment. I looked at that kid shaking and poking the dog to try to get the dog to come around and I placed myself between the yard bird and the truck. "Look shit for brains; see that kid over there, your not touching this animal. I'll take care of it. Now get your big ass in the truck and motor on out of here. Pronto! Mumbling to himself the worker did an about face. Climbed into his truck and roared off. I returned to that little boy, What the Hell do you say to an innocent kid. There's no words, no manual. The kid doesn't understand death that well. He's five years old. Anyway, I knelt down and pulled the kid close. Little guy, I'm so sorry your pal has gone to heaven. You go into the house with mom. I'll take care of your buddy.

The crowd has already sauntered off. I wrapped the poor creature in a blanket and roared off to the meadows. Before that I went to Chaplin's Box and begged for a decent box which they so generously donated. Placing the dog and blanket and all in the box, I buried that creature in a peaceful setting near the river. Then I got a hold of Ed Tooken, the dog warden, I told him I needed a golden retriever puppy like yesterday. Well old Ed came through. Together we went to 10 Hudson, Apt. 3K. The little kid opened the door and when he saw the puppy his eyes were as big as saucers. I say to you my heart felt warm with joy for the kid.

Harland jumps in so, "Lance what's your point?" "Come on Hank, it shows a cop always leaves an impression, good or bad that can be everlasting. I'll tell you it was one of those rare times when I felt joy for another human being. That kid was ecstatic. Here's the point Hank, when my first book, "*The Badge, The Street, and The Cop*" was published, the kid now a man living in North Carolina, called. He told me he'd never forgotten that day and that his respect for cops never languished. It was a nice phone call. He'd wanted to thank me so many times. He went on to say when ever he passes a blue and white he flips a little salute. I'd long forgotten that indecent, with all the breaking news of this age it appears trivial but not to that kid. Like he said, "Lance my world was shattered but not for long. You saw to that, thank you and God bless."

Chapter 13

He walked slowly scanning left to right observing the night traffic and those on foot scurrying into the night with secrets known only to them. He was lonely and depressed. He wore a high collard jacket and a hat pulled low over his forehead in an attempt to mask the horrific scars that masked his neck and face. The result of Napalm dropped to close to his lines in the Nam. He fished in his pants pocket and felt a tinge of panic. Only loose change jingled there. He was in disarray. Flat broke and about to be evicted from his flop house apartment. He'd sought assistance from the V.A. but was dismissed with a curt "can't help you sorry." Bitterness enveloped his being like an out of control cancer. He'd served his country, suffered grievous wounds, scorned by women, for he was hideous to them. Fuck'em all he thought. He snorted to himself reflecting on a conversation he'd over heard in an all night cafe. Two shits stains conversing, expounding on how great America was. "Yeah, great for the rich fat cats who need not worry about their next meal or a cot to sleep. Well, enough he'd use the training he'd received in recon at the expense of a fat cat government, to etch out a living, to sustain his hunger and thirst."

For small creature comforts, he passed a street walker, nodded hello. She bared her teeth in a wide smile. Displaying her jagged broken teeth, "hi honey, looking for company." He grunted a horse, "No thank you," and continued walking. "Shit," he thought, "poor bitch trying to earn some bread to last another day. America the beautiful, where veterans and impoverished were rewarded with alleyways strewing with human garbage and the eternal stink of urine as a last chance refuge from natures cruelty. He slowed his pace for his objective moved into view. He stood in a dark foyer reconnoitering the T&W Convenience store. Cloaked in darkness he had good position. His view of the interior revealing a lone female clerk and a lone customer exited through the door with a lone brown bag in his grasp. "Now," he thought, "the areas isolated." Looking both ways he trotted across the street. Satisfied no souls were about. He flung open the door marching up to the cashier he leaped over the counter. Grabbing the clerk, he pressed a pearl handle 12" knife to her throat. Whispering, "walk to the door with me and lock it. Put the closed sign out. Move or I'll slice your throat." Trembling and sobbing the clerk obeyed. Whispering, "Please don't hurt me." "That's up to you bitch."

The clerk, a pert brunette, Mary Jasper, inserted a key and twisted it to the right. He heard the lock snap. "Ah," he thought, "We're locked in." His loins pressed against her firm buttocks tingled with a warm sensation. He hasn't had a woman in years. He'd not planned a sexual attack, but his desires had heightened with the sensual contact with the cute bitch. Satisfied the door was secured and the closed sign hung, he marched his captive to the wall lights. Flipping them off one by one, the store was in semidarkness. Dragging the clerk to the rear of the store, he found what he was looking for. The door to the storage room was inviting. He moistened his lips and could feel his cock throbbing. Yes, screaming for release. His lust mounted to a fury. He had to have this pretty thing and longed for her soft nakedness. He flung open the door and shoved her inside. Whimpering, she crashed into the wall, wind sucked from her lungs she collapsed to the floor. He stood there hungry, ogling her, anticipating the rapture. She stirred terror radiated from Mary's eyes. He chuckled, and then burst into hysterical laughter. Finished with his private joke, he stared at Mary long and hard.

In a hoarse voice, he ordered her to strip naked. She coward against the wall with tears streaming down her cheeks, she was due to go off duty. Recently married, looked forward to joining her husband for their habitual nightcap. She groaned, as the male demon reached to her ample breasts. He began squeezing and kneading them. She could hear his heavy breathing, feel his hot breath and without warning he tore her blouse from her torso. He ripped her skirt from her hips, as she stood shaken in her bra and panties. "Aah," he groaned female flesh. It's been an eternity. She glimpsed at his face stifled a scream. A mask of horror stared back it her. His hands continued their offensive assault. He ripped her bra from her body where upon causing pain as it sailed loose through the darkness. He dragged her to a pile of flattened card board. Flinging her on her back, the knife gleaming in the soft ray of light filtering through the partially opened door, reaching down he tore her panties. Yanking them hard down her legs he flung them to one side. He marveled at her young beauty the ample tits. Silk like bush that surrounded her honey pot. In a fury he pounced on her. His mouth wrapped around her right breast. He was sucking greedily while his finger was probing her secret treasure between her thighs. She yelped in pain, pleading for him to stop. Excitement coursed through his veins. He spread her legs and his tongue lapping at her womanhood. She whimpered in shame, out of control, he tore off his pants. His organ was throbbing with the thrill of the hunt. He entered her thrusting hard and quick. Pumping with a fury, his manhood pulsating into her like a piston. He groaned with pleasure as he exploded within her. Spasm after spasm, finally he lay still and felt the soft body limp beneath him. As he lay on top of her body, he heard the soft cries and felt the wet tears on his shoulder. "Fuck," he thought. "Fuck! Fuck! Fuck! She can identify me. Well, like they trained me. Rise to the occasion and leave no trail. Dispatch your enemy quickly without hesitation or a second thought, he plunged the knife into his victims chest twisting the blade to and fro several times. The body beneath him yelped softly. Mary body went limp for the last time. Blood spewing from the deep chest wound. Oozing onto the floor, he rose slowly, glanced at his victim and with a crooked smile exited the store room. Proceeding briskly to the cash register, he relieved it of its contents. "Not bad," he thought a sweet piece of ass and $350 in cash. "Fuck you people! Fuck you all! Meet and fear, Ex-Staff Sergeant Bill Howser former recon. Yeah, hell is about to explode catch me if you can. It's my turn suckers, time for fun and games!"

Officer Lee Hotchkiss was in a somber mood cruising south on Main Street. He was reflecting on an earlier call. He'd responded to a pregnant woman who had given birth to a still born, and the mother and family devastated. His tour had been quiet up till then, "Shit! He thought. What a tragedy. Poor little tyke the little girl had had no chance, never took life's first steps." He struggled emotionally when it came to the innocent. "So quickly done, why I was begun the words rang hollow, but how true to the moment."

"Aw fuck it. Get off it. Can't dwell on this shit or you'll self destruct. Guess I'll head over and see Mary to see her off safe." He turned right onto Charter Oak. His area of patrol, had begun to experience urban decay, bordered up businesses scarred the landscape. Debris pock mocked the streets. The area played host to transits and homeless, who wandered the neighborhood, desperation and wild looking eyes propelling them where. Fuck nowhere, mumbled Hotchkiss. He came to a stop as he entered the T&R parking lot. The convenience store's interior lay in darkness. The stillness frayed his nerves. "Something amiss here," he whispered. Why is Mary's car still here? He studied the parked blue Honda parked quietly and immobile at its usual space abutting the westside of the building. Killing his lights he exited his cruiser quietly. Scanning ahead he approached the business quietly. He was tense deep in his gut he felt a tinge of foreboding not a sound or movement emitted from the interior. Reaching the door, he pushed gently. It swung opened a slight squeak penetrated the silence. "Shit! This sucks something fucked up here." Retracing his steps he sprinted to his cruiser. Reaching inside he lifted the radio mike from its console. "Unit 8, dispatch" "Dispatch, come in unit 8." "Unit 8, can you roll me a backup, 86 Charter Oak Street at the T&R Convenience. Make it a 107F for now. Place looks deserted but wide open." "Dispatch 10-4, unit 8. Unit 6 head over to 86 Charter Oak. Backing unit 8 on a 107F I'll put you off at 22:15." "Unit 6, 10-4 dispatch" "Unit 6 to unit 8." "Yeah 6, unit 8's on." "Lee, be there in two." "Okay, 10-4 unit 6. Come in lights off. Can't tell what I've got here." "10-4 read you. I'll come in quiet."

Hotchkiss faced the store front and his anxiety level at a higher pitch. The closed sign on the door acting like a neon beacon. Advancing in a crouch position, revolver in hand, sweat trickled down his armpits. Experience set off an alarm in his brain placing him in a defensive mode. Danger signals rippled through his being. The arrival of unit 6 startled him and his reflexes propelling him to the ground. Officer Greg Smyth joined him in the prone position. Both studied the building cloaked in darkness. It radiated a sensation of dread. Both officers ruse in unison charged through the door dropping to one knee weapons in hand. They peered into the darkness gaining time for their eyes to adjust. The interior laid quiet only the soft hum of food freezers, cut through the quiet. Hotchkiss moved to the wall. His fingers found the light switch, yelling, Police!" He flipped on the store's interior exploded in a flood of florescent lights. Both officers back to back scanned the interior. Smyth nudged Hotchkiss pointing to the cash register. Its drawer opened and a trail of loose change strewn about the floor led directly to the entry door. "Fuck," whispered Hotchkiss, "Where the hell is Mary."

Slowly and methodically the premises was searched and found secure. The two officers ignoring the counter area where sat the opened register. Evidence would be safe guarded at the extreme. Satisfied the main area was secured they advanced to the green storage door. Discipline ruled the moment. Cautiously Hotchkiss turned the knob. Smyth revolver pointed straight and true gestured the go ahead. The door swung open and both officers entered cautiously. Cloaked in darkness, Hotchkiss located a dangling over head light and yanking the chain which bathed the room in light, the two officers recoiling at the scene confronting them. There on the floor, the naked twisted body lay Mary caked with blood. Her sightless eyes gazed into eternal darkness and her mouth agape in a final agonized silent scream. "Oh fuck!" yelled Hotchkiss, Raising a fist into the air, "Mother Fucker, the prick or pricks finally got the kid! Jesus fucking Christ! Greg notify dispatch, Tell'em to send everything, poor kid Christ, $5.50 an hour for this, go on Greg or use the phone, no you can't its on the counter. Don't go near it, use the car radio."

"Unit 6 to dispatch," "Dispatch, come in unit six." "Six, we have a 10-89 here at 86 Charter Oak. Notify the DD and watch commander. Scene is secured. Looks like a 10-82 and 10-88 led to the 10-89, six out." And with a short pause then the dispatcher's raspy voice "10-4 unit six" dispatch unit 43, "Unit 43 go ahead dispatch." "43 you copy?" "10-4, 43 on the way, 86 Charter Oak, from Park and Putnam, eta 3 minutes."

A small group of officers stood conversing in the parking lot. Detectives and evidentiary services personnel busy at their ghoulish task. Powder marked the areas dusted for prints, photos taken from various angles. The M.E. had come and gone. Ordering the body removed to the coroners office. Detective Mark Foley whispered to his partner, "Joe fast ado. Shit, the prep left all kinds of evidence for he is a real flaming asshole. I've lifted a dozen clear prints and the poor kid had a clump of his hair clutched in her right hand. Also there are blood and skin scrapings galore under her nails. No eye witnesses though. The boys are canvassing the area. Nothing concrete so far. Well, we've just about wrapped it up here. Have the meat wagon haul her away. Poor kid, it sucks. But we've got some good shit here. We'll get this slime ball. My guess he lives in the area. Come on, let's head to the barn and get the ball rolling." Both dicks glanced quickly at the draped body and beckoned to the waiting hearse. They watched as the victim was placed gently on a gurney and inserted into the black vehicle. It departed slowly with tail lights marking an amber trail in darkness for it slowly disappearing into the lonely night.

He felt euphoric and was drunk with his successful venture as he slithered along the sidewalk. He'd gotten a cute piece of ass and absconded with $350.00. He'd live well for a couple of weeks. He felt a tinge of regret that he'd hurt the girl, but his marred face was easily identifiable. He'd had no choice. "Aw, fuck the bitch for she was a lousy clerk. No devastating loss. Expendable that's what she was. Just like me and my buddies in the Nam, expendable." His throat felt dry and his hands shaking. "Yeah, bout that time, need some fire water. A couple of tastes will calm me. Always has." He grunted with gratitude as he saw a neon light up ahead announcing his favorite watering hole. The blinking sign read, "Fearless Bar and Grill." He hastened his gait, craving the fiery liquid that would calm his nerves and relieve the tenseness that shackled his body. Reaching the door, he sighed with contentment. Pushing the door open he entered the semi dark interior. Headed straight to the bar, he chose a stool located at the end away from wary and nosey customers. Reaching into his right pants pocket, he retrieved his pot of gold. Placing a twenty on the bar, he signaled the bartender. He needed a drink and fast. He could ill afford a flashback now. "Come on!" he bellowed. "Where the fuck is the service?

Fucking asshole," He whispered, "makes maybe 300 clams a week and acts like pukey Washington bureaucrat." His suppressed anger took hold. "Innkeeper gets your ugly ass down here. I'm fucking sick of waiting, God Damn homo." Al Deaton had been bartending for years. He had built immunity towards obstinate drunks. But on close inspection he realized this asshole was wired. He slowly approached the end of the bar. Now face to face with his heckler, he asked softly, "Yes sir, what'd you have?" "Bout time worm lips, give me a double of V.O. and a miller draft. Be quick! I'm in a hurry." Al studied his adversary noting large crimson stain on his shirt for he had red specks on his right hand and face. Nodding cheerfully "yes sir, coming right up. Thanks for your patience." Al headed to the array of whiskey bottles. Poured two fingers of V.O. into an oversized shot glass. He spotted his friend Charlie Lee coming towards him. He beckoned him close, Charlie asked no questions, "Will ya, do me a favor? Take a walk to the dining room, use the wall phone call the police. Tell them I've got a fucked up individual at the bar. He's loud and abusive. Oh and tell them he's covered in blood, probably nothing but who knows. "Okay Al, I'll take care of it, no sweat."

He downed the whiskey in one gulp and followed up with a long pull on his beer. The fiery liquid warmed his stomach. He banged on the table yelling "Hey moose face! Bring another double. Hurry up shit for brains! What the fuck they pay you with, rubber ducks!" He laughed at his pun. Looking around he realized no one was listening. Preferring to show him, "Au, fuck you all useless fucking draft dodgers I'd kick all their asses."

"Unit 6 and 8, attention 43, the fearless Grill, 286 Main Street, see the bartender, has a 107F creating a disturbance, Units off at 0115." "10-4 unit 6" "10-4 unit 8" "Roger unit 43" Officer Smyth in six had been pondering, enraged at the terrible death suffered by the T&R clerk. Murdered like an animal, raped, no dignity, no mercy shown, fuck the world! It is depraved. He gunned his cruiser and headed towards the Fearless Grill. Officer Hotchkiss had left the T&R reluctantly. He'd known the victim for some time. He had made it a ritual to be present at closing time when possible. His heart was heavy and his emotions mixed. He felt he'd failed her, should have been there. Yet he'd been on a motor vehicle accident. Fucking fender bender "It was a dent in a car, worth a life? Fuck," he thought. Society just doesn't get it. Everyone thinks his or her complaint stands alone in importance. "Where the fuck is our priorities?" Yelling out the window, "Shit! Dogs running rampant, killings, rapes, burglaries, robberies, larcenies, muggings, assaults, and we have to respond to garbage calls. Wake up people! Your being butchered and it's gonna get worse!" He screeched to a halt in front of the Fearless. His brother, Smyth in unit 6 already there, leaping from his cruiser, he sprinted to Smyth's side. "Ready Bro., Let's see what we got. Time to be zookeepers again" "Lee you take the front. I'll go in through the rear door. That way we flank the son of a bitch." "Yeah, right Greg. You never know."

Hotchkiss strolled into the bar. Al, the bartender flashed a grin and pointed to the end of the bar and said "him. He's being a pain in the ass. Several patrons left in a huff because of his shenanigans. I want him out. Please Lee take care of it for me." Officer Hotchkiss stood 6 feet for he was muscular well known street cop. He tolerated no nonsense and had little patience with the human critters who roamed the streets seeking innocent prey. He strode to where a belligerent male was busy harassing a young couple seated at a booth behind him. Hotchkiss stopped short, leaving 3 feet between he and the subject. He was about to confront when heard, "excuse me sir, may I talk with you?" Spinning around on the bar stool, the subjects eyes narrowed. His eyes were slits and he hated fucking cops "What you want cop? I'm relaxing, ain't hurting no one, get the fuck away. Fucking Nazi, fucking fags from Washington send you?" "Whoa, hold on pal. Just want to get acquainted is all." Hotchkiss tensed as he spotted the crimson stain on the shirt and red specks on his hands and face. "Look pal don't fuck with me," Hissed Hotchkiss "What's your name?" "Howser, Bill Howser. "What's this, an infringement of my rights?" From the corner of his eye Hotchkiss caught sight of Smyth advancing on Howser's right, coming up fast and quiet. "You keep running your mouth, Howser; I'll jam your rights up your ass. Then I'll rip out your gizzard and use it for grass fertilizer. How's that for starters?" Howser grew ridged. He exploded in rage. Grabbing his beer glass he rammed in into Hotchkiss face. Blood spewed from under his right eye.

Propelled back from the force of the blow, partially blinded by blood flow, he couldn't know Howser was advancing at a gallop. Knife in hand, he was in attack mode. Officer Smyth drew his weapon and in one swift motion cocked the hammer and leveled his piece at the whirlwind human descending on a vulnerable wounded Hotchkiss. "Halt he bellowed, halt or I'll shoot!" Bar Patrons fled in every direction. Some sought cover under tables. Two leaped behind the bar. The bar had suddenly grown quiet. A soft lonely song emitted from the juke box, and only the labored breathing of three men, two in blue the other in black competing with saddened lyrics of a popular love song. Howser spun about his eyes and locked on Smyth. In a flash, he reversed direction with a demented look on his face. Spittle flowing down his chin and he took up his charge advancing quickly on Smyth. Flipping the large knife from hand to hand in a crotched manner, he screamed, "Fuck you, and Fuck you! I'll cut your balls just like I did in the Nam!" Smyth orders to stop were unheeded. Howser was feet away. The whites of his eyes on glowed with angry fire. Smyth took two steps back. Blam! Blam! The shots resounded through the bar, echoing onto the street. Flame 3 inches long spit from the 38's barrel. Smoke cascaded towards the ceiling. Cordite filled the nostrils. The force of the rounds, piercing into flesh, knocked Howser backwards with a look of disbelief on his face. Blood flowed from his mouth. He uttered a soft groan and collapsed face down to the floor.

The bar had long been closed. Patrons questioned statements recorded. Evidence techs had completed their tasks and gathered lethal evidence linking the deceased Howser to the heinous crime at the T&R convenience store. Officer Hotchkiss was treated at Hartford Hospital and his wound requiring several sutures. Officer Smyth forwarded a detailed report and witnesses confirmed he acted in self defense. Bill Howser's body was shipped to the morgue and on completion of the case was laid to rest in a pauper's grave. Mary Jasper was laid to rest several days later. A young wife cut down in the flower of youth. Hundreds attended her funeral. Terry eyed family members left with a lifetime scar imbedded on their souls. Darkness would cloak a part of their hearts the rest of their days. It was another chapter of a senseless act of violence for a tragedy that occurs to frequently in our violent society. For

Bill Howser, he was buried alone and dishonorably. Forgotten was the story of a young man in the prime of youth who answered America's call to the colors and who suffered horrific wounds that disfigured his face resulting in a monstrous existence. Scorned, ridiculed, ostracized, lonely, bitter, frightened, betrayed by an ungrateful government and loathe by a segment of society. His soul cloaked in darkness. He faltered and eventually his spirit collapsed and in a fury his actions resulted in a horrific tragedy. There is no condoning his action. There is no honorable excuse, only God can be the final judge. Mans law terminated a rabid animal. However, we all share the blame. Veterans, who have lived the living hell saw the demon, should and most would be treated with honor. Maybe just maybe, if more concern, interest and gratitude were shown episodes within theses pages would cease. Politicians render great speeches, stroll from the podium from which they forget and disregard the very words written for them. It's up to us, the little guys to comfort and welcome our own.

Etched on a coin the lonely little penny are the words, "In God We Trust." Hey, it's time to believe and embrace those very words.

Cop Talk

Good Ass Reaming

The Lucky Leaf Café was busy for a Thursday morning. Guests were loud and merry as a company party was in progress. The juke box was blaring and its melodies to couples dancing to various rhythms. LaPore, Jardin, Ray, and Harland sat quietly observing the party goers. Harland staring at one obese couple snorted. "Christ, the floors shaking and no wonder they're playing the elephant waltz." "Aw, fuck came back Ray that ain't music that's just a lot of mumble jumble noise. Bunch of jackasses making weird sounds with fucked up implements. Shit I'm getting a headache. Our hole has gone to Hell."

Jardin chuckled. "Hey Lance, you remember the time we tossed Dirtbag. "Yeah," laughed LaPore. "That was some show." "Right Nick," both slapped the glossy table and their laughter inviting attention from several patrons. "What was that all about," smiled Ray. Jardin pointed at LaPore, "go ahead you tell it, after all was your brainstorm."

"Okay, well guys, Dirtbag was on loan to crime suppression. Assigned to downtown, the business district, merchants were suffering a rash of snatch and grabs, and shoppers were being mugged daily. There was an epidemic of crime in the area. Anyway, Dirtbag always the actor, plays the role to the hilt, should have gotten an Oscar for his role. Here's how it went down. He dons a long trench coat that had seen better days, along with scuffed combat boots and to top it off sports an earring in his ear. He even puts on a little French beret tilted on top of that scrubby hair of his. Yeah, you get the picture. All of that and he's sporting that disheveled beard of his. Anyway he's assigned to that hot spot with orders to make some collars take the pressure off the palace guard.

Well on Friday, I've got unit 42, as my assignment. You know north central boss, Jardin here assigned to beat 14. It's a quiet tour, so I spot Jardin at Main and Church. Hard worker that he is, holding up a building with his back skirt watching, love those minis, huh Dick? I pull the cruiser over, beckoned to Dick to hop in. Fuck head heads to the car, like he's got a load of shit in his pants. Motorist's line up behind and are pissed but because it's a blue and white show great restraint, smart fuckers, wouldn't you say. Anyway, fuck lips finally slides in beside me, stinks like a tipped over outhouse, cause he guzzled beans all night and is generous with his gas outlet. He stares at me with those ugly sunglasses. He always wore to camouflage his fucked up eyes, got more red in them then a jar of Heinz ketchup. He burps in my ear," "Hey sarge, what's going down and how's it hanging?" "Dick, one's up and one's down, but the old soldier sweating between them is a-okay. Dick, I say, you know Dirtbag's on that undercover detail. He's out there today." "Yeah, that fat fuck, he'd have to catch the fucks right in the act. Sure as hell can't chase them down." "Yeah, I've noticed he's put on a few pounds, it's all that Gneiss Ale. Dick I'm bored shitless. Let's go toss the big ape." "Oh, no Lance, not again, he got all pissed off last time." "Aw fuck'em, let's have some fun. Besides I'm the sergeant, you must obey slave. Obey." "Aw, shit Sarge. He's gonna get fucking pissed off if you fuck with him again." "Fuck'em again I say. Be good for his blood flow. His arteries are probably clogged with all kinds of shit. Hey, there he is." "Where?" "Come on, Dick, right there. The big ugly fuck, see'em? Right in front of the five and dime store" "Jesus fucking Christ sighed Jardin, the fuck is scary looking. Look people are giving him a wide berth." "Well, wouldn't you? I'll bet the dipshit shit his pants to enhance his role. Shit to fuck, this is gonna be fun. "Aw, but Sarge, all these people." "Aw fuck'em. They won't have a clue. Think we're collaring a bad guy. The way he looks, the herd around us we'll be happy." Pulling to the curb we both jumped out. Dirtbag spots us scoundrels and hisses, "Fuck you, fuck you, you assholes, not this time." He turns and starts running south towards Asylum. "What a sight looks like a fucked up duck with burning hemorrhoids." We're laughing our asses off. Shoppers all around us are transfixed. Gaping first at Dirtbag then at us. Everything's going great, it's hilarious, then the show went sour. Some wannabe security guard in the bank saw what was going down through the bank window. He thinks we're after the smelly fuck. Roars out of the bank and tackles Dirtbag. They roll into the street landing in a pile of slimy street shit. Dirtbag is snorting at the fucking wannabe, growling "get the fuck off me! I'll fuck your pretty little ass!"

The two of us are bent over roaring with laughter. People think we've gone mad. Anyway Dirtbag flips the guy off him and flees down Asylum. Didn't want his cover blown. The security guard walks over to us all pissed off. "Jesus officer's I tried to help and your standing here laughing. What the fucks so funny. Well we tried to smooth him over, poor bastards covered in grease and shit and fucked up his nose. Too no avail. He was not hearing it. The little pussy marches into the bank and puts in a call to I.A.D. I figure here I go again another reprimand or some shit. So good old Brian Meli blasts my ass. Dick's off the hook because honorable fuck that I am, I took full responsibility. Meli ecstatic, forwards the complaint to the Chief. Next morning I'm standing asshole to teakettle at attention in front of Bernie. Hoping the old man got laid the night before and had his morning java. He's stares long and hard. "You know the way, had his method gotta give the guy credit. His look could be intimidating. He lights up his perennial Camel, snorts and grunts, "You French fuck! Have you gone completely bonkers? Are you out of your fucking mind! High noon down town. You gotta fuck with Officer Trevost! Jesus, Lance sometimes I think you've lost it! Why must you always fuck with the guys. Meli wants your ass in a sling! The bank is pissed. Citizens called in by the dozens! I mean what a picture's been painted here. A bank security guard scuffling with a derelict in the middle of the street and two of my finest are bent over laughing doing nothing. God Damn it!! If you gotta fuck around to keep the edge off, at least wait for the grave yard shift. Your lucky, shit for brain, if you weren't such a dame good line boss, I'd fry your ass in camel shit! Anyway, you've got bigger problems. Dirtbag is really pissed off. I gotta see how you get out of it with him this time. Now get the fuck out of here. Oh and if you need to take the edge off, play with yourself only in private. Fucking nut. Oh yeah consider this a verbal, going in your file that way I appease that fuck Meli. Lance, you got that nerd staying awake nights hoping and praying he nails your French ass. GET OUT!"

All four laughed hysterically. Harland, "Hey Lance, you think the Chief laughed when you left?" "Yeah, I heard him through the door as I was leaving. "Yeah, Bernie was alright. He could play act shit. He needed laughs too. That chair was a hot seat. Maybe that's what kept him from going over the edge, assholes like us." "Yeah, the boss appreciated an honest sense of humor, just couldn't let it show." Ray kept it going, "Yeah your right. He suppressed it but there was the time he kicked ass, huh Lance." "Oh yeah, when was that," piped in Jardin. "Oh fuck you Dick," you were in on rasped LaPore." "Okay," Harland discharging gas, hands upraised, "pray tell I'm innocent and all ears."

LaPore lit a Lucky, exhaling smoke he began. "Okay, I was assigned to the 10-6 watch line boss. One nice May day. I report for duty, well you know the blue and whites were always lined up like tin soldiers in view of the Chiefs office. Well anyway, this day the Chief is hosting a meeting with some VIPs, two bank presidents and two CEO's from Aetna and Travelers Insurance Companies. They're discussing who the fuck knows what." Jardin cutting off LaPore continued, Sarge Lance here heads to his blue and white chariot, opens the drivers side door and a yellow smoke bomb activates filling the air with a beautiful yellow smoke. The Chief and his guests witness the action. The Chief has his back to his guests. He sighs audibly and whispers, "those fucks and that fucking LaPore. God damn, of all days! Him and his God Damn boys constantly fucking with each other!" The Chief prays that's the extent of the prank. But oh no, LaPore stands there in a yellow cloud. "Bastards!" He yells, "aw fuck it!" He turns goes to the trunk to check his gear. Opens the trunk and two red smoke bombs activate. Now the whole building is garnished in a red and yellow hue. Secretaries, maintenance workers all gaping in astonishment. The Chief cradles his head in both hands. swearing softly and reciting epithets of doom for the pranksters. The VIP's remained silent engrossed in the situation. Astonished how daylight has turned a misty red and vomit like yellow. LaPore meanwhile is gesturing towards the river bank. Repeatedly gesturing with his middle finger. Bernie follows his gaze and spots six heads bobbin in the weeds. Laughing hysterically. He grabs his binoculars' from a drawer and attempts to home in on faces. But they've disappeared.

It takes LaPore good twenty minutes to sign on the line. He's oblivious that the Chief along with the VIPs witnessed the entire event. Anyway, Bernie red faced swivels around in his chair. He's flushed with embarrassment and a little angry to say the least. He mumbles his apologies but the Lords of the Realm done zipped up their briefcases and in gentlemanly fashion respond, "it's okay Chief. Beautiful color scheme, we believe we've rapped up our business here and will leave you to your busy schedule." The Chief escorts them from his office. Barks at Pearl, "Have commo reach out to that asshole LaPore. Order him to my office immediately and I mean right now!" "Oh Fuck!" yells Ray, ass reaming time, huh Lance." "Yeah, you crazy fucks Bernie rid me of my hemorrhoids that day."

Jardin continues, so Lapore reports to the Chief. Bernie is facing out the window. Contemplating homicide on his sergeant. He swivels about quickly, rises from his chair. "You French Fuck!! You Asshole!! God Damn it!! I just reamed your ass last week and you pull this rainbow stunt right under my nose! Doesn't make a fuck to you who I was entertaining, does it, Lance? You and your gang are all fucking nuts! You all belong in the H block in booking! No delay that, in cages, in the cellar, out of sight of the world! What the fuck do you have to say, Sergeant?" "Huh, What? Damn, Chief, I was as surprised as you. I didn't plant those smoke grenades. You saw what the fuck could I do?" "No you didn't plant them, but the buys you fuck with did. It's a tug of war between you and your squad. I think you fucks requested L.S.D. on some hit, or piss pour booze. Maybe your all celebrant your old ladies know your all nuts and won't fuck. Can't says as I blame them. All right Sergeant Schultz you've pissed me off. I have a damn good idea who orchestrated this operation, but fuck'em. I'll pick em off one by one, your the first. Effective immediately your being assigned to the grave yard shift. Yeah, that's right midnights. I'll separate you from that Looney bunch that's led by a loaded pistol. Now you can go play in the dark and by the way kick that night bunch in the ass, wake up their livers. Maybe your the sugar to the spoon. Motivate those fuckers. Oh, and if you behave like a good little boy maybe, just maybe, I'll bring you back to your squad. Keep your balls to the wall Sergeant. Now get the fuck outta here, and Sarge hit the coffee shop on West Service Road. It sucks It'll keep you going and lively, with a little wave." "LaPore was dismissed."

"Damn," hissed Harland, that's why you left us. The old man got pissed."
"Well what the fuck!" yelled LaPore startling several patron. "He was
right we were a bunch of screw balls." "Yeah, whispered Jardin, but deep
down he loved us. and why? We did the job and had fun doing it."

All four nodded agreement. Filled with their own nostalgic thoughts.
they emptied their beers uttering good byes, they strolled from the bar.

Chapter 14

John Carter sat to the rear of the bus. The huge blue and white grey hound paced itself bound for the city of Hartford. It had departed Norwich, CT at 14:15 hours. Carter surveyed the scenic views, drifting along outside his window. He was an angry man, one who suffered severe psychological mood swings. He chuckled softly to himself, pleased that he had bull shited doctors at Norwich State Hospital in that he'd gained control of his emotions. He had grown to hate the institution which housed him those past five years. His eyes were dark and menacing as he glowered at fellow passengers. John delighted in their discomfort as he rambled on talking to himself.

John Carter was a strong man with a burley build and he had spent time in the mental ward for various crimes, where a violent temper had propelled him into the arms of the law on several occasions, leading to his incarceration, "Fuck'em all!" He shouted. I'll show them all, I'm the man. Someone fucks with me, I'll hurt them. His loud boisterous exaltations led passengers to ignore him, granting him a wide berth. The interior of the bus quiet, with travelers weary and nervous with the sudden outbursts of this wild black man seated alone in the rear of the bus. Several times he was admonished and given warning by the bus driver. Even threatened with removal, he suddenly grew quiet and eyes darting frantically to and fro for anger sending tremors through his body. Shaking, he seethed with rage but remained silent. He was determined to complete his jaunt into Hartford. "Shit," he thought. "I'll fuck up that city. Make the fuckers pay. Ha, Ha," the thought of creating carnage calmed him. He relaxed and sat back in his seat closed his eyes and fell into a fitful sleep.

Officer Fred Horhardt was enforcing traffic violations on Pratt Street and assigned to the traffic division, he practiced his art on a police Harley motorcycle. His task at the moment, issuing traffic summons to double parkers in violation on Pratt Street, at 15:30 hours. Pratt Street was a beehive of pedestrians and vehicular traffic. Located in the heart of the business district, thousands of employees were completing their work day and flooding the area either shopping or negotiating their way home. Many employees reveled in the sun filled afternoon happy with the enjoyment of treats at local eateries. Many of them would browse through various shops allowing the employees to filter through merchandise which had sparked their interest. Few paid much attention to the motorcycle cop performing his duties. Noting his presence they passed by thankful they would not be on the short end of a traffic ticket. Officer Horhardt cycle parked securely on the north side of Pratt Street and continued his chore advancing east toward Main Street tagging vehicles in arrears. Occasionally he would request a wrecker to tow vehicles that were creating traffic jams, annoyance and a potential danger to pedestrians.

Fred Horhardt was a veteran cop. One who had served his apprenticeship in the trenches and had received recognition for his service. He had been assigned to the prestigious motorcycle squad which shouldered the bulk of traffic enforcement within the Hartford police traffic division. His tour of duty for this shift was nearing completion at 17:30 hours. He would head into the barn shed his equipment and exchange comments and jokes with comrades and embark on his homeward journey. Fred looked forward to a night of solitude with is wife and two children. Finishing the tow of a pickup truck, he took a breather, "Shit," he thought, another double parker. "Asshole," he thought. This bird's got balls parking half on the sidewalk. Well, he'll learn, fuck him now I'll need a wrecker. "Crossing to his cycle, he spoke into the mike. "Cycle 10 to dispatch," "dispatch go cycle 10." "Dispatch, need a wrecker for a 1968 Chevy. Color blue. Bears Connecticut commercial tag is CMHM1030. 66 Pratt Street." "Dispatch 10-4 cycle 10, Halprins responding from Main and Buckingham, eta 7 minutes. Roger that cycle 10?" "10-4 Dispatch."

John Carter sat mute in his seat satisfied that the passengers were departing the bus. Now alone, he rose from his seat and strolled leisurely down the isle exited the open door and stepped into bright sun light. Its warmth comforting passersby on Union Place, as he stood transfixed gazing left then right debating where his travels would take him. His soul was cloaked in a dark rage. He harbored dark thoughts within his spirit. He turned and walked briskly south towards Asylum Street. John then turned left and headed east on Asylum seething with volatile anger. He glowered at pedestrians as they sauntered by. "Fuck" he spat aloud. "I'm ready, I'll unleash a little of hell on this city!" He continued his march and halted on Trumbull Street and then took a left onto Trumbull crossed over to the east side. Raising a finger in an obscene gesture to passing motorists, he came to Pratt Street, halting in his tracks as he gazed east towards Main Street. "Ah ha," he thought, a tremor of excitement coursed through his body. He spotted his prey. Two hundred yards distance, writing a summons was a motorcycle cop oblivious to his presence. "Fuck, I need a weapon." He peered down an ally. Whooped with joy for there lay a large axe handle lay solitary and inviting not three feet from him. Half running, he retrieved the thick handle. Exited the alley he advanced towards the unsuspecting Officer Horhardt. "What a gift," thought Carter. "His back is to me. This will be a slaughter." Foot by foot he advanced. His stealth placed him within two feet of his chosen victim. He whipped the stick high in the air, swinging it in a downward ark. The swish sound as the stick bit into the air, cutting its path towards the back of the unsuspecting officer engaged in his duty.

Officer Horhardt engrossed in issuing a summons never knew what hit him. Horrific pain to his lower neck with the bright stars and flashes, he collapsed to the ground. As horrified bystanders watched Carter grabs the officer's revolver. Raising the weapon, he fired a single shot into the officer's head. Laughing with menacing roar, he glared at scattering hysterical pedestrians. Then turned and walked briskly toward Main Street with the axe handle and officer's revolver, brandishing, in a determined air to have his anger fulfilled, towards terrified citizens. He thought, "This is too easy and now I have a weapon."

Pedestrians rushed to Horhardt's aid only to find him unconscious. Hysteria filled the air and women screaming and men scrambling for safe refuge, the brave souls assisting the wounded officer screaming, call an ambulance! Notify the police! Someone anyone do something!

Hartford police operator, Joan Wilson, was humming a soft tune. Phone lines had been steady and about normal for this shift. Suddenly, the switchboard lit up like a Christmas tree. Excited voices on every line she pushed, screaming get officers to 66 Pratt Street! Get an ambulance! You've got an officer down! He's been shot and it's bad! Very Bad! She directed the calls to the dispatch center, keeping dispatchers in a frenzy to handle the volume of calls pouring in. Sergeant Robert Tallace pressed the alert button at his console. Beep, Beep, Beep, "attention all available units respond to 66 Pratt Street. 10-0 officer shot and down. First unit on scene ascertain and advise KCA 330, the Hartford Police 16:05 hours. "

Blue and whites throughout the city lights and sirens screaming descended on Pratt Street. The business district was in siege mode one of their own was down. The area was quickly saturated with somber faced cops with weapons at the ready. Citizens ran to individual officers excitably pointing towards Main Street. Soon the airways were congested with information. Splitting the air, looking for a black male approximately 6' feet wearing black pants and shirt. A small black beret and has in his possession an axe handle and an officer's revolver, last direction of travel east towards Main Street.

Lieutenant John Maconiel and Officer Justin Cole reared up in their blue and white next to the fallen Horhardt. The officer now semi conscious saw the world through a blurry mist. Maconiel squeezing his hand uttered, "Okay Fred, We're here you'll be okay. Breathe easy. Try not to move, a 10-10 is enroute. The guy's are everywhere. We're getting the son of a bitch." Horhardt gasped in pain. Feebly he whispered in the lieutenant's ear. "Tell my sweet heart I love her." "No sweat Fred, you'll tell her yourself." Maconiel then spoke into his portable. "Unit 50, dispatch all units. Officer Horhardt holding on, dispatch I want Pratt Street shut down. Do you copy?" "Dispatch unit 50, 10-4 unit 14, from unit 50, shut down eastbound traffic on Pratt." "Unit 14 dispatch, 10-4

I copied already on it." Confused citizens milled about the area, but were moved along by uniformed cops. Other officers were interrogating potential witnesses, while scores combed the area for the shooter.

As dispatch was broadcasting information about the shooting over the airways, Officer Bill Grippe was cruising south on Main Street. As he approached Pratt Street, the beep, beep, beep officer in trouble alert pinged over the air, stalled in traffic. He took little notice of the shadow that past his front with adrenaline flowing as he ingested the radio transmission. He failed to see a burley black male appear to the front of his cruiser. As he gazed outwards, the muzzle flash of two shots echoed through Main Street. The windshield of officer Grippe's cruiser exploded in a shower of shattered glass. Grippe grabbed at his face as two powerful blows struck him in both cheeks. Excruciating pain cascaded from his face. He slumped forward hard on the steering wheel as blood spurted from his face as he lost consciousness.

Carter roared with laugher as he did an about face and sprinted south towards State Street. Panic enveloped the crowds as they watched in horror as shouted phrases of a cop shot on Pratt Street still hung in the air. Now in full view a second officer had just been shot. Bedlam embraced the area for pedestrians running amok, terrified, and confused. They looked for safe exits only to be restricted due to the massive traffic bottleneck. The result of blue and whites screeching into the area double parking zigzagging throughout the business districts hunting for a cop shooter. Phone calls deluged the dispatch center a second time.

Sergeant Tallace, sweating profusely, once again hit the alert tone, beep, beep, beep, "signal 10-0, signal 10-0, officer shot at Main and Pratt." Having no available units, he sighed audibly, "Any units in area, check, confirm and advise." Scores of officers rushed to their brothers' aid. They observed his cruiser immobile in the middle of Main Street. Noting the officer slumped against the steering wheel. Trembling hands pulled him from the vehicle and laid him on a blanket. Checking his life signs, Officer Bob Giovanni, roared over his portable, "GET a 10-10 TO MAIN AND PRATT! WE'VE GOT A SECOND OFFICER DOWN!

OFFICER GRIPPES BEEN SHOT IN THE FACE, JESUS WHAT THE FUCK?"

Sergeant Tallace monitoring the airways ignored the obscene transmission. "Dispatch to units at Main and Pratt, message copied a 10-10 is enroute. What's the condition of Officer?" "Dispatch he's unconscious but breathing. We're working on him and dispatch, looks like the same bastard. Witnesses confirm, black male, wearing black pants, black shirt and the beret ran towards State Street. Info is hot, suspect last seen approximately 3 minutes ago. He's still armed and is attempting to lose himself in the throngs of pedestrians mingling in the area. "Okay, dispatch copies. Attention all units suspect is same as previous broadcast. Units converge on State Street. Party has been last seen that location. Use extreme caution. Suspect still armed."

A chaotic scene unfolded in the downtown business district. Scores of blue and whites parked haphazardly. Their strobes casting red fingers of light, which danced off walls and reflected from glass windows, cast a surreal brilliance to the area. Buses were stalled, and traffic flow came to an immobile state. Horrified pedestrians cemented in place as they watched in fear. Scores of armed police fanned out and scour the neighborhood. Sirens wailing in the distance as additional police and ambulances thundered into the hot spot. A massive dragnet was in effect. Every available officer was thrown into the hunt. A cop shooter on the loose was a cop's worst nightmare. Angry, frustrated, they would do their damndest to apprehend this sick animal. It was a given. He could not escape. Every officer was tuned to the same page. Harness this prick one way or another.

Chief Culligan arrived on the scene escorted by Major Dellaher. Command and control established the man hunt roared into high gear. Numerous reports guided the officers towards the suspect. Suddenly the voice of Officer John Tobin spilt the airways. "Suspect at State and Market. He's crossing over Market trying to negotiate the bridge. Move in. Move in." Scores of officers converged on the area. Carter, unthinking was trapped. Standing alone in the middle of Market Street, he realized that he was suddenly surrounded by numerous cops. Weapons trained on him there was no chance of escape. Dropping his weapons he threw himself to the street. Lying in the prone position arms outstretched, he surrendered meekly. Laughter replaced by fear, would the cops do him in? Alas no, discipline and professionalism ruled the day. Lieutenant Mulchaey and Officer Jim Butcher exploded on his person. Cuffed behind his back he was roughly pulled from the street and hurled into the caged rear seat of a near by cruiser. Mulchaey, his voice trembling spoke into his portable, "unit 52, dispatch, suspect in custody, State and Market. Weapons secured enroute 10-2 to detective division,. "Dispatch unit 52, 10-4, a good job, good job to all." Chief Culligan grabbed a near by portable. "Unit 300, to unit 52, be advised stay with the suspect. Make certain he's secure. "10-4, Unit 52 to unit 300, understand chief. Party is and will be secure."

Officers Horhardt and Officer Grippe were rushed to Hartford Hospital. They were taken to the O.R. where their wounds treated by teams of surgeons. Both recovered after lengthy and painful rehabilitation. Both returned to active duty and enjoyed distinctive careers. Respected by their brothers and sisters in blue, they retired with honors. It is fitting here to borrow the military slogan:

"Some gave some, some gave all, I salute you my brothers' fare thee well."

Chapter 15

The wind whistled its cold tune through the city streets and alley ways. Winter was fast approaching and the hawk had already entered the city and taken refuge. Lapore stomped his feet on the pavement attempting to warn them from the night chill. This grave yard shift sucks. He grumbled as he assigned to foot beat 12 in the heart of the business district. Glancing at his watch he noted it was 02:20 am. Traffic was light at this hour. What vehicles were careening about was cabs; Mac trucks bread trucks, and produce and bakery vehicles. All racing to deliver their goods on time thus ensuring restaurants and various other businesses would be prepared to feed and service a hungry city. A cold mist caressed LaPore's face, forcing him to constantly dab at his eyes, which were tearing from the cold sting. As he continued in patrol mode, he couldn't help but gaze at the tall buildings which adorned the downtown district. They stood as sentinels guarding a proud city. Lights flashed on an off in several buildings which cast a glow on the streets. Giving the impression of dancing sparks of light bouncing off windows and walls. It made for a partnership with street lamps creating a surreal yellowish hue in the night.

LaPore continued west on Pearl Street with his head swiveling side to side, and always watchful, checking alleys and side streets for any unusual activity. For a moment he lapsed back through time. It was a year ago that he had suffered a severe head wound on this beat in an altercating with three crack heads. He shivered at the thought. Three bore holes were needed to relieve blood causing pressure on the brain, of course his buddies had been brutal, and stating there was no brain so where is the pressure. He noted no parked cars in his area of patrol so he'd not have to tag overnighters. That was a break.

As he approached Haynes Street, his sense of smell was suddenly assaulted. A strong smell of smoke filled his nostrils. "What the fuck? Where's it coming from? He quickened his pace as he reached the corner of Hayes Street. He got his answer, smoke and fire was bellowing from a fourth floor window obviously unnoticed as no alarms had been sounded. Retracing his steps he ran East on Pearl to a waiting fire alarm. Shattering the glass with his night stick, he activated the switch which would alert fire headquarters automatically. He then turned and ran toward the burning building knowing it was a residence for seniors, many who were elderly and infirmed.

As he sprinted towards the lure of smoke, Officer Charlie Grasso pulled up in a line unit sensing his beat a needed help. "Lance, what you got!" He yelled. "Charlie, right there at 16 Hayes Street, smoke! Fire! Call it in! Call it in! I've pulled an alarm, but we need ambulances and everything else!" Grasso compressed his radio mike, "unit 10, working fire, 16 Hayes Street, Lots of fire on top floor. Beat 12 pulled fire alarm. They could hear apparatus from Pearl Street fire house. Notify them this looks like its goanna be a two or three alarmer." "Dispatch unit 10 copy. All notifications are being implemented." "Roger district 10 including gas, water, electrical, this look's bad." "Dispatch, unit 10 10-4, got you covered."

LaPore and Grasso knew they could not wait for fire personnel. Together they entered the building forcing the main door open so as to gain entry. Once inside, they were in a dark interior. Each took off in separate directions. Yelling fire and banging on doors. By now smoke was snaking its way along the floors and walls. As the officers continued their ascent into the building the heat and smoke had gathered strength. The two officers were no longer knocking on doors but kicking them in. Lives were in peril here. They had no time to lose. Lives of elderly were already affecting an escape. Down the smoky stairwells, directed by the officers Grasso and LaPore continued their frenzied search of the top floor. Satisfied it was empty; they turned to make good their escape. Suddenly, both ends of the hall burst into red hot flames. The floors radiated intense heat. The two officers were trapped with no air. Both soon collapsed in a heap and pictures of family danced before them, then blackness.

The eerie quiet of the night had exploded into a beehive of activity. Fire apparatus arriving on the scene quickly and professionally, knew they had a dangerous working fire here. Battalion Chief James McCarthy immediately called in a 2nd alarmer. Engines were laying their lines and fire fighters advanced on 16 Hayes in attach mode. Now water was being directed on the heart of the fire. Firemen continued to advance driving the smoke and fire backwards. Spotlights from engines pockmarked the building zoning in on hot spots and trying to ascertain if any victims were trapped. Firemen were now attaching the beast vigorously. Firefighter, Charles Borowski, knew two police officers had ascended to the top floor, but had not seen them return. Turning to his captain, he yelled, "There's two cops located on the top floor! They haven't returned! Myself and O'Leary are gonna look see!" "All right, but be careful. I have no spare air packs, do what you can. Go with God."

The two firemen raced up the smoky stairwell. Three at a time, upon reaching the top floor, they could hear the roar of the flames and there was no sign of the cops. Borowski looked at his partner O'Leary "Shit the fuck. Why the fuck did they come up here? Were they gonna piss on it." "Aw Charlie, don't get pissed. They were concerned about life. Isn't that what we and they are about." "Yeah, you're right. Let's find them; crazy fucks probably saved a lot of lives tonight."

Crawling along the floor to conserve and find oxygen, the two firefighters were able to find the two officers unconscious lying on the north side. Implementing the firemen's carry, they were sweating profusely and gasping for air, were successful in carrying the officers safely to waiting ambulances. Both Borowski and O'Leary acted with great courage and exposed themselves to severe injury or even death, but never wavered in duty. The fire department remained on scene for 18 hours. The fire was bought under full control and only several seniors suffered nonlife threatening injuries. Once again the Hartford Fire Department had shown bright. Their quick action and professionalism saved many lives and preserved adjoining properties.

Both officers, LaPore and Grasso, were under oxygen for 24 hours as a result of fire in the lungs. The brotherhood between police and fire was once again a solid operation. This writer can never thank the fire fighters, Charles Borowski enough for his heroism. For there are no words, to express the fact that I watched my kids grow because of him. Rest in peace Charlie you are truly a hero always will be. I salute you and always remember you in my prayers.

Chapter 16

Frank Rizzo was busy finishing his chores in the bowels of Hartford Hospital. His duties were that of Janitor and fire watch assuring that the huge furnaces and air conditioner units ran smoothly and safely. While powering the majestic structures of Hartford Hospital, his was not a high salaried job but it paid his bills, fed his family and afforded some creature comforts. He was excited to complete his tour as this was the weekend. He was to begin building his surprise for the pride of his life, his angel, his six year old daughter, Lisa. Supplies had already been delivered and covered with a tarp to prevent his little girl from suspecting what was to be erected. Frank had studied books, conversed with hospital carpenters picking their brains. His dream was to build his daughter a doll house in the rear yard, second to none. This was Lisa's dream and he was determined to deliver. For a solid year Frank and his wife Ellen had pinched pennies to follow the dream. Checking the valves one last time, he wiped his hands and brow and exited his work place. Nodding at his relief John Murray and with a word assuring him all was a go with the heart of Hartford Hospital.

He strolled into the crisp night, inhaling the cool scent of fresh air. Anxious to get home, he found his old 54 Ford, petted it's hood and muttered come on old girl get me home, to momma and little angel. Pulling into the rear yard, he glanced at the hump in the yard covered by blue tarp. Smiling to himself, he would begin his chore early the next morning. He entered though the rear door and the aroma of home cooking filled his nostrils. "Ah, home made stew," his favorite. Both his wife Ellen and Little Lisa fell into his arms. The three shared an embrace of love and warmth. Happy with each other and their humble 5 room ranch home.

Small talk dominated the meal hour. Outside dark had spread its tarp on the landscape. Finishing up supper dishes and after a family conversation, Little Lisa now bathed was ready for her nights rest. Frank as always, bundled her in his arms and humming a soft tune placed his little angel in her bed. With a soft kiss and embrace, he slowly closed the door and with a contented sigh, headed toward the living room to share a quiet evening with his wife and best friend Ellen, sitting together on the couch they enjoyed the soft music of Perry Como. Words of love emitted from the antique record player. They sat in silence for no words needed to shatter their solitude. This was a happy home. Love, understanding and sharing were the basis of its foundation, rendering it strong and invulnerable to outside demons.

Frank tired, had fallen asleep on his wife's shoulder. Safe and warm slumber had overtaking him. As Ellen stroked his hair, she noticed slight trembling coursing through his body. She was startled as soft moans escaped his person. Intuition of womanhood alarmed her. She knew he'd been experiencing pain in his lower and upper back for the past month, but both she and Frank had attributed his discomfort to the hard regimens of his job. Arousing Frank arm and arm they sauntered off to the warm safety of their bedroom.

The next morning, Frank attempted to rouse from his bed early. Being Saturday, it was his day off. This was D day, when he would begin his labor of love. The erection of the doll house, but pain exploded in his upper back and shoulders. He experienced strong nausea and found he hadn't the strength to lift himself from his bed. Weakly he called to Ellen who was busy preparing breakfast. Alarmed at the weakness of his voice and his grayish hue, as she entered the bedroom, an anxious dread filled her soul. Frank, what's wrong! Honey, what is it?" Frank now in a wet sweat, rasped, "I can't move and I'm having trouble breathing." Ellen noted the glazed look in her husband's eyes. Fear pierced her soul as she observed his labored breathing. She grabbed the phone on the night table and dialed the Hartford Police. A tired voice came on the line. "Hartford Police, may I help you?" "Yes, Ellen cried my husband is having difficulty breathing and needs help!" "Yes, ma'am, what is your address?"Oh officer, we live at 29 Campfield Ave. Please! Please send help! "Yes ma'am, I'm dispatching an ambulance and a cruiser as we speak. Hang tight, help is on the way."

Ellen couldn't control herself. Constantly pacing in the large cold waiting room at Hartford Hospital, her husband of eleven years was currently being examined in the E.R. 1. When she last saw him he was being administered oxygen and tubes were affixed to his arms supplying life saving nutrients. Frank she feared was very ill. She prayed and waited alone. Her soul distressed in fear. She had left little Lisa crying with a neighbor. Poor soul, she wondered what was wrong with daddy. Hours passed. Finally the door to the waiting room burst open and a white clad figure approached her. "Hi, Mrs. Rizzo, I'm Doctor Hurley. We've got your husband stable for the moment. But we are going to admit him for a battery of tests. Something doesn't mesh here. As I'm sure you're aware. He's on his way to one of the wards. He's pretty sedated. You may as well go home. You look exhausted. Rest assured we'll take care of him." "Thank you, doctor. If there's a change will you please let me know?" "Of course, Mrs. Rizzo, that's a given."

Alone in the quiet of her dark home, Ellen shook with fear. Her husband and daughter were all she had. Both she and Frank had been orphans. There was no one else. Tears coursing down her face, she gazed at a religious photo hanging on a foyer wall. Please God, Please spare my husband. He's a good man." Exhausted, she collapsed on the bed falling into a restless sleep.

The ringing phone roused her from slumber. Gazing at the night clock it read 6:30 am. Fearfully, she clutched the phone, "Hello," she whispered hoarsely. "Hello, Mrs. Rizzo, Dr. Hurley here. I am sorry to call at this hour, but I must inform you your husband's condition had deteriorated very quickly. I believe we're losing him. Can you come? He's in room 8W 35." With a shriek she dropped the phone, threw on her worn brown jacket and flew out the door and quickly entered the old Ford. Throwing caution to the wind, she sped towards Hartford Hospital.

The rain pelted the soft earth, monuments to the dead, their life stories etched in their souls, stood guard at the gravesite. Ellen, holding Little Lisa's hand, ignored the tears cascading down her face. A sparse crowd was in attendance numb with grief. Ellen hardly heard the priest's burial words. Life was now in turmoil. Ellen and Lisa alone in a cruel world and would be forced to survive. Ellen didn't know how but whispered a silent prayer directed towards her husband's humble casket. "Frank, I love you. I'll take care of our Lisa." Turning from the grave, she dropped a single red rose. It settled in the center of the casket. Raining, it gave the appearance this lonely rose was crying and taking her daughter's hand in tears, departed this quiet refuge.

Days turned into weeks. Ellen surviving on insurance money sat lonely and depressed hours on end in the small living room. She was stunned by the fast moving cancer which devoured her beloved Frank and took him prematurely from her. There was enough money for a time but eventually Ellen knew she would have to find work, with little skill she contemplated returning to school. This thought enthralled her, for she'd always dreamed of being a nurse. "Shit!" she exclaimed to an empty room, "that's just what I'm going to do." Ellen enrolled in the Hartford Hospital School of Nursing. She was trying her best to cope and to make a life for her and little Lisa. At times the moment would catch her and tears would burst forth. But she'd take a deep breath and march on. There was no choice. Survival was now paramount in her mind.

Ellen was busy baking a cake. Her daughter was to have school chums over for a visit and a sweet treat was what the doctor ordered. The screen door barged open. It was little Lisa. "Mommy can I ride my bike." "Yes, but stay on the side walk and don't go far, okay angel." With that little Lisa scampered happily out the door.

Humming softly to herself, Ellen was taking the baked cake from the oven. She was startled by the piercing sound of sirens resounding in the immediate vicinity. A dreadful premonition encompassed her being. Flying out of the house she ran to the street facing north on Campfield Ave. She observed flashing lights and a large crowd fearfully looking left and right. Little Lisa was no where in sight fear propelled Ellen towards the flashing lights. As she drew near, she saw several police vehicles, a fire engine and an ambulance. She gasped in horror, lying in the road was the twisted green metal of a small bicycle. My God! It's my Angel! Oh God! OH! NO! NO! NO! This can't be, she screamed!" Approaching the scene a hysterical Ellen was restrained by two police officers. She could see a small body lying on the gurney in the ambulance. Screaming insanely at the officers, she broke free and climbed into the ambulance. Attendants were working feverishly on the small figure. Ellen could see she was breathing but blood oozed from several injuries and she was unconscious. An officer entered the ambulance, "ma'am, is this your daughter?" "Oh yes, officer, yes, "is she okay?" "Well, she's banged up, some, but should be alright. The ambulance is about ready to head to the hospital. Will you ride with them?" "Oh yes, but my house is unsecured." "No problem, what's your address?" "29 Campfield, officer," "Okay, we'll secure the house for you." "But my keys are on the counter." "No sweat, little lady, we'll bring you the keys." "Okay, thank you so much, you're so kind, thank you."

Once again Ellen found herself pacing in the ER waiting room. It was a repeat of several months ago when she lost her husband so tragically. Tears welled in her eyes as her heart pumped in fear. She could not stand to lose her angel. She screamed startling several people in the waiting room. "You wouldn't be that unkind God! She bellowed. Have a heart show mercy, that's what you're all about, aren't you?"

The door burst open and a young female in a white smock approached her. "Mrs. Rizzo, I'm Dr Shirley, your daughter is okay. She's banged up and has a compound fracture to her right hip, but in time should do okay. It will be a long process with a lot of rehab. Her youth should get her through. She'll need to be admitted for some time. She needs care and rest and the love only you can give her." Ellen hugged Dr. Shirley and together they entered ER 2 where a teary eyed Lisa smiled with joy upon seeing her mother.

Ellen was enjoying a hot tea, at the table, when her doorbell buzzed softly. "Hmmm, who could that be?" For it was getting dark and a lone in the house she was apprehensive about answering the door. Peeking out of the window corner, she observed a white police cruiser idling in front of the house. Ellen caught movement at the door and could see a burley police officer standing at the door. Once again he pressed the doorbell. Ellen responded quickly opening the door to allow the police officer entry. Officer Joe Hubiac stood transfixed in the doorway removing his hat he simply stated, "good evening, Mrs. Rizzo I'm officer Joe Hubiac, of the Hartford Police, Accident and Investigative Unit, I'm here to fill you in on the circumstances resulting in the accident involving your daughter. May I please come in?" Ellen somewhat flushed was able to stammer, "Why yes, officer. Please come in. Why don't you sit in the recliner? It's old, but cozy and comfortable. Hubiac headed directly to the recliner. As he positioned himself comfortably, Ellen stated, "I've just boiled some water, would you care for some hot tea?" "Why, yes ma'am, that's very kind of you and if you wouldn't mind, could you add cream and two sugars please." "Can do, officer, it will be just a moment." As Ellen prepared refreshments, Hubiac scanned this humble home, noting the furniture was cheap but clean. The house appeared to be neat and fresh and there was an old bookcase in a corner that was the refuge to numerous books and family portraits. Yes he thought this is a comfortable cabin.

His scrutiny was broken by Ellen's sudden appearance carrying a tray with two cups of steaming tea and assorted cookies. All she had at her disposal. Seated across from each other, Hubiac began the conversation. Mrs. Rizzo, I'm sorry for your daughter's injuries. They appear to be long term in the healing process. Thank God she's alive. The motorist responsible for the accident is an 82 year old man, who is a diabetic and apparently suffered a seizure propelling him onto the sidewalk where he collided with your daughter while riding her bike. He is also at Hartford Hospital. He went into diabetic shock, but doctors feel he'll be okay. Now due to the circumstances, I hesitate to ticket the old gent. But I need to know if you're comfortable with this decision. I am going to submit a report to D.M.V. requesting they terminate his license. I believe this course of action to be the correct avenue to take. What's your feeling, if I may ask? Ellen had listened attentively, with an awkward smile, she responded in a soft voice, "Officer you're the professional. Whatever your decision, it's okay by me, my little girl alive and that's what matters and only that.

Hubiac smiling back, thank you ma'am, that's kind and generous on your part. However, I will give you some sound advice. "Your daughter's injuries are serious, as we both know, there's a chance she'll never walk normally. I pray that's not the case, but you must prepare to protect her's and your future. The operation of the vehicle has good insurance; if I were you I'd silicate the services of a lawyer. Your little girl will need financial security down the road. Think long and hard Mrs. Rizzo, no one likes the words sue but, in this case it's imperative for you both."

Ellen eyes, down cast, stared long and hard at the floor. Her response was low almost inaudible, yes, officer, I believe you're right. My life's been in turmoil for several months. What with the loss of my husband and now this frightening event. Thanks for the sound advice. Hubiac studied Ellen for a long moment. "I hope you don't mind my asking. And I don't mean to pry, what happened to your husband, Lisa's dad?" "Oh, he died tragically of cancer. You know officer we just don't know here. He was full of energy and excitement to build his little girl a dollhouse in the back yard. It will never happen. The materials are still piled in the yard covered by a tarp. There was just the three of us. We have no relatives' so I guess the materials will rot as they sit or I'll try to sell them. Oh, I'm sorry officer. I did not mean to dump my troubles on your shoulders. Brushing away tears she asked more tea, sir? Officer Hubiac sat quietly, "No ma'am thank you. I have to get back on the line. I wish you the best here's my card should you have any future questions. Please heed my advice. Protect you and your little girl. Sorry for your troubles." With that Officer Hubiac let himself out into the damp night. His heart was heavy as he made his way towards his waiting cruiser. Entering same, he turned the ignition, "shit," he thought, "there's always grief in this fucking business, always."

Officer Hubiac pulled into the all night diner. He had spotted unit 42 parked. He knew this was LaPore. He liked this sergeant; felt maybe he could find some solace regarding the sad lonely woman he'd left sitting there with nothing but memories. LaPore was enjoying a coffee and kidding the waitress about how it tasted like diesel oil. He loved to tease and could take it back. "Hey Joe," barked LaPore. "Hitch you ass to a seat. How about some java? You look like shit, like you've seen a ghost or something or maybe you looked in a mirror." "Aw, sarge, your no beauty you know. I hear when you walk into a men's room, all the toilets flush, is that true?" "Fuck you Joe. At least, I don't fuck a duck. Truthfully Joe, what's up? You look down and drawn. What's eating at you?" "Aw sarge, you know this fucking job. I just left a nice little lady at 29 Campfield; her little girl got fucked up in an accident yesterday. Car vs. bike, bike lost. That little girl has probably suffered a life time of injuries and get this the dad died three months ago and was in the process of building a doll house for the kid. He got cancer and like a ravaged bull that exploded, result, doll house was never started. The materials are still in the yard rotting. Shit, this job sucks, they've got no relatives, nobody to help I'll tell you sarge regular folks, they just don't get it; don't see this shit on a regular basis. I'm hurting inside for that mother and kid, hurting."

LaPore lit up a lucky exhaled blue smoke towards the ceiling. "You know Joe, your right. This job is mostly grief but sometimes out of grief can come some joy. You say this woman has no one, not true old trooper. She's got us. Let's rustle up some of the boys and see what we can do."

Saturday morning came quickly. Ellen had prepared herself an egg sandwich and coffee. She was excited for she was to see Lisa this afternoon and had brought her a stuffed rabbit. Walking to the kitchen sink, she was surprised when two blue and white cruisers pulled into her driveway. Six officers in jump suits began removing tools from the trunks. Saws, hammers, and nails suddenly appeared, as well as other instruments. One of the officers she recognized as the cop who'd come to her home two nights ago. Exiting through the door, she greeted the officers. Hi, Officer Hubiac, what's up and why are you guys here." "Well Ellen, if I may call you that? These lugs need a lesson in carpentry. So with your permission we're going to erect that doll house." Ellen gasped aloud tears cascaded down her face. "Oh you blue angels. Oh go for it. Oh, thank God. I can't thank you enough."

Throughout the day, the sound of cutting and banging resounded through the neighborhood. Slowly, but proudly the doll house came to life. Between short breaks of coffee served by Ellen and smokes, the labor continued. Finally at 4:00 p.m, the doll house stood tall. It possessed a certain beauty. Officer's Trevost, Ray, Hubiac, LaPore and Bobby Z, admired their hard work. Laughing and slapping each other's backs, each taking credit for performing the bulk of labor. It was good natured fun a job done as a labor of love. Ellen Rizzo stood on her porch and tears flowing down her cheeks. Her husband's dream stood proud and gleaming. She felt his spirit nearby and knew he was pleased and would now rest easy. As the boys in blue finished their task, they affixed a police logo to one side of the house. It was a round Hartford police logo with the words "Post Phobias Nublia" entwined in same the Latin words transcribed meaning "after the storm, the sun." On the front of the house, placed over the entry way, was affixed a three by five metal disk. Etched on same were the words, in memory of Frank Rizzo, husband, father, and a good man who left his mark. As the group of officers stood affixed a crisp salute to Mrs. Rizzo and then enter their blue and whites and in a plume of dust were gone.

Mrs. Rizzo would never forget this act of kindness. Her daughter would spend many a happy hours at play in this structure of love. Yes, they were thankful and though the media or a few others would know of this generous act, what no one knew was the peace and tranquility that embossed the officer's hearts for the rest of their days. Until this day the doll house still stands in a home's yard in California with a red rose affixed to its roof.

Chapter 17

A cold rain pelted the parking lot of Arthur's Drug, forcing patrons to move quickly to and from the store to their waiting vehicles. Rapid like water cascaded about the lot carrying debris and depositing the contents in the gutter of Sigourney Street. Traffic on the street was snarled due to the deluge like rain which restricted visibility throughout the city. Flash flood warnings had been advised throughout the city. Several streets submerged in two to three feet of water. Police and fire personnel were kept busy responding to numerous emergency situations. Downed wires stalled vehicles with occupants trapped within. Numerous streets were closed due to flooding and traffic needed to be deviated in several areas.

Jerome Murphy and Willie Byron exited the rear of a store burdened with large bundles of garbage, which was to be deposited in the large metal dumpster located in the North West portion of the parking lot. Moving quickly so as to escape most of the deluge, they arrived at the dumpster wet and sour, both bitching that the garbage could have waited until the storm had subsided. "Hey Jerome, fuck this, shit man!" yelled Willie. That manager, he be crazy. His ass should be out here." "Yeah bro, he's a mother fucker, alright. Treats us like shit. We'll fuck it let's just get it done." "Hey Jerome, wait a minute, you hears that?" "What man, what you hearing, mother fucker, sounds like a cat" "Yeah, man there's a cat in there, could be wild or something. "Shit, don't open the door, the mother fucker come outta there like a raged lion. Could chew us up." "Yeah Willie, you be right something in there howling. I don't know." "Hey, that not be a cat. Wait a minute, sounds like a baby crying." "Yeah, that's what that sound be. It's a mother fucking baby." "Willie, you be crazy. How a baby get in that shit hole?" "God damn Jerome, it didn't walk in, some mother fucker put it there. You go get us a flashlight and have that dip shit manager call the police. Move boy, we got us a small person in trouble in this tub of shit."

Willie flew into the store approaching his manager, John Drew. He blurted, "Mr. Drew, Jerome and me, we thinks there's a baby in the dumpster. Hears crying and gurgling sounds needs us a flashlight, can't see inside that shit hole." "Willie, is you on crack or pot? Come on, a baby you say? That's crazy!" "It may be true, Mr. Drew, you comes see for yourself."

John Drew stared hard at Willie. His actions telling him something, grabbing a flashlight the two headed to John Jerome at the dumpster. Together they opened the large heavy metal door. Drew ran the flashlight back and forth over the large mounds of garbage. A small movement to the right of the door caught Drew's attention. Suddenly a loud cry emitted from a small clump of blankets. "My God!" Drew exclaimed. It is a baby. Jerome was quick, immediately jumping into the much to retrieve the small vulnerable mound. "Wait Jerome!" Yelled Drew, don't disturb anything. There may be evidence for the cops. "Fuck the cops," snarled Jerome. "This baby been exposed in this shit. He gets exposure and be dead. Let's get him inside, warm and dry. "Willie, go call the cops!" ordered Drew, Now! Use my office phone." Willie stumbled several times enroute to the office. Finally dripping wet and excitable, he retrieved the phone and quickly dialed the Hartford Police. The phone rang and rang. Come on mother fuckers answer the God Damn phone. Finally a female operator came on and in a tired voice stammered, "Hartford Police." Willie explode at once into words, "God Damn, you best get the cops over here to Arthurs. We got's a baby in the dumpster. Yeah that's right a baby and it be alive for now." "What's your name, sir?" "Willie, my name's Willie. The police will see me there. Hurry, it be in the back of the store in the parking lot." Willie dropped the phone and ran back to the dumpster where Drew and Jerome now had rescued the baby from the dumpster and were sprinting to the rear door of the store. All three crashed through the door shouting, We've got a cold wet baby! Gather anything warm! Startled customers gave way to employees who struck out through the store in search of warm items for the baby.

"Unit 16 and 14, attention 43." (line sergeant) "Author's Drug, 190 Farmington. Make it a check welfare for the moment. Report of a baby found in the dumpster. Rear lot, caller reports infant is alive. An ambulance and fire department also being dispatched. First unit on scene advise as to situation." "10-4 unit 16." "Roger unit 14" "Unit 43 10-4 on the way."

Drew, Willie and Jerome, had tenderly placed the infant in a warm plastic box wrapped in blankets. The baby was lethargic and making small mewing sounds and was covered in grit. An attempt had been made to clean the infant as much as possible, but on the advice of a nurse shopping in the store limited, their ministrations so as to reduce any chance of injury or exposure. As the three males and assisting nurse, cared for the infant. Three cruisers pulled into the rear lot. "Unit 16, dispatch." "10-4 units 15, 14, and 43. arrival 11:15." Drew pointed at Willie. "Go tell the cops we're in here. By the pharmacy. They're headed towards the dumpster. Hurry up, Willie! No time to waste. Ain't got that luxury, rather this baby don't!"

Willie ran outside. Out of breath, he yelled to the cops, officers in the store, we've the baby in the store. Over by the pharmacy. Officer's Smith, Davis and Sergeant LaPore, dashed into the store and approached Drew and Jerome. With Willie at their side, they observed a small infant in the plastic box. LaPore grabbed his portable, "Unit 43, what's the eta of that ambulance?" "Dispatch unit 43, they've just given an arrival. "Oh yeah, I see them. Thanks dispatch, and dispatch be advised we do have an abandoned infant here on scene. Notify the watch commander and detective division. Have the dicks respond like yesterday." "Dispatch 10-4 unit 43. Be advised juvenile division is enroute to your location. Detective division are mired in a triple shooting." "Unit 43 10-4 dispatch. In form Juvenile infant enroute to Saint Francis. Have them report here first." "Dispatch 10-4 unit 43 are you set for the moment?" "Affirmative dispatch. Dumpster secured and what minimal witnesses are sequestered in the managers office. Juvenile dicks will see them there." "Dispatch, ah, ah, juvenile states they'll going to proceed to hospital first." "Unit 43 dispatch belay that, inform those detectives, I want them here. I've locked down the store. Anyone and everyone who's been here for the last hour is being detained. Tell them to get their asses here. The baby can't tell them anything for Christ's sake." "Unit 43 off. We have used enough air time." "Dispatch unit 43, your message has been copied. Juvenile enroute to you KCA 330 the Hartford Police 11:25."

LaPore had assigned officer Davis to secure the dumpster. He then ordered Officer Smith to detain all customers currently in the store and to place the establishment in lock down mode. At the moment, he was sitting across from Drew, Willie, and Jerome. They could volunteer little information other then finding the infant. None had observed any suspicious activity by the dumpster. LaPore checked his watch. The ambulance had whisked the baby away immediately. The fire department had an engine standing by the dumpster illuminated by it's powerful search lights. Crime scene tape ringed the dumpster. LaPore thought long and hard hoping he'd covered all bases. Reaching for the phone, he dialed St. Francis and asked for and was connected to the ER. Explaining who he was and was told by a tired nurse that the rain baby was currently being examined and receiving nutrients through an I.V. line. She could offer nothing further at the time. LaPore thanked her and disconnected. Looking at the ceiling, he uttered to no one particular. "What make of animal could do this, Damn this world is full of shit heads, monsters and demons.

Lieutenant Mike Donroy, juvenile division commander sat at his desk reviewing the report forwarded to him on the rain baby. The name designated by the circumstances which the baby was found in a major north eastern, in a dumpster. "Damn," he thought. "I'd thought I'd seen it all." He set the report in front of him on his grey steel police issued desk. Had noted the infant had been stabilized and currently housed in the pediatric ward at St. Francis Hospital. His two detectives, Bradley and Jones had interviewed a dozen potential witnesses to no avail. No one saw or heard anything. He drummed his fingers on his desk perplexed. His division was up to its ass in cases, three on going sexual assaults, two endangered run a ways and a suspicious child torture. Also four child abuse cases. "Shit, what the fuck?" he muttered, need some help here in a bad way. Reaching for the phone, he dialed ext 200. Chief of Detective's Reynolds, answered on the third ring. Chief Mike began, I need to draft a couple of guys from other plain clothes divisions. He explained his dilemma. Chief Reynolds listened sympathetically, "Mike no can do. Vice and narco has a big sweep going with the feds. Homicide is in a gun fire of its own, three homicides, four rapes, and last night a multiple shooting. Burglary is involved in a sting operation with the statees. Maybe patrol can lend you a couple silver shields. Let me call Dellaher and run interference for you. Okay, I'll get back to you A.S.A.P." "Okay chief, but at least try to get me some experienced silver shields. And thanks chief, the line went dead as the chief disconnected."

Donroy set back looking at nothing for his mind was in overdrive. Have to contact DCYF, Welfare Department, see if we ascertain what or if any of their clients were pregnant. Hit the street walkers, they may know something. God Damn it someone does. "Shit, you can't drop a baby and business as usual." The knock on Donroy's door startled him. "Come in! He bellowed. Officer's Trevost and Ray entered the office. "Good morning Lou. We've been assigned to you on a temp basis. Captain Henrich told us you'd bring us up to snuff. We're here and awaiting your orders. "Damn, Donroy," thought Reynolds acts quick like lightening, and he's got me two good guys. There is a God. He smiled at the two officers. Pull up a seat, troopers for the smoking lamp is lit. Let me fill you in and bring you up to date. You're going to be busy beating the bushes and burning shoe leather.

Both officers leaned forward and listened attentively as the Lieutenant brought them up to date, on rain baby's case. He informed them that he'd already contacted DCYF and the Welfare Department and they'd informed him that case workers would be checking their caseloads, as too pregnant females and get back to him. The Lieutenant instructed the two officers to canvas the area. Maybe just maybe they'd hit pay dirt. The Lieutenant then dismissed them with a curt nod. As they exited his office, he watched them with a bemused look, thinking they'd need the help of St. Michael's Legion to solve this case.

Office's Trevost and Ray spent the first three days of their assignment canvassing apartment buildings in the Sigourney Street area with frugal results. They then turned their attention to the street, working nights and badgering the hookers, dopeies, homo's pimps and just plain old Joe citizens. Again with negative results DCF and the Welfare Department had checked with the Lieutenant with negative results. All their reported pregnant clients were healthy and staying the course.

The officers were frustrated. They'd interviewed a hundred people and still the barrel was empty. They'd left word with informants to keep a sharp eye and attentive ear. The days passed then weeks. After three months, there wasn't a clue. Rain baby, it seemed arrived with the storm. Numerous tips were checked out to no avail. It was beginning to appear that perhaps a hysterical woman in transit may have disposed of her burden there in the dumpster. But the officers had to thread carefully. For this was the appearance someone purposely gave off. Trevost and Ray returned and questioned Drew, Willie and Jerome repeatedly. "Did it appear that the baby was thrown into the dumpster or placed gently? Was the baby entwined in the garbage or on top? Was the baby wet or dry? Did they see any nervous white woman loitering that night as rain baby was Caucasian. The interviews were depressing. They were getting no where. What little leads they had, when followed up they led to dead ends. Pressure was mounting the media and sympathetic public clamoring for justice. The demand to find the monster mother of this defensive child was escalating to a frenzied level.

Lieutenant Donroy had added two of his detectives to assist Trevost and Ray. Reacting to the intense pressure, surrounding P.D.'s had been checked hoping for leads directing them to missing pregnant females, nothing. Results were all too frequently being repetitive and negative. Trevost and Ray were alone in the juvenile division office. The tick tock of the wall clock agitated them. They were busy pouring over past interviews, laboring to see if there was something, anything that may have eluded them. The hour was late. They were about to wrap up this night's tour, as they headed for the door, the shrill ringing of the phone stopped them in their tracks. Trevost walked to the phone, picking it up softly whispered, "juvenile division, Officer Trevost." The phone was silent then a soft female voice spoke up, "you the man working the rain baby case?" "Yes ma'am." "Well, then you listen and you listen good, you way off base. You need to go to 38 Atwood Street, 2ⁿᵈ floor, there be a young white girl lives' with an older dude. You see she be frail, looking bad, health ain't good. The dudes no good, made that girl dump that baby. You males sure you go see her in the morning sometime. The dude, his name be Ben. Ain't there then, this girl frightened, needs help, her name is Samantha. Go soon, talking crazy about killing herself. You hear me officer?" "Yes ma'am, Can I have your name?" "Please, you don't need to know that, you just do what I says. You solve case and help that girl and maybe put that mother fucker, Ben away, he's the monster, not the girl!" The phone went dead. Trevost locked eyes with Ray, "we may have just got the key to the lock, my friend. Tomorrow we open the door."

Lieutenant Donroy arrived at his office promptly at 07:30 hours, heading directly to his desk, anxious to study the previous night's reports. Setting down his coffee, he began perusing the unusual reports submitted by patrol personnel. Satisfied there was nothing requiring his immediate attention, he gathered reports logged by his investigators. One caught his eye immediately. He studied the report at length, left on his desk by Officers Trevost and Ray. The contents brought him to full attention.

"Sir, at 11:35 p.m. on last night's watch, these officers received an anonymous phone call relating to a young girl, residing at 38 Atwood Street, 2ⁿᵈ floor. The caller implied said female was in trouble and had been in a pregnant state. Female no longer pregnant and no baby observed in her surroundings. Caller feels female is being held against her will and stated has been severely physically abused. The undersigned will be reporting for duty at 0800 hours to await further instruction and orders."

Don Roy sat back in his chair. Lit up a Marlboro and contemplated the information he'd just digested. Grabbing his daily personnel roll, he noted two of his detectives would be tied up in court and another was out of state on an ongoing investigation. Yet still, he had two others on loan to the state police on a mutual investigation involving a pedophile.

Shit, he had no one to assist the officers. He'd have to trust their experience and street savvy. It was his dilemma and they'd have to go it alone. "Fuck," he muttered. *It is what it is.* They've handled themselves professionally these past months and had dedicated themselves and spent long hours displaying their intelligence and zeal to resolve the rain baby case. He'd let them run with it for he had no choice. They'd either make it to the end zone or punt.

"Well sir," began Ray. "We're going to check out 38 Atwood and get a feel on things. Ascertain if there is a young female at that location and take it from there. Hell's bells, sir it's the only solid lead we've got maybe we stumbled on a break. Whatever, we'll take it. Maybe lady lucks smiling on us!" Donroy locked eyes with both officers. "Okay," he blurted. "Check it out but go slow and easy. This girl is more than likely scared shitless. Try not to push her into the abyss. Tread softly and make use of that street sense you possess. Alright I'm sick of looking at your ugly faces. Do your thing and good luck. Oh and remember, there's that dude Ben. Use caution here. We don't know who he is as of yet. But, he fucking well will know who you are. One more thing I've checked with dispatch. Sergeant LaPore's in charge of that sector. Check with him. Let him know what's going down. Cover your flanks. He'll supply you with whatever assistance you may require. Make damn sure you reach out to him. Okay, scram I'm busy."

Trevost (aka Dirt-bag), and Ray signed on the line with dispatch and were logged on 09:15 hours. Dirt-bag, riding shot gun reached for the radio mike. Compressing same, he uttered, "unit 254 to unit 42," a moment's pause and then the loud response came. "Unit 42 on go unit 254" "Hey Sarge, can we meet up with you somewhere?" "That's a 10-4, 254, name your pleasure." "Sarge, how about the Chicken Coupé parking lot?" "10-4 254 eta of about five, okay" "10-4 42 meet in five 254 out"

Unit 254 was already parked rear in facing Asylum Street, when LaPore arrived. Pulling alongside, LaPore quipped, "morning shit stains, what's up?" "Hey, Sarge uttered Dirt-bag, still playing with your rubber duck." "Fuck you Dirt-bag. Come on give it up, what's going down?" "Wow, a serious sergeant, we have here Ray, very serious. I'm concerned he's not getting laid or his assholes on fire." LaPore laughed softly. "Dirt-bag as to your first observation, check with your old lady, bet she was smiling this morning." "Damn Dirt-bag, snorted Ray; he just squashed your balls." Dirt-bag laughed. "Awe, fuck him, we all know stripers are pricks. "Okay Lance, here's the scoop; we're going to 38 Atwood Street, 2ⁿᵈ floor. Got a tip that rain baby's mommy may be held up there. Not sure how good the information is, but we're going to nose around and see how it plays out. Either we piece the puzzle together today or we don't. We thought we'd bring you in on the deal. LaPore lit up a Lucky. "Umph, 38 Atwood, we've been there on several occasions. Listen, let's get unit 16 over here. That's Jardin; he knows that area like he knows his old lady's ass. Let's not go in blind. If memory serves me, there's a big dude lives there. Bad ass fucker got a yellow sheet as long as your nose. Dirt-bag, hang tight let me get sixteen in on this." "Yeah okay, needle dick responded Dirt-bag, no disrespect intended Mon Sergeant."

LaPore, Jardin, Trevost and Ray, had been buds for years. Now the four in serious mode had plans for the handling of 38 Atwood Street. Jardin had confirmed LaPore's fears that a bad ass dude named Ben Oliver resided at that address. He had a rap sheet for assault, injury or risk of injury, sexual assaults and violation of the Mann Act. He loved young girls and was known for pimping and terrorizing his girls. Ben Oliver was in to sex slavery and was also known to carry a fire arm. LaPore had the floor. "Okay dick, I've notified dispatch to put you off the line. You and unit 14 hover in the area of Atwood Street. Dirt-bag and Ray will do their thing. I'll also play the area, but let's keep the blue and whites out of sight. I want to surprise that asshole Oliver and not the other way around. We all Set? Everyone knows what to do? Okay, let's move and Dirt-bag, Lou, be careful. No tombstone courage here. If this Ben guy appears we're in a fight, right Dick?" "Yup, you got that right, Sarge, retorted Jardin." "Guys before we set up I just want to instill one thing I learned from Major Rome, the old state police Major Crimes Commander. He said to me once, young sergeant, remember the courts protect the rights of the accused; it's our job to protect the rights of the victim. He was right on. Let's hope this lead proves true so rain baby can grown and rest easy. Keep your backs to the wall, okay let's roll."

Dirt-bag and Ray headed to 38 Atwood Street. Unit 16, Jardin and unit 14, Paul Reyes took position in the rear of a doctor's office at Collins and Atwood. This place them in a 30 second arrival time should the shit hit the fan. They were 254's immediate back up and had chosen a strategic position. Unit 42, LaPore played the area keeping close while conducting roving patrol. Dirt-bag and Ray parked their dark rusted unmarked in front of 46 Atwood, electing to walk the 100 yards to 38 Atwood in hopes of disguising their presence should Oliver occupy the apartment or return suddenly. Three steps and they were on the front porch.

Ray rang the door bell to the name of Oliver located on the second floor. Several minutes elapsed with no response. Ray hit the bell several times at last they heard the creaking of a stairway for someone was responding. Both officers held their breath. The door suddenly burst open. Standing before them was a petite, very young girl. She stood all of 5 feet and maybe and it was a maybe weighed in at 100 lbs, perhaps less. Dirtbag displayed his shield and I.D. "Good morning, police. We're hoping you can assist us. We're looking for Samantha. Would that be you?" The girls eyes lit up with fear. A slight tremor observed by the officers. At first she stood there mute, eyes wide and moisture covered her bottom lip. With a soft voice she finally responded, "yes sir. My name is Samantha. Why are you hare? How can I help you?" Ray took the lead, "Could we go inside? We need information. We believe you can give us. We don't need nosey neighbors eves dropping." "Ah, okay. Come on in. But my apartment is a mess. I apologize in advance. I don't get much company." All three ascended the stairs and entered a dark musty smelly apartment. The officers were greeted by a stench of urine and human sweat. They were in the living room which contained a torn dilapidated couch, a broken recliner and a table top TV with the screen smashed out. One picture adorned the walls. A poor replica of a Reuben nude. The canvas torn and shredded. The rug on the floor soiled and pocked mocked with various stains which contributed to the fowl odor that permeated throughout the interior of the apartment. She closed the door behind them and went and sat on the couch and waited silently. She appeared to have a look of resignation on her face. Both officers took note of the horrific bruises on both her arms. Also it was obvious she was attempting to disguise a black eye with much to much make up. It was caked on her face and her upper lip appeared swollen and she made a feeble attempt to conceal her nervousness. Again Ray took the lead, Dirt-bag had hung back. Remaining by the door, "honey are you in trouble here? We're not here to hurt you, trust and believe, we want to help you. Will you let us?" Samantha stared long and hard at Ray. Her breath came in small gasps. Her trembling had grown more profound. She emitted a long hollow sigh and then it began. A cascade of tears streamed down her cheeks. She emitted a long low wail and covered her face with both hands. Words of sadness exploded through hidden hands. "I'm no good, God hats me. The world will hate me and worse my little son will grow to hate me." Ray waited patiently. In a whisper he asked, "your son, where is he?" She dropped her hands and with a bemused smile gazed deep into Ray's eyes. He shuddered. It was as though she was peering into his very soul. Softly and sadly she answered, "you know you found him in that dumpster. May God forgive me."

Ray stared at Dirt-bag. The room was quiet only passing vehicles on the street broke the stillness. Ray speaking softly, "Samantha, How old are you?" With a shrug she answered, "I'm 15, but I feel 70. My soul is dead officer." She stood and screamed louder. "My soul is dead! I'm going to Hell. Do you hear me? I'm destined for Hell!" Ray continued with his questioning. "Do you live hear alone?" "Ha," she laughed bitterly, "no way. I live with an animal. I live with Ben Oliver and entertain his friends. He's a pig. He's the Devil and he's going to kill me for talking to you. That bastard took my baby! He threw him in the dumpster. Threatened to cut me up if I said anything." "Honey, where did you have the baby? What hospital?" asked Ray. "Hospital," she roared. "Right here. This was my ward. There on the couch. The pig kept me prisoner, When I began to show. He wanted no one to know. Tired to give me an abortion. Hurt me so gave up. Said he didn't want to bruise my flesh. Was making to much bread, because I'm young and tender. Beat me daily and forced me to fuck and suck all kinds of men. All pigs, with no heart or soul." She was near high-strung and Ray attempted to sooth her. It was now paramount to calm her.

Suddenly the rear door burst open. Standing there was an apparition from hell. Ben Oliver, 6'1, 250 lbs of muscle, he stood his eyes blazing hate as he glazed at the three some. He had a swarthy complexion, pock mocks map on his face, eyes of coal that emitted evil. He held a large hunting knife in his right hand. He growled, "who the fuck are you two assholes? You here for some pussy. Show the bread or best you beat feet out of here." Dirt-bag stepped into the middle of the living room. "Asshole! You listen and listen real good, we're the police! and right now I'm looking at a big piece of shit! You want to dance, shit for brains! Leap like a frog otherwise sit the fuck down and shut the fuck up!" Ray had grabbed his portable. "254 to unit 42. We've found rain baby's momma and Satan has just arrived from hell." LaPore responded immediately, 10-4 254. Unit 16 and 14, did you copy?" "10-4 42 on the way." Very good responded LaPore in 42. My eta one minute."

Oliver stood in the doorway transfixed for the moment. Reaching behind he retrieved a large hunting knife concealed in his belt. With a loud snort and demonic look in his eyes, Oliver charged at Dirt-bag. But Officer Trevost, now in defensive mode was prepared as Oliver came at him. He side stepped placing in left foot, so as to trip Oliver and negate his insane attack. Oliver tripped over Dirt-bags foot stumbled losing his balance. Falling forward in a slash the powerful Dirt-bag reached out with his left hand grabbing Oliver by the hair. With his right hand he reached around and locked on to his belt. Using Oliver's momentum, Dirt-bag ran him towards the wall. The officers adrenaline in full rush, he threw him forward. Oliver was propelled toward the window. Screaming there was a raw shattering of glass and he was airborne. Tumbling in a free fall two stories to the grassy landscape below.

LaPore had just arrived on scene when he gazed astonished as a body flew out of the window and landed feet from him. LaPore sprinted to the whimpering pone body of Oliver screaming in pain and fear. LaPore now joined by Officer's Jardin and Reyes, approached cautiously, LaPore kicking away the hunting knife. Oliver began screaming, "that mother fucking cop! He threw me out the window!" LaPore grinning, "Don't lie to me you piece of shit. You were attempting to escape. Thought you were superman and could fly." Turning to Reyes, he ordered, call for a 10-10 (ambulance) then pick up beat 23, he's to go to the hospital with this asshole and hug him tight." Dirt-bag leaning threw the window, yelled down to his brother officers, "Nice job good apprehension. The prick thought he could fly. Hey, Sarge when your secure down there, see us up here. We've rain baby's momma." "Okay Dirt-bag. Give me 10. Oliver now under police guard was transported by Maple Hill ambulance, where it was ascertained he suffered two broken ribs and his right shoulder broken in several places. Admitted, he couldn't take a piss without a blue solder smothering him with kindness.

Samantha was brought to police headquarters where juvenile detectives along with a DCYF worker unraveled a story which was demonic in its magnitude. Samantha, 15 years of age, had been born in Chicago. Her father left one day never to return. The mother was an alcoholic and was seldom home. Finally she to disappeared one night and walked away unseen never to look back. She etched out a living on the streets using her young body to forge for food and occasionally a cheap motel room. Most of her young life was spent in alleys. The rear seat of automobiles where sex hungry men from all walks of life satisfied their lust with her youthful body. Eventually she'd saved enough money to travel to New York City, where she continued to pry her trade seeking shelter in bus terminals. Grand Central Station, under railroad trestles and in cheap smelly hotels with men of all ages and creeds. She related how her life was filled with despair and fear and loneliness, until one day she was approached by Oliver in a grey hound terminal. He had promised her the world, a good life, hungry for love and affection she reached for the dangling bait.

Oliver brought her to Hartford where he began a ritual of beating her. Forcing her into prostitution. Her dream world collapsed. She'd become his sex slave and was to terrified to seek help. Alone and forlorn, she'd felt abandoned by what she perceived to be a sick society. She'd become pregnant by whom she had no idea. It was Oliver who took the baby and dumped the little soul in the dumpster. Oliver when released stood trial and pleaded guilty to numerous counts of assaults, engaging in prostitution and sex for hire, injury or risk of injury to a minor, kidnapping, violation of the Mann Act and assault 2 on a police officer. An unforgiving judge handed down a sentence of 20 years with no chance of parole.

The belabored Samantha was placed in the care of the House of Good Shepard. Rain baby was given up for adoption by young Samantha. The decision made after a tearful reunion by mother and son in the chapel of the House of Good Shepard. The baby was whisked away by Catholic Family Services and placed with adoptive parents. Their identities known only to God.

Samantha remained in the residence of the House of Good Shepard till she reached the ripe age of eighteen. She was then encouraged to vacate the premises. Alone on the streets again, with no friends and no where to go she wondered the streets of Hartford, Eventually finding her way to the Buckley Bridge where on a dark rainy night, her soul tortured by remorse, cast aside by an apathetic society, she jumped into the night. Her tragic young life brought to an end in the frigid water's of the Connecticut River. A tragic ending that occurs all to frequently across the land. May she and all the tortured souls who have joined her rest in peace.

Chapter 18

Tony Fontana and his wife Gail exited the Franklin Italian Club. They'd just completed a dinner of fine Italian cuisine and several glasses of aged wine with several friends. However, they'd had to cut the evening short as Gail had an early day at her workplace in the morning. Breathing in the crisp night air, they headed for their vehicle. A very handsome black 64 BMW, parked in front of the club. Entering their vehicle they failed to notice an old beat up Ford parked in the lot directly across the street facing the club.

Muzzy Vallero and Louie, the blade Cavaliere, sat quiet in the secluded darkness of their vehicle. Their beady eyes locked on the BMW. Satisfied that the couple were in the vehicle, Vallero brought the engine to life. The Ford shuddered as the old beat up engine coughed causing the worn body to vibrant intensely. Muzzy gazing at Louie whispered, "Make ready, we'll tak'em down at Franklin and Brown Streets. Be cool, aim straight, we can't fuck up or we'll sleep with the fishes in the Connecticut River." "Fuck you," Muzzy shouted. "The Blade, don't miss, you know that asshole."

Both men were hired hit men. Lured from the Chicago area for the job at hand. Fontana revved up the BMW pulled away from the curb and headed south on Franklin Ave and headed to his home in Wethersfield. A stone's throw from the city's border. Gazing in his rear view mirror, Fontana noted an old Ford that pulled out of an empty lot and take a position close to his rear. His heart skipped a beat as the ford sped up and over took him. Suddenly pulling around with the intent to pass on his right.

Officer LaPore in unit 2, was stalled in traffic on Brown Street. East bound when he observed a black BMW and an old beat up Ford roar through the intersection of Franklin and Brown. Suddenly he saw orange flame spew from the Ford and heard the retort of two popping sounds. Gunning his cruiser, activating his strobe light, he pulled out of the line of traffic and hooked a right on Franklin Ave., pursuing the BMW and Ford, two more retorts emitted from the Ford. "Shit Fuck!" exclaimed LaPore. "That's gun fire! What the fuck do I have here?" Grabbing his mike, he keyed same. "Unit 2 dispatch" "Dispatch unit 2" "Dispatch be advised I'm south on Franklin Ave., near the Wethersfield line, pursuing a BMW and an old beat up Ford. Shot's have been fired from the Ford. The target being the BMW. Request backup units and notify Wethersfield P.D." "Dispatch 10-4, unit 2. Dispatch units 4, 6, 8 attention 43, unit 2 pursing two vehicles south on Franklin Ave. A BMW and an old beat up Ford. Use extreme caution shot's have been fired. Repeating shots fired, vehicles appear to be heading into Wethersfield." LaPore applied the metal to the pedal and soon closed the gap between the dilapidated Ford and the show piece BMW. The BMW hooked a sharp left into the parking lot of The Old Hose Co. dust and gravel spiting into the air. Both vehicles came to a sudden stop. The screeching of brakes resonating throughout the lot only now as both vehicles stood idling, the blue and white of a cruiser stood as a sentinel between them. LaPore revolver drawn, lunged from his cruiser. Fontana, like a cat, sprang from his car, only to halt in his tracks, as the officer barked, "Stay in your car. I don't have time to fuck around here! Get back in your vehicle now!!" Fontana obeyed by reentering his vehicle. Anger enveloped his being as he watched the officer exchange fire with the Fords occupants. He'd only wanted to help the cop, instead he found himself cradling his wife in his arms attempting to calm and sooth her with reassuring soft words of comfort. As the officer crouched behind his cruiser, Fontana watched in horror as the passenger of the Ford exited and headed towards the rear of the vehicle. His interest to flank the cop thus rendering him helpless and exposed to certain destruction. Fontana felt chills as the night erupted in a chorus of vehicles clouds of dust and bits of small rocks pelting his BMW. Numerous cruisers careened into the parking lot. Their search lights flooding the scene. A voice commanded authoritatively, "Drop the gun!!" "Shit bird or eat dirt, your call! Do it now!" Louie the Blade stood transfixed in the glaring lights and knew they'd been had. Dropping his 45 to the ground, he raised his hands. "Okay, cops, Okay." Muzzy surrounded by police was ordered to exit the Ford. Hands in the air. Both were thrown to the ground and searched and routinely cuffed.

Tony Fontana observed the ongoing episode with gratitude and admiration for he knew him and his wife had flirted with death. Pulling her close he whispered hoarsely. "Honey, I would have never thought cops would save my ass." Muzzy and Louie, the blade, were thrown into a cruiser and whisked away to police headquarters. The area was roped off and crime scene tape ringed the immediate area. Sergeant Rich Green confronted Fontana, "well Tony who the fuck are they? God was with your ass tonight. Somebody wants your butt eliminated. What shit's going down?" "Aw sergeant," replied Fontana. "I don't know who the pricks are and I don't give a fuck." "Yeah, well that's fine, Tony. But your going to the station anyway. Lots of people want answers to lots of questions after tonight. You and your wife okay?" "Yeah, I'm fine, Green. The old lady's shook up but a couple of shots will negate her fear. Before we go to the station, I'd like to thank that cop, privately. If you don't mind. Who is he?" Sergeant Green pointed at LaPore, "that's him." "His name is Lance LaPore, officer to you. He's fairly new, but has the makings of being a good one. Make it quick. You know the drill. The dicks are waiting with great interested to grill you at the P.D."

Thanks, Sarge, Fontana strolled over to where Lapore was standing. Checking a bullet hole in the passenger door of his cruiser, he turned facing Fontana as he approached. Fontana, hand out stretched came up close. Shaking hands, he simply didn't forget. You do that uniform proud. My wife and I are thankful you do. If someday I can return this act of courage with a helping hand, you'll learn how to reach me if you already haven't with that Tony Fontana walked briskly into the night took his wife's hand and both entered the rear of a n waiting cruiser, which exited the parking lot, turning north on Wethersfield Ave. LaPore watched as it's taillights grew faint. Finally evaporating into the darkness.

Sergeant Green approached LaPore. "Hey, had you known who's ass you just saved from the butcher block?" "No sarge, but I guess I'll find out soon enough." Green turned to several veteran officers. The group expelling soft chuckles. "Well, kid that dude is Tony Fontana, and he's an up and coming top prospect in the Mafia, thought you should know. Anyway kid, nice job, well done. Head into the barn. Start your paper work. The dicks have a lot of questions to ask and the media is clamoring for information. They are circling like wolves for dying prey. Look across the street they're already here." "Christ sarge, I know they were shots fired, but shit it's not like a rare occurrence." "Kid your alright, but your a cherry. Don't you know you broke up a hit on a top mobster. Jesus, your learn, okay scram, head for H.Q." With that the sergeant departed heading towards his cruiser.

LaPore stood transfixed for a moment. His hands had only now ceased shaking. The taste of bile was biter in his throat. He'd exchanged fire with two men and was now informed they were hit men. "Fuck he thought, what the hell did I stumble into." Gazing at the starlit sky, he entered his blue and white whispering, "thanks to his God." He'd escaped this encounter unharmed. Compressing his mike, he whispered, "unit 2 on the line enroute 10-2 (headquarters)." The voice of the dispatcher responded "10-4 unit 2 enroute 10-2, 21:20." As Lapore exited the parking lot, he observed several media vehicles and two plain clothes units turn into the lot. "Hmph," he grunted, "must be true. Obviously I stumble onto something out of my league. Oh well, it is what it is." He accelerated towards H.Q., curious as to what awaited him.

LaPore pulled into the east lot of headquarters and entered the building and acknowledging the nods of brother officers, took the elevator to the third floor. Exiting same, he headed directly to room 3. It had embossed, in black lettering, over the overhead, gleamed the words, Detective Division. Once inside the busy complex, he was beckoned by Detective violet. As he approached the waiting detective, his eyes scanned the interior. Seated in the northwest corner was Tony Fontana and his bride. Both were busy answering questions fired at them by Detective Dutch Leonard, but managed to wave. He touched his hat in acknowledgement and sat in the chair Detective Violet directed him to. The questions directed at him were routine. What tipped him off? What alarmed and registered in his brain that propelled him into so expedient action. Simple, he smiled, the pop, pop of gun shots and the tongues of flames spewing from the dilapidated Ford. He was questioned for approximately twenty minutes. As Detective Violet terminated his interview, he was instructed to submit and forward his report through proper channels. He was also advised better still, warned to show the media that the head of the detective Division would handle the press. The interview ended when Detective Violet smiled and whispered, "good job kid. Glad your okay. Get back on the line and be safe." LaPore walked into the night. Breathing deeply he whispered softly, attempting to communicate with his deceased father, "Well old shoe, lucked out tonight. I know you were there beside me, rest easy old warrior, our name will never be tarnished."

The years marched on from time to time he would read about various exploits where Fontana was suspected to be involved but never proven. Now and then it would dawn on him that' he'd disrupted a hit by the mob. He wondered how the two hit men had fared in prison. Then shrugged it from his mind. "Who cares? They were punks who struck in the dark, like rats, now they were where they should be and would despise being caged.

"Unit 42, 42 come in." The sexy female's dispatcher's voice roused him from his nostalgia. "42 is on go. Dispatch, 42 meet up with unit 14, 22 Brook Street. He's requested a supervisor, he's at apt E-3. That's the residence of Angel Reye's." "10-4 42 enroute 22 Brook Street., e.t.a. 5 minutes."

LaPore front parked at 22 Brook Street. Officer Rick Haron was waiting in front. Standing with him was a petite pretty Spanish girl, holding hands with a girl, he guessed to be nine or 10 years of age. "Yum," thought LaPore these Spanish women are hot. "Wouldn't want momma knowing my thoughts, chuckling, he sighed no sir, no way, she'd roast me, the burning bed repeated."

"Hi Rick," exclaimed LaPore. "Morning Sarge, listen I've a problem here. Oh Angel meet my Sergeant." LaPore gazed into the darkest eyes he'd ever seen. "Hello Angel, how can we help?" Angel was scanning the street. Fear clouded her eyes. She was trembling and tears trickled down her checks. "No can talk here," she whispered. "Go to my apartment, quick, eyes are watching, Please come quick, quick." She turned trotting to the apartment building's door. LaPore and Haron in close pursuit, reaching apartment E-3, all four entered into a dimly lighted apartment. Smells of Spanish cooking permeated the air. It was a small apartment with sparse furniture, but the interior was neat and clean. Old photo's adorned the walls and candles were casting a warm glow. Their shadows dancing slowly along the walls.

"Policia, please, please sit, I have story to tell. Bad story. Make me angry and sick. I have coffee. Maybe you like some? Both LaPore and Haron uttered "a no thank you." Settling themselves in their chairs, "Okay Angel. Shoot tell us your story," uttered LaPore. He glanced at Haron silently commending the officer to himself for having the foresight to have another officer with him in the presence of this lovely young woman.

She began, "My little girl here, her name is Carmen. There be a man playing with her, taking sex pleasure with her in many ways. But she not be alone. This man he be taking advantage of many young girls, only everyone's afraid to talk to Policia. This man very dangerous, he's member of a Cuban group. They hurt people real bad if you cross them. My little girl needs help." Once said, she simply pulled the little girls pants down to the ankles. LaPore and Haron gasped in horror. The girl's legs masked in purple and yellowish gashes. Angle pulled up her shirt and the area of her girlish breasts were pocked marked with bite marks and red welts running down past her naval. LaPore was horrified, he could not believe what he was seeing. His gaze lingering on the ugly wounds. He noted the big eyes of little Carmen, full of fear and confusion. Anger shook his being rattled his soul. "Angel cover your daughter, please. Rich, he glanced at Haron, call for evidentiary services. Have the respond to this location. I want photo's. These are not old wounds as you can see. She's has no phone, use the car radio. Have them respond A.S.A.P. And rich also have juvenile respond. My gut tells me this is going to be a horror story. I want us on top of this from the get go. Okay go." "Right sarge, you got it," touching his cap, Haron exited the door at the quick step.

LaPore turned back to Angel. May I have the coffee now. Please and do you mind if I smoke?" "No, is okay," she replied, "but must give one to," she smiled. LaPore attempted to converse with little Carmen. To no avail. Frightened she held tight to her mother. No sound escaped her lungs. LaPore studied her intently. "Damn," he thought. This poor creature has been through Hell, needed to get her medical attention. Shit need to roll her to the hospital now. Evidentiary and juvenile can meet us there. Where the fuck is my brain? I'm sitting on it today." He locked eyes with angel. "Come with me we're going to get your little girl checked out. Okay with you?" "Oh, yes officer, thank you. Just let me get jackets for us." "Okay, meet us down stairs." He ran down the stairs and met unit 14. "Rick, belay my first order. Inform dispatch to have those units connect with us at St. Francis. That little girl needs medical attention, first. We'll do our digging at the hospital." "Roger, that sarge."

LaPore followed unit 14, Officer Haron, who transported both angel and her daughter Carmen to St. Francis Hospital. While Young Carmine was being examined by medical personnel, LaPore and Haron initiated the investigation by questioning the mother in a private room adjacent to the ER. Angel answered questions carefully and was deliberant in her responses. The suspected make was one Louis Montelvo, a member of a cruel Cuban sect called Le Mulchardos. Known to inflect torture and even death to those who opposed or crossed them. It was evident too the two officers that Angel was indeed terrified, but a mother lion goes to great length to protect her young even at the cost of her own life. The officers departed only when Juvenile Officer Ross and Carmen arrived and relieved them. Juvenile would now handle the follow up. LaPore was abhorred to learn, as he was leaving that young Carmen suffered various bruises about her body. That indeed she'd been sexually assaulted and suffered a torn vagina.

Stepping into the crisp night air. He turned to Officer Haron, "Rich it never ends. Sometimes I feel we're shoveling shit against the tide, but we've got to keep at it. For the poor and meek we're all they've got. Haron pulled a pack of Marlboro's from his pocket, offering one to Lapore. He sighed, "yeah sarge, your right, up town doesn't really give a shit for the little guy. They talk the talk but don't walk the walk." "Right on Rich. Well, let's get back on the line. By the sounds of radio traffic, it appears like the old town's heating up."

Both officer's signed on the line, returning in harms way. Two day's later, LaPore was summoned to Juvenile, where he met with its Commander Lieutenant Donroy who filled him in on the Carmen Reyes case. Apparently, they had five other active cases involving girls age's 9-12. But the families involved were to frightened to talk. The girls had clamed up and cried hysterically when pressed to talk. DCYF had been brought in to no avail. They also had failed to break the silence. Frustrated their case worker compared questioning the victims as talking to a stone. Montelvo had seen and questioned. But had only sneered and laughed, refusing to cooperate. He'd simply rose and strode from the office. Donroy obviously angry stated, "He smelled like a pig was cocky, arrogant and defiant. So far Lance the only hope for a break is through the Reye's kid. Angel it seemed had the balls to stay the course. Anyway, Lance wanted you to know we're moving slow but no stone will be left unturned." "Thanks Lou, for taking time to fill me in. That son of a bitch is a piece of shit! Hope we can press his balls in the vice." "Hey Lance, how do you really feel? Chuckled Donroy. Okay sarge, hit the street with your troops. Keep your back to the wall." LaPore touched his cap, "Aye, aye, Lieutenant. Thanks." With that, LaPore rose and exited the Juvenile Division and stepped into the night.

The next several weeks revealed additional reports of young Spanish girls being sexually molested by an animal. All within LaPore's sector. Try as he might, not to take this personally, he could not. This was occurring on his watch and the information filtered to him enraged him. The count now stood at 10 young females, ages 9-12 who had been sexually molested. It was an epidemic he could not fathom and caused him restless nights. His troops were also on the edge. They were all fathers and this blight scarred their souls.

Sitting across once again from Lieutenant Donroy, he spilled his guts. "What's happening here Lou? What the hell are we doing? We know who the shit stain is. What the hell are you and DCYF doing?" "Easy sarge," retorted Donroy. His voice rising a couple of decimals. "We're on it. The man hours we're expanded on this are acute. No one is talking even your Angel Reyes has had a brain fart. Yeah, we believe its Montelvo, but no body, I mean no body is pointing the finger. Never question me again sergeant. You know my rep. I've thrown all my resources to cage this prick. But without direct testimony, you know as well as I, we've got shit in the barrel. You take care of patrol, understood?! Leave this to us." "Yeah Lou, your doing great, every night I hear about an additional assault. Don't worry sir, I'm out of here."

LaPore felt his heart pumping. His blood pulsating through his being. He felt anger and frustration. What the fuck? How could this be happening? Proceeding from Juvenile Division, he headed directly to the Detective Division. "Ah, the dick he wish to see was alone in his cubical typing furiously at a report. He approached Detective Dutch, leaning softly not wishing to startle him. As he drew close, Leonard looked up with an appraising eye, smiling he pointed to a chair. "Have a seat sarge. You look like shit. What, your hemorrhoids on fire?" LaPore pulled up a chair. "No Dutch, just pissed and frustrated. You know how this game is, sometimes it sucks! This is one of those times." Leonard pushed away from his pile of papers and leaned back in his chair, Lit up a Salem and said, "What's up Lance, you got a stone in your shoe. Have at me, maybe I can help."

For twenty minutes, LaPore divulged the on going horror in his sector. Leonard listened attentively and sympathetically. When LaPore finished, Leonard locked out his eyes and stared into LaPore's soul. "Listen Lance, you know God Damn well Lieutenant Donroy's the best, especially when it comes to kids. You and I know we have to work within the law. We don't pick and choose and we can't work around it. What's your bitch. Huh, young sergeant, juvenile's on it. They can't perform the miracle of the fish. Come on, lighten up giv'em a some slack for Christ's sake."

LaPore lit up a lucky. "Look Dutch, Angel Reyes told me what went down with her daughter. Isn't my testimony bona-fide and good enough to put this prick Montelvo away." "No Lance it's not. At this point in time it's hearsay. She's not talking and neither is anyone else. You know better. Jesus, your acting like a pubic, right out of the academy." LaPore stood red faced. He glanced at his idol. "Fuck, Dutch. Doesn't this badge stand for anything?"

Detective Dutch Leonard sucked in his breath, staring hard and sympathetically at Lapore. He whispered softly, "**Sure Kid**", it stands for:

A career of frustration

A life time of despair

Fear

Courage

Anger

Tears

Now and then you get a high, but mostly low's

And in the end demon's in the night

Get out of here sarge, do your thing, but remember you live with whatever action's you take, right or wrong."

A week had gone by with no break through on the Reye's sex case. He'd attempted to visit Angel, only to be greeted by a stern faced woman who chose to ignore his pleas to cooperate with the Policia. Leaving only when the door slammed in his face. Frustrated he continued to patrol his sector. He'd experienced a busy week. Four shootings, 5 stabbings and three armed robberies, several muggings and numerous assaults, his was a busy venue, no question. His thought process suddenly exploded when the dispatcher's voice blared over the airway. "Units 14 and 17 take a suspicious act, 22 Brook Street, apt. 3C, unidentified caller, states he heard a loud commotion early in the morning. Now there's no answer at the door and caller states he was expected. LaPore hit the gas. His cruiser leapt forward and with his mind a whirlwind. "Angel Reye's Apt, Shit, hope they're okay. "

Imagination in overdrive, he arrived at 22 Brook, just as units 14 and 17 roared to a stop. The three officers flew up the stairs in a moment they stood on the third floor landing. They were greeted by a cold silence. Officer Haron knocked on the door. No answer. He repeated knocking several times, but to no avail. LaPore yelled, "Angel it's the Policia! Open the door!" Like a stony graveyard, only silence was their response. A creak to the rear, had the officers turn in unison. The door to 3B was slightly ajar. A face of an elderly black women peered out at them. She be in there. I've been up all night and heard a little set to around three o'clock this morning. But no one's left. She in there alright. The door slammed tight and the old lady was gone.

The officers remained transfixed for the moment. Both patrolman studying LaPore seeking direction. LaPore wiped his brow. Sweat formed on his face. Stains forming under his armpits. Yelling, "Watch it!" He took a step back aimed his right foot directed a strong blow under the door latch. There was a loud crack as the ancient door flew into splinters buckling under the onslaught. The door groaned and fell from the door frame. The entryway to apt 3C lay opened and unhindered before them. Weapons at the ready, the three officers advanced cautiously into the semi-darkness. The apt was stuffy and an eerie silence engulfed them. LaPore risking it, flipped the light switch on by the doorway. The living room exploded in bright light. There before them seated in a recliner, the form of angel Reyes greeted them. Her head lulled to one side. Her eyes opened a fixed black stare appraised them. LaPore whispered softly "Angel, it's the police are you okay?" No response then the three officers halted in their tracks. Soft moans of alarm escaping their souls. Their dangling from Angel's left arm, the glint of the hypodermic needle. Lifeless eyes glistened under her left eye. LaPore felt the carotid artery. Nothing the pulse of life silenced forever. "Damn!" exclaimed Officer Haron, "Shit!" uttered Officer Jones. "Mother Fucker! screamed LaPore. "Fuck to Hell! Check the rooms! Look for the girl, Carmen!" He yelled. "Carmen, come honey, its the Policia! Come on honey, come out!"

Receiving no response, the three officers fanned out into the apartment. It was officer Jones on entering the bathroom, who yelled hoarsely, "Oh

Fuck, sarge, Rich in here, oh my God! Son of a bitch! "LaPore and Haron rushed to the door. Their souls twisted in mournful rebellion. There in the tub immersed face down the water was the frail naked body of little Carmen. One glance was enough. Officers could see the girl was gone. Her young life slashed in a moment. LaPore tears welling in his eyes, nudging Jones, "notify the bureau, also inform the watch commander." Turning to Officer Haron, he muttered, "secure the apartment door, no body enters except the dicks. Oh and Jones, make sure evidentiary services also responds. You know the drill. Let's not contaminate the scene anymore then we night have." Glancing over at the slim lifeless form of little Carmen, LaPore's brain snapped a photo that would haunt him for the rest of his days.

The dicks arrived, evidentiary doing their thing with dusting and photographing and neighbors being questioned. One senior dick glanced at LaPore. "Something stinks like camel shit here. There's no signs of a drug catch here. Could this be her first try at it? "Shit, Lapore, no signs of a struggle, neighbors report only a moment of two with sounds of an argument. No one seen entering or leaving the premises. Lighting a camel, Detective Sherrod continued scanning the living room. "Lance!" he barked, "what do you think, murder suicide?" LaPore, his emotions in turmoil, stared at the somber face of Sherrod. "No, Ed I don't. But someone made damn sure it would shape that way. Look Ed you need me here?" "No sarge. We'll wrap it up here shortly. The M.E.'s come and gone and the meat wagon is standing by. Not a hell of a lot more to gain here. Thanks for securing the scene. You and your guys are okay." Lance stepped close to the detective. His voice almost inaudible. "Ed you may never be able to prove it. But I tell you Angel here and her little girl were murdered. She, pointing at the lifeless body of Angel Reye's, was about to stir up a hornet nest, we all know it. Dig Ed, dig hard." Sherrod place his hand tenderly on LaPore's shoulder. "Hey Sarge, you know it, we always do but this, this looks tough. We've got goat shit. Lance and you know it. Go easy, Lance. Don't let this Montelvo fuck lips eat up your guts, won't help." "Yeah Ed, your right but the prick will continue to harvest other kids. It's us the blue soldiers who have to cage this animal. "Yeah Lance the world is a zoo and we're the zoo keepers. LaPore nodded whispered a soft "see ya" and flew literally, flew from the apartment. His heart heavy. His eyes wet with moisture as he descended the stairway. He thought, "yeah, once again the law fails. Once again two innocent victims were the prey of a social animal. The scumbag figures he's home free. He'll have a thousand alibis, no doubt, but home free, we shall see. Oh, yes we shall see."

LaPore continued to scrutinize the case from a distances, checking frequently with Detectives Sherrod and Leonard. Progress was nil. Dozens of witnesses interviewed, the neighborhood canvassed relentlessly. All leading to a dead end. Montelvo had been questioned several times. But as LaPore had thought, was able to provide a solid alibi. What the sleuths had uncovered was Angel Reye's had no history of drugs. Those that knew her were emphatic that she abhorred them and never allowed its use in her presence. The medical examiner in the solitude of his lab had discovered slight bruise marks on little Carmen's rear shoulders. His diligence and investigative prowess led him to believe and unveil to investigators that young Carmen had been held face down in the bathtub by someone of superior strength. Still it wasn't enough the question remained by whom?

Time lapsed into months. The case unresolved. No new leads had developed. Some in their official capacity leaned toward Angel. That perhaps frustrated b y life she'd taken the life of her child and her own. LaPore wasn't buying this train of thought. Whisper's still abounded in his sector. That Louis Montelvo was indeed responsible that he was still enjoying his sexual fantasies with young girls. There was a fear that gripped the area. LaPore had made several attempts to converse with other suspected victims. But was rejected by wild eyed parents and had many doors slammed in his face.

He was summoned to the patrol division's operations commander. There he was strongly warned and advised to back off that he was dangerously close to interfering with a homicide investigation. His stern face deputy Chief informing him that he was an H.P.D. line sergeant and the case was in the hands of trained investigators. "Back Off!, Lance" He was ordered. "There are policies and procedures we follow, you know the drill.

Your a supervisor, your threading on peoples toes. Cease and Desist. God Damn it! Your a cop do what's right here." LaPore rose from his chair touched his cap. "Yes sir, your right, but you forget one thing." "Yeah sarge, what's that?" LaPore stared hard into his deputies eyes. "I'm a father, first."

He'd visited with several prosecutor's in vein attempts to convince them of his testimony and was rejected continuously and respectfully told his evidence was not enough and not to return. Frustrated and angry, he found himself in the chambers of his favorite judge, a cops judge. His honor listened sympathetically to his pleas and never interrupted the sarge at he spilled his case. When LaPore finished, he stared at the Judge, whom rose from behind his desk. He turned staring out his large window which offered a scenic view of the city. Back to LaPore, his hands clasped behind him, the judge spoke softly. "Lance your pissing people off. Everyone feels bad but the law is the law. There's just not enough to follow up on. Your testimony is hearsay. I know the frustration you feel. I experience it every day in the court room. Ever wonder why the scales of justice she wears a blind fold?" His honor turned facing LaPore. Placing his hands on the desk he snarled, "You Lance are one hell of a cop. One hell of a street boss, and your a street cop, If you don't know what to do, who the hell does?!" LaPore touched his cap respectfully, "Thank you sir." Departing softly and quietly from the judges presence. He returned to his blue and white. in a plume of smoke he headed for his sector.

He headed to Farmington and Sigourney. Parking his cruiser in the rear lot of Arthur's Drugs and entered through the rear. As he approached the cafe area, he spotted his prey. Frank the pigeon Mangie sat sipping a coffee. He was reading a newspaper. LaPore approached from behind and nudged the patron sitting to the right of Mangie. When the middle aged male turned, he was looking into the eyes of a cop. His cap adorned in gold braid. The officer spoke in a whisper. Sorry bud I need this seat. need to converse with this gentleman seated next to you. The customer smiled and left quickly. The pigeon gazed at LaPore. "Shit sarge. I've been cool. Why the hassle?" "No hassle Frank, I need you to get a message to your boss. Like yesterday. Here's a private number he can contact me at. I'll wait there half and hour. "Okay." The pigeon took the piece of paper and shoved it into his pocket. "Okay sarge, I'll contact him right away." With that he swilled his coffee and was gone.

LaPore drove to his quiet hide away. It was a quiet refuge in his sector where he could unwind and plan different strategies for his sector. Firing up a lucky, he sat back contemplating his next move. The tick tock of the clock broke the silence. Within fifteen minutes the phone rang. He reached for it on the second ring. "Hello, LaPore here. There was a slight chuckle from the other end. "Well, well sarge now that your wearing all that brass, how are they hanging?" "Hey Tony, what's new? How's business these days?" Fontana laughed there's always a deal to be made sarge. Now what's on your mind?" LaPore took a drag on his smoke. "We need to meet somewhere out of the way. Out of the city and soon. Is this feasible for you?" Fontana stared at the wall full of intrigue. "What could this cop who'd saved his ass years ago want?" Drumming his desk softly. "Sure sarge, West Springfield, you know the place. How's tomorrow night? Say seven o'clock." "Sounds great Tony and thanks. See you then." The phone went dead. Well thought LaPore, the die is cast now we set things in motion.

LaPore pulled into the parking lot to The Out of The Way Cafe. This was perfect. No roving eyes or pineapple ears to eavesdrop. He entered through a side door and found the interior in semi darkness. Adjusting to the dim light, he scanned the room. "Ah," seated up against the northwest wall was Tony Fontana. He beckoned him to his table. LaPore approached cautiously, while taking a silent deep breath, and thought there they are. Two bodyguards sat at the opposite wall keeping sharp watch on their boss. Fontana began, "What's your pleasure? What'll you have?" "Rye and water, Tony. Good to see you, glad your in good health. How's your bride?" "We're both fine sarge, now let's can the shit. Your not here socially. What the fuck can I do for a straight cop?" LaPore took a sip of his just arrived rye and water. "Okay, Tony, here's the scoop, he commenced to relate the Angel and Carmen Reye's deaths. Also expounded on the epidemic of several assaults on young girls in his sector and how whispers and the statement of Angel and her daughter pointed to Louis Montelvo. How his sector was in lock down mode out of fear of the Le Mulchardos, led by one Louis Montelvo. He continued to explain how the law was stymied that their hands were tired due to the stringent laws of evidence. "Tony" he finished, it's a dead end. The law is crippled here and we know its that scumbag, but there's no way of caging him."

Tony had sat still and attentive. His eyes shown coal black. The thought of children being brutally exploited had put fire in his soul and enraged him. He gulped his scotch, threw back his head and in a guttural voice asked, "What is it you want Lance? What the fuck? This is a cockroach, What you want of me?" "Tony I want the scumbag out of the city by plane, train, bus, auto, walking, I don't give a fuck how. But out of the city. Can you help?" Tony remained silent for several moments waiting for Lance's reply. "Out of the city, that's all you want? No problem, he'll be moving real soon." "You need info as to where he lives, description?" Fontana laughed loudly, "Nah, sarge we know who the shit stain is. You know us we have a lock on everyone. No sweat. Rest easy. The census of the city will be minus one. We'll give him a one way ticket to East Bum Fuck. Make him an offer he can't refuse."

Fontana extended his hand. Two men one for the law and one facing it smiled. "Take care Lance and thanks for years ago. Your request will be honored." With that Fontana rose and merged into the night. His body guard on either side. LaPore finished his drink and then exited the bar. Driving home his brain somber. He contemplated what he'd set in motion. Soft music emitting from the car radio. He remembered the words of one of his mentors, a major in the state police. Remember young sergeant, the courts protect the rights of the accused. It's your job to protect the rights of the victims.

Louis Montelvo had left the city on unexpected business, just as Tony Fontana had promised. And because of that, the assaults on the young girls had ceased in LaPore's sector. The families were all so grateful because their fears had been put to rest. The people in the sector never knew what actual happen to the feeder of young girls and they did not want to know. For knowing their children were safe meant everything to them. Thanks to our soldier's in blue.

Author's Note

Although I made an honest attempt to convey a broad spectrum to this case, it is still a condensed version. The leg work, patience and dedication placed in effect by juvenile officers to solve this case was impeccable. Yes the police enjoyed a huge break with the anonymous phone call, and there's no denying it broke the case. But this writer always admired the character and self discipline of Juvenile officers. I admit I could not have performed as a juvenile officer. What these men and women investigate and witness on a daily basis is boggling. It has to scar one's soul. One most remember they to are fathers and mothers and what they uncover is what is being done to our children across this land is horrific. They deal with the broken twisted bodies of children. They witness the life long anguish that tattoo's their very soul. Predators feast on our children and you and I must share the blame, for we do not pressure the courts to do away with these rabid demon's. Imagine the horrors that young Samantha experience surviving in bus terminals, subways and alleyways. Used and abused not only by street animals but by men of education and influence. There are those of you who will disagree with me that is your prerogative but until you hold a lifeless child in your arms and look into the eyes of the victim's parents. I say you don't know what the hell your talking about. As for me, I wish to go on record in saying, thank you to all juvenile officer's across this land. It's the toughest assignment in police work. Thank God for these officer's. They are in a league of their own. To you the reader a warning. Stay close to your kids. Be mindful that demon predators are lurking in the shadows. To all my brother and sister officers who read this book. a reminder, the courts forever go one step further to protect the rights of the criminals, it was my job and now yours to protect the rights of the victim.

Our court system bends over backwards for the demons. They forget and fail to follow up on the victim and the victims survivors who suffer a life time of horror, grief, and anguish. Pining for the loss of their child or loved ones. What will it take for we the citizens of this country to remove the blindfold from the scales of justice.

Chapter 19

Lieutenant Andy Hanzi sat at his desk reviewing the previous nights activity reports from field investigators. Sitting upright in his chair he snorted something's wrong here. Glancing back at the reports, his feeling of dread jumped at him as though struck in the eyes by a poker. He noted that vice and narcotics detectives had dispatched four junkies and five street hookers to the hospital for a sickness with weird symptoms. His investigative experience found him at the file cabinet where he sifted through numerous reports and through his persistence discovered that occurrences of this nature had been deluging routinely his division and the patrol operations as well. "What the fuck chuck?" He whispered, "What are we being besieged by poor drug quality or what? This is bizarre."

Alone in his dimly lit office, he fired up a Chesterfield, then sat back experiencing a deep feeling of brooding and concern. At 08:30 hours, he dialed ext 206, the tired voice of Captain Reynolds answered on the third ring. "Morning Capt., Andy Hanzi here. Got a couple of minutes? I'd like to run something by you." "Sure Reynolds," exclaimed shoot Andy, always got time for my drug and vice czar." Hanzi chuckled softly, "well Capt. I've noticed my guys have been shipping street junkies and flash paddlers to hospitals at an alarming ratio. Weird like symptoms and they all suffer loss of weight and appetite, like overnight. Now boss I know we're not talking about health nuts here, but this don't sit right in my gullet. Also I pursued patrol calls for service and noticed a steady incline in sick call runs. I don't like it Capt., your guys in itell stir anything up?"

Reynolds grunted into the phone. "Well Andy all I can tell you is there's suppose to be some kind of a disease that allegedly gets transmitted through sex, possible dirty needles, etc, etc,. Medical investigators out of Atlanta area scorning the country and intentionally to ascertain what the hell's happening and to get a feeling as to what might be the cause. All I know it's occurring world wide and there's been reported deaths are world wide and nationally. No one has an explanations or answers to the how's and why's. Right now the information I have before me is the sickness has been prevalent in homos, junkies and hookers. I must warn you Andy, this is sticky business. No one knows for sure yet as to a cause. There's a whole lot of speculation and theory and nothing concrete as to transmission or exact linage to what I've told you. However, based on what you've brought to my attention, I'll have one of my investigation teams roll on this to try to get a solid grip of what the hell bug or bugs are there." Hanzi sighed, "Okay Capt, thanks and would you please keep me informed. My guys deal with shit everyday you know." "We all do, your guys, patrol, EMTS, nurses, doctors, teachers, they pay. Everybody's in the same arena on this one. I'll make this priority one for itell. Thanks for the info."

Reynolds disconnected. Hanzi sat starring at nothing in the dim lights, a feeling of foreboding slowly enveloping him. Reynolds also deep in thought, exited his office. Hanzi had confirmed what he feared obviously some type of epidemic was infiltrating the city. It was his job to go deep on this information and knowledge at this stage was minimal. His travels brought him to the commander of patrol. Deputy Chief Davis was busy studying a wall map of the city. His concern at the moment, a rash of muggings that were occurring in the northwest sector. Reynolds entered with a slight cough, Davis who spun around startled from his concentration. "Ah, Frank, good morning, he grunted." "Good morning Chief," replied Reynolds. "Can I steal a minute or two of your time?" "Sure pull up a chair, coffee? Just made some fresh." "Sure Chief, need a surge here feel a little tweaked this morning." Deputy Chief Davis poured two cups, both veterans preferred theirs black and strong. Such a brew stirred the innards and started their day with a fuel like petrol.

Chief Davis sat silently, "okay Frank, What's you got, I know this isn't a social call. Reynolds tapping the desk, glanced at the wall map that pierced the wall directly behind Chief Davis. Speaking softly he began to enlighten Davis regarding what information he possessed obtained from the conversation only moments ago, which he had with Lieutenant Hanzi, Davis listened attentively occasionally sipping his coffee. He never interrupted allowing Reynolds to continue his orientation. When finished, Reynolds sat his cup on the edge of the desk. "Chief, I pray to God I'm wrong but my gut tells me we've a new demon lurking in the streets."

Davis swiveled in his chair staring at the dikes restraining the Connecticut River. Spinning about he faced the itell commander. "Frank Let's do this quietly for the moment. I'll direct records to retrieve a list of sick calls. Ah let's say, for the past six months. You set to work with your guys. Check the hospitals. What ambulances we deal with, even those in the private sector. Let's use caution here, we don't want to cause a panic at the same time the media has been poking around. There's a shit load of whispers throughout the country. Let's see if we can't get a handle on this quick. You know what to do. In the meantime I'll touch basis with other departments. Let's pray we're not up against a tidal wave. And Frank I should have a firmer picture in a copy of hours. So will you. Let's meet here at 14:00 hours. If we have a bleak picture, we'll have to inform Bernie (the Chief). Knowing him he probably suspects something's amiss and is just waiting for our visit." "Okay chief, Reynolds rose from his chair, exiting the office he was oblivious to secretaries only now reporting for work. His mind was in overdrive, functioning on all cycles. There was work to be done expediently.

Captain Reynolds had dispatched a team of investigators to area hospitals. He'd also been in touch with medical investigators located in Atlanta, Georgia. He'd been on the phone for hours with intelligence commanders from large or moderate sized cities, New York, Boston, Baltimore, New Haven, Bridgeport, Waterbury. A dark cloud was coursing through the country. A sickness of epidemic proportions was enveloping the nation. It's tentacles reaching deep into the lost soul populace. Good men and woman were confronting this peril head on attempting to discover its source and how to counter an attack. He'd been given a name for this black death like disease. It stuck in his claw and it wretched in his gut. It howled at him like a wounded demon. He wrote it on his calendar. The word jumped at him and tore at his heart and tormented his soul. He continued to stare with transfixed eyes.

"AIDS!"

While Chief Davis and Captain Reynolds were busy collecting data, the press was also digging. Investigative reporters were uncovering a monster sickness running a muck that would strike fear in the hearts of men. The world would shake and quiver and years of dedicated medical labor would lead to control but it would take years. Reynolds and Davis had presented their findings to Chief Culligan. With that, a meeting with medical minds, educators, clergy and media personnel had been placed in motion.

"Aids Virus Grips the World," the article went on to reveal how a social disease was being transmitted worldwide leading to slow painful death. The world reacted in shock and terror. This was new and horror gripped their hearts. This disease led to a hard death. The revelation of this disease led entire governments to band together to reach for all resources known to man to combat this dreaded illness. Hospitals were being deluged, clinics overwhelmed, doctors in private practice weary from examining an onslaught of patients, who, because of actions known but to them, were in fear of contracting this disease.

First responders were met by bitter frightened souls who'd been condemned to death by this black death. The victims would advanced on. Their would be rescuers, spitting and shouting, "Now you'll get the aids!" It was a nightmare world and existence. In its infancy no one possessed the knowledge on how to deal with these tortured souls. There were no policy or procedures, but as this plague advanced educated men and women formulated and constructed means to deal with the onslaught.

The world was mired in despair. Those with the dreaded disease were shunned and let to die lonely, tortured souls. True, many dedicated people reached out to those unfortunate souls inflicted with the Aids virus. Many researchers dedicated their lives to discovering a cure.

Today there is control. Thousands walk this earth with the HIV Virus, but due to the tireless efforts of medical personnel and the fruits of their labor the ills remains dormant, at least for now. One has no revelation as to what the future holds. There's no doubting the world is a sinful place. Is this the wrath of God? Will the bug reappears stronger and immunity over come our enemy or will man continue in it's victorious breakthrough? Every city and town felt the sting and the wrath of the aids virus. We all existed in its shadow. One must live practicing common sense in protecting one's self. More educated people have and will write on this assault against man. I can only reflect on the hardships of first responders during that turbulent era. Cop's drawing their revolvers on aid's assailants. Refusing to transport them. They feared for their families and who can blame them? They'd been kept in the dark and very little education was given them in how to deal with this menace.

One had to be there to appreciate the magnitude of this terror. Looking into the eyes of a aids victim was like peering through the windows of Hell. They were lost dying souls with no hope, no one to turn too, no where to go, only the grave offered a glimpse of relief from their pain and suffering.

The author can remember one night in the Detective Division a young girl sick and exhausted was being questioned as she'd had been a rape victim. The investigators were perplexed asking how come your not upset or at least hoping we apprehend the scumbag? Staring at nothing she softly answered, "Why don't I worry about it? The prick is a dead man." The dicks startled, asked, "why?" Her answer, Because, I have aids, now so will he. He's a goner." She laughed quietly and left. Gone into the night to what fate bestowed her. There are thousands of stories, broken hearts, millions of shed tears, during this tenure. I hope God in his compassion showed mercy to the victims and compassion to their survivors.

The medical profession warrants a hearty salute from all of us. For the dedication, sacrifice, courage and zeal in combating a deadly disease that left its mark in history. Let's pray they find a permanent cure and it gets wiped off the face of the earth and never returns.

Chapter 20

A clear blue sky gazed at the scene unfolding beneath its comforting tarp. The sun shone fiery. Its rays reaching to comfort and embrace the sea of mourners in attendance who were lined three deep surrounding the humble outdoor chapel. Those grieving sharing memories stood in respectful silence. Intent on observing the sea of blue that snaked across the quiet cemetery. Marching in a crisp cadence the loud authoritative voice of a sergeant, strong and resonating throughout soldier's fields, leaving them with butterflies in the stomach and goose bumps as the triangles flags burst into view. Old Glory, the city flag and state flag flanking her. Yes, they paved the way for those who had given all. Tear streaked faces lined the ranks for this day brothers gone in glory would be forever remembered.

As the sea of blue approached the muffled drums and thunder of hundreds of feet pounding the pavement reached the spectators. Heading the marching contingent, seven officers carried blue gold pillows. The American flag folded triangularly sat proud and crisp atop each. White stars gleaming in the sun, approaching the chapel, the command detail right and left obliges. Responding to this command the marching contingent of blue soldiers broke half to the left, half to the right. Surrounding the black granite alter which adorned the middle of the chapel. Detail halt. Hundreds of officers froze in their tracks. The wind sighed audibly within tree tops. Birds ceased chirping. For a moment the world was frozen in silence. Detail left and right face. The command echoed loud and clear through the cemetery. Hundreds of officers responded crisply facing the chapel. Detail Attention! The color guard marched slowly bearing the colors to their respected position. Seven officers bearing the triangular flags stood to the front facing the family members and guests honoring this hallowed ceremony. Not a sound nor breath could be heard. The soft ripple of the flags flapping in the soft breeze fueled the respectful atmosphere.

Father Cleary Police Chaplin, strode to the small podium. "Ladies and gentlemen, brothers and sisters officers, we gather here to pay homage and remember those who made the supreme sacrifice. Those who felt it was worthy to give their all in order that others should live in peace and solitude. Our officers are truly soldiers in blue who daily wage war on our streets, battling drugs, rapists, robbers, sex fiends, murderers, the list is endless. Technology produces new and horrific crimes everyday. The world grows complacent, uncaring, apathy reigns supreme, yet these good men and women leave the safety and comfort of their homes so we can live life to its fullest. How do you ask a man to die for someone else's mistakes or greed? Yet everyday, somewhere in this land a blue angel falls performing his duty. Words cannot convey what I feel in my heart for our boys and girls in blue. Without them, this country would suffer utter chaos. We can only thank our God for their presence, their courage, and their dedication to mankind. Here surrounded by graves, we will remember those who gave their all within these hallowed grounds. Our brave dead lie in the arms of the Lord for by his own words. He declared blessed are the peace makers for they shall see the kingdom of God. You know I've known many officers in my function as Police Chaplin. I often wondered where the courage to charge head on to a gun bearer comes from, or to enter a burning building to save a child or pet. To suffer abuse and walk in fear on a daily basis. Fear of the unknown, who ever that cop approaches is unknown to him. But that subject knows who you are. Why guys, why, what makes you go there? What makes you tick? What drives you? I'll tell you, love of your fellow man and dedication. I and all here and society must and should be extremely grateful. I could salute the ranks all day. But have found over the years. The great myth of being a cop is that it can be left behind. In finishing I want to read this poem handed me by one of our officers prior to this ceremony."

My Dad

When dad leaves home at night
I lie in bed and pray
that God is walking by his side.
As he labors through the night
I wonder what horrors he
might have seen
and where his soul has been.
Sometimes I feel his sweat and fear
and often see his tears. Oh I love
the color blue that's what dad's about
he serves both you and me, takes
risks when out the door, for peace
and harmony.
Yes, dad you fill that color blue, with
pride and courage to, you see my friends
my pop's a cop and he is at the top.
Head bowed Father Cleary hands clasped
whispered, all the tears, sweat, disappointments,
fear, grief, heartaches, hardship, loneliness
build a stairway to heaven, that says it all. Thank you.

The command attention thundered through the air carried by the wind. Officers ram rod straight stood proud and tall. Silence enveloped the throngs of participants as Deputy Chief Joe Buyak strode to the podium. Erect and proud, his voice crisp and clear thundered through the cemetery, "Commanding the following officer's will answer to the roll!"

"Officer Thomas Horton," Silence!
Then a voice from the ranks
"Sir Officer Thomas Horton, End of Watch 11-22-1919"

"Officer Henry Jennings," Silence!
Then again from the ranks
"Sir, Officer Henry Jennings, End of Watch, 8-25-1964"

"Officer Harvey Young," Silence!
"Sir, Officer Harvey Young, End of Watch 8-25-1967"

"Officer Francis X Fenton," Silence!
"Sir, Officer Francis X Fenton, End of Watch 3-28-1969"

"Officer John Daly," Silence!
"Sir, Officer John Daly, End of Watch 7-29-1977"

"Officer Edward Cody," Silence!
"Sir, Officer Edward Cody, End of Watch 4-16-1979"

"Officer Thomas Toohey, Silence!
"Sir, Officer Thomas Toohey, End of Watch 5-16-1996"

The seven flag bearers stood erect facing Deputy Chief Buyak, "Sir, the officers have answered the roll. They rest in peace in honor, in peace, as they served their final watch." Chief Buyak saluted the flags, whispering, "Final watch noted and logged, may they rest in peace."

Off in the distance, seven blue clad officers raised their riffles to the sky. At the command fire, three volleys were enacted as the officers and throngs of participants stood at respectful attention. The sad soft notes of taps echoed from a distant knoll enrapturing and captivating those who honored these hallowed dead.

Chief Buyak addressing those in attendance softly stated, "This concludes our ceremony. Thank you for mourning our departed brothers. Post Phoebus Nubila. After the storm the sun."

Chapter 21

The old comrades sat at their favorite table. Over the years the Lucky Leaf Cafe had become their sanctuary. A private place where they could gripe and share their griefs and troubles. A comfort zone to all. At times it acted as their church, their confessional. There was no race or creed, no one cared what religion of choice one practiced. All that mattered was the color blue. Photos of old times cops and action shots covered the walls. Mementos brought from brothers long gone. So many had now answered to the top cop. So many volleys of rifle fire laid down for old comrades. The mournful wail of taps played repeatedly over the years filled each with a sad nostalgia. In that their hearts and souls these old soldiers in blue, knew they had given their best and had risked life their very souls to safeguard their community. But father time had caught them and had them in his clutches. Soon they would join the ranks of those who lay waiting in peaceful repose.

Their eyes glistened with wet tears. They knew this was their final roll call at the Lucky Leaf. It was LaPore who stood. Saluting his old comrades, he chose the words of General Washington to bid goodbye and farewell to his brothers in blue, alive and dead.

> "It was the best of times, the worst of times.
> We laughed, we cried, we made merry. Now
> we must say adieu. And if we meet again
> We'll smile and if not this is a good ending."

Some think of them as cynics, hard core, but their eyes did not glimpse what those bearing the blue witness everyday. Their minds did not snap horrific photographs that linger in the soul haunting them in their sleep till the end off their days.

Farewell

"My friends I was fortunate in life in so many ways, I was raised by good honest parents who taught by example and instruction. The foundation to life's structure, love, compassion, generosity, patience, humor, honor, integrity, responsibility, accountability. I had forty eight years with a great woman who bore me three honest children. Who stood by me through the highs and lows. Who's passing left me devastated. Like a rudderless ship I was foundering but God was kind, for I learned that in the spring the rose grows. Lives in beauty through the summer. withers and dies in the fall. But comes spring another rose takes its place. So it happened I found my second rose. My current wife Lisa, who is so full of love and zeal for life. She has paved the road to my final years with happiness and taught me the value of smiling again. I thank God for her. How wonderful it was to have served my country in the military, second to none, Ah, yes, U.S.M.C., Semper Fi to you all. What an honor and privilege it was to serve you as a peace maker. Being a cop was a ticket to the greatest show on earth. Along the way I came in contact with wonderful people. Yes, I saw the demon many times. It is the reason I do not believe in Hell, its here all about us, under the disguise of pimps, pedophiles, drug dealers, murderers, rapists, con man, burglars, robbers, the list is endless. But in retrospect it was a career I loved, cherished and honored. I sincerely hope my contributions helped make for a safer community and I pray I left a profound influence on those I made contact with.

As a son of the city, I thank Hartford for allowing me to serve as one of its finest. The city allowed me to fulfill my boyhood dream. I attempted honestly to give you the reader an insight and a feel for what your blue soldiers address across this great country on a daily basis. I bid you farewell and pray that the byways of life is kind to you. Follow your dreams, remember to support your police they keep the Hun at bay. Keep your kids close and hug your mate everyday.

If the hands of time were hands that I could hold,
I'd keep them warm and in my hands.
Hand and hand we'd choose the moments that should last.
The lovely moments that should have no future and no past.
The summer from a top of a swing
The comfort and the sound of a lullaby.
The innocence of leaves in the spring.
All the happy days would never learn to fly
until the hands of time
would choose to wave goodbye.

Life is to short. Thank you for the privilege of serving you and I hope you enjoyed the read. May God be kind to you and yours with gratitude and respect I bid you adieu."

"Semper Fi!"
Leo P. LePage
Sgt. Hartford Police
1961-1986.

About The Author

Leo LePage is a former marine and served 25 years in the city of Hartford and 17 years of that service was as a line sergeant. He also is the author of The Badge, The Street and The Cop.

CPSIA information can be obtained at www.ICGtesting.com
Printed in the USA
BVOW07s1118150614

356345BV00003B/142/P